BRENDAN

THE 13th VOTE

Red Light Green Light Publishing Co.

TORONTO, CANADA

THE 13th VOTE

Published by Red Light Green Light Publishing
Toronto, Ontario, Canada

Copy Editor: Arlene Prunkl (PenUltimate Editorial Services)
Proof Editor: Emily Stewart (Shelf Potential Editing & Creative Services)
Developmental Editors: Rev. Doug Van Aartsen and Oksana Sharonina
Cover Artist: Tim Barber (Dissect Designs)
Interior Artist: soe_the_arts (on Fiverr)

Book Layout: tigaboys (on Fiverr)

The 13th Vote / Brendan Gavin. -- 1st ed.
ISBN 978-1-7774829-1-6

Dedicated to my wife, kids, and Hazel.

My fondness for challenge greatly exceeds my ability to appraise the effort needed to overcome them.

——BRENDAN GAVIN

CONTENTS

PROLOGUE

DAWN

One Day before Landfall

Alyn's image startled him as he saw it reflected in the polished silver door. Deeply lined and sallow, his face showed the toll that the last few sleepless nights had taken. However, no amount of rest could have prepared him for the treachery that he'd witnessed moments ago. Plotting behind the silver door were six Congress members who, by the fuzzy math of proportional representation, held nearly enough power to decide the fate of thousands. Alyn gritted his teeth and tensed himself, possessed by the impulse to rush back in and put an end to all of it. But the heavy weight of reason bowed his head and slumped his shoulders. He sighed and closed the door.

Click.

The sound of the latch comforted him somewhat as the thick door shut tightly and muffled the ruckus behind it. He closed his eyes and breathed deeply as he took in the quiet of the empty hallway. It felt like a cool breeze on a hot day, at least from what he remembered. They had left Earth so long ago that even this memory had started to fade.

"Governor," said Chung, who had just rounded the corridor's gentle curve. Her pursed lips and furrowed brow told him everything he needed to know.

"Captain," he answered with a curt nod before he bolted in the opposite direction.

Click.

He entered his quarters a short while later, relieved to hear the door latch again, as if it had sealed off the lunacy behind the silver door. But he was not safe here. Like the flu bug they struggled to contain, the madness could infect him too, for ideas could pass up corridors, enter through doors, and infiltrate the refuge of his self-imposed quarantine.

In a daze, he made his way to the room's center, collapsed on the white leather couch, and inadvertently knocked over a porcelain vase as he kicked his feet onto the glass coffee table. The sight of the red tsubaki flower lying limp on a soaked carpet would normally have triggered him, but a far grander problem weighed upon his mind.

The vote.

The six would conclude their votes soon, and, given the way things had been going when he left them, it would be his that determined their fate, the last remnants of Earth.

The doorbell chimed and startled him. He went to the door and peered at the face on the video screen. It was Commander Jacob of their sister ship, the Renascent. The slightly younger man stood tall in the crisp lines of his white dress uniform; his eyes, starkly framed beneath his peaked service hat, held a mirthful charm, and his mouth was closed in stoic confidence. On the whole, he projected far more optimism than the situation warranted. Alyn opened the door, wishing the commander's visit were under different circumstances.

"Eleazar, come on in. Glad you could make it," said Alyn with what he hoped was a warm, authentic smile. In fact, it was fabricated to hide his shame over what had transpired behind the silver door. He gestured to the couch. "Have a seat."

"Thanks," Eleazar replied as he removed his cap, tucked it under his arm, and made his way to the center of the room. He stared at the flower and vase on the wet carpet as he sat.

Alyn fixed a half-smile on his face and took the upholstered chair directly across from him.

Eleazar smiled politely. "Since it's just you and me here, I gotta know, did you really think we'd find it?" He leaned back and shook his head. "Hell, after three years?"

Alyn beheld the planet framed in the window behind Eleazar. Primis. Their new home. So similar to Earth in size, atmosphere, and climate, and its day was just two hours greater. The seas teemed with oxygen-producing microorganisms and phytoplankton, and the mineral-rich land gave life to fungi and lichens only. Only time would tell how the animals, plants, and other living creatures they had brought from Earth would establish there, but Primis's nascent stage of development meant that they would face little competition. While not a bespoke garment to attire their civilization, Primis was definitely made to measure. A needle in the proverbial haystack. Finding it was lucky. Getting here had been a roll of the dice. Desperation and chance alone had righted their rickety ships as they wobbled a precarious path down the Milky Way. Humanity had just removed its celestial training wheels, and though they were teetering, they hadn't fallen. Yet.

Eleazar had waited patiently as Alyn had reflected on his answer. "Honestly?" Alyn said. "It was nothing short of a miracle."

"Finch? The miracle worker? He'd be pleased to hear that." Alyn suppressed a disdainful frown as he pictured the billionaire entrepreneur, Zylas Finch. The man's ego was rivaled only by his ability to charm shareholders out of their cash without regard for the necessity to return them a profit. But even Alyn had to admit Finch's Rift Gate was well ahead of its time. They'd never have covered four light-years in just seconds without this remarkable technological advancement.

"Let's not anoint him yet. We were, after all, over six million kilometers off target." Alyn left out the obvious fact that they had also burned just about all their fuel and had to make landfall tomorrow. He hoped Finch had another miracle up his sleeve.

Eleazar chuckled and shook his head in wonder. "Six-point-five million klicks to be exact."

They smiled in amiable silence for a while before things became serious again. Alyn spoke first. "Given our predicament, I'll assume this meeting will be one of official business?"

Eleazar nodded in agreement.

"Very well." Alyn pulled back his sleeve and pressed in the top pusher of his wristwatch.

Eleazar said, "One way or another, tomorrow, we make history."

Alyn stared downward at the flower and gave a series of nods before saying, "Yeah. We sure will." Slowly he raised his head and met the other man's gaze. "So then. Let's hear your idea. How do we get out of this mess?"

They talked for about twenty minutes before they embraced and said goodbye. Alyn leaned against the doorframe and stared as Eleazar passed around the bend in the corridor, out of sight.

Click.

The door latched closed, bringing with it two jarring realizations: whichever decision he arrived at today, they would never meet again and, more disturbingly, the memory of this moment would haunt him until his very last breath.

Zzzz. Zzzz. The little red light on the intercom panel flashed in tandem with its buzzer.

"Yes, Dara," he said.

A reedy computerized voice replied, "The Dominus's six Congress members have recorded their votes."

"And how did they vote, Dara?" Almost unconsciously, he held his breath.

"Six votes were cast in favor of the proposal."

Madness!

"Governor. You are required to register your vote to Congress no later than 00:00 Earth Time."

Alyn went completely still, as if he could turn himself invisible and they would all forget about him, but it was no good. After all, they had sent her to remind him of the futility of avoidance.

Dutifully, Dara said, "Sir?"

"Affirmative. I understand, Dara."

Driven by restless energy, he moved across the room and planted his hands on the windowsill. Like twin pearls in a deep black ocean, two planets glowed softly in the sun's cool bluish light. A deep urge had stirred inside him ever since he had first cast eyes on them two days ago.

Hope. They had not had hope for quite some time and oh, had they suffered from its lack, but like lime to scurvy, hope had reconstituted their spirits, straightened their backs, and squared their jaws and shoulders. Who was he to take that away from them?

He knew in that instant what decision he would make, though in truth, he had always known—he just would not admit it to himself. But with the clock close to midnight, there was nowhere to hide, not from Dara, not from himself, and not from those who would live with the consequences.

"Dara?"

"Yes."

"Notify the others that I am ready."

"Yes, Governor."

He stared out the window and spoke with a clear tone and measured cadence. "Governor Alyn Frederick reporting to the official log of Earth's Own Ship Dominus on this 27th day of June, 2035, Earth Time."

CHAPTER ONE

CHAOS

Year Fifty-Six after Landfall

N*o!*

The protest, more whisper than scream, perked up the young boy's ears, and he sat perfectly still, hairs raised on end while he waited for the plea to sound again. Had he imagined it? As the seconds ticked by, their silent march comforted him a little, and he relaxed and continued to play with the small toy horse Grandpa had given him. Moments later, however, the silence vanished again when he heard a muffled movement from where the plea had come. He raced downstairs and through the hallway, opened the door at its end, and saw her.

"Alyn!"

Her face, framed by the door, was centered amid a thousand camera flashes exploding all about her. He covered his face and shut his eyes tightly until the lights faded, and when he looked out again, he saw snow-covered trees surrounding him, their bottom halves encased in a thick fog, and the toy horse, now life-sized, grazed upon the grass nearby. But what most alarmed him was the sound of sobbing. Mom! He would not hesitate, not this time, and he mounted the horse and rode down the hill and followed the sound through the dense branches until he broke through the forest's edge. There he laid eyes on a grand lake, frozen solid, with a solitary figure standing upon it near the shore.

"Mom?"

The figure turned to him solemnly. Her white robes flapped in the hard, cold wind that blew her hair and obscured her face. "No," she said.

Alyn spurred on the horse and charged out onto the frozen water.

CRACK!

He pulled the horse up and checked the ice below: a single hairline fracture marred its glass-like structure. Just as his fear subsided, a greater terror overtook him when he surveyed the lake again. Mom had disappeared. He scanned his surroundings and saw her farther up toward the center of the lake.

"Mom!" he said with a desperate shout as he urged the toy horse forward, faster this time. He had just about closed the distance when he heard the frightful noise again.

CRAAACK!

The hairline fracture had widened tenfold and lanced out from the shore past him, but the ice appeared safe for the moment, so he scanned the lake again to find her. She stood near its center, back turned and hunched over slightly, with a hand covering her face as she appeared to weep uncontrollably. The fissure creaked and popped as innumerable crystalline cracks spidered outward from its core. He had little time left, but he steeled himself against any other course. This time, he would save her.

He hastened the horse into a gallop, and in that instant, she took him in with woeful eyes and cast them aside moments later.

CRAA—AA—ACK!

The ice splintered in a million fragments and opened up a great hole beneath her. She toppled into freezing water that gushed up and enveloped her and took her down into the lake's depths.

Alyn's head jerked back against the headrest as he woke abruptly from the dream. How he had dozed off was anyone's guess. The driver had prattled rapid-fire over the last two hours, and the springs beneath the thin upholstery prodded him mercilessly with each bump in the road. Thankfully he was almost home. The vehicle rattled and shook as it started across the bridge that spanned the river, the loud noise answering Alyn's prayers as the man paused to focus on something in the distance.

"Grant's a smart cookie—*one of the best damn governors we've ever had*—but she made a mistake with all this," the driver said as he extended a finger from atop the car's steering wheel toward the side of the bridge.

Alyn followed it and spied the factories in the distance—squat gray cubes clustered around the ocean shoreline, lifeless and weathered. The driver explained that they had been brought from Earth and reassembled there, churning out the needs of the fledgling colony while it struggled to gain its legs. It was why so much of Primis resembled Earth: the houses and buildings, vehicles, and consumer goods were made of parts and materials furnished from the same assembly lines and molds. But times had changed. The colony was now on firmer footing, confident and advancing, and as a result, these factories puffed the smoke of industry no longer, having been replaced by modern ones.

"My dad worked in that one thirty years. Retired full pension. But those days are over—ever since she gave those contracts to those damn corporations and they rebuilt them far into the Frontier where you can pay people peanuts. Even then, just a fraction of the jobs are left since the four horsemen moved in—Automation, Robotics, Big Data, and AI. Bottom line is more important than a person's right to provide for their family."

"Yeah, true," Alyn said. He had no time for politics and it was better not to encourage the chatterbox. That was the thing about ride-share programs—you never knew who would pick you up. Admittedly, Yehven wasn't that bad, just lonely. He had been recently divorced and lived alone, far from his adult children, who both had moved into the Frontier.

"Tell you, though, I *do* like her. Tough gal, that one ... only person in government who gives a damn about the little guy and the only one willing to push back against the Foundationalists. She'll rain hell on them after the cinema bombing a few days back. I know the polls are running close, but mark my words, she'll win the election."

"Right."

"Speaking of governors, you said your name was—uh—*Alyn Frederick*? Any relationship to *the* Alyn Frederick, you know—the late governor?"

"No. None at all." Alyn Frederick Jr. lied again, for he could predict the next words that would come from Yehven's mouth:

Your grandfather was a good man.

One of our great Founders.

The colony would never have progressed so far without him.

You must be so proud.

Alyn *was* proud of Grandpa. He just wasn't in the mood to talk, not after today's events, and even less so now because the wobbly car was making him sick. By now, he could taste bile in his throat, which meant it was time to leave before things got nasty.

"No, eh?" Yehven looked askance at him. "Some coincidence, huh? I read he passed away a few years back. Too bad. Was a good man."

Alyn rolled his eyes. "Over here is good," he said, pointing ahead to the vehicle charging station just past the end of the bridge. He could take the river path home and it'd be good to catch some fresh air.

Yehven yanked the wheel to the left, eased the car into the empty lot, and brought the vehicle to a halt. "You sure? I can take you the whole way."

"Yeah. It's just a short walk from here."

"Well, it's been great getting to know you. You're quite the conversationalist." Yehven extended his hand.

Alyn shook it, dumbfounded by the remark. He had actually said very little in comparison to the driver.

"Enjoy your trip home. I wish you well." The man's eyes drifted off for a moment before they came around to him again. "That reminds me. About that girl at school. The one you told me about back there? I forgot to share the secret. Would you like to hear it?"

"Sure."

"Don't be afraid."

"Of what?"

"Of asking her out. It's that simple. It's all here." Yehven pointed to his temple. "It's in your head. Don't think too much, you know? You'll know when it's right. Trust me."

Alyn nodded and delivered his best impression of a sincere smile. Don't think too much? Was he kidding? That was the worst advice he had ever received about women!

"Thanks for the ride." He stepped out onto the asphalt, closed the door, and waved as the car sped away from him.

He walked the short distance back to the foot of the bridge and stopped where the trail began its serpentine path alongside the river. He gazed out across the water, deep into the Frontier, and looked for the little prairie town where he had come from, but it was indistinguishable in the twilight. The new space port's towering beacon provided the only clue to its existence. Its little red light stood alone, stoic and courageous, as it blinked starkly against the coming night. Alyn looked up into the sky above it. The twin moons and thousands of twinkling stars shone brightly as the last sliver of the sun dipped below the horizon. As if on cue, a choir of bullfrogs crooned to the hand of some unseen conductor, their jubilant chorus echoing into the silence and rejoicing that night had conquered day. Alyn exhaled a slow, deep breath, awestruck by nature's beauty, and humbled by its scale and timelessness. How was it that the universe was so orderly when he, something much less grand, roiled with chaos?

The moons, discontented with their lot, glared down and cast their judgment, as if to say, *We've danced for eons, pirouetting in perfect, unerring unison. You, sir, share none of this burden, carry none of this weight. What's your excuse?* It was a good question.

But Alyn had an answer, as any good supplicant would, and it was the very reason why he now stared up at them. For mere hours ago he had stood not just in front of two discerning witnesses, but an audience of two hundred. Their admission paid with hard-earned wages, they settled in comfortable seats justified in their firm belief that they should be entertained, each face stamped with a smug smile that declared, *I honored my part of the bargain, now you—make me laugh.*

It was to be Alyn's moment, the moment he would rise above his fear. He would delight the discriminating spectators and, buoyed by their approval, screw up the courage to finally ask out Dorothy Dinh. He had fallen hard for her the first time he'd set his eyes on her glossy black hair, brown eyes, and warm, thin-lipped smile, and on that Friday night stage, they would cross eyes and deliver the lines they had practiced and polished in the weeks prior. The audience would lean in, teetering on the edge of their seats, and hang on every word and gesture. And their scene would culminate in laughter and tears, ovations and roses, and finally when the curtain dropped and the night fell, she would look at him, and he at her, and she would take his hand.

But it hadn't happened that way, not even close. Yes, he'd made them laugh, but not in the way he had envisioned, for somewhere deep inside, the fault lines of panic had opened up and an abyss of fear had swallowed his nerve. He'd frozen. Simply stared out at the audience, mouth agape and eyes wide, stricken by stage fright. In utter humiliation, he had fled the stage at the audience's mocking laughter, hitched a ride in Yehven's car, and now stood before the moons, asking, *Is this excuse enough?*

The moons did not answer.

He shook his head as he shifted focus back to the present moment and checked his wristwatch. Moonlight danced along its shiny titanium case and frolicked through the large domed crystal as he drew his sleeve back to take it in. He loved looking at Grandpa's old Centauri I Holographic Time. Its crisp lines and Earth vintage had a timeless beauty that never ceased to captivate Alyn. Of the thirteen built to commemorate the Great Voyage fifty-six years ago, seven or fewer remained in working condition. The words *Transcend Our Limitations* were engraved along the top curve of the polished silver case back and *The Great Voyage* ran along its bottom. Centered between these the number *13* was engraved in thick bold numerals. For all its grandeur, the fact that it had been *there* when Grandpa had left a dying Earth and partaken of the great events of their age—the Great Voyage, Landfall, the Dark Days, and the Settlement—spoke to a greater pedigree. The watch had borne witness to those trying times, and it, like Grandpa, had survived them all.

Alyn rotated the watch's crown a half turn counterclockwise. Iridescent red numbers sprang to life and floated just above the black dial. They read 5:00 p.m. He wondered about Dad. Had he eaten? More so, what state he was in? His father's mental health had seemed to worsen ever since Alyn left for school three years ago, and it was anyone's guess what he'd walk into now.

Alyn turned his back to the moons and gently popped in the earbuds that he had produced from his knapsack. Just two taps on his sleeve's FabricTouch interface and he could push it all away for a time. With the first tap, he chose his favorite genre—1990s heavy metal. With the second, the song "Enter Sandman" by Metallica. Its up-tempo beat and harrowing power chords set him off with a hop as he bounded down the trail with the recurrent head nod common to fans of the genre. He entered the park about ten minutes later and passed the seesaws, swings, and jungle gyms sitting idle in the dusk. He made for the far exit, noticing the smooth sand underfoot before he looked up and immediately dug his heels into it. He lowered his earbuds slowly as his eyes locked onto the figure standing just ahead of him.

"Frederick? That *you*? What? You stupid? What are you doing back in town?"

"Damon? Hey ..."

The young man emerged from the gate and closed the distance between them quickly. He was several inches taller and much broader than Alyn and walked with a confident swagger. "I thought all the college sissies hated this town," he said. "Why aren't you and your sissy friends in the library, studying Marxism or writing poetry?" Damon stopped a few inches in front of him and blocked his path to the gate.

"Well, you know. Came to see Dad."

"Dad? Your dad?" Damon sneered. "You mean the drunken stooge who the paramedics found ranting face down in your front yard the other day? Shit. I was the one who found him. Thought he was dead but when I got close, all I could hear was him talking about beaming at the speed of light, and how it makes you sick and crazy. That's what he kept saying. I heard it! What an embarrassment. And you? A chip off the old block. Seems greatness skipped two generations."

"It's just that—he has his problems. You know?"

"What about you? You got a problem?"

Damon reared back with a cocked fist and struck him in the face. Alyn hit the ground hard, his knapsack taking most of the brunt, but the sharp edges of the textbooks inside pierced into his back, knocking the wind out of him for a moment.

Damon hovered over him and scowled. "I haven't forgotten the prank you pulled on me in senior year. I never got the chance to personally show you how I felt about it, you know, with the teachers around and all. But I got a memory like an elephant, I never forget. Now you get up so I can prove it to you."

Alyn tasted the blood that oozed from his nose and trembled in anticipation of the next series of blows.

A new voice came from the darkness. "Hey, dickhead. You wanna tussle? Let's tussle. You and me!"

Alyn craned his neck around to see who had just spoken. It was Donel. Donel? What was he doing here?

"Saved in the nick of time again, Frederick, you chickenshit," Damon said. "You always seem to have others fight your battles for you. Donel, my beef isn't with you, so you fellas have a good night." With that, Damon turned on his heels and left the park through the back gate.

Donel stood over Alyn and lowered a hand to help him up. "What an asshole," he said before stooping to pick up the earphones that had fallen off in the tussle. He cleaned them on his shirt quickly and popped them on for a few moments before returning them to Alyn. "Still listening to this archaic stuff? Music has literally advanced light-years since Earth. No wonder you're single."

Alyn ignored him. He'd heard it all before. "Hey, Donel. What are you doing here?"

"That any way to thank the guy who scared away the boogey man?"

"Sorry. Thank you. I thought Damon would've outgrown that by now. I mean, it was a simple little prank."

"It's not every day a guy gets two dozen spiders in his pants, Alyn. S'pose it's something he's bound to never forget. Like an elephant."

"I suppose. So, tell me. How'd you find me?"

"What? Oh, c'mon. It's Year Fifty-Six after Landfall. *Everyone* has the Friendzee app on their phones by now. Mine alerts me only when my *best of friends* are in the vicinity. Lucky for you, you made the cut. See here." Donel stuck his phone in Alyn's face.

Blinded by the bright screen, Alyn drew his head back. "What's that?"

Donel lowered the phone. "The app settings. The green checkmark against your name says you opted in."

"But I didn't, Donel."

"Yes, you did." He paused as if considering something. "Ah ... but you wouldn't remember, would you? The last time you were home? At Troon's party?" Alyn gave him a blank stare. "You were shit-faced."

Alyn gave a half-hearted smirk before several droplets of blood dripped down at his feet. He sniffed and held his nose in a futile attempt to staunch the flow.

Donel looked down. "I'll say one thing, he clocked you good." He reached behind him and produced a white handkerchief from his back pocket. "Here."

Alyn took it, tilted his head back and placed it on his nose. "Thanks."

"What brings you home?"

"Came to see Dad."

"You mean your acting debut had nothing to do with it?"

Alyn stared at his friend in shock.

"C'mon, Alyn. It hit my social media feed. Your deeds travel much faster than you do, especially the foolish ones. So, what happened?"

Dorothy's smiling face came to mind, and he couldn't help but watch it again as it turned from joy to absolute horror. That was the last look he remembered. "I froze. Right in front of an audience of two hundred and now I'm the laughingstock of the school."

"As I said before, no wonder you're still single."

"Hmm ... some friend."

Donel flashed a genuine smile. "Buddy. Come out tonight. Han is hosting a party. It'll be good and we'll drown your sorrows in copious amounts of alcohol. We can prime at my house before. Dad's liquor cabinet is well stocked as Mom's been on his case after the holidays. He's out of town and she goes to bed at like, 9:30, so come just before then. She'd like to see you and all."

"That should work. I'll check in with Dad and swing by after." Alyn had no intention of doing so. The thought of all those people judging him was just too much.

Donel's face softened but he moved quickly to hide it. "Good. Listen, I gotta run. Need to pick up some milk before dinner."

"Okay. See you later then."

"Catch ya on the flip side, Frederick." Donel's white teeth gleamed in the moonlight as he gave his trademark farewell and then trotted out the front of the park.

Alyn exited the park at the opposite end, fuming. He wasn't sure what he was angrier about, that Damon was such a prick or that his father was such an embarrassment. His dad hadn't always been like that. Times were good when he was younger. Dad was just like all the other dads then, easy going, nice but firm when the situation warranted, industrious and funny on occasion too. What had changed over the past several years? What demons had crept in and pushed him to the brink of madness?

The gate squeaked as he pushed it open and clanged as it swung back and shut tight within its latch.

"Hazel!" The scrappy, yellow cockapoo rushed over to greet him, tongue panting through a wide, toothy grin. Her small body swayed back and forth in unison with her bushy tail. "Hey, girl!"

The dog leaped and knocked Alyn back on his tailbone, and he laughed as ten kilograms of kinetic joy smothered and licked him. He had missed his pet these past few months at school, and apparently, Hazel had missed him too. Alyn held the handkerchief tight to his nose and fended off the blissful attack with the other hand. Eventually he managed to get up and start for the house. Hazel nipped at his heels as he approached the porch stairs, where he paused to scoop up the dog's orange ball. With a flick of his wrist, he sent the ball flying across the yard, careening off the fencepost and rolling under a small opening in the woodpile. The canine darted across the yard to fetch it out. Alyn smiled as Hazel labored to get to it, and, not wanting to wait, he climbed the steps and opened the door.

As he entered, he noticed something strange about the alarm console that adorned the wall beside the entranceway. Its little battery compartment was open and two shiny batteries sat on the kitchen counter below it, next to their plastic cover. Strange. It wasn't like Dad to have anything out of order. He peered around the cupboards and into the kitchen, and what he saw shook him to his core.

His father lay in a pool of blood upon the tiled floor. Spatter radiated out in all directions from his motionless body, the crimson droplets filling the open spaces and walls as if flicked from a bushy, saturated paintbrush. A stranger squatted near him and rested a blood-soaked knife on the floor—calmly, as if it was no big deal. Strangest yet was that the man now rolled back his father's sleeve and inspected his arm right up to his elbow. He paused and gave a dissatisfied huff before he did the same for the other arm. He appeared to find nothing there either. In frustration, he grabbed Alyn's father by the collar and shook him violently. "Where is it?" the man shouted.

His scream tightened Alyn's throat and sent a cold shiver through him. What was this? His eyes saw clearly but his mind simply could not grasp what was playing out in front of him. He felt faint but quickly roused himself, retreated around the edge of the cupboards and, leaning against them, placed a hand on the counter to steady himself. Somewhere, on the fringe of his perception, he heard the sound of a battery as it rolled down the countertop. Had he nudged it? Silence followed briefly as it sailed off the edge and plunged to the tiled floor, ringing out like a thunderclap.

Startled, the stranger got up and peered around the cupboards. Alyn stared back, frozen in place.

The whoosh of rushing wind and smack of pelting rain startled Sergeant Peters. From his vantage point in the kitchen, he could see through the hallway that a man had just entered the front door. After a brief struggle against the torrent, the man slammed the door shut, shielding himself from the elements and dampening the noise so it was quiet again. He wiped his feet on the entry mat and hung his trench coat and tan trilby on the rack in the front foyer. Both dripped wet and seemed to sag under the weight of the water. Peters knew the guy. Detective Elroy Marcus. Though they weren't exactly friends, they had interacted on several investigations over the years. Marcus fumbled in the breast pocket of his weathered blazer, produced a red handkerchief, and used it to clean the fog from his eyeglasses. Stooped and sullen, he worked his long bony fingers over the lenses, slowly and deliberately, without a glance around or word uttered. He had a weariness about him now, as if he had lost his spark, and it was no surprise to Peters after what had happened to him.

“Nice Roosevelts,” said Peters, trying to break the ice with something light and complimentary. “I’m in the market to replace my horn-rims. Was thinking ’bout a pair.”

Marcus placed his glasses on, tucked the handkerchief back into its pocket, and donned a thin pair of latex gloves that he’d mysteriously produced from another unseen pocket. He entered the kitchen. Peters wasn’t sure if Marcus had heard him or ignored him; either way, the detective’s eyes had not left the dead man lying in a pool of blood.

“What’ve we got?” Marcus said, turning to Peters. But he stopped short at the sight of the navy-blue blazer hanging on the chair near the kitchen’s island. He continued to stare at it for several moments before he met Peters’s gaze.

“Oh. Heh.” Peters reached over and snatched the blazer. “It’s hot in here.” He folded it over his arm and cleared his throat. “Ahem. Male. Forty-five years of age. Owner of this house. Name’s Joseph Frederick.”

Marcus squatted near the body and regarded it carefully.

“Scene is yours, Detective. However, if you don’t mind, how long do you need to wrap this up? I’s at the end of my shift when the call came and I turn back to day shift tomorrow. It’s a drag you know.”

“Not long, Sergeant.” Marcus’s attention remained focused on the body. He nodded slightly twice and repeated, “Not long.”

The victim lay straight on his back as if down for a nap. A bloody handprint was near his head, its crimson fingers spread out at an angle from the body and pointed toward his feet. It was accompanied by a single pawprint, also stained in red, near the side door.

Marcus lay down beside the man, at a distance so as to not disturb the pool and spatter, and closed his eyes for a good thirty seconds or so, after which they sprang open. He angled himself into a sitting position and pushed himself up from the floor with his left hand. He wobbled a little before standing, then turned and regarded the print with deep intention. Several moments later, he put his hands on his hips and cast his eyes around the room before making his way through it, stopping at various objects in situ. A brown suede wallet and a sleek unblemished smartphone lay on the island countertop in the center of the kitchen. Marcus flipped the wallet open, lifted the cards out one by one, and thumbed through the cash. He gazed down at the mobile phone but did not pick it up, and for good reason—they were a magnet for fingerprints. The lab guys freaked when they were smudged, and they'd do a more thorough sweep of the phone's contents if they were in a good mood, but he tapped the bottom corner of the screen anyway.

"Strange," he muttered to himself. The phone's screen lit up and displayed a digital page from the *Observer*'s classifieds section with an ad titled, "Car for Sale." Frederick's car's make and model were listed there, along with the asking price and his address.

Next, Marcus squatted beside a desk lamp on the floor that was broken into two pieces. He brought his eyes down to floor level and examined the threaded seam that connected its halves together, concluding this undertaking with a furrowed brow. He lingered by a dog bowl full of untouched kibble and also at a blood-stained white handkerchief on the floor.

"No murder weapon?" Marcus said under his breath.

Peters grew nervous at the question. As an experienced officer, he knew the three lessons of crime scene investigation. One, defer to the investigating detective; two, speak only when spoken to; and three, if you must speak, stick to the facts, stupid. Detectives were a funny bunch, he thought, and Marcus topped the list. Who knew how he'd react if Peters broke the code? He remained silent and watched the detective over the next thirty minutes as he perused at his own pace, seemingly oblivious to any other presence.

Nothing escaped his attention. The window over the clean, empty sink that was open a crack. The immaculate countertop, with its row of neatly arranged cream-colored tin cans that read TEA, COFFEE, and SUGAR. The various contents of the drawers and cupboards. Marcus scrutinized all, pausing here and there to get their measure before moving to the area near the back door where two double-A batteries were situated on the floor. Marcus stared at them, apparently lost in thought, for much longer than Peters thought was necessary before the detective looked up at the wall-mounted alarm console, its front cover was swung open to expose the feature keys. The plastic panel that covered the emergency battery compartment had been removed, and the two open slots revealed where the batteries had likely come from. Marcus moved close to the unit and read the text printed on the tiny yellow service tag stuck to it. He then unlocked his phone and dialed a number, alternating his focus between the tag and the phone until he was done. He spoke with someone for a minute or two before he hung up.

"Strange," he said. "Alarm company said there was no service call scheduled at this address for today. It was to be tomorrow."

Peters nodded but stayed silent.

Marcus directed his gaze to the thermostat anchored on the wall beside the alarm console. It was set at eighteen degrees Celsius.

The wind wailed again as Marcus exited through the back door and into the rain. Peters stood in the doorframe while the detective cast a wide net over the backyard. The intermittent clangor of metal on metal drew him to the rear gate, where he studied it closely for a while before something else caught his attention. It was a neighbor, who waltzed through the laneway and struck up a conversation with him. He followed her into her backyard next door.

Peters moved back into the kitchen and waited. Several minutes later, Marcus stepped in through the rear door and entered the kitchen with that expressionless face. What did he make of the scene? Marcus must certainly have a theory. It was said that he was the best, known throughout the precinct as a phenomenon—the guys called him the Sage.

The Sage crouched in front of the body again, gazing ahead to a point far into the distance, again lost in thought. He drew in a slow, deep breath, closing his eyes before exhaling. Peters grew more anxious by the second.

"Strange thing that neighbor said. Thought she saw someone out of the corner of her eye running through her backyard as she took out the trash. Frederick's dog was barking something fierce so she couldn't be sure with all the noise, so she went down the side of her house to investigate—but found no one. Strange since the space is hemmed in by a fifteen-foot fence and blocked by a large shed at its end. Saw it with my own eyes. There's no way out unless you're an Olympic-caliber athlete. She said it was about five hours ago." Marcus paused and glanced about the room casually. "Anyway, whaddaya think?"

Peters fumbled his words as he said, "As you can see ... lotsa defense wounds ... hands, wrists ... arms and all, but the big one is right there." He pointed at the victim's chest. "The perp stuck 'im. See. There, under the sternum. Right in the heart. Hell of a blow, man. Probably killed him before he hit the floor." No sooner had the words left his mouth than he knew he'd broken the first damn rule. *Shit.*

However, Marcus didn't seem to care, just stared absently at him for a moment before he took in the body again. "Not exactly," he said. "Looks like Mr. Frederick survived at least a few minutes before he succumbed to his wounds."

"How ya know?" *Shit.* Peters admonished himself for breaking the second rule. But Marcus seemed to entertain the dialogue for now. It was odd, but so was Marcus.

"His position on the floor, mostly. He's not all jangled up. No contorted angles of the arms and legs that happen when a lifeless body hits the ground." Marcus produced a classic ballpoint pen from inside his blazer and clicked it on. "There," he said pointing to the left of the body. "The bloody handprint couldn't have got there from its current position. Arms don't bend that way. Poor soul must've propped himself up on his palm after he was stabbed."

"Huh." Peters nodded in appreciation.

"Another thing is strange. Why not take the money, the cards? Those phones are worth a king's ransom these days. And where's the dog?"

Peters decided to remain quiet for now. It was safer.

But Marcus persisted in engaging him. "So, how long d'you think he's been lying here?"

Here he goes again, thought Peters. *Why's he putting me on the spot?* He tapped a fingernail on the countertop's hard quartz in an attempt to release some of his nervous energy. It didn't work, and his mind raced even faster. Maybe he could cut his losses? Tell Marcus, "I dunno, Detective," and it might end there? Perhaps flattery would get the detective off his back. Maybe "I'm really not qualified, Detective" or "It's above my paygrade" would extricate him from the situation? Probably not, but it was better to play it safe.

"Fucked if I know, Detective," he said with an air of indifference.

Marcus looked him in the eye for the first time that day. "Nah, Sergeant. Gimme your best guess. It's a freebie," he said, pulling a hand toward himself as if to say, "C'mon, I dare you." He settled in, perfectly still, and waited for an answer.

The man was an odd one indeed, but Peters's buttons were being pushed now and he'd be damned if he would flatter him—rules or no rules. *Ah, fuck it!* However, Peters's contrived bravado failed to deliver the goods as he said, "Uh ... hard for me to say, Marcus. I mean, I ain't no detective, but I seen more'n my share of these right? So, judgin' by the blood, I'd say maybe three and a half hours max."

"Hmm ..." Marcus closed his eyes again. He drew a hand to his chin and scratched it absently. "Good guess, Sergeant. The room's ambient temperature and viscosity of the pooled blood indicate two things. That the body hasn't been moved and that it was here three, maybe three and a half hours." Marcus's eyes shot open. He rose to his full height the instant afterward and gazed down at the body.

Peters nodded slowly in acknowledgment and gave a silent prayer of thanks. He'd gotten off easy.

"However," Marcus went on, "we're both wrong. It's been lying here about five hours and eight minutes."

With a mix of fear and admiration, Peters trained his eyes on the Sage who, true to form, had demonstrated his investigative prowess. *How had he done it?*

Marcus walked to the front door and stopped to gather his coat and trilby. As if in answer to Peters's question, he pointed to an area just behind the officer, who in turn spun around to take a look. A small digital alarm clock sat unobtrusively on the counter, hidden behind a can of processed meat and a bright-colored margarine container. It was slightly off-kilter, and its power cord was stretched to its limit, held in place only by its two copper prongs, both bent and protruding slightly outward from the wall receptacle. Despite its dejected state, its red digital numbers blinked through the cracked Plexiglas. It read 5:08.

Peters, in his excitable state, almost blurted out his thoughts. *So the clock was knocked during the struggle and reset itself to 12:00 at the time of the murder!* Once reset, the clock had counted the time from the murder to now. Amazing! But this time, he breathed them out silently instead. Marcus turned to go. Peters followed and paused at the open door, mouth agape, and watched him the entire way to his car.

Marcus eased the car into the fast lane. He knew the route back to the precinct from the Frederick house, so he could focus his mind entirely on the case. He stopped the car at a red traffic light and pushed the little green button on the steering wheel to initiate audio. "Station. Connect me to Albert," he said, speaking into his dashboard's computer interface while at the same time reaching for the cigarette box that had fallen to the floor. "Detective Marcus, E., Registered Detective. Acorn 1-0-8-7.0." His fingers hit pay dirt just as the voice answered.

"Intelligence Protocol Session initiated to Registered Detective Elroy Marcus. Numbered Acorn 1-0-8-7.0. Pursuant to section 6.1.47 of the Police Authority Act, this session will be logged and recorded for security and compliance purposes."

Marcus cringed at the tinny, computer-generated voice of Albert. The creation of the late Zylas Finch, the famed innovator who had developed the Rift Gate that brought them here from Earth. Albert was a government-funded project, a quantum leap in artificial intelligence from all that Marcus had heard, that had been a mainstay on the police force now for about eighteen months. That was exactly eighteen months too many.

The traffic light turned green. Marcus accelerated slowly while he flicked the lighter mechanism with one hand, lit the cigarette that hung from his mouth, and took a soothing drag before he cleared the intersection. His nerves relaxed immediately on the exhale.

"Detective Marcus. How may I be of assistance?"

You could go away, thought Marcus, that'd help, but there was no other choice—humans no longer worked the intelligence desk since Albert's arrival. The state-of-the-art computer system was all he had to work with.

"Albert. Invoke a Deep Level Analysis on subject Joseph Frederick of 31 Oak Park Avenue. Include a twenty-six-hour PBA."

"Detective, I am not aware of that acronym."

"Of course you're not. Means predictive behavior analysis."

"Thank you, Detective. I have updated my slang dictionary. Now gathering sources."

For the next minute and forty-six seconds while Albert retired in thought, Marcus did too. His mind drifted back to the crime scene, scrutinizing every detail from every angle as if seeing it all for the first time. It was important that he miss nothing. As intelligent and artful as prosecutors may be, they needed Marcus to tie motive, intent, and the act itself into a cohesive story, and ensure it was backed by solid evidence. They, with their advanced degrees and haughty vocabularies, jousted in the sanitized, oak-paneled courtrooms, while he, the unsung journeyman, trod into the muck and filth of the mad world in search of truth. Often, the truth was reluctant to step forth, like roaches in the shadows that scurried under appliances when the light flicked on. And so he examined the various objects, states, conditions, or people that bore witness to the crime, for these gave insight if one would listen, and listen he did until the sum of their testimonies brought the truth to light.

Marcus's unique methodologies had led to the development of his Crime Condition Model, a multidimensional way of looking at crimes. Photos and video left out information and, if exclusively relied on, produced two-dimensional thinking. Instead, the CCM cast a wider aperture—things like temperature, weather, landscaping, architecture, even building materials, through to the layout, furniture, and all other manner of items were incorporated. These silent observers were brought together to divine the human motivations, behavior, and actions that led to the crime's perpetration. By creating a multidimensional mental map and committing it to memory, he could replay it at whim, forward to back, back to forward, side to side, and more. It allowed him to break any convention that could blind him from seeing patterns and inconsistencies, and it was best to do this immediately after leaving the scene before the images, sounds, and smells started to fade. Marcus ran through the CCM in reverse, and then again once more, starting halfway in and randomly moving about the crime scene wherever his mind drew him. It was during this time that his intuition nudged him a little. Something wasn't adding up.

Albert chimed in. "Fifty-seven sources have been obtained relating to Joseph Frederick of 31 Oak Park Avenue. Of these, twelve are protected sources and thus will require a search warrant. The remaining are unprotected sources or public records and will not. Advise if protected sources are in scope." Marcus didn't have a warrant in hand, and with the assailant on the run, he was up against the clock and losing time.

"Protected sources are not in scope, but submit the warrant application now."

"Yes, Detective. Search has now been initiated. Results will be transferred in an estimated time of two hours and twenty-six minutes."

Marcus broke the link, shook his head, and grimaced as he recalled the day that Albert had been unveiled to the world. The papers had rejoiced, as though it were the second coming of Jesus. Headlines like "Ushering in the New Age of Crime Prevention," "Crime's New Boss," and "Harnessing the Power of Data for Good" contained some of the platitudes used to sell *him*. Albert the miracle worker, champion of rationality, and protector of children, was touted as the epitome of virtue and all that was necessary to keep evil at bay.

However, Marcus knew exactly what he really was. More Frankenstein than God, Albert had been concocted of piece parts of vendors' software, hastily slapped together at great cost and with great urgency, the result of which was entirely predictable without the aid of a computerized brain—an ineffective, complex machine that despite being touted as never having taken a day off was prone to so many unplanned outages that the most devout atheist would resort to prayer. An army of well-payed data scientists, Albert's high priests, were devoted to the deity's service and care; they maintained, updated, and patched him, and their numbers swelled with each major code release. How could the government afford this upkeep? Up until now, the only casualties on Albert's march on consciousness were the dozen researchers who had lost their jobs just before his launch. They were now *redundant*.

Redundant. Where had that word come from? How had it become attributable to human beings? These were people, working people, Marcus's kind of people, but to anyone on the outside, they were just faceless entities shuffled aside in the name of progress. Their names, contributions, and legacies reduced to a seven-figure entry in the savings column of the well-promoted but nonetheless fabricated business case that was used to evangelize him. None of this mattered. Albert, the destroyer of careers and devourer of balanced budgets, hid behind a grinning mask, the product of marketing hocus-pocus conjured by advertising wizards incanting from the grimoire of opinion polls. And it worked.

Children were the easiest targets. Schools brought them by the busloads to venerate the wonder of science and human ingenuity. And then there was Albert's annual birthday party! Attendees were among the movers and shakers of society; their limousines arrived, one after the other, to offload their haute couture–clad occupants onto the red carpet. Servers mingled among the crowds with trays of Albert cupcakes, "I love Albert" buttons, and his own flavor of Albert lollipops. A multi-piece orchestral band played Albert's very own theme song while the mayor and governor (not ones to let any ounce of goodwill go to waste) reveled in the hoopla and used every iota of their time, charisma, and Albert's brand recognition to promote their government. Trust us to bring you justice, peace, and happiness—just come forth into the pews and kneel. It was absurd. For all his cognitive computing power, Albert didn't realize that he was a useful idiot, a puppet made to dance from strings tied to politicians' fingers. But no one else realized it either, for that matter. *Never let the truth stand in the way of a good story.*

"Detective?" It was the dispatcher calling in. It sounded like Rachel, the old broad who was about to retire. Her monotone voice and I-don't-give-a-shit attitude gave a clear indication that she was ready. Giving him no time to respond, she said, "Marcus? Are you there?"

"Yeah. Marcus here." At least she'd used his surname. It was proper. She must be in a good mood, as he couldn't remember a time when she had done that before.

"Detective, you're needed at the intersection of Armstrong and Glenn."

Marcus knew the intersection well. It was New Times Square, a major commercial hub of shops, restaurants, and tourist traps loosely modeled after the old one. It would be packed with people this time of day, so a robbery or assault was the likely reason.

"What is it?"

"Public vandalism, Detective."

"What the f—?" The surprise got the better of him but he managed to stop short of swearing. She was a lady, after all.

"Excuse me, Detective?"

"Public vandalism?"

"Yes, Detective. You need to make your way there. At once."

"Get one of the other detectives. I got a murderer running loose."

"It's coming from the top, Detective. Get your ass over there." Rachel clearly had no problem with swearing at a man.

Coming from the top? Marcus was puzzled, but nothing would be gained by arguing it out with her. "Confirmed and en route," he said. "Marcus out."

She had already hung up.

A quick flash of the police lights and a short burst of the siren cleared the way as he made a U-turn onto the highway that would take him to the scene.

CHAPTER TWO

A SIGN

The paint-flecked door creaked and moaned at being forced into a frame that wasn't quite plumb. Victoria tugged again and nestled it in place, produced a key, and locked it. She turned away from the back of her semi, and in two paces cleared the three wooden patio stairs that led downward to the path that bisected her garden. The carrots looked as though they were doing well, but the kale appeared downright strange, as if something had flattened the leaves. It seemed to be making a comeback, but—

Owww! She pitched forward, bewildered by a violent thump, and somehow managed to regain her footing just before she tumbled into the vegetables. She stood and pressed her hand to the back of her head where she had been struck. What was that? But more importantly, was her camera okay? She reached around her hip, opened the top of the tanned-leather camera bag, and pulled it out. After removing the lens cap, she inspected it, powered it up, and surveyed the body quickly before putting it back. *Whew.* It was unharmed.

She breathed a sigh of relief before noticing that her foot lay squarely on the kale plant. *Its comeback is finished*, she thought as she extracted her foot and swung around to seek out her assailant. It was one that was all too familiar: a black and white killer of—up to now—only plants. A soccer ball. It wouldn't add humans to its hit list despite its dogged determination. She scooped the ball up and marched down the path through the back gate and along the alleyway to the Johnsons' yard. Without pause, she opened their gate and saw two young children sharing a perch on an overturned bucket, a vantage point that allowed them to just see over the fence into her backyard. They wobbled on tiptoes and seemed perplexed by the missing ball.

"Jonni ... Jora Johnson," she called out. The kids looked her way so quickly that their careful balancing act was upset by the sudden change in equilibrium. Their surprised expressions turned to fear in the instant it became clear to them that they were about to fall. *Oh no!* The desire to catch them overtook her completely but she couldn't react from this distance—all she could do was watch it happen, seemingly in slow motion. When the dust settled, Jora rose first, looking about her with bewilderment as if she knew she had gotten away with something she shouldn't have. Not a scratch could be seen as she'd fallen right on top of her brother Jonni. What were big brothers for? Jonni had fared worse. He picked himself up, sniffling and shaking, as if the wind had been knocked out of him, but she would check to be sure. Oh, that Jonni was so damn cute. She had a soft spot for him, and in his current state, it became much softer. All thought of the sinister soccer ball flew out the window.

"JJ One, let me see you," she said as she kneeled down at his level. "Here. Let me get that." She brushed away the dirt and twigs that clung to his corduroy jacket and pants.

"Mom will be mad," said Jonni, tears welling in his eyes as he began to shake.

"Oh? Why will she be mad, sweetie?" Victoria spoke in a sugary tone that did nothing to placate him.

"She told us not to get dirty. We're going to see my uncle, you know?"

Jora chimed in. "He's joined the Eloration Corps, and Mom says we get to see him in his luniform."

Victoria hiked up Jonni's pants and straightened his shirt. "*Ex*-ploration Corps, huh? In *uni*-form too, eh? Lucky you." Victoria had an idea. She looked at Jonni. "Okay. Now, let's get you dressed proper, just like your uncle—an astronaut in the Exploration Corps!"

He stopped abruptly, eyes meeting hers, vacillating between sniffles and thoughts of outer space. He was under her spell for now, but she would lose him again if she didn't keep the momentum going. She needed to act quickly.

"JJ One. As a good officer, you need to stand straight while your admiral inspects your dress. Only the good officers go to space, and a good officer must have a clean uniform and stand at attention."

The boy stiffened in that exaggerated way that kids do when impersonating soldiers and added a right-handed salute to the mix. She placed his matching poor-boy cap on his head and squared it perfectly, allowing just enough space to let a little curl fall down the front. There. She had his full attention.

"Corporal Jonni. I award you this medal symbolizing the planet Tribus that you have just discovered." She presented the soccer ball to him and his eyes widened in the instant before he snatched it from her. "Our world is grateful to you. You have found us a new home and saved our civilization. Just like our Founders!" He was now in full make-believe mode, staring ahead in pride, eyes wide.

Victoria cast an eye over the yard before she pointed to a vine-covered arbor that separated the front from the back. "Corporal Jora, you will pilot the ship to that Rift Gate and enter it, just like our Founders. And like them, on the other side, you and your brother will explore a new galaxy and find a new world that we can colonize. When you find it, please report back to me at once. But before you go, you are commanded to pose for the official mission photograph that we will put in the history books."

She removed her camera from the bag, positioned Jora next to Jonni, and lined up the shot. They did the rest, posing silently and proudly. Picture taken, the transfixed siblings hurried off to explore the far reaches of their backyard in search of a new world. Satisfied that they were all right, she left the yard and started down the road that would take her downtown.

Victoria arrived at the bottom of New Times Square about twenty minutes later and spied a large crowd near its center, about two blocks up. All throughout it, heads tilted and hands pointed up at a large billboard sign several stories above the street. Without breaking stride, she reached into her bag, took out her camera, and readied it.

"Watch it!" said a woman's voice from in front of her.

Victoria brought her eyes up from the viewfinder. A stylish young couple came into view, sporting a variety of shopping bags and looking as if they had sprung off the cover of a fashion magazine.

"Oh, a—" began Victoria, feeling contrite as the woman interrupted her, raising her hand in derision. With a disdainful huff, she tugged on her man's arm and coaxed him on. They stepped around and passed her as they continued their conversation.

"It's those damn Foundationalists!" said the metro male from behind chic tinted eyeglasses. He gestured at the crowd. "No way this is anyone else. Just a bunch of low-bred constitutional literalists living out in the Frontier."

"That's prejudiced. They're not all like that," replied his companion, a woman whose self-assuredness matched the height of her stilettos. The sound of her heels clacked off the pavement and faded as they disappeared in the crowd.

Victoria neared the large billboard. The sentence that adorned it stunned her. While it was crudely fashioned, its intent was clear. The vandal had somehow climbed up and spray-painted over some of the sign's original printed text. What the painter lacked in artistry, they had made up in courtesy, as the paint color matched the sign's background. It made it easy to read. The phrase that remained read:

Tyra nt—for Hi r e!

"Tyrant for Hire," said Victoria, muttering under her breath. "Clever. Clever."

Tyra Grant's portrait filled the sign's left third and the makeshift words stretched across its remaining length. **JOIN THE FIGHT** was crudely scrawled across the bottom in dripping neon-red paint.

Tyra Grant. The governor of Primis. The most powerful person on the planet, for now anyway, for she was up for reelection. In addition to traditional print magazines and signage, Tyra deployed an unrelenting barrage of holovision commercials, digital signage bursts, radio spots, and psychographically tailored social media spots to drill her campaign slogan into the minds of the people: *Tyra Grant—Forward! Higher! Together!* A five-dollar can of spray paint had undermined the millions of dollars it had cost her, if the sarcastic chatter around the sign was any indication. Guerrilla warfare at its finest.

How had the painter gotten up there to change it? There was no obvious way that Victoria could see to climb up. The billboard was secured directly to the building's façade, and there was no visible access to the rickety metal gangplank that ran the length of the sign's base about ten meters below the rooftop. The painter must've plied their craft from upon it; however they got there, it was not a feat for the faint-hearted.

She snapped pictures from every angle before her mind focused on *the story,* and then she mingled among the crowd and tried to connect with anyone who could help her to tell it. Finding the story was a journalist's greatest challenge, but Victoria enjoyed it because she genuinely liked people—and it showed today. Like a butterfly in a wildflower garden, she floated effortlessly from conversation to conversation, borne by a warm smile and unbridled enthusiasm. People leaned into her like blossoms in the breeze and shared information as if it was sweet nectar. Her ability to harvest it set her apart from her peers and was the reason why she had been promoted from intern at the *Observer* to the city assignment desk in just five years, a startling achievement for someone under thirty.

However, the story would not be found today. Two dozen interviews later, she snapped the camera back in its bag and cursed her luck. Her charm had failed. She'd yielded a basket of disjointed theories, all lacking credibility and most with little basis in reality. She'd heard everything from "the shadow government of the patriarchy is bent on usurping a powerful woman" to "the Business Improvement Association is enacting revenge for Grant's zero-tolerance to plastic straws," and even the most absurd suggestion—that it was Grant herself trying to evoke sympathy!

"Ugggh!" Victoria said, cussing so loudly that she drew glances from more than a few passersby. Frustrated and desperate, she approached the area cordoned off with yellow police tape. She saw someone she knew.

"Marcus?" The man swiveled his head left and right before finding her. "Marcus. Over here!" Victoria made eye contact and a moment or two later, he broke off from a conversation, walked over, and stood in front of her on the other side of the yellow tape. "Hey, you!" she called out, happy to see him.

"Victoria. Long time."

"Working on a Sunday? No day of rest for you, huh, Marcus?" She drew out the last bit.

Marcus smiled a tight-lipped grin. "'Take no part in the unfruitful works of darkness, but instead expose them.' And I shall, be it Monday, Sunday, or any other day of the week."

Victoria returned the smile and regarded him earnestly. "So what do you make of that? Foundationalists? Finally graduated to color by numbers?" She pointed at the sign. "You think they're behind it? I mean, the signs are all there, aren't they?" She realized the bad pun after it escaped her mouth, but if Marcus had too, he didn't show it. Measured Marcus, always great in a crisis but not so much for a laugh.

"All the signs are there," he replied.

"Can you believe it? 'Tyra Grant—Forward! Higher! Together!' Who in the communications department came up with that?" She paused and, with mouth agape, shook her head several times. "Crazy, isn't it? It was screaming to be vandalized by some wall-climbing Banksy."

Marcus's eyes glazed over, his mind clearly somewhere else, deep in thought.

She waved a hand in front of his face. *"Maaaar-cus?"* she said in the sing-song way she would call a child. He was back and looked at her again. "You wanna grab a coffee?"

He glanced at the crime survey team for a moment. "Sure."

They settled into a boutique café half a block from the scene, chancing two seats that afforded a good view of it. And lucky too—Marcus would be less irritable if he could keep his eyes on it. A waiter arrived and took their orders before dashing back into the main building.

"Why would the Foundationalists do *this?* It's no secret they're against Grant's government, but"—she paused, searching for the next word, and waved a hand in front of her while she shook her head slightly—"but this, this is like kicking the hornets' nest! I mean, going after Grant *here*"—she pointed to the cobblestones beneath them—"in the epicenter of her power!"

"Right," replied Marcus with a slight nod of his head. "Don't make sense."

"Or perhaps it was to send a message to Grant. You know, message could be, like, to scare her, let her know that they can strike anywhere, anytime, including in the heart of *her* city?"

"Hmm." Marcus nodded again slowly as he studied the digital screen that hung from the restaurant's outer wall. It played highlights from last night's baseball game.

"I didn't know you were a fan?" she said, both to get his attention and mask her irritation at the same time.

Marcus heaved a heavy sigh. "Well ... sort of." The waiter returned and placed their drinks on the table. "Can I pay now?" Marcus asked him, appearing happy to change the subject. "I may have to leave abruptly."

"Superhero, eh? I've got a place where you can change," said the waiter, laughing at his own joke. Victoria joined in too.

"Something like that," replied Marcus, his look deadpan.

"Together?" The waiter grinned broadly. They both nodded and with the confirmation, he removed the receipt from his waist pouch and handed it to Marcus, who took it and reached into his breast pocket.

Victoria gave the waiter a frosty glance before glowering at Marcus. "Hey!" she said. "I got this!"

"Oh, no you don't." Marcus brought out a worn, ancient-looking wallet, the size of a small paperback in thickness, a real guy's wallet.

She reached across the table, snatched it from his hand, and placed it on her lap.

"Victoria. C'mon. Give it back."

"No, Marcus. I most certainly will not give it back."

"It's not right a woman pays."

"What? Why not?"

"Not the way it should be."

"The way it should be? It *should be* that you've stopped using cash by now. It's *soooo* dirty and gross too." She scowled. "Here," she said to the waiter, offering him her thumb. She pressed it on the mobile payment device that he produced from the other pocket of his pouch. "Keep the change." She glared at Marcus as she returned the wallet and decided to ignore his archaic views for the moment. What was the point? Marcus was Marcus. Traditional, yes, but he meant well.

"Say, you know anything about this?" Marcus said, addressing the waiter as he pointed casually to the vandalized sign.

The waiter tucked the device into his waist pouch. "No, nothin'. It was done by the time I got here this morning."

"What time?"

"I opened at six. My turn to get the ovens going. Pastries take time, you know?"

"Hmm. Saw no one, eh?"

"Nah. Just the usual weirdos. Like Max over there," he said as he pointed toward the adjacent park. There stood a grimy, disheveled man who belted a discordant tune while he urinated on the trunk of a large tree. "You could ask him, I guess. Maxie's harmless. We sneak him the leftovers at the end of the day and in return he doesn't panhandle here. Customers don't like it, you know?"

"Sure. But why sneak?" Marcus said.

"Well. The boss don't like it. Thinks it's enabling him. So we do what we do under the radar. Only problem is we won't be here after next week. Maxie there won't starve, but he's gonna have to work for his food and there'll be none of the girls who take him to the clinic."

"Er ... what's going on? You guys, closing up shop?" Victoria said.

"No. Boss is bringing in self-serve kiosks. Supposed to use state-of-the-art AI. You'll be able to order your food through a voice-enabled device right here at the table. Supposed to be able to remember what you ordered before too, makes recommendations, you know, like food pairings and the like. All I know is, the wait staff will all be gone. The few bus people that remain will have their hours cut to part-time and just shuttle orders from the back."

"Why is that?"

"It gets around the living-wage policies. Since Grant brought in LW last year, all these business owners are pissed. Looking for ways to beat the system. Part-timers are not covered by the law, so they don't have to offer them benefits and can pay them peanuts."

"I had heard the government was going to license Albert's software but had no idea it was this far along or, to be honest, that it could be used in the business of selling coffee and tea."

"Well, leave it to the rich. They might be greedy but they're not stupid. Ironic, though, how they were able to use Albert, a gift of the government, to circumvent its own law, one that was supposed to make working people's lives better—not *worse.*"

Victoria let that sink in while she wondered what else she could say to this man who had just lost his job to a computer, but she couldn't come up with much, so she simply added, "I'm sorry to hear that. However, I wouldn't bet against Grant. She's intelligent, tough too. She'll rein in the fat cats. In the meantime, what are you gonna do?"

"My cousin's got a catering business out in the Frontier. Got some government contract supplying the new space port. Been asking me to join her for a while now. Honestly though, I can't stand it out there. No diversity and it's so wide open, not like here. But it's work, so I'll probably join her next month and we'll see."

"Ah. Good, then." Victoria thought about what a great story this was. Businesses taking parts of Albert's cognitive model and incorporating them into their own computing environment had dire implications for the working person, if this was any indication. How the government reacted would be the major factor in how this played out. Yes, there was a good story there, maybe even a feature. She scribbled a note on her napkin because even good ideas were easy to forget. "Well, good luck to you."

"Thank you. Hey, gotta hustle. Take care," the waiter replied before darting back inside.

Her note taken, she leaned toward Marcus, rested her elbows on the table, and steepled her hands in a power triangle. "Let's get back to it."

Marcus's eyes drifted down toward the table and remained there for several moments. He blinked twice and looked up at her as if something occurred to him. "Maybe it's simple. Grant's up for reelection in six months. The Foundationalists are no fans. Remember the Anti-Terrorism Act she pushed through Congress? Put a crimp on their operations and who knows the kinda damage they could've inflicted since. An army marches on its stomach, a revolution on dirty money."

"So it's revenge, then?"

"Possibly."

"Stranger things have happened, I guess—right?"

"Yeah. You could definitely say that."

"What do you mean?"

"Artist left a half a can of spray paint up there."

"So what? Maybe he's a pro? Doesn't need all that paint?"

"No. What I mean is the *can*, the *actual* can—it's cut clean through. We found the top half of it up there and paint splattered all about. Like someone took a hacksaw and cut through it, except it was perfect, like a surgeon did it."

"Why would the criminal do that and leave it there?" said Victoria. She stared off into space and absently tapped her chin with her index finger as she considered her own question. "Where's the rest of it?"

Marcus shook his head. "Dunno. That's even stranger."

"A symbol, maybe? Maybe they're trying to say something with it. I mean, why else would they leave it there?"

"Maybe."

"They're recruiting! Think about it. There's no better place to advertise—I mean, businesses pay top dollar to get in the Square. Think about all the eyes out here every day—it must be millions."

Marcus went silent again and stared at the crime scene. Victoria wrinkled her mouth. They were getting nowhere. She needed the scoop, but without an inside track, she had only news—not a breaking story. She tossed back a large gulp of coffee and sighed. Marcus turned his attention back to the table. He seemed to have gotten the hint.

"Except."

She perked up, her eyes now riveted on him. "Except? Except what, Marcus?"

"You said eyes, right? What other eyes are about in New Times Square?"

For a moment, she was puzzled, and her head drifted upward while she considered the question. She snapped it back down moments later to meet his gaze. "Video cameras! There must be a dozen around here."

"Maybe dozens." He gazed deep into the Square as if spying them all at once. His wristwatch vibrated before she could follow up, and he reached into his breast pocket and produced a phone that looked older than his wallet. It wasn't even N-1 technology, N-12 maybe, like the kind that came from Earth.

"Marcus here." He listened intently for nearly a minute before he hung up. "Victoria, I gotta go."

He rose to his full height, shoulders back, hands on hips, with his eyes cast beyond the crowds, gleaming with intent. Like a bloodhound, she thought, latched on to the scent, consumed by the need to catch his quarry.

"Hey, one thing. Let me know about the videos, will you? I really need this, Marcus."

His eyes drooped as he gave her *that* smile again, the one formed at the confluence of happiness and pity. She didn't know what angered her more—that he did it from time to time, or that she never called him on it. Its unspoken message was clear. He liked her, yes, but he didn't think she could cut it as an investigative reporter. That she was too naive to swim with the sharks in the crime-infested water. Sure, he was being protective and that was natural, after losing his family and all, but she would prove worthy of the job. She would prove it to him, prove it to everybody. Just as she always did.

"You bet. I'll call you. Bye, Victoria." He left the café and disappeared into the crowd.

Victoria looked out into the Square, her eyes ranging far and wide, searching for something—*anything*—that could offer a clue to what had happened here. They fell upon the green digital newspaper download box that sat by the curbside. It was one of the *Observer*'s, and though it was not the clue she had hoped for, it reminded her that it was time to return to the office. She ordered a taxi from her mobile and abruptly left the table to wait at the curb.

About twenty minutes later, she said to her driver, "Could you let me out a bit before my stop, please? It's such a nice day. There by the white van. I'll walk from there."

The car stopped and she stepped out onto the sidewalk that ran alongside the four-story row houses lining both sides of the street. It smelled different here. The air's earthy tones and sweet fragrance were a welcome embrace in contrast to the bouquet of perfume and excrement that she had just tolerated in the Square. Spring charmed people from their homes and coaxed them into the streets, the basement-level shops, and the sidewalk cafés that were nestled under the green-leafed canopy that extended from one end of the block to the other. These fig trees were among the few that grew on this planet, their vitality owed to some quirk in the local microclimate, and though they hadn't ever borne fruit, their vigorous growth gave the neighborhood its distinctive character.

Victoria strolled down the boulevard and arrived at the *Observer* about ten minutes later. The four-story Italianate brownstone anchored the row at the east end of the street, its style and location in the seedier edge of the city standing in stark contrast to the tall glass skyscrapers of their competitors in the core.

She ascended the stairs two at a time, pulling hard on the thick wooden handrail, and stopped to fix her clothes on the landing. With wrinkles smoothed adequately, she cast a glance above the arched doorway before her. The *Observer*'s official coat of arms was chiseled into the keystone between a pair of ornately carved corbels. It was a heraldic shield sectioned into thirds. A spyglass was emblazoned in the top-left third, a sword in the top right, and a feather quill occupied the bottom. Broad fig leaves supported the shield on each side and a twentieth century worker's hat topped it. An old platform scale crested the shield, which lay in a flowing fabric torse, and the bottom of the mantle read:

Vigilate Cognitionis Verum

Goosebumps trailed the electric shiver that arced through her every time she viewed the regal symbol and its words of truth. She was *born* to seek out injustice, *built* to talk truth to power, *called* to aid the powerless, and *privileged* to give voice to the marginalized. That these were the *Observer*'s highest virtues was awe-inspiring. Oh, how lucky she was to work there! Aside from the meager paycheck, of course, which barely covered her lifestyle, the *Observer* gave her something more valuable—*meaning*. Recently, a major news corporation had offered to double her wages, but that money came with strings that bind; it held sway over what stories she could report, and what truths she could bring to light. It was a farce, really. Big-news journalists masqueraded as stewards of enlightenment—it made her sick—but in reality, they served at the corporations' behests, solely for the purposes of the elite. The *Observer* was different, the underdog of papers, it was said, and it felt good to play a role in that. Yes, they were small, but they were the last bastion of veracity in a world sustained on spin. Those who conspired to advance the interests of the patriarchy, big business, and dirty politicians would find no safe haven within these walls.

Victoria made her way through the front hallway, greeting familiar faces as she went, and badged through a set of glass doors that led into the gallery. The newsroom was full of activity. Peers yelled across their desks, barked through headsets, rapped frenetically on keyboards, and dashed about as if life depended on it. A chaotic scene to an outsider, but a synchronistic order could be interpreted if you knew the language. Over there was Xio, the eager intern who hadn't developed a reporter's instinct but compensated through sheer work ethic, playing the phone like a musician, tapping keys for leads, her face marked by a desperation to keep up with the conductor. Gregory, the IT guy, surveyed the tangled mess of wires that hung inside the closet-like computer room. He could be seen through the glass wall, hand on chin, brows knitted, flummoxed by the stubborn machines, his paltry budget and the role of miracle worker foisted upon him. There too was Brenda, the copy desk chief, astonished that just two-thirds of the print space was allotted for. With deadline looming, she paced the floor with barred teeth, roaring at journalists for fresh meat. Sure, it was crazy, but for all its turmoil, it was a wonder—and Victoria *loved* it.

Victoria sat down at her desk. It was neat and uncluttered ever since she'd gone paperless. It had been a challenge at first, but with persistence, she had founded a paper-free oasis in a desert full of tree-killing hordes. It was her mission to convert them all eventually. She logged into her computer and waited for her apps to connect to the cloud. While she waited, her mind drifted to the event in the Square and the conversation with Marcus. It appeared to be a simple act of vandalism, but Marcus didn't seem sure. Why?

At that moment, a melodic *ping* projected from her computer speakers. A message from Saam, her editor, popped up in the instant message window. It read: *Come to my office when you get in*. Saam's impatience was legendary, and so she rose abruptly from her chair and darted toward his corner office. Just as she rounded the last corner, someone jutted in front of her. The next thing she knew, she lay sprawled on the floor, as white printer papers, liberated from their stack, floated pleasantly above her. When they landed about her, the serene view was replaced by a face glaring down at her.

"Victoria. My *office*!" said the frowning face. It was Saam, who otherwise appeared unmoved from the impact. He started toward his office. "And Xio!" he said, raising his voice, "Pick up these papers and get them to Copy right away."

Victoria straightened, smoothed out her skirt and carefully beelined for Saam's office. It was twice as large as any other in the building. It featured windowed corner walls, a polished mahogany desk, and a bookshelf bulging with motivational books common to upwardly mobile executives. She could guess their titles without even looking: *How I Became so Smart and Accomplished—and You Can Too!*; *Leaders Are Not Born, They Are Made*; or even *12 Ways to Satisfy Your Ego at the Expense of Others*. Precious shelf space was cleared at deliberate intervals, the books replaced by framed portraits, each of Saam locked in a collegial embrace with the movers and shakers of Primisian society. There was cricket star Roddy Arkasian, gamer extraordinaire Wendy Svrivasta and even Governor Grant—and she was certain that he knew none of them. *Never let reality stand in the way of a good selfie.* Other curiosities were placed strategically around the room so one's eye could not rest anyplace without seeing something that begged the question, "Oh, are you interested in such and such?" Which elicited a well-rehearsed response that equated to something like, "Well, yes. You see, I am not just accomplished in my current career pursuits—no sir (or ma'am), I am well-rounded, interesting, and accomplished in many, many others." The last five years had made Victoria fluent in the lingua franca of the chief executive office and though it was revolting, she accepted it because she had to.

Saam got right to the point. "So what did you find out in the Square?"

"Best I can tell is that it was the Foundationalists."

"Best you can tell?"

"Well, the writing. It points directly to them. I mean ... it's all there."

"So what's the story, then?"

"The election's in six months. They don't want her to win. And her opponent is like, not a hawk, right? Heck, he even stated that he'll open a dialogue with the Foundationalists and maybe give them concessions in exchange for peace. It's a good story for us, Saam. Grant was raised by a single mother, just a step up from poverty. Despite the hardship, she climbed the male-dominated ladder of politics. She opened up doors for all women and now is besieged by a bunch of ignorant constitutional literalists on the right. She needs our help, Saam!"

"Yeah. She does and I'd like to give it to her, but we need to be sure. You got any hard evidence?"

"I've a source in the police department. I hope to know more soon."

"Hope is not a strategy, Victoria. Don't rely on your source to do your job. If it comes up goose eggs, you got nothing. Okay?"

"Well ... yeah, sure. Okay, Saam."

"Good. There's another matter I wanted to discuss with you. I got a request from the Interstellar Exploration Corps."

"Uh huh?" Curious, Victoria leaned forward, clasped her hands to her knees, and waited.

"This is hush-hush for now—you got me?" He lowered and deepened his voice for effect.

"Sure. I mean ... absolutely, yeah."

"Okay. The government will soon announce an expedition to fly a spaceship to our sister planet Secundus in two months. It's something about finding resources that aren't abundant here and that we'll need in order to fuel the mission to Earth, but politically—and this wasn't mentioned on our call—it's clear that there's huge political gain for Grant, you got me?"

"Uh huh. Yeah. Course."

"They want a reporter embedded on the expedition. For some reason, and despite my fiercest objections, they specifically requested that *you* be the one to join them."

"What?" Victoria leaned back in her chair, aghast. "Me?"

"Yes. You. Apparently, Grant likes your social justice orientation, thinks you'll be a good fit." Saam paused to let it sink in. "Now"—he raised his hands, palms outward, just above his shoulders—"there are some things they want you to know. There's danger. If you think about it, it makes sense. It's the first ever space flight since the one that brought us here. Equipment failure, space sickness, a botched landing, these are just some of the possible risks. Now, I'm assured that our best scientists are all over preparing for this, but it's a first for us, you know?"

"Yeah. Yeah ... for sure it is."

"Good. Glad you understand. Oh and I need your answer by tomorrow morning."

"Tell them I'm in," replied Victoria, not missing a beat. There was no way she was going to miss this opportunity. Steeled in her chair, she stared deep into Saam's eyes and squared her jaw. Saam rose with a series of quick nods, and Victoria held his gaze and followed. He knew her as well as anyone, so there wasn't much more to be said. After a long moment, Saam extended his hand and she shook it, and with that, his expression changed from one of irritation to pride. She smiled and left the office, wondering what it could all mean.

◎◎◎

The street sign was cast in the moon's warm glow, so it was easy for Alyn to read it as he stood in the long shadows of the dank road. Tovarish Avenue. He had arrived. It was a good thing too since the wave of nausea that had swept over him about four blocks ago threatened to overwhelm him. But he'd have to fight it a little longer to avoid notice from the man who appeared from the darkness on the opposite side of the road. The man's aimless, slow shuffle implied that he had nowhere to go, and after what seemed like an eternity, he passed out of view.

With a hand upon the signpost, Alyn stooped over and retched onto the sidewalk. A wave of dread enveloped him as he pondered his father's violent death. He wiped his mouth on his sleeve before he steadied himself and straightened. Who had murdered him? And why? The whole thing seemed bizarre. Like an illusion. He wasn't supposed to be here, alone on some dim street corner, and the thought swallowed him whole into a dark pit of despair.

He thought of Mom, just as he often did when the gloom floated in and his mind drifted back to his twelve-year-old self, alone in the house when he'd heard the voice from somewhere on the main floor below him. "No!" it had said, hushed and muted, as if the intent was to be heard but not widely noticed. Alyn had strained in silence just to make sure it was real. When the voice shrieked less than a minute later, Alyn couldn't make out the words, but he recognized its tone and character. It was Mom's. He followed it down the stairs, through the hallway, and stood before the doorway to the garage. What was she doing in there? He turned the knob and opened the door. He froze dead in his tracks at the sight of Dad, who was straddling her as she lay face-up on the floor. His back was turned to Alyn at a slight angle that was just enough to see his hands wrapped around her neck. He squeezed and pressed his weight downward. He was killing her.

She looked over at Alyn with bloodshot eyes, wide and wild with fright, but her reaction was stranger yet as she seemed more alarmed to see *him.* She snapped her head back so as not to disclose his presence and re-engaged in her life-or-death struggle, clawing at Dad's face and arms, ripping at his hair, anything to free herself.

He remembered how he had grabbed the hammer from the tool bench and, without hesitation, raised it high as he approached his father from behind. How the rage had overtaken his being and seized his mind while paradoxically, in that moment, he felt strangely calm. In control. As if he floated outside of his body, regarding it at a distance, and it seemed no more aware of its actions than a robot driven by malicious code. He was just about to strike, to drive the hammer deep into his father's skull, when Mom yelled.

"No, Alyn! He doesn't know what he's doing!" she said.

A flicker of recognition washed over Dad's face as he turned and saw the hammer. His grim expression transformed into one of deep shame, and with it, he loosened his grip around her neck and raised himself up slowly. His slumped shoulders and downcast eyes were in utter contrast with the man Alyn had just seen; he looked more than weary now, confused and exhausted, as if the power that had possessed him ebbed and leaked into the shadows from where it had come.

Alyn trembled like a leaf in a hurricane as he considered this. How had his father become such a monster, and even more startlingly, how could he himself have become one? For when he grasped the hammer, Alyn had glimpsed a part of him that he otherwise hadn't known existed and that was now impossible to deny. A brutish part of him that held the most savage of impulses, that could override his rational mind and takeover—one powerful enough to drive him to kill his own father. And it terrified him.

"You need help, Joseph," Mom said as she raised herself up from the cold concrete floor. She coughed several times and pushed aside her hair and wiped away her tears. "This can't go on. You need to stop! You cannot fix the sins of the past!" She ran into the house, weeping. That night, the police came and took Dad away.

His mom's sobbing haunted him the rest of the night. For a time, he had watched over her as she lay nearly motionless upon her bed. Like a broken-winged sparrow, she was hurt and vulnerable and he had to live with the fact that there was nothing he could do to mend her. Her normal stately bearing was overcast by a depressive cloud that followed her everywhere in the weeks afterward. She barely spoke to him for the first few weeks as she merely went through the motions of life. Friends and acquaintances came for tea and listened compassionately, but despite their large numbers and abundant goodwill, there was no lasting improvement in her demeanor. It was maddening. Alyn had thought his actions had saved her that day, but they hadn't in reality, for she just seemed to get worse as she slipped away a little more each day. He tried to be the perfect son, cleaning the house, doing his homework, even cooking his own meals—he didn't want her to fret about him one bit.

Then one day, almost six weeks later, she cupped his face, fell to her knees, smiled, and pressed her forehead into his. He had reached her! Broken through that miserable fog! She had a chance—or so he thought. The next day she ended her life.

Alyn went to live with Grandpa for a while. He had pulled some strings to fast-track Dad's rehabilitation and before long, his father came home. Though they settled in again under one roof, things were different. They were father and son, yes, but in name only. Alyn could never forgive him for opening up the large hole inside that Mom had once filled. In essence, both parents were gone, and aside from Grandpa and his best friend Donel, he had no one in his life who truly cared about him. And all the while his dark self brooded, lingering in the shadows and waiting for a reason, a necessity, no—*for an excuse*—to come forth again. But, neither necessity nor excuse would have the opportunity to coax it out as the crushing weight of Alyn's disgust pressed it downward and sealed it away, entombed it behind a thick wall of will and denial, and covered it over with layers of repressive sediment. He was determined that it would not rise again to see the light of day; it would not control him ever again.

Alyn's thoughts came back to the present. He could waste no more time out in the open, so he slipped through the alleyway between the three-story buildings that abutted the street. Without a moment's notice, he leaped from the pavement and with the grace of an acrobat, sprung off a discarded crate, and anchored his feet on the red-brick wall while he grasped the metal downspout simultaneously with both hands. He clambered up the pipe and onto the small second-story roof that extended over the front porch. Spring had arrived late this year and the morning frost that tingled his dew-soaked toes also produced an icy film that covered the window before him. He puffed warm air onto it then wiped his sleeve to clear a spot so he could peer inside. Satisfied by the result, he gently rapped on the window, froze himself in place, and listened for a reply. There was nothing. He rapped again. Still nothing. Undeterred, he rapped harder, and the old iron window frame vibrated in its seat, creating a loud thud that was certain to alert everyone in the house.

Just then, a startled face came into frame and peered out the window. Donel's narrowed eyes fixated on him for several moments before they settled back into their normal position. In the next instant, his friend loosened the latch and flung the window open. Alyn slid through the opening into a bedroom, the chilly air chasing him through before the window was slammed unceremoniously shut by the wind. Alyn stared blankly while he took a seat on a wooden chest nestled in a dimly lit corner. He closed his eyes, drawing in a deep breath, before slowly opening them again and facing his best friend.

"What was wrong with the front door?" said Donel, who stood before him.

Alyn gazed at a point seemingly below the hardwood floor.

"And why are you so early? You were supposed to be here just before nine-thirty."

Turning his head, Alyn shifted his eyes upward to face his friend.

"Well?"

He snatched the small wastebasket from the floor and retched in it.

"What the hell? Why'd you come if you're sick?" Donel glowered at him with disgust. He reached over and grabbed a tissue box from his bedside table. "Here," he said, handing it to Alyn. He then seized the wastebasket and with a grimace, lifted the plastic garbage bag within it, tied it up, opened the window, and launched it out over the roof and into the alleyway. He produced another bag from within his closet and set it into the wastebasket. "There you go. Just in case you need to go again."

His friend sat on the edge of his bed and faced him from the side. "Been drinking already? You were supposed to wait for me!"

Alyn gained a measure of composure and wiped his mouth with his sleeve. "Sorry, Donel. It's just ... they murdered him. It all happened in front of me. As if it were all a dream. But it wasn't, Donel. It was real." He could scarcely believe he was saying the words.

"*Murdered?* Who? Who are you talking about?"

"I've never seen so much blood. There was so much of it. Everywhere. Didn't know we had that much."

Donel's eyes widened like saucers as he straightened and brought a hand up to stroke his thin beard. He rose to grab a footstool and sat on it, now eye to eye with Alyn. "You need to look at me now. Good. Take a breath and tell me—*what the hell happened*?"

Alyn's eyes zeroed in at a thousand yards as his mind went back in time. "I got home ... just after I saw you. I came in through the laneway and the back door." He shook his head and pressed his lips tightly together before continuing. "Something was strange when I got in—I knew it—so I turned the corner into the kitchen. That's when I saw him."

"Your dad?"

"Yeah, and someone else. A man. I saw him squat down beside Dad ... he was lying down on the floor." Alyn slowed, still staring vacantly as silence hung for several moments. "Funniest thing was, I think he was trying to steal his watch."

"What? Are you sure?"

Alyn didn't respond, just stared at Donel, who got the point quickly.

"Oh. So what did you do?"

"I ran at him. Surprised him, I guess ... and he bolted and squirmed out the side door. I went after him but tripped down the stairs, and when I got up, he was gone. So I went back in to see about Dad—so—"

Alyn stopped before the story got away from him, surprised at how effortlessly the lie fell from his lips and how easily Donel accepted it. In truth, he hadn't pursued the man. It was Hazel who had rushed in from the yard, Hazel who had charged the man and given chase. In an unbelievable irony, fear had gripped him twice today. Alyn Frederick Jr., grandson of the revered, fearless Alyn Sr., had remained still as ice as he'd locked eyes with the intruder. How could he reveal his fright to his best friend, when he could barely admit it to himself?

Donel replied without hesitation, "And he was dead?"

"No. Not at that time. He was in a bad way, though. Must've been a dozen or more cuts. I tried to stanch the bleeding but ... shit ... it was coming out everywhere. Then his eyes opened and he perked up a bit. He was weak, breathed these deep ragged breaths, but he could talk. Told me to stop. Said it didn't matter anymore. Like he was prepared for his death—almost at peace with it, you know? But then, the strangest thing happened—he looked at me and pointed to this." Alyn pulled his sleeve down and held up his wrist for Donel to see.

"A wristwatch? Really?"

Alyn nodded.

"Lemme see it."

Alyn took it off and handed it to him. Donel turned it over and back and brought up to his eyes to examine it. "Nothing here jumps out at me. Looks like ... well, a watch. A classic, though. Thing's got a center crown you unscrew to set the time and the two pushers to stop and start the timer function. Don't make 'em like that no more. Where'd you get it?"

"It was Grandpa's. As you can tell from the engravings on the back, it came over with him from Earth. Dad gave it to me a few months ago when I left for school this year. I thought he had lost his marbles, right? But he lay there and pointed to it, and clear as day he said, 'Your grandfather and I tried to atone for his past sins, and this watch is the key to doing that. I wish I had more time to tell you—but just know that it holds two secrets. The true legacy of our name, and the power to redeem it. There are those who want to abuse that power, and so they will come for it. Listen carefully, for the secret to unlocking it lies in the simple instructions that Grandpa has told you many times before—to move forward, see your past, ponder your present, envision your future, fill yourself with purpose, then the hardest part—*act*.'"

"What did he mean by all that?" Donel said, looking flabbergasted.

Alyn paused in reflection. His mother had said something similar in the garage, about the need to atone for Grandpa's sins, but it still meant nothing to him. Grandpa was good, pure, and unblemished, unlike Dad in every way. What possibly did he have to atone for? "I asked him the same thing! But he was fading in and out by then, said there was no time to explain, so he said these final words, 'They came for it today and so they will come now for you. Trust only yourself. Run. Hide. I love you, son.' That was it. He seemed to drift into a deep sleep, and he was gone. Just like that."

"Alyn. I—I'm sorry." His friend's expression said it all as silence seized the room. There was little more he could say, nothing he could do to heal the deep sense of loss that had overtaken Alyn. "So where the hell have you been since then?"

"I searched for Hazel for a while but couldn't find her in the dark, so I sat there in the park for God knows how long trying to figure it all out."

"That's just it, isn't it? It doesn't make sense. An old watch. Murdered for an old watch?"

"I know. There's no sense to any of it. It's so strange. I mean, Dad unraveled in his later years—you know that—but he channeled his demons inward after Mom died. He didn't go out and create enemies."

Alyn's mind spun, topsy-turvy, from all of it. He would never speak to his dad again, and despite their differences, it tore him apart. They could never reconcile either. All of what might have been was irreparably lost as Dad joined his mother and grandparents in death. Alyn Jr. was now the last of the

Fredericks. A name forged by rocket fuel and stardust, relegated to such a frightened and pathetic vessel. A wave of isolation crept in like a rolling fog, intermingled with deep sadness and crushing guilt in an odd concoction of feelings. Like a pent-up geyser, agony roiled within him, compressed by his stoic attempt to bottle it up. He wanted to give in to it, let it burst forth in tears, but not here, not yet, and he attempted to force it back down with an equal measure of rage. But cracks soon formed, and all his attempts to contain it were abandoned. The pain erupted with fury and poured out of the depths of his soul, surging forth, and smashing the wall of fear wide open. And as the tide ebbed, something seemed to awaken within him, as if a giant guttural roar were exploding from the hole in the wall and into the wide-open space of his soul. His dark self could be contained no longer; like a lion, it emerged from the shadows and glared about as if seeking some prey. Finding none, the lion gnashed its teeth and growled.

"Alyn? You okay?" Donel seemed alarmed.

Alyn gathered himself. Something inside him had indeed changed. "Yeah." In truth he wasn't okay. He had lost everything, was on the run, and had nowhere to go.

Donel put a hand on his shoulder. "I'll help you find whoever did this. I got your back. You can count on that."

"Thanks." The word hung in the air for several moments, and Alyn took the opportunity to think on things a bit more. He needed to do something. But what? Who was looking for him and why? His nerves piqued at the thought. Thankfully he had a friend like Donel. Wait. *Donel.* It would be relatively easy for the authorities to connect the dots and realize that he and Donel were close. After all, they had been best friends since first grade. And if the bad people Dad talked about could make that connection ...

"Donel. I need a favor."

"Sure. What?"

"I need to get out of here."

"But you just got here."

"I told you what my dad said. I need to run, hide. I need to get out of the city—and soon."

"For sure, but for starters, you can't go anywhere this late so jump in the shower and get that blood off you. I'll lay out some fresh clothes, get you some food too."

"I'm not that hungry, Donel."

"Well, you gotta eat and there's lots of leftovers. I'll pack you a knapsack with some food just in case."

"Naw ... thanks, but I think I need to travel light."

Donel brought his hands up to his chin and looked at the ceiling for a moment. "I'll go out and grab some cash then. If there are people tracking you, best to stay off the grid, right?"

"Yeah. Good idea."

Donel opened his door a crack and surveyed the hallway. "All right. Coast is clear. You know where the bathroom is. Towels under the sink. Don't be long. Mom's still up downstairs. Now, I don't know the shit you're in but probably better no one knows you're here."

"Yeah."

"Best you rest before you head out again. Take my bed and sleep while I'm out." Donel was halfway through the open door when he whipped his head back toward Alyn. "Any idea yet where you'll head to?"

"Not yet. But I need to find out the truth to all this. Who killed Dad, and why. I'll shoot past the moons if I have to."

CHAPTER THREE

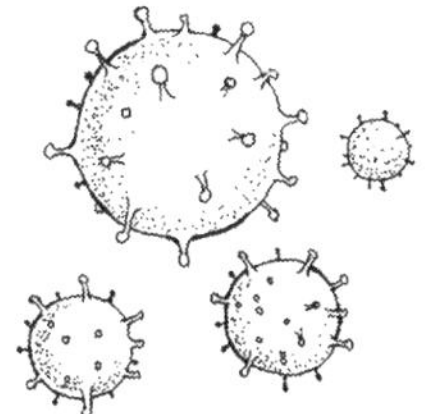

IMPROVISATION

Tyra gazed upon the crowd from inside the lobby of the Primis Rehabilitation Hospital. Its tall, tinted-glass panels had a sepia-like hue that created the illusion of an old photograph, and it made her feel as if these events had happened before.

"Podium's set up, ma'am," said the voice behind her.

"Thank you, Charmagne. Give me two minutes." Tyra emptied her mind and focused on her mantras. She needed to be on her game today.

A wild cheer greeted her as she stepped outside about two minutes later. She warmed to it instantly and raised her hands high in the air, causing the crowd to roar with even greater zeal. A good start! However, the thought vanished as she skipped into the parking lot and stumbled on her approach to the podium. A downward glance illuminated the source of her mishap—the microphone's power cord. It lay unsecured on the asphalt and awaited a foot to snare. An inexcusable hazard to her health and worse yet, her brand! Her image would suffer horribly if the press got even *one* grainy pic of her sprawled on the ground, but thankfully, she regained her balance without breaking stride.

Smile. Wave. Perfect. Well maybe not. The accursed microphone wasn't positioned appropriately to her height! Was it asking too much to set up the damned podium properly? No! *Someone will be fired today,* she declared in a silent act of defiance. As pleasant as that would be, it would have to wait, and she paused to adjust the microphone herself. *Straighten. Position. True.* By now, the throng of onlookers were waiting patiently, all eyes eagerly cast toward her.

And thus she began. *Timing. Authenticity. Charm. On!* She beheld each person warmly, uniquely, face to face—even the members of the press. Oh, the press! Their red-dotted reticles followed her relentlessly, dialed in to every utterance, movement, or quirk—not in the pursuit of truth, but to expose *flaws.* And the knives would unsheathe once those flaws were discovered, but there would be no Ides of March, for there was little utility in a death stroke; no, a simple cut and twist would be all it took to open the wound and allow the parasites to devour her slowly. But even parasites could be beneficial. After all, the natural world showed that some parasites actually *helped* their hosts. A symbiotic relationship, it was called, and that was exactly the kind she had built with the press. It had taken years to train them, but she'd done it, and like Pavlov's dog, they salivated in her presence and greedily accepted the scraps of information she tossed out. They loved her for it, and now, hoisted upon their shoulders, she rose to the top of the political hierarchy, cresting a reciprocal wave of ingratiation. *Give them what they want, and they will give you what you want!* It was all so easy once you understood the game and were willing to suspend reality to play it.

Tyra rested a hand on her heart. "My fellow Primisians. I stand before you humbled by the greatness of our remarkable achievement. Here *we* are, millions of kilometers from our cradle, in a world our Founders settled for us. After many decades of hardship, we now stand on our own two feet." She removed her hand from her chest and pointed a finger at the ground beside her.

"The Founders of Primis have bestowed their legacy upon us and we, the inheritors, accept the duty it demands of us." "But first, let us acknowledge their gift, the gift that made this possible." *Rhythm. Volume. Control.*

She raised her hands and head up to the sky in an expression of grateful adoration. "A gift freely given, like all gifts are, but few gifts are rendered with such personal cost. We know the story. Two starships traveled across the galaxy and limped into orbit, battered, bruised, and carrying fuel sufficient for only *one* of them to land. On that fateful night before Landfall, the crew of the *Renascent* gave the *Dominus* its remaining fuel and in doing so, gave *us* life! Who among you would give your neighbor the last of your fuel so that they could sustain themselves over a brutal winter, knowing full well it would be your families' last? We may not understand from where our Honored Ones summoned the courage to make that very choice, but nonetheless, we remember it and honor their sacrifice! A sacrifice for the *greater good*," Tyra emphasized, with her hands resting flat on the podium, her eyes closed, and a slow bow of her head.

She brought her eyes back again on the crowd. "Since our founding, there have been those who have followed their example—like the brave men and women lying in the very hospital beds behind me, they who have given their backs, limbs, and minds to safeguard the very freedom we take for granted. Some gave their lives so that we may live in the world that our Founders desired for us and that our Honored Ones bequeathed to us. The patients here all have suffered greatly from fighting the terrorist organization—the so-called Foundationalist Resistance Army. They all have sacrificed their futures in some way, and it is because of their example that *I* stand here before you today. I will magnify their resolve through the lens of our government and focus it on burning out the ants that infest our good society and seek to destroy its roots. Recently the FRA has sought to intimidate us by bringing their sordid message into the very center of where we work, play, and live. However, like our Founders, we do not intimidate easily, do we? Like them, we push back! And so, I stand here and declare that we demand the FRA surrender or face the wrath of our might! Those who seek to tear down the fabric of our civilization will receive no quarter. To this end, the time has come to approve the proposed measures our government requires to eradicate the evil FRA. Congress can no longer sit idle, debating syntax and semantics from safe and comfortable seats. It is time for *action*."

Reason. Passion. Fire. She reached them. Armed with the weapons of eloquence forged through the years, and the symbols of civilization forged through many more, she deftly wove a narrative that connected them to their past, present, and future. It gave them an identity and once they had adopted it, it was easy to manipulate them because it harkened to something nobler, better than themselves, and they knew it. They knew it and loved it and would rather die than give it up! It was easy once you knew the playbook; in fact, she could see the instant that she had succeeded in turning them. They went still, eyes and pupils widened, heads nodding with a slight turn to one side, and the most peculiar aspect of it all was that they did so unconsciously—*in unison.* Uncanny! Now it was time to hammer the nail home.

"Our Founders sought to move the human race *forward*, and they chose to go *higher* into the reaches of space, and to do it *together*, so that no person would be left behind. I ask you to do the same with me, to join me in this *just* war against terrorism. I ask for your *votes.* Through your votes we will tell Congress that enough is enough, that our civilization will flourish and not expire from this planet!"

The crowd teetered on the brink of euphoria. *Strong. Fortified. Determined.* She had them! A less skilled orator might've left the podium buoyed by their approval—but not Tyra Grant, no. She wasn't done yet. "We will not be bullied, not be pushed, and not cower in the corner like some defeated cur. Despite our foe's resolve, ours is the greater. We will not stop, nor put our progressive plans on hold for even a second. No, we will go *forward*, *higher*, and we will do so *together*!"

Tyra looked down at the podium and paused deliberately, as if to compose herself before she gazed upon the crowd. "Today, I announce the re-establishment of this planet's own Interstellar Exploration Corp., whose purpose is to summon the best of our energies, to marshal our greatest strengths, to challenge our minds, and to task our creativity, and *ultimately*, to re-establish contact with our brothers and sisters on Earth! In just two months, the *Dominus II* will launch from Punarmilan Space Port and land on Secundus, for there we will gather the resources needed to build the Rift Gate that will take us home!"

The crowd exploded into a raucous roar, fists and voices raised. Each person had a strong connection to Earth; like some evolutionary imperative, it pulled at them, made them feel a bit less than they were, and like a shaded flower bent toward sunlight, they yearned for any notion that they could re-establish communication and perhaps, even return one day.

She had better go before the tide of adulation displaced her good sense. With a final nod and a raised fist, she exited through the crowd in her bodyguards' wake and leaped into the large black SUV that awaited her, all the while reveling in the cries of adoration that diminished only as the rear door slammed shut.

"Ms. Grant, the usual Tuesday stop?" asked the driver.

"Yes."

A video call appeared on the small communications screen that adorned her driver's headrest. It was Szrina Dvorak, chief administrative officer of the Exploration Program.

"Dvorak. How go the launch plans?"

"Governor. All goes well," she replied.

Tyra almost rolled her eyes. With Dvorak, everything was great, excellent, or even stupendous at times. "Well" was decidedly a downgrade, so Tyra waited for the other shoe to drop.

"The *Dominus II*'s tests are completed and we commenced engine burn-in first thing yesterday morning. Food stores are at eighty-five percent completion, a full week ahead of schedule and—"

"Cut it out, Szrina. What did you call for?" Tyra was careful not to cast it as a problem, lest she utterly burst Dvorak's bubble. She was good at her job for the most part, and it wouldn't serve Tyra's interest to demoralize her.

"Ah. You see, it's—it's the task force, ma'am. As you know, we've continually hit our recruitment targets."

Tyra thought, *yes—but you omitted the fact that you didn't hit your contingency targets, leaving yourself exposed if something unforeseen should occur.* She suspected that was exactly what was coming.

Dvorak continued. "However, something unforeseen has occurred."

Tyra gritted her teeth.

"The entire crew of Cawnpore Barracks has been quarantined."

"Quarantined? A full barracks? What is the cause of this quarantine?"

"The Interstellar Flu."

"The IF? What do you mean, the IF? That was eradicated decades ago!"

"Well ... ahem ... yes. That was what we thought. There has been no recorded diagnosis of it since year twenty-seven, but here it is."

"Are you sure?"

"Positive. Our doctors have compared the DNA sequences from the archived strain to the active one. There is a one hundred percent match."

"And the other crew, in Carlow Barracks? How are they?"

"They are all fine. They have been tested and monitored. Not one person has been affected."

"How has this happened?"

"We have found the source of the virus. It's the ship itself. The strain had lain dormant all these years. An engineering crew engaged in the last bit of servicing had picked it up from deep within the waste recycling system."

Of course, she thought. Germs. No single person or entity had halted the progression of human history more than germs. How ironic that they would show up just in time to thwart her own progression? The Interstellar Flu had first been encountered on the *Dominus* during the voyage from Earth and had quickly spread to the *Renascent*. The common influenza virus mutated in zero gravity and became a more virulent strain. The ships' enclosed spaces, stale and humid air, and numerous niches created the perfect environment for the virus to take root, and when placed within a population having a higher density than any city on Earth, created a killing zone, cutting down swaths of settlers from every walk of life and profession. No group was safe. The young, the mature, the old—all paid their price. The fact that it lurked there, hidden for decades, was the truest testament to nature's authority over human endeavors, but despite this, she could not give in and let it alter her plans. She would have to improvise.

"What is the current status, then, of the program?"

"The ship is being disinfected and the process is expected to have no effect on its readiness for launch. What will have an effect, however, is the shortage of crew since we have nine hundred potential carriers of the virus. We will need to exclude them from service all together."

Her blood boiled. How had Dvorak not contained this in time? *Control. Calm. Focus.* It was useless to get angry. It never served any good purpose—no, she must think instead. "Could we staff the ship with those remaining?"

"No ma'am. The original designers engineered it in such a way as to require a large contingent to operate it. The devil makes work for idle hands and so they ensured that everyone had productive work to do."

Nine hundred men and women—out—just like that! It had taken over six months to recruit them and the launch was to occur in just two months—and one month before the election! There was no time left to recruit replacements and without them, there would be no launch, and without the launch, the vote was a toss-up. The polling was close, well within statistical margins of error, and a successful liftoff all but guaranteed a tip of the balance in her favor. A delay could swing the momentum to her opponent and that can't happen! There had to be a way forward, but whatever it was, she couldn't see it and so she placed the onus back on Dvorak.

"What is your plan?" she replied in a measured tone devoid of urgency.

"Well. Our officer core and navigation team remain at functional capacity. That's good news. So, we simply need to fill up the maintenance and labor ranks for the most part, and we have a legal means of shoring these up quickly. Section 7.9.6 of the Constitution gives us the power to conscript."

Of course! They could pull the crew from the citizen population! It would solve the problem quickly, yes, but she didn't have to consider it for long to realize it created another one. Conscription was unpopular and would roil the voting public. Compelling those to serve would almost guarantee nine hundred votes to her opponent. Nine hundred would become ninety thousand when the negative sentiment was magnified through their mothers, fathers, brothers, sisters, friends, colleagues, acquaintances, and more. It would be a disaster. She might as well hand the election to her rival.

"Dvorak, we must delay the launch."

"Yes ma'am." Dvorak replied, her eyes dipping for a moment or two while the words sank in.

"Wait ..." An idea took hold of Tyra. She might have a way to reverse the current course and do so in a way that wouldn't cripple her chances.

"Yes ma'am?" Dvorak's eyes widened and sparkled with hope.

"Proceed with the conscription. However, do not pull from the free citizenry. Instead, pull from the criminal elements. Empty the jails. First, anyone convicted of a violent crime, and if you need any more bodies, offer reduced sentences for nonviolent ones or deals to those awaiting trial. Get those ranks filled, trained, and ready to ship out."

"Ma'am! That's—that's brilliant!" It was the first time she had seen Dvorak stammer. "Right away."

"Oh, and connect with Ms. Dufour. This might play well with the under thirty-five cohort. There's a rehabilitation angle here that might earn us votes. Have her test it on her focus groups before she rolls anything out."

"Yes ma'am!"

This is what leaders must do, thought Tyra. Find ways to move forward. And move forward she must.

Twenty-five minutes later, her motorcade of dark-colored SUVs stopped in front of the entranceway to a large cemetery. Stepping through the gates, Tyra went up the herringbone-bricked lane that crossed through the center of the graveyard, her blank eyes no more noticing the blue sky, the songbirds, or the majestic trees than did its denizens. She approached a grave near the back and signaled her bodyguards to give her some privacy. She stood before a marble stele. Its thick base supported a rectangular main stone, and a small sculpted cherub sat peacefully on its peaked gable. She breathed deeply before reading the inscription for what must have been the thousandth time.

Sacred to the memory of
CAROLINE.
Wife of Robert Grant
and Mother to Tyra.
Who died on the 21st day of
January 040
Aged 53
Hark! A voice. It cries from heaven;
Happy in the Lord who die!
Happy they to whom 'tis given.
From a world of grief to fly!

"Hollow," she said under her breath as the anger bubbled and rose from deep within. *Clarity. Righteousness. Power.* The unpleasant sensation almost enveloped her entirely before she interceded to diminish it. She cleared her mind and worked her mantras, and as the fury subsided, she realized that both jaw and fists were tightly clenched. She stared sharply at the grave as if her thoughts could penetrate it. *Foolish woman! Why had you done this?* She had posed this question many times, and each time the answer was the same. Nothing. Mother's life was an infuriating enigma, made no sense, didn't calculate, especially near the end. Any rational mind in possession of the facts knew what life was. It was all that is! There was nothing after death. Not even darkness. Nothing. The choice between living life and succumbing to death was an easy one. You fight! Hang on to every scrap, battle for every shred, claw your way through whatever you must until the candle burns out. What you do not do is cut the wick before its time! Oh, how Tyra had tried to help her, convince her to listen to reason. To listen to the doctors who said they could give her more time. They might've even extended her life for years. But oh, she was stubborn!

Thus, Tyra had resorted to legal means to take control of the situation. However, after all the paperwork was filed and every loophole explored, this effort failed too, since there was no justification to transfer power of attorney to Tyra. Mother, according to the quacks, was "perfectly rational." But she wasn't in reality. The rational were inoculated against that viral religion she refused to part with. Prudence, science, ethics, these were virtues of the modern age, not some oppressive morality portrayed in a stone-aged soap opera. Most had discarded those stories like a worn-out rag when they arrived here, but Mom remained swaddled in them like a comforting blanket. Why? The common sentiment was to leave it back on Earth, but Mom was anything but common or sentimental. No. She clung to that archaic belief system like a log in a raging stream and no logical lifeline would convince her to abandon it. She was the unshakeable, immovable rock and when the time came to decide, she chose "Jesus" over "daughter." And it was that decision that had brought Tyra here, standing on a bright, cold spring day, in the center of a cemetery. Alone.

The solemnity of the situation settled in, bringing with it a cool draft of remorse that extinguished the fire that blazed within her. *Desolate. Sorrowful. Crushing.* With thoughts untethered by rage, her mind drifted back to happier times. Her fifth birthday party and riding the rocking horse for hours, tuck-ins with kisses after story time, driving to debate club and singing in the car the whole way, and of course, of Mom working extra shifts to put her through college. It was that sacrifice that pained Tyra the most: its toll, when viewed in retrospect, was illuminated in the crags and lines that riddled Mom's once youthful face and in the stoop that formed in her narrow little shoulders. Tyra had scarcely noticed in those days; after all, a parent's curse was to be taken for granted by the child. But Tyra only realized it now, and it was too late. If only she had more time. She would tell her.

She said her last goodbye, left the cemetery, and entered the back seat of the SUV. She pushed the green button to open the audio, then the yellow one next to it that initiated the noise isolation technology. Her employees were handpicked for their loyalty, but she could not be too careful. The last thing she wanted was for anyone to overhear this conversation.

"Albert?" she said, while peering into a handheld mirror and reapplying mascara that had smudged in the cemetery.

"This is Albert. What may I do for you, Ms. Grant?"

"Connect me to Charmagne." Moments later, a face filled the small video screen.

"Charmagne?"

"Yes ma'am."

"Get me a meeting with Mr. Krieger. This afternoon."

"This afternoon? He's the keynote at the Building Trades Union Conference. He'll be—"

"Get me the damned meeting with that bastard. No excuses."

Little bells tinkled through the air as Marcus opened the door and stepped into the Spread Eagle Tavern. Its clean, nondescript carpet was enclosed by pine wainscoting, deep-grained and lacquered to a shine. Gleaming brass beer taps lined the matching pine bar, each flanked by a wide and shiny handle. Like a peacock's feathered display, they projected their colors and flamboyant brand logos toward the door in the hopes they would catch a mate. He sat down at the bar before them and nodded a greeting to Cyrus, who, true to form, awaited with drink in hand. A real pro, that one.

"Whaddaya think, Marcus? Rockets gotta chance this year?" He stared up at the baseball game that played on the holovision behind the bar.

"Bullpen's much stronger with the pre-season trades. Doesn't hurt they picked up Dominquez." The old bartender nodded in agreement and let it be. Marcus swigged his drink and zoned out as he watched the game. Sometime later, he checked his watch. It'd been almost two hours since he arrived.

Cyrus eyed him with concern. He rested a hand on a tap handle and placed a glass under it. "Switch it up, Marcus? Something lighter?"

"No thanks." Marcus rose from the stool and produced several bills from his pocket. He placed them on the bar.

"That's too much," Cyrus said, a look of disgust marking his face. "Lemme give you some back."

"Nah. Tell you what, then. I'll take this newspaper home. I want to read about last night's bombing."

"More than a fair trade, Marcus. See ya around."

He entered his car and punched the dispatch number on the dashboard computer, verified his identity, and spent the next three minutes waiting in a queue for Albert. There was no end to the irritation he suffered when it came to Albert, and to top it off, the computer would get all the credit once the case was solved. Newspapers wouldn't miss a beat, running headlines like "Albert Does It Again!" Social media would explode with memes like "I sure wish I had a guy like Albert on my team!" And radio talk shows would proclaim that "The super detective can't be beat!" Marcus's role would be relegated to an understudy and it was more than a man could take.

"Albert?"

"Yes, Detective?"

"What was the domestic profile of the deceased?"

"Born Joseph Stephen Frederick in the fourth year After Founding to parents Alyn and Jane."

"Alyn Frederick?" Frederick wasn't exactly an uncommon surname; however, Alyn was in a class of his own. "The governor of the *Dominus*?"

"The same, Detective."

"Interesting," said Marcus absently before he drifted deep into thought. The governor? He remembered Alyn Frederick's place in history from his college studies. As he recalled, the technological challenge of moving settlers across the vast expanse of space was overcome by Zylas Finch and his team of scientists. They practiced the tools of the trade—logic, rationality, objective observation, and lots of math—to devise the Rift Gate, the propulsion engines, waste recycling systems, and even the cryogenic chambers that housed most of the passengers.

However, a greater problem awaited them once the technical ones were resolved, and it was one that even Finch was ill prepared to wrestle with—*human nature.* The cruelest parts of human nature could easily flare up given the right conditions and wreak havoc on the expedition. What would happen to thousands of people separated from their world and cooped up in a tin can for years? No one knew. Human nature didn't play nicely with the empirical models plied by the numbers people. It neither fit neatly in an objective box nor conformed to a logical framework, and it was anything but rational. No equation could predict the outcome, so the traditional scientists looked to those that could. Earth's finest philosophers, thinkers, and social scientists were sequestered in a remote area near Banff, Canada, to work through the problem. Fortunately, they had good data to draw from. Thousands of years of human history.

One idea was to control the cosmic citizenry by imposing martial law for the duration of the voyage. Under this regime, the ship's commander would have the authority to adjudicate maritime law and enforce it through a police-like organization. The greatest flaw, however, was that it would create two distinct classes of people—one that had the power to withhold resources and another that lacked the power to do anything about it. The potential for abuse by the commander and his armed coterie was akin to packing gunpowder into a most precious keg. A single match, applied to a very short fuse, would spell disaster.

Another idea was to provision a constitutional government of the sort that had backstopped Western societies for centuries. Under it, there would be no division between the ship's military branch and the people it was sworn to protect because the former would be subject to the latter. Twelve elected members of Congress would call the shots through the mechanisms of democratic processes. A thirteenth would be elected by the twelve to act as the governor in order to serve two roles—to be the council's spokesperson and to cast the tie-breaking vote in circumstances where the democratic process was insufficient to work out their differences. Alyn Frederick was the thirteenth vote.

Curiosity piqued, Marcus said, "What did you find from the protected sources?"

"Detective, your search warrant for the protected sources was denied."

Marcus frowned into the dashboard console. What was this damn computer good for? Umpteen millions of dollars for what, exactly?

Honnnnk!

Marcus snapped his attention back to the road. In the time it took to glower at the dashboard screen, he had drifted into another lane and almost into a cargo truck. He righted the car and stared back at the computer momentarily in order to make his point.

"What do you mean my warrant was denied, Albert?"

"The twelve protected sources were deemed not to have any practical application to the case."

"What? You *are* kidding, right?"

"No, Detective. I am not."

Marcus seethed. The bureaucracy never failed to surprise him. Though it was rare for this to happen in such a serious crime, it did on occasion, especially when notable politicians like Alyn Frederick were involved. Likely, there was some wildcard buried within the protected sources that would embarrass the government, but as it stood, he'd have to play without a full deck.

"Fine! Gimme what you found then—*and* can tell me!"

"Subject Joseph Frederick, age forty-five. Primary occupation: Retired. Formerly self-employed as owner and operator of an electronic component engineering firm. Spouse: Sarah Woodford, deceased ten years ago by suicide. Son: Alyn via spouse aged twenty-three. No other children."

"Parents?"

"Deceased."

"Outstanding debts?"

"Only one. A forty-eight-month automobile lease contracted four months ago."

"What is the total owing on the contract?"

"$30,506."

"Total cash in all bank accounts?"

"$412,798."

"Other assets over $5,000 and total estimated net worth?"

"Just the home, Detective. Given a market-comparable resell price, Frederick's total net worth is estimated at $795,000."

"Transactions over $5,000 settled in the last year?"

"None."

"Greatest income in any year?"

"Gross or after tax?"

"Gross."

"$123,934.23."

"Anything to suggest he had a romantic interest?"

"None."

"What probability?"

"Less than one percent. My analysis of subject's historical volumes of emails, text, chats, and GPS data produce no statistically relevant trends."

"Any warrants or arrests?"

"Yes. One."

Marcus took his eyes off the road and stared at the dashboard computer console again. "An arrest ten years ago at subject's home. Subject arraigned on domestic abuse charges but they were subsequently dropped."

"By whom?"

"Spouse Sarah Woodford." He knew it. It was common. What wasn't was the dearth of information relating to the murder. Marcus sighed and focused his eyes back on the road. It didn't make much sense. Guy was the son of a father who was practically Primisian royalty, though judging from his home, modest financial status, and marriage, he led a quiet, perhaps even humble life outside of the spotlight. Sure, he hit his wife. Marcus hated assholes who did. It was wrong to be sure, but he had seen enough of these cowardly pricks to know that it didn't necessarily amount to anything more nefarious than an insecure SOB who took his life's frustration out on someone who couldn't fight back. Marcus sighed. There was no reason to suggest this jigsaw puzzle would assemble into anything more than a burglary, but something about it was wrong. What was it?

"Has the DNA test been run yet—I mean *processed*—on the bloodstain found on the handkerchief?" Marcus corrected himself quickly. Albert didn't do too well with vernacular.

"Yes. The DNA results were processed exactly seven minutes and thirty-four seconds ago."

"Well? Anyone identified aside from the victim?" Marcus was perturbed. Even a child would have inferred why he had asked the question in the first place.

"Yes. Alyn Frederick's DNA was found at the scene."

"Joseph's father?" he asked incredulously.

"No. His son."

Marcus dialed in to the significance of this information and chastised himself that he allowed it—and Albert—to surprise him.

"What degree of confidence?"

"One hundred percent. Blood tests are completely matched over all Y-chromosome and mitochondrial markers." This was it. He had to find the boy.

"Albert. Run—uh—*process* predictive behavioral algorithm number seven."

"Fourteen sources have been obtained relating to the current whereabouts of Alyn Frederick of 31 Oak Park Avenue. Of these, three are protected sources and will require—"

"Protected sources out of scope!" Marcus replied, cutting off Albert in mid-sentence.

"Thank you. Search has now been initiated. Results will be transferred in an estimated time of twenty-nine seconds."

Twenty-nine seconds later: "Analysis indicates no social media usage, no communications media and/or GPS travel was undertaken by Alyn Frederick Jr., in the last twenty-six hours."

That's it! He's on the run or hiding. Marcus needed to find out where. "Who might Alyn Jr. seek out if he was in trouble?" he said, carefully crafting the sentence to ensure Albert understood.

"Ontological analysis of social media and communications suggest Donel DeCruze. The frequency and proportion of their communication occurrences are categorized into themes common to 'friendship.' They interact in virtually analogous social media circles and partake in very similar activities, all of which suggest that Alyn Jr. and Donel are very close friends."

Marcus had a hunch. "Albert. Has Mr. DeCruze made any financial transactions in the last twenty-six hours?"

"There is just one. Mr. DeCruze withdrew five hundred dollars from his savings account earlier today." That was a tidy sum of money. Donel was aiding his friend.

"What's Donel's address?"

"79 Main Street."

Lucky. That was only about five minutes away. "Albert. Load Donel's address into the GPS."

"Completed."

Marcus hit the gas, maneuvered through traffic with one hand, and operated his mobile phone with his other. He didn't want to route this call through Albert. The less he had to deal with him the better. The phone connected on the first ring.

"Hey, Victoria. I need some help."

"Hey, Marcus! Wait—hold that thought. I got news for *you*. Hot off the presses! Pardon the bad pun, but I need to tell someone. Like, you won't *believe* this. Guaranteed you'll be surprised when I tell you. It'll only take five minutes—promise!"

"Okay, okay. What is it?"

Over the next ten minutes or so, she combed over every detail of her appointment with the Exploration Corps. He wasn't surprised by it; after all, she was a talented woman—even if a tad verbose—and after congratulating her, said, "Victoria, I'm timing out here and got some business to take care of that can't wait. So real quick then, there's something I need you to do."

"Sure. What do you need?"

"I'm in pursuit of a suspect. Surname is Frederick. That sound familiar?"

"Yeah of course. The Fredericks were kind of a big deal in the past, you know? The old man's name was Alyn, the governor."

"Right. His son Joseph was murdered today. Alyn Junior, the grandson of Senior, is the prime suspect."

"Wow! Well ... how can I help?"

"Something feels strange about the crime scene, something's not right. No clear motive, nothing appears to be taken either. Even a wallet full of cash was ignored. I need to better understand this family. Could you mine your media resources for me and come up with a sort of—I dunno—profile of them?"

"Sure, Marcus. I'd be glad to help. When do you need it by?"

Marcus was nearing the address and needed to settle into surveillance mode. "Soon. Listen, I gotta go."

He hung up just after he heard Victoria asking, "Hey, Marcus, did you find me the scoop about the sign—"

CHAPTER FOUR

FLIGHT

Marcus parked across the road from 79 Main Street to keep an unobstructed sight line to the house and also to allow for egress should vehicular pursuit occur. If it sounded textbook, that was because it was. Chapter 12 of the *Officer's Introduction to Detective Methods* handbook spelled it out just so.

A vibrant streetscape filled his windows—dogs and their walkers, joggers, cyclists, and the like—so he relaxed a little, lit a smoke, and pulled a long, satisfying drag from it. The tip flared with red embers as he inhaled and flickered for a moment before it ebbed and darkened on the exhale. He took a thin metal flask from the glove box, unscrewed the cap, and took a quick haul from it, tucking low in his seat so he couldn't be seen. The alcohol hit his brain immediately, sending warm tingles throughout his body.

Mind at ease and nerves settled, he scanned the newspaper in between glances at the house—fully aware that Chapter 12 wouldn't approve. The headline read "Brazen Blast Kills 22." Shit. "Triple the number of the last one," he muttered as he continued down the page. There was no mention of who the casualties were, but the Central Union Bus Terminal was a zoo at lunch hour when the explosion had occurred, so it was not surprising that the numbers were high. Though it was no consolation, the bomber couldn't have chosen a worse place; the terminal was full of security cameras. Rolph, the investigating detective, might catch a lucky break and God knew he needed one. The media attention and political pressure mounted each day the bombers remained at large.

A terrified scream jolted him upright. He swung around toward its source and simultaneously grabbed the pistol from its holster that lay on the passenger's seat. Craning his neck and torso, he angled between the front seats, eyes and gun aligned toward the rear window as he removed the weapon's safety. He sized up the situation instantly. The assailant was in full view, clear as day, caught red-handed and unapologetic, bursting with ill intent. This breed of villain was common in these parts, unpredictable, with a blatant disregard for authority and predisposition for violence. Marcus was genuinely out of his weight class and ill equipped to handle this aggressor. It was a toddler, a boy of about two or so. The little thug simply stared at his victim, emotionless, like the psychopaths he had interviewed in his past. The boy's remorselessness was in stark contrast to his target, who had screamed bloody murder with an undulating shriek that had grated on Marcus's nerves.

The victim appeared to be his sister, about six. She looked down at an ice-cream cone stuck to the sidewalk, upended at a cockeyed angle, and he reflexively ran the crime scene through the CCM to deduce what had happened. The likeliest scenario saw Mom, oblivious to all but the need to safeguard her charges across the busy intersection, waiting for the pedestrian light to turn. The pint-sized hoodlum had seized the advantage, reached out of his stroller, and snatched sister's ice-cream cone. The ensuing tug-of-war left no winners. It wasn't Mom's fault. She was just a casualty of the dynamics of parenthood, which now demanded that she contend with a very pissed-off daughter and a son who, while devious by adult standards, didn't know any better.

Marcus settled back in his seat, returned the gun to its holster, and upon reflection, affirmed that if given a choice, he'd have changed places with that mother in a heartbeat. He smiled, and with the threat level downgraded to low, his mind drifted into memory.

◎◎◎

“You’re a miserable person, Clarise. Just face it.”

“Fuck you, Marcus.” She struggled to open the baby monitor’s battery compartment. She huffed in frustration, shoved the monitor into his chest and transitioned fluidly to the countertop to dry some dishes. Marcus took it, opened it effortlessly, and inserted the fresh batteries that had rested upon the counter. He slid the panel back in place with a click, powered the unit up, and handed it back to her.

“You know the girls are not toddlers anymore. They don’t need that thing.”

“Marcus, if I could just get some help. Your help. You think just because I don’t work, I have all this time—”

“I don’t think that,” he replied, turning away from her and walking to the other side of the room.

“The kids, Marcus. That’s all I think about, it’s all I do. Making lunches every day before they go to school, doing their laundry, getting Grace to her piano lessons and making sure she practices. Getting Mary to study math and making sure she brings her textbooks home. It’s a full-time job, Marcus! You don’t see that. Don’t see what I do.” Clarise worked the monitor’s buttons to set the time.

“So I—”

“And this house.” She looked at him with disgust. “You and the kids don’t give a shit. Stuff everywhere. Who cleans it? I do! Not you, not them. Me! Look. Your blazer on the fucking chair. The usual, Marcus. I bet if I looked there, there’s another one under it. Socks there next to the couch. Your dishes on the table. I can’t take it any longer. I don’t know what to do.”

“Fine. Look. I’ll help more,” he said with arms wide and palms open, followed by a long sigh to help neutralize the tension.

"You? Help more? Help? You won't help more. All you do is work! All you care about is work! You never take a day off. That's all I am asking, Marcus—take a few days off to help more." Her eyes welled up with tears.

"Okay. Okay ... I'll take a day off next week."

"Marcus, I need help now. Not next week."

"Look, I got it, but I can't right now. You know this! We're in the first week of a fucking murder case. It's the actor and you know how they feel about these goddamn celebrities. Anyone famous and the press is all over. Shit. You *know* how important that first week is. If I don't invest the time up front, we'll lose so much good intel."

"Tell your boss you need time off. Get someone else on it."

"There's no one else."

"No one? You mean the whole department will shut down if you take a fucking day off? Marcus is so important that the world stops? C'mon. Who are you fooling? Take some time off. I need help, Marcus!"

"I will. I will."

"No, you won't. Mr. Detective, the *Sage*, it just burns you to have to come home, to leave that world where you feel so important—but guess what? You're important here *too.* Important to your damn children! And how about your wife?"

She looked to be at her wit's end in the attempt to get the device to function. "Who designs these damn products?" she said, exasperated. "They promise they'll work for you but they *never* do. Just like my husband!" Frustrated, she hit the face of the monitor twice with the heel of her hand.

She was too much. Never thought things through, never applied logic to the situation. Sure, he wasn't perfect, but my God, the guys at the precinct weren't even close! The majority of them caroused in the night clubs with a frequency and intemperance that defied belief. And the cheating! That shit was rampant in his profession. He didn't do any of that. Imagine if she was married to one of *those* guys. If she could just step back and see how good she had it. Right?

Anger roiled within him. "Stop it! You know how much those cost? Shit. You'll never be happy, Claire. It's because you were born on that damn rock. That cold fucking island where the sun barely pokes its head out of the clouds. And that's it, you're all like that. Miserable. You'll never change. You'll never be happy."

"Fuck you, Marcus!" Tears streamed down her face as she wound back and pitched the baby monitor, it narrowly missed his head before it careened off the kitchen cupboards and smashed into several pieces onto the floor. By the time he picked them up, she had run upstairs and slammed the bedroom door.

◎◎◎

"Detective Marcus?"

The voice snapped him out of his reverie. It was Albert addressing him coolly over the commlink. "Satellite has detected movement on a roof of the domicile under surveillance."

There. Above the covered porch, just as Albert had called it. A male, young, probably early twenties, shimmied feet first through a window above it. Clearing the opening, he gained his balance before extending himself to his full height. He treaded carefully down the sloped roof before he sat and dangled his legs over its edge. Shifting his weight, he turned and dropped, and started to clamber down the downspout.

It's him. Alyn Frederick. Electrified, Marcus clicked his seatbelt off, left the car, and in three strides cleared the road. He could just make out Alyn's figure through the branches of a large tree that stood between them. He was already halfway down the pipe.

Alyn hung from the roof's shingled edge and locked his feet tightly to either side of the sturdy iron downspout. He shimmied down the pipe, alternating his hands quickly, and heard a commotion coming from the street when he was just past halfway. He stopped to look. A man in a dark blue suit lay sprawled on the grass abutting the sidewalk. It was clear that he had clipped the stroller pushed by what looked like a very pissed-off woman, and she in turn stopped to settle an upset little girl. He couldn't hear actual words over her shrieks, but it was clear that the mother was tearing a strip off the man. The most curious thing was the toddler in the stroller who watched it all as if nothing was happening. The man, on the other hand, looked embarrassed and bewildered as he stared at the woman.

There was something else about him, though. His air. The way he picked himself up and disengaged from her as if he had a vital purpose. What could it be? The man, now having restored his equilibrium, picked up his hat, rose, and looked directly at Alyn. How could the man have known that he was there, tucked behind the tree, hanging from a roof in the alley—unless he was looking for him? It was a cop!

Alyn's heart beat rapidly as he landed hard, feet first, on the pavement.

Run!

"Frederick!" yelled the cop, who was now halfway across the yard, charging forward toward the tall chain-link fence that separated them.

Alyn pivoted and launched himself down the alleyway in a ragged sprint, dodging garbage, building materials, and other castoffs. *Who is this man? How did he find me?* Those questions were quickly displaced by more practical ones. *How will I lose him? Where can I hide?* Alyn had a decent lead on him, but he was convinced that it wouldn't last for long. *Grim* and *determined* were two words that described the man's bearing, and if his resolve matched, then he was dangerous indeed. Alyn's skin prickled at the thought and his breath become shallower, less rhythmic, as fear seized him again.

Why waste my breath? Wouldn't it just be easier to stop?

It was a point worth considering. Running was a sign of guilt, wasn't it? Maybe he *should* stop, tell the cop what had happened? Convince him it was all a mistake? Besides, the truth was on his side. Yes, pull up! He could go quietly to the station, talk this all out. It would all work out in the end, wouldn't it?

He remembered yesterday's peculiar harbinger. *They'll come after it, and so they will come for you. Trust only yourself. Run. Hide.* Though he was uncertain of the meaning of his father's words, it was best to obey them, play it safe, and buy himself time to figure this all out. With single-minded purpose, he charged forward, and in that moment, something awakened deep inside of him.

The lion.

It arched its back, stretched its front legs, and then sprang forward.

Alyn burst into the market square and dodged to sidestep a vendor balancing a cage carefully on his head. Alyn glanced the man's side, sending white feathers in the air as the chickens within the cage squawked and flapped their wings in protest. The poultry purveyor gave a derogative cluck, but Alyn dashed ahead without heed, bobbing and weaving through the throngs of people with great abandon. He did not look back at his pursuer, knowing full well he was right there, knowing he would not tire, and knowing he would not stop.

Alyn had to think. Had to do something to shake him. With that in mind, he ran farther down the fare and ducked into the first door he found.

Marcus looked east down the long thoroughfare that bisected the market. There were an incalculable number of places for Frederick to hide, and the throngs of shoppers wouldn't help either. He leaped on a wooden crate in order to see above them. The chickens within it cried foul, and their owner screamed at Marcus, who gritted his teeth and stared down on him so fiercely that the enraged vendor backed off to tend to his customers.

Marcus rotated his watch's crown, raised it to his mouth, and said, "Albert. Convey location of suspect."

"Detective. Suspect's location is indeterminate at this time. Suspect was last seen by satellite approximately 17.6784 meters east from your current location."

So he was close. Marcus spoke into his watch again. "Albert. Do you use the difference in walking speed as the means to identify the runner relative to the others in the market?"

"No."

Frustration set in. Alyn's escape was imminent and Albert was wasting time. Why could he not infer the intent of the question?

"Then what means do you use, Albert?" replied Marcus, screaming into the watch.

"A combination of physical attributes."

"Which ones?" Marcus was shouting now.

"Physical dimensions like shoulder area, head circumference, clothing and skin color patterns, and gait where observable. These are run through an identification algorithm that creates a unique numeric score. Speed is an unreliable characteristic given that it can be modified easily by—"

Marcus cut off the communications link, angry that the computer was choosing this time to be verbose. However, what was clear from Albert's expansive monologue was that there could only be two explanations for Frederick's disappearance. The first was that Alyn had modified his appearance in some manner to fool Albert. It was possible. Alyn could've donned a large hat or coat and in turn, corrupted Albert's algorithmic score. It wouldn't be hard to do in a market like this. There was ample clothing for sale, of all different shapes, sizes, and colors. However, one thing made this very improbable. The vendors. The density of people in the market greatly increased the potential for theft, and so merchants eyed their customers like hawks. The only other explanation was that Frederick had found cover from the satellites by running into a shop. That was it. He must have hidden.

Marcus stepped back down to street level, eyes focused on Frederick's last known position. He paced an estimated eighteen meters and checked each vendor's place of business thoroughly—under tables, behind hanging textiles, around crates, and any other places that afforded concealment. Coming up empty, he continued on to the first storefront. It was small and nondescript, having few of the flashy trimmings that adorned the façades of its neighbors. Marcus approached its glass door and paused to read the white stenciled words painted across its top section.

Interstellar Exploration Corps
Community Relations & Outreach Office

The IEC? Alyn Jr. would be crazy to hole up in there! There couldn't be a better place to make the arrest. But maybe that was the thing? Maybe he had guessed as much, had known Marcus would think so, and given the desperate situation Frederick found himself in, had taken the gamble. Yes! As far as places to hole up, it was the perfect place.

He spied a small white sign that hung behind the glass at the door's center, the word Open imprinted upon it in bold red letters. Marcus shoved the door forward. It squeaked a sharp retort and waved the white sign in surrender as he burst inside. By now, he was out of breath, but managed to hold himself upright, chest out, projecting confidence. His eyes had trouble adjusting to the dim light, and he could scarcely make out a figure sitting on a plain gray metal stool at the side of a gleaming stainless-steel counter, behind which a woman stood, outfitted in a sergeant's full-dress regalia. Frederick's face was just visible in the half-light, and he was looking back at Marcus with a calm, serene expression. What was this? Were his eyes playing tricks on him? He shifted them mechanically to focus on the officer. She returned his glare with a scornful expression but said nothing, as if expecting Marcus to account for his insolent behavior.

Marcus took the advantage and said, "Alyn Frederick! You are under arrest for the murder of your father, Joseph. You will place yourself in my custody and come to the station for questioning."

The sergeant's eyes shone with a sharp keenness as they regarded Alyn carefully, but her face gave no indication of what she would do next. The kid, in contrast, sat there tired and glum, as if he had given it his all but knew it wasn't enough. Marcus produced handcuffs, brandished his badge, and moved forward to cuff the young man, who stood up passively and presented his hands.

"Officer! You will stand down. You will *end* your pursuit of this young man," said the sergeant with a shout as she strode out from behind the counter and into the space between the two men. Though she was a head shorter than he was, the military woman stood toe to toe as if she were his equal and seemed prepared to prove it.

Stunned but undeterred, Marcus said, "And why the hell would I do that?"

"Officer. Recruit Frederick has been fully attested and is now a non-commissioned soldier in the Interstellar Exploration Corps."

"What the ...?" Marcus lowered the pitch of his voice while raising its volume at the same time. "How?"

"Our processes do not concern you, Detective, but I assure you they are one hundred percent legal. I should also inform you that as a condition of service, Recruit Frederick receives all rights and obligations herein. His obligations, though considerable they may be, are his to bear and are of no interest to you. His rights, however, are. He will provide service to this government and by pledging to do so, has the protection of the state. You may leave now, sir."

"You're shittin' me," said Marcus.

"No, Officer. I am not." The sergeant went still and hardened like concrete. Marcus needed to try a different tack. Softer, maybe. She wasn't going to give in through intimidation.

"Look. I'm sorry if I barged in here and created such a commotion. I'd been chasing him and, uh—well—I ain't as young as I used to be, so sorry for my reaction. Now that I've caught my breath, Sergeant ...?"

"Dryer."

"Ah. Sergeant Dryer. I'm Detective Elroy Marcus of the PPD. Pleasure. This young man, you know, he might just be a murderer. How's *that* gonna sit with the government?"

"Fine, Detective Marcus. In fact, murderers and delinquents are in vogue at the moment."

"What?"

"Haven't you heard? Grant's desperate to fill her starship, so she signed the executive order to fill them with anyone she can muster—including criminals."

"Modern-day press gangs, huh? And that's okay with you?" Marcus attempted to appear unfazed despite the fact that this news unsettled him.

"Okay with me? Detective, my duty is to the state. How I feel is of no consequence."

"And could I change your mind about this one little thing? Look the other way?"

"Detective Marcus, you of all people should know this. Duty is that which you *must* do, not what you *wish* to do. Goodbye, Detective."

CHAPTER FIVE

CONTRITION

In a sullen stupor, Marcus watched as the sergeant beckoned Alyn toward a nondescript door that she had opened behind the counter. Alyn rose from his stool, its steel legs grating along the floor and piercing through the silence that had overtaken the room. His footsteps thudded on the cold concrete floor, each carrying the answers that Marcus needed farther and farther away. Speechless and confused, all he could do was stare as Alyn approached the door.

Just then, Marcus said, "Son." Alyn turned his head and looked him in the eyes. "I know it wasn't you." They stared at each other for a second or two before Alyn turned his head back toward the open door and exited. Dryer followed, pulling the door behind her. It clicked tight. He was gone.

And for good too. Marcus had no jurisdiction over the Interstellar Exploration Corps. Even *if* he could coax a court order from the District Judicial Authority, it would be worthless due to the colony's unique Second Amendment. It gave the federal government the right to draft citizens into military service for any "just and necessary" reason. That "just and necessary" was subjective, allowed the politicians some latitude in its application, but despite this, it had only been exercised once, several years after Landfall, in the time known as the Dark Days.

In those early days and for several years after the crash, shelters were hastily thrown up, and all living organisms were summarily released from the ship. The absence of some species and the haphazard introduction of others had opened a Pandora's box of ecological torments. Successive waves of pestilence and famine swept through the colony, leaving sickness and death in their wake. Mother Nature was a cruel matron and doled out harsh lessons that the colonists, in their deprived state, were all too fond to imitate. They cowered like frightened sheep as the scythe of tribulation swung relentlessly, shearing off their noble fleece and exposing the nasty and brutish character underneath it. The murderous strife that followed threatened the fledgling civilization, and so Governor Frederick had reconstituted the IEC to keep order during the first ten years after Founding. It was the only means to keep people's hands off people's throats and feuding clans from choking out civilization.

Though the IEC was designed to move humanity across space, it proved to be a convenient way to organize a military force given that its legal, procedural, and operational frameworks were established already. It gave the government a legitimate means to forcibly end vendettas, crush insurgencies, and bring peace to the colony. When the dust settled and the swords turned to plowshares, few could disagree that it had worked. And thus the authority to muster a pacifying force, which was so central to the colony's existence, was ratified by the twelve members of Congress with zero dissent. Like it or not, the Second Amendment superseded any other jurisdiction. And as a result, a key witness would escape the clutches of the justice system today, leaving Marcus with many questions and few answers.

He pulled into his driveway at dusk, exhausted by the rain-induced gridlock. He covered his head with the newspaper as he dashed up the pathway leading to the front door and in that moment, noticed the weeds bunched between the patio stones. When had they sprouted like that? He ascended the small set of stairs before scooping up several more newspapers that cluttered the front porch and fumbled them as he pressed his thumb against the security reader.

He entered the house. Turned on the lights, opened the blinds in the dining room and kitchen, and switched on the gas fireplace in the living room to warm things up. In the kitchen, he set upon the fridge and sized up what he might have for dinner. Thankfully, there were sufficient leftovers to cobble together, but first he needed a drink. He deserved one, though he would've had one even if he felt he did not. It just tasted a little better when it was justified. He inspected the row of bottles lined across the shelf above the fridge. What was he in the mood for? Scotch? Rum? Tequila? Yes, tequila. He poured an ounce and a bit, pounding it back with a single tip of the glass. The alcohol hit his brain immediately, sending him somewhere else, somewhere pleasant, where the pressures of the day struggled to find him.

About an hour and many more tequilas later, he slumped into his chair by the fire, full from the meal and weary from the day's events. He now sipped Scotch from a glass that was closely guarded by the bottle that supplied it, they both waited dutifully on a side table next to his chair. He flipped through the HV channels absently before stopping on the twenty-six-hour news network to check the baseball game highlights. The news cycle had just wound up again, so he'd have to sit through all the sex, lies, and violence before the sports came on. There was no escape in it for him—heck, he lived through it every day, so he zoned out and stared at the screen, drawn in by the bright colors, fluid movement of the ticker, and rhythmic cadence of the anchor. Several more Scotches reinforced his relaxed state, and with eyelids weighed down by the pull of the spirits, he sank deeper into his chair and went over the crime scene, from the moment he had entered Frederick's street through to when he'd left it. Backward and forward, forward and backward, then in complete disorder, over and over again, before he fell fast asleep and dreamed.

A pair of seagulls squawked bitterly at each other, and Marcus spied the object of conflict upon the ground nearby. It was not a French fry, apple core, or some other discarded digestible; rather, it was a black and white calendar page labeled with the month of June and curiously, the day of the 13th was circled in red felt-tipped marker. Marcus wondered why they would fight over something like that—he'd never seen them tussle for anything inedible. It was more than silly, but then who really understood what went on with birds?

He dismissed the thought and with that, the birds' cries melded into the background, replaced by the crashing of waves on the shore and the din of beach life. It was like heaven. The taste of salty air on his lips and warm sun on his skin invigorated his spirits. He sat on a beach chair nestled in a small, shade-giving tent that formed a semicircle around him, and that was when he spotted Claire's book in the chair next to him. Funny. Its cover was totally blank and colored a brilliant white. A coppery-red feather bookmark was inserted between some pages near the end. He had never seen a book with a white, bare cover nor a bookmark of such a beautiful shade before. Where was she?

"Maaar-cus," came a voice from somewhere behind him. It had a song-like quality and cadence that he instantly recognized as Claire's. He stood and turned toward the direction it had come from but there was no one there. Not a single person. He lingered a moment longer and, satisfied he wasn't crazy, turned back and sat down. He was perplexed for some time before the feeling subsided, replaced by a warm sensation that wafted over him. Hope. Yes, she'd be back soon. Nothing to worry about.

He looked out across the water, amid the throng of people, and zeroed in on his children who played gaily with each other, laughing and splashing. He smiled and the warm feeling came over him again, as if time had stood still and God had singled him out and smiled back at him. Marcus reached into the plastic cooler beside him and hauled out a soda from under the ice. Black cherry cola, his favorite. He twisted the cap and paused to admire the little wisp of vapor that danced at the bottle's tip and vanished moments later. Then he admired the condensation beading upon its surface. Magnificent. He brought the bottle up and as he tilted his head to take the first sip, he noticed that his kids were gone. In fact, so was everyone else. He was alone on the beach.

Marcus lowered the bottle and stood. Where had they gone? He must find them, keep them safe. He strolled along the boardwalk looking here and there, peering into the adjoining shops, but all were empty. He called out to them but his tongue, like coarse sandpaper, could not shape the words and his throat, like baked clay, fashioned only a hoarse rasp. He remembered the black cherry cola and brought his hand up to swig it, but it was gone too. Where had *it* gone? He stumbled about for several minutes before ducking into a sandy alley in between shops that led to the parking lot. If he could find his car, he was sure he would find his family. He started toward where he thought he had parked, and a short distance later saw a nurse dressed in light blue scrubs. She appeared to be cleaning a set of invisible tools. Marcus stopped her and asked, "Have you seen my wife?" He noticed his voice changed, ever so slightly, as if he was pleading, and it alarmed him.

"No," she replied, now writing feverishly on a paper sheet pinned to a clipboard.

"Have you seen my kids? Two children. Twins. Girls. About yea big?" He held his hands just below chest level to indicate their height.

"No," she said again and returned to her task.

Marcus moved passed her and not far along came to a uniformed police officer, whom he asked the same questions. The officer said nothing, just looked at him with a subtle expression that scarcely surfaced through his stolid face. What was it? Disgust? After some time, Marcus found his car parked alone in the center of the lot. The wind had blown sand all around it, about a foot or two high, and tall sprigs of grass had sprouted in these mini dunes. How much time had passed?

A man leaned back against the front of the car. As Marcus approached the man from behind, he paused to look inside the back window. No one was in there. He rounded the front of the car and stopped a few meters in front of the man, a Catholic priest in flowing black vestments, his face motionless save for his jaw that chewed a single stalk of tall grass. What was the expression it wore? Pity? Marcus was about to ask him something but couldn't remember what it was. The priest spoke first.

"Elroy. I haven't seen you and your family for some years."

"Father Jack. I've lost them."

The priest looked out into the large dunes that bordered the parking lot.

Marcus followed his gaze and saw them. Grace and Mary! Their backs were turned but he knew it was them. He would know them anywhere. They wore the classic pinstripe shirts and hats of the Rockets. They loved attending the games, or more so eating the peanuts, popcorn, and cotton candy, and couldn't wait to tell their friends what a time they had had. Oh, how he missed them. They frolicked amid the sand and tall grasses, stooping here and there to pick flowers and toss the ball in a game of catch. Strange though. They seemed oblivious to the fact that they were lost.

Marcus hurried over, but halfway there, a loud cheer, as if a stadium full of fans were celebrating a home run, burst forth from every direction. In that instant, the children slid down a large dune and dropped out of sight. He ran to where he had seen them last but there was no one as far as his eyes could see. They had vanished.

At once, a violent crash permeated the air from the direction of the car and startled him so terribly that it sent him into a protective crouch. Slowly, he straightened and looked back toward the vehicle. It was completely destroyed, looking as if it had been crushed and then torn in two. Curiously, there was no sign of what had caused the crash; not even a speck of dust or sand floated nearby it. Maybe someone was injured? He was about to start back to it when a voice called out to him from behind.

"Hi, Daddy!"

It was Mary. Standing next to her was Grace. They both beamed. God, he was so glad he'd found them! The urge to rush and wrap them both in one giant hug and tell them he loved them and missed them was all he could think about. Before he could move or even say a word, Grace said to him, "A shepherd has lost his way."

Marcus awoke with a start and the dream vanished. How long had he been asleep? He cranked the lever on the chair to straighten himself before he reached tentatively out across the table, fingers spread wide, searching for his glasses in the dark. Despite this care, he sent the bottle of Scotch toppling over, sending it clanging to the floor. He was amazed that it didn't break, but he could tell by the relative ease of moving it that it was empty. He found his glasses, put them on, and peered at the holovision, which still blared the news. He squinted to read the time on the ticker. It read 5:08.

It all hit him. The dream, the shepherd, the time—it was clear now. He jumped from his chair. He had an important visit to make, and it couldn't wait a minute.

◎◎◎

Tyra exited the casino floor and entered the hidden corridor. The sound of her footfalls on the rough plywood floor echoed harshly against the unfinished walls and exposed pipes. It was dusty and smelled like raw-cut wood and plaster, mixed with a hint of urine. She made her way toward an unpainted metal door that lay at the end and noted how the Bauhaus hallway was so different from the luxurious trappings at the other end. It was true here, as in life, that there was the thing you wanted people to see and the thing you tucked away that you didn't.

Tyra punched the passcode and opened the door. The pungent smell of new carpet hit her right away. It pushed back the foul odors from behind her, and like a time machine, triggering her olfactory system to project a mosaic of vivid memories. Memories of her childhood. Happier, more innocent times. Where time was an esoteric concept and the future existed in the land of unrestrained dreams. Most children departed this land in adulthood, weighed down by the baggage of fear and self-doubt, never fully understanding that their dreams *could* come true. If only they knew this. Young Tyra did.

Her transformation had begun after her father left. Just faded glimpses remained of those days, not of her father, whom she couldn't remember, but of her mother, who for a time was violently ill. She threw up in the toilet for weeks after his departure. Tyra held her hair once so it wouldn't fall into the grimy bowl and watched as she sobbed uncontrollably, both trying their best to ignore the stench that filled the bathroom.

After a time, things started to look up for Mom. She worked a series of casual and part-time jobs before she finally found full-time work at the city library as a purchasing agent. As a child of six, Tyra didn't know what a purchasing agent was, only that Mom was very excited about starting her new job. She went to work that first morning dressed in neatly pressed clothes, which she had ironed with ritualistic fervor the night before. One night soon after, during bedtime, Mom put the storybook down, kissed Tyra on the nose and snuggled in to her closely as she lay on the bed. She smelled nice, like lavender shampoo, and her soothing tone carried the higher pitch she used when she was excited.

She said, "Honey? Mommy's receiving her first paycheck tomorrow. Sweetheart, it's more money than we have ever had before. Now, we're not rich by any stretch, but I think I could take a little bit of it and buy you something nice. Would you like Mommy to do that?"

"Uh huh."

"Okay, then. What would you like, sweetheart?"

"New carpet."

"What, honey?"

"A new carpet, Mommy. A blue one. I want one in my room."

And so it came to be about three weeks later that the creaky wood floor in Tyra's bedroom was replaced by new blue carpet–sending her instantly to the moons! Its warm, plush presence made her room a very special place. Her sanctuary. *Luxurious, beautiful, safe.* All from something as innocuous as a blue carpet. And she owed it all to Mrs. Harmon.

Mrs. Harmon was an old family friend, and she watched over Tyra while her mom worked. Tyra liked Mrs. Harmon for she was always well dressed, very pretty and nice, and worldly too, telling her wondrous stories of travel and adventure that were more common to the early days when the world was bigger and untamed. She lived in a grand house that stood a good distance back from the road, situated on over four acres of land, standing tall and majestic on a hill that commanded a view of the wilder country that surrounded it. It had a steeply pitched roof with front-facing gable, intricate gingerbread trim, a turret topped by a witch's hat, many windows and shutters, and a half-width asymmetrical porch that extended along the front. The stately nature of the home never ceased to enthrall Tyra when she closed the car door and turned to take in its grandeur. A path led from the driveway to a regal fountain in the center of the front yard where a dozen copper fish gathered in a ring and spat water toward its center. Here the path split in two, a wider walking path went across the yard and snaked its way around the house and into the dense forest. A narrower path led the front door, meandering through a copse of topiary trees manicured with great skill using every geometric shape imaginable. It terminated at a gate that opened into a beautifully arranged garden of all manner of flowers and where birds would shade in the fruit tree that blossomed white in the spring. It was heavenly.

But it was the blue-carpeted playroom, just off the kitchen, that was her favorite place of all. Mrs. Harmon kept it stocked with toys for her granddaughters whom she watched over too. Tyra had never seen so many toys in all her life! Dolls and their houses, a cash register and various sundries of plastic produce, canned goods, vegetables, meats, coins, hair combs and brushes, mirrors, and many more wondrous things were at their disposal. Playing "Grocery Store" was her favorite! Hours would float by while she and her playmates alternated between cashier, customer, and the most coveted role—*boss*. The little thespians and their supporting cast of dolls and puppets garnered a perpetual string of standing ovations from the invisible audiences who paid top dollar to attend. The scrumptious smell of Mrs. Harmon's oven-fresh cookies was the one thing that would break them out of character. They'd crash into the kitchen once the signal was given, climb up the giant bar stools like little monkeys, grabbing and scoffing the treats as they teetered and wobbled before they washed them down with tall glasses of lemonade. Mrs. Harmon made wonderful lemonade. Squeezed by hand, even! Tyra had never seen anything like it. To see it produced before her eyes and to taste it immediately afterward was like magic! And so, the day would go on in her happy place and before she knew it, it was time to go.

When she arrived back home, the difference was stark and jarring. Her house looked meager in comparison to Mrs. Harmon's; it was drafty, and there was no toy-filled, blue-carpeted refuge to escape to. And she knew why. She was poor, Mrs. Harmon was rich, and it was as simple as that. *Money*. Even in her child's mind, she understood that money could bring an entirely different reality into being, and that was why she decided early on to design her life in a way that she would have it. Lots of it! Her first step in that long journey was to get her own sanctuary, her own room with a blue carpet. There she could think. There she could dream about the woman she would become. Someone rich, someone to be admired, someone who could stand on her own two feet. Someone who needed no one.

Now, she crossed the room and made her way to the large oak desk at the opposite end, pausing to look at the painted portrait of her mother that was placed upon it. A young woman stared back with wide bright eyes and a broad smile. Her face lit up the canvas with an optimistic expression, as if she had just started her life, beholden to no one and bound by nothing but her dreams. As always, Tyra was saddened at how little she remembered of that smile, and she experienced more than a twinge of guilt, for she was the reason it had faded. A life unlived was not a life at all.

Tyra thought about how far she had come, what heights she had gained since her earliest dreams, and she laughed out loud at the incongruity of her present circumstance. After all, she was now waiting, hidden in the bowels of a casino, for a criminal. The building of the Grand Centaurium Casino had been a major plank in her last election, sold to the public on the promise of jobs, reduced personal taxes, and the boosting of local retail sales. With the election won and mandate approved, she had made it happen, but it hadn't been easy. A host of do-gooders and NIMBYs had done their best to stop its construction, but she'd prevailed anyway through sheer will and a combination of guile and charm. Ironically, votes had nothing to do with it; after all, she had polled to win by a landslide in this district before she championed the casino's creation. Her personal legacy didn't play a factor in its support either. Rather, it was all about securing her power base, since many became rich off its construction and now *owed* her.

And no one was indebted to her more than the Centaurium's owner, Jan Krieger, whose personal wealth had skyrocketed overnight. Thanks to Tyra, his casino occupied prime Primis City real estate, had been constructed with generous government grants, and paid only a fraction of the property tax rate.

Krieger paid his debt to her in loyalty, backdoor kickbacks, and in the customization of the very room she stood in. She used it on the occasions when she wanted to stay off the radar. The location was perfect for this sort of thing. People from every walk of life frequented casinos—from the salt of the earth to the scum. No one was out of place here. Not even her. She would not have to conduct these meetings in dark alleys, abandoned warehouses, and other clichéd locations. This was better than those. And so was she.

A man entered and closed the door behind him. He looked rough, wiry, all angles and no planes, as if hewn from the coarser material of society with a set of old blunt tools. Handsome was not the word to describe him, but his average looks were more than compensated for by his confident stare and swagger. He stood behind the chair across from the desk and stared down on her. Dark irises closely matched the black of his pupils, giving the impression that he peered from the depths of his soul, deep into hers.

A feeling of panic flitted inside her. Though just a spark, its suddenness compounded her unease. She needed to smother it out before it found dry kindling. *Calm. Attention. Control.* The sensation dissipated into a smoky wisp while she leaned forward and neatly stacked some papers to mask the effort. All the while, he just stood there silently, square, hands on hips, ready for a challenge. In the next moment she almost laughed out loud since it was clear she had already won. He was not some indomitable thug come to stare her into submission; he was just an actor playing a role. The eyes gave him away. The same eyes used to manufacture fear did not have the ability to hide it. *Fear. Doubt. Submission.* These were inscribed in them, faint but legible. The top of his eyelids and brows were positioned high on his face while the bottom widened and flattened. More clues seeped from his façade: his shoulders were lowered slightly, and his feet angled a few degrees from center, one of them tapping almost imperceptibly. She waited some more, knowing he would be the first to break the silence.

"So?" he said.

There it was. "Have a seat," she replied.

He stared blankly for several more seconds before his eyes lowered in the instinctive signal of defeat. He sat down. She waited for him to settle, and then waited a little more to unsettle him. She had him, and they both knew it.

"You came alone?" she said.

"Yeah. Just me."

"Where is your boss?"

"Tied up. Gives his regards."

"Has more important things, does he?"

"Yeah, well. He's an important man."

"So he is. Let's get down to it, shall we? Your botched job in the Square? How would you rate it, Nicholas? On a scale of your choosing?"

"Please. Call me Nikko."

Tyra stared at the man for several seconds without as much as a blink.

His fingers tightened their grip on the armrest as he shifted and drew back in his chair. "It ..." He hesitated as if thinking.

"It *what*?" she said, drawing out the words for effect.

"It ... look ... I thought it would help the cause. *Your* cause."

"You *thought*, Nikko? I needed a job done. A simple one. Mr. Krieger chose *you* to plan and execute it. I paid him handsomely, I might add, and all I got in return for my investment was disappointment. So tell me, Nikko, what exactly were you *thinking?*"

"Well, after we talked, me and the lieutenants sat down to figure this all out, you know, map out our plan, so we got together the night of the Patel fight. You remember that night, right?" Tyra nodded, raising her eyebrows in exasperation. Nikko leaned forward in his chair. "Well, we were havin' a coupla drinks, trying real hard to do right by you. Know what I mean? But we couldn't come up with nothin', all sat there lookin' at each other over a bottle of Scotch." He leaned back in his chair, more relaxed now. "It was getting late by the time Inez came up with the idea. Said it would create the buzz you were lookin' for, make a splash—"

Tyra interjected, unable to indulge the asinine narrative any longer. "A splash? A splash, Nikko? This wasn't a splash. It was more of a fucking tidal wave. You embarrassed me in front of the world, plus you left behind a half can of spray paint!"

"You wanted publicity. We got you publicity. Now everyone knows who you are."

"Sure they do. My name was all over the news—print, web, holovision, social media ... you got that right, Nikko. Problem was, you got the story wrong. You put it in peoples' minds that I am a *tyrant*. That's not good press, Nikko. That's *bad* press. Bad press won't get me elected!"

"All press is good, isn't it? That guy on Earth said it—it's worse to be talked about than not talked about, right?"

Tyra lowered her head. *Fury. Disappointment. Derision.* It was useless. There was no getting through to this idiot. He couldn't be helped, couldn't be reasoned with, and couldn't be saved from himself. It wasn't entirely his fault. Nature wasn't kind to the petty criminal. Sure, she had imbued him with characteristics useful in the underworld—impulsiveness, independence, a willingness to take risks, high social awareness, and little conscience. However, he was *stupid*. If Nature's bounty included intelligence, he'd have become a lawyer.

She chastised herself for allowing her anger to flare up. Nikko was inconsequential, so it didn't matter much, but she promised herself she would work harder at emotional regulation for the times it was truly needed. She composed herself and looked at the dimwit, working her facial muscles to project a calculated mixture of sorrow, understanding, and empathy. Smiling warmly, she said, "You're right, Nikko. It was a success when you consider it that way." Pausing for a moment as if to consider her next words, she said, "Thank you."

Nikko grinned and exhaled deeply. "My pleasure," he said. The counterfeit smile she returned passed as legitimate if Nicholas Nylund's smug demeanor was any indication. "I'll give the boss your regards." He rose and left the room.

A side door opened just as soon as the main door clicked closed. A slender and attractive thirty-something woman entered. She was impeccably dressed in her usual pencil miniskirt, this time gray, a white blouse, red high heels, and a fitted baby-blue blazer. Her hair was tied up tightly in a jumbo bun and held together by a chopstick, and all was accented by a stylish belt, necklace, and a pair of computer-interfaced designer glasses that synced with the tablet she held at her side. She carried a coffee cup in her other hand and waited silently just inside the doorframe. Tyra looked at her for a moment and nodded once. The woman left abruptly.

Tyra was alone again with her thoughts. Imagine the nerve! With a thud, her fist thumped the desk before she violently swept her arm across it, knocking off the neatly stacked documents. That useless tool thought that the media coverage that she had received was a good thing? Something to be proud of? No. It was a huge step backward. The headlines read things like "Grant's Crime Rant," "Encircled in the Square," and "Foundation Crumbles Grant" while the holovision pundits insinuated that she couldn't control crime in general nor in her city specifically. It was a critical blow. Crime was the voter's greatest priority and that halfwit handed the pole position to her competitor in the race! He was supposed to create sympathy for her cause, not make her look weak this close to the election.

It was almost more than she could take, so she spent the next half hour in meditation to think through her options. She couldn't change the past, but she could find every advantage that it bestowed to make a better future. That was what she always had done, ever since the blue carpet. Today would be no different. She would take back the initiative! She left the room and exited through the unsurveilled passages to the garage bay, entered her car, and made a few calls to execute her plan. It would take a good deal of work to recover from this hand, but it would be well worth the effort once she was done. Make lemonade out of lemons, she thought. Yes! Lemonade from lemons.

◎◎◎

The Woman in the Pencil Skirt hurried down the brightly lit hallway, zipping past slow movers and smiling cheerily at familiar faces as she went. She saw two female greeters up ahead. They flanked the casino's main entranceway, their heads and tails covered with grand feathered plumage and silver sequined fabric that covered little else. And there was Nikko Nylund, smiling at one of them. He flipped his dark sunglasses down and uttered something she couldn't hear. He would be at his car soon.

She quickened her pace and passed the two scantily clad women, entered the front foyer, and spied Nikko below. He was strolling toward a black town car at the curbside, its rear door held open by the valet. She descended the stairs to street level, surprising herself with her own dexterity in six-inch heels, and was within ten feet of the car in seconds.

Just as the door shut, she said sweetly, "Oh, Mr. Nylund? Mr. Nylund?" She waved a hand above her head and layered on a smile of red lipstick and perfect white teeth.

Nikko looked out from the back seat and removed his sunglasses. His eyes squinted, and upon seeing her, he lowered his window. "Hey, doll. What can I do for you?" He grinned and unabashedly looked her over, top down, bottom up, and then reluctantly back to eye level.

"Mr. Nylund! I'm so sorry to bother you. Ms. Grant asked me to give you this." She produced a piece of paper that had been lying flat against her tablet. "She needs you to sign it," she said as she sped up to cover the last six feet between her and the window. She stumbled as she neared it, lurched forward, and at the last second pushed up against the chrome sill to steady herself. The coffee flew into the car, cup and all, emptying over Nikko.

"What the fuck!" Nikko shouted, the leering smile now turned upside down.

"Oh gosh! I'm so sorry, Mr. Nylund. I don't know what came over me. It's these darn heels, you see. Oh my goodness. It's all my fault!"

"Driver, get me the hell outta here!" Nikko barked. "And you," he said, glaring at her like a rabid dog, "whatever the fuck that is—tell Grant she can come give it to me her fuckin' self!"

The car sped away and left her standing at the curb alone. Remarkably, there was not a drop of liquid on her. She straightened her attire, brushed the dust off her clothes, and fixed her hair and glasses. Next, she bent down to pick up the sheet of paper. Not a drop marred either of its blank white surfaces.

◎◎◎

Marcus turned from his driveway onto the road and headed to the precinct. He poked at the dashboard's colorful touch screen buttons in an attempt to connect to Albert. Nothing. It was his third failed attempt, so he gave up and pushed the little red Help button instead. A recorded voice greeted him. It was human this time.

"Central Services help desk. This call will be recorded for quality and training purposes. Please hold the line and the next—"

"CS help desk. This is Nigel. How may I help you?"

"This is Detective Elroy Marcus. I think the link to Albert is broken."

"No, Detective. Link's fine. Albert's just getting a tune-up today."

"A what?"

"A tune-up. You know, like an upgrade? Giving him some new code and a few bells and whistles to boot."

"Like what?"

"Not entirely sure. They don't tell us much but I hear tell that they're applying an AI boost. He's gonna be much smarter."

"Much smarter how?"

"Rumor is, he'll be able to wipe your ass now but will refuse since he'll know his union rights." Nigel laughed heartily at his own joke. Marcus didn't join in.

"When's he back online?"

"Later today if all goes well, but these big platform upgrades, sheesh, they never do. He was supposed to be back up last night but got a bad set of code injected in him. Very strange since the QA team is top-notch, but I hear the full-timers are slowly being replaced by automated testing systems, so you never know." Marcus recalled the waiter in the café and wondered when this shit would end.

"So he's sick, is he?"

"Yeah. But when Albert sneezes, the whole world gets a cold right? It's like we can't do nuthin' without him anymore. You wouldn't believe the amount of calls we're taking because of it."

Marcus disconnected and entered the precinct at 7:00 a.m., thirty minutes before the morning shift started. He proceeded down the main corridor when a man exited an adjoining room in front of him.

"Elroy?" said the man as he raised a hand in greeting.

"How are you, Rolph?" The men clasped hands for a moment.

Rolph rested his hands on his hips as he straightened and smiled. "I'm okay. Just wrestling with an inflamed appendix. Gotta get it removed soon. Gettin' old like the rest of us, huh?" Rolph looked away quickly before he settled his gaze back on Marcus. His face softened as he lifted his chin to ask, "How're things with you, El?"

"Gettin' old. Just like the rest of us," repeated Marcus with a mirthless laugh. "Say ... the bombing investigation. You're the lead, right? How's it going?"

Rolph raked his fingers through his hair. "A strange one. Never seen a crime scene with so few clues. Like the Foundationalists went pro."

"Andrews! My office."

Marcus looked down the hall past Rolph. The captain leaned out his office door.

"Praetorius," Rolph said with a whisper and a slight shake of the head. "Gonna tear me a new one because of it. See ya around, Marcus."

Marcus took the elevator down to the basement. Exiting, he noted how bland it was down there, all doors and windowless hallways, not even a union safety poster to liven things up. It made sense to him, though. This was where they kept the computing hardware—the Big Iron, as the techies liked to call it—the stuff that powered their cars, computers, and communication devices. Things like Albert. This was his home. Like a true celebrity he subsisted in seclusion, surrounded by thick walls, bulletproof doors, armed guards, and myriad security protocols, all with the sole aim of keeping the public out. Windows, posters, and pretty aesthetics just weren't in the playbook when the budget was disproportionately directed to Albert's development. Hell, Albert's version upgrade was probably a pretty penny. How much was *that* costing the taxpayer? He had no clue, but the upgrade couldn't have come at a worse time. He was certain of that. Clock ticking, and with his suspect on the lam, Marcus could ill afford the time to do things the manual way, but without Albert, it was the only way.

He followed the signage for Digital Surveillance and arrived at a set of double steel doors. A security keypad hung on the wall on one side, and on the other, a video camera that pointed down toward it. He hit the buzzer button on the keypad and turned to look at the camera. The doors swung open after a moment. It seemed like something out of a movie, the kind where a light mist trailed out of a darkened doorway and revealed the villain in dramatic fashion. However, there was no light mist, no villain, or anyone for that matter, so Marcus strode into the middle of the room searching for a sign of life. There happened to be many, existing solely in digital format on the video screens mounted upon no fewer than a dozen metal desks. People on screens went about their daily activities. There an elderly woman struggled to lift her groceries into her trunk while a young couple ignored her as they strolled by, heads buried in their mobile phones, safe from guilt. On another, a legion of shiny new SUVs fought their way out of the city. Like salmon on the run, they surged and pushed up the expressway with single-minded purpose, absent of courtesy or grace. What was this world coming to?

More curious was the single office chair that held court among the screens. As he pondered its significance, he heard the sound of shuffling feet behind him and turned.

"Detective Marcus, it's been a long time. How are you?" The man approached and clasped his hand in a warm greeting.

"Zukher. You haven't aged a bit." Marcus's lie drifted through an earnest smile, for in truth, the man looked much older now than he remembered. His hair had surrendered to a gray that had clearly advanced over the years and it had thinned greatly too. He wore the same clean, white lab overcoat but it was threadbare now and slightly too big for him, and when combined with his stooping posture added several years to his profile. However, his owl-like eyes, nested under dense, unruly brows and staring back from their vantage point behind thick trifocals, had a youthful appearance that didn't fit the rest of his persona. Marcus looked around the room. "I like what you've done to the place."

"Ha! I remember when we started thirty years ago. We were using Helium storage media then. Helium! It was the height of technology those days and we thought we were so advanced. We could record over two hundred thousand daily hours of video in this room. None of us fathomed then that there would be any need to have more. Oh, this place was bustling then, twenty-five analysts, if you can believe it. Now, there's just one. Me."

Of course, the single chair, Marcus thought. "Only you? How's that possible?"

"Possible only because I've been around so long that they don't know what to do with me. Kinda like a nostalgic item you have no real use for but can't seem to throw away." Zukher laughed jovially. "Seriously though, Detective," he said, his voice drawing to a whisper as he moved in close. "It's because I am in possession of some video of a, shall we say, an *explicit* nature. It would make some very important people look very, very bad." He finished with a wag of his finger.

Marcus was stunned. "Really? Who?"

"Naw. Just kidding," said Zukher with an endearing chuckle. "Had I, they'd have killed me by now. They figure time will do it for them soon enough."

"So what happened to the other analysts, then?"

"They've dropped like flies over the past five or six years. It started with attrition, people would retire or change jobs and they simply wouldn't replace them. Then, over the last eighteen months, the axman cometh. The last three packed up their bags a couple of months ago."

"But the number of video cameras in the city has increased like crazy since Grant's government implemented the Anti-Terrorism Act a few years back?"

"Yes, yes. We were recording over one million daily hours from this room once the Quantum Storage technology replaced the Helium-filled disk drives. This new technology was so fast, efficient, and cheap that it no longer was the limiting factor."

"What was, then?"

"Political will. What else? Let me explain. Once Grant removed that barrier, we were open for business, and happy to oblige too. You see, we had thought it would reinvigorate our budgets, allow us to hire staff again, restore this place to its former glory. We *finally* had hope again. But all of that was dashed."

"Dashed? How?"

He reached out and clasped Marcus's shoulders. "I lived a long life. When I was a young adult I was as a child, but as I got older I became aware of many, many things. One was my shelf life. Like a perishable good, we all expire, something we all know eventually, Detective, but we don't apply this thinking to our careers. Sure, we think about the beginning and yearn for retirement near the end, but we tend to ignore the periods in the middle. It's somewhere there that a person's ratio of their productive output relative to what they earn starts to get all out of whack. I realized this early on, and *intended* to ensure the top part of that equation always offsets the bottom, for if it becomes unbalanced, there awaits a young woman or man who will supply the energy to topple it. Sure, they may not have your experience, but they bring vitality, an openness to new ideas, and are willing to work for *half* of what you make. I always thought that would be my downfall, but ..." Zukher paused, threw his hands up, and looked crazily around the room. "It wasn't."

"Who, then?"

"Ha. Some detective you are!" Zukher leaned in close. "The analysts fell prey to someone with far better eyesight, unmatched intelligence, and whose unique physiology allows him to work indefinitely. However, it was no young man or woman."

"Albert."

"Yes. He simply outmatched the analysts at every level. He can compute teraflops in seconds, perform facial recognition in less time than we blink, run thousands of concurrent algorithms like a million Einsteins and compare records against all databases in existence *instantaneously*—all without having to step out for a sandwich, go pee, or possess any urgency to update his social media accounts in between." The old man's posture sagged as his eyes drifted to the floor. "And now he's come for me."

Marcus was saddened at the abrupt change. He was like a different man. And why wouldn't he be? In one cruel stroke, his identity and purpose had been cleaved away by the sharp mind of a machine. Words could not close such a mortal wound, and so Marcus offered silence instead, a poor salve, but one that wouldn't make it worse. He let it sink in for what seemed to be appropriate to the situation.

At length, he said, "Zukher, you *are* one of the finest." Zukher looked up, eyes bright again, a little smile creasing his face. Marcus smiled back, pausing again for several moments before he continued. "Listen. Mind if I switch gears?"

Zukher blinked twice, reined back his smile, and refocused his eyes. He was back to business. "Sure. Sure."

"That thing I called you about? Find anything?"

"Why, yes! I am delighted you sought me out, Detective, but you needn't have come all this way. You could've asked Albert. After all, he's in charge now."

Marcus drew a sigh of relief: he hadn't mentioned Albert's upgrade. A little white lie wouldn't hurt. "I'm old school. Wanted to see what a real pro thinks, not some expensive tin can."

Zukher chuckled again as the energy seemed to flow back into him. "Well then. Let's see what this pro came up with. Here. Please. Sit." Zukher tapped Play on the screen in front of them with a stylus he had extracted from behind his ear. The video was of the crime scene in New Times Square; a good portion of Grant's defamed billboard and its immediate surroundings were in view.

"How close is the camera?" said Marcus.

"About ten meters above the roof and a hundred away from the sign. It's positioned diagonally, about forty-five degrees to the southern corner."

Unfortunately, a quarter of the sign on the north side was not in frame. Nothing moved except a pigeon that pecked nervously at its feathers. It was perched on the railing of the metal gangplank running alongside the sign's length. Just then, the image seemed to twist and fold in on itself for an instant before it returned to normal, but this time, a person stood on the gangplank. The pigeon was gone. Marcus peered in closer. The person's build and gait pegged him as a man but that was all Marcus could surmise at that point. Zukher rewound the video.

"You see this here? The image experiences some jitter so we can't see how the guy made his approach. For all we know, he appeared out of thin air, but I checked historical photos of the building and can confirm there is a ladder on the north side. He must've used it and climbed down from the roof."

"What would cause the jitter?"

"Detective, the video camera is just one half of the puzzle. It's the network that's the most important part. In fact, most of our budget is spent setting up and managing it. The network connects the camera to our central storage pool where the video is recorded. Now, this camera uses a wireless network, probably because it was cheaper than running a cable all the way up the building. Wireless is very reliable but is prone to distortion from magnetic disturbances common to large urban centers. This one is only a split second, but it's just enough time to obscure the image."

Marcus nodded. Zukher continued with the playback. The perp spent the next three minutes plying his craft. Speed favored over artistry, his wild movements focused on ticking the box and nothing more. When finished, he stepped back, took in his masterpiece, and then looked back toward the street to determine whether he was being observed. It was at this stage that he faced the camera. Zukher froze the image at this point and zoomed in on the face.

"There is your man."

Marcus squinted hard at the face, trying to identify features from the grainy picture that was more than a little out of focus. "Can you get it any better?"

"You mean can I touch a button and have the computer extrapolate the image to create a high-resolution 3D image? No. That is only in detective movies, Detective. The image is only as good as the information that the camera captures. This image wasn't captured in Life Definition, you know, like they use for the HV films. It's for basic security only. This is what you get. However, you're in luck. There is just enough information to run our advanced facial recognition algorithms."

"Please. Could you?"

"I took the liberty of doing so before you came." Zukher shuffled over to the printer and handed Marcus a printout. "I've also uploaded it to your mobile account so you can access it later."

Marcus read the report. "Nicholas Nylund."

"Goes by the street name Nikko. See the second page."

Marcus tapped a fingertip to his tongue and wet it before he turned the page and ate up the words as if he was famished. "Yeah ... it's all here," he muttered, mostly to himself. Apparently Nylund had done some time at federal prison for embezzlement, but had mostly stuck to petty crimes—

burglary, intimidation, assault. He had filed taxes the previous year under the employer Khufu Entertainment Inc.

"A real winner. I'll leave it in your capable hands from here, Detective." Zukher gestured as if wiping his hands. "I am now out of my element. And don't get out of yours, Detective. There's a machine waiting."

"Thanks." Marcus turned to leave when a thought entered his mind. "Zukher?"

The old man's head perked up and his eyes brightened, wide yet again.

"You—uh—you mentioned that you know how to set up a communications network, right?"

"Yes, Detective. Why?"

"Could you find a way to send a signal to a spaceship?"

"Did you say—a *spaceship*?"

A few minutes later, Marcus left Zukher and made his way to the assignment room to view the shift schedule. It was accessible on his mobile phone, but last-minute changes frequently occurred, someone calling in sick or last-minute swaps. The Centralized Service Group processed these change requests, and the whole process of inputs, checks, balances, and output meant it was four hours before the electronic schedule was updated. Captains needed to manage their staff in real time, so they reverted to whiteboard and erasable marker to account for these intraday changes.

Marcus scanned the monthly schedule that stretched from one end of the room to the other. Finding the current day, he looked down the column and matched it to the row with Sergeant Peters's name in it. Scrawled in black marker was 8:00 p.m. to 4:00 a.m. He followed it backward across the row, each day with the same time written in, until he got to the date of the murder, where Peters's assignment was written in red marker: 7:30 a.m. to 5:30 p.m. It had been changed at the last minute. He had the right man.

Excited, he turned and in two long strides reached the door. Just then it opened abruptly, and a figure stepped through. Marcus rocked back on his heels for a moment, and once settled, he adjusted his glasses and peered at the person before him. It was none other than Sergeant Peters.

"Peters."

"Detective Marcus? Hey, good to see ya again. How ya been?"

"Fine. Let's talk. Me and you, okay?" Marcus looked back into the room briefly. There were too many people around. He gave a quick head tilt toward the outside of it. "C'mon."

Peters gave him a blank stare. "Ah ... okay. Sure, Marcus."

Marcus led him out into the hall, over to an empty bench seat near the elevator bank that was flanked on both sides by large palm trees. He gestured for Peters to sit. Peters looked perplexed but shrugged and sat. Marcus sat down beside him.

"Peters." He uttered his name just firmly enough to bring a seriousness to the conversation. Scaring the sergeant now would ruin his shot at solving the Frederick murder. Finding the balance between carrot and stick required good judgment and a lot of luck. Marcus had one advantage, though. They were cut from the same cloth. Peters was a veteran cop and a respected one, anyone would've said so—up till now anyway. The rumors that floated through the precinct told of a loyal, family-oriented man.

However, as Marcus had heard it, Peters's partner was into some dirty stuff—drugs and taking payoffs mostly. Peters had confronted the crooked cop one day, tried to bring him back to the flock, but he had refused the offer and, with his back against the wall, panicked and shot Peters in the left shoulder. Peters refused to fire back, and despite his injury, managed to disarm him. But the most admirable thing was that Peters refused to rat him out. In exchange for his silence, his partner agreed to take a leave of absence and wound up in a drug rehabilitation treatment center shortly thereafter. Peters reported the affair as a firefight with unidentified street muscle. That was the unofficial story, and if it was true, and a lot of guys believed it was, then Peters was a stand-up guy. That he put his own career on the line to give his crooked partner a second chance spoke to the kind of man he was.

"Peters," Marcus said again.

"Yeah."

Marcus thought it best to start small. "Whaddaya think about the scene the other day?" He watched Peters's face closely.

"Well, you know. Pretty standard stuff. We, uh, we see this stuff all the time, right?"

"Yeah, we sure do." There were no tells yet, but he didn't think Peters would come clean without a little pressure applied, and so he'd apply it, slowly but deliberately. He continued with the plan. "You were the first on the scene, weren't you?"

"Huh?" Peters looked bewildered. That was the intent. Place an innocuous question out there, one so irrelevant it would make him wonder why it had been asked in the first place, and one that would seem to indicate that Marcus knew something he was trying to hide. If Peters had planned to deceive, he would've mentally prepared for a more direct line of questioning. He was a cop, after all, and knew about interrogations, but he wouldn't have contemplated this slow pitch coming over the plate. Like the classic change-up, it would leave the batter guessing—should I? Shouldn't I? Whether he swung quickly or after some deliberation would be the most important indication, and Peters's hesitation told Marcus that he was hiding something.

"Yeah," Peters said after he had regained a modicum of composure. "I was the first officer to secure the scene after it was called in by the neighbor."

Marcus nodded several times with raised eyebrows and pursed his lips as if in agreement before he looked away and down at the floor.

Peters relaxed some more and said, "What's this about?"

"What's this about, Peters?" Marcus repeated with an affable chuckle as he brought his eyes back up to meet the other cop's. "It's about a lot, much more than it would seem to an outsider. To an insider, say, like me and you, it's about everything. It's about a veteran good cop, who joined the ranks young and with a purpose, and that purpose was to make things just a bit better, better than they were before. It's about a career where service and loyalty were put first, and from the story I heard, even put before personal safety."

Peters remained quiet. He could have left at any time but he didn't, and that encouraged Marcus to press on.

"You know, my dad was an asshole. Tough guy, gendarme on the *Dominus*, survived through the Dark Days, and like many of them back then, well, he was hard, real hard, you know?"

Peters nodded, his face changed as if from a glimmer of shared experience.

"I went to see him in the hospital just before he died," Marcus continued. "Was gaunt and stooped, even the tattoos that covered his shriveled old arms looked tired. What struck me most was that the crusty, calloused SOB looked *scared*. Unsettled me, 'cause I never seen that look on his face before. Hell, he could've taken a dozen rebels with only a toothbrush in his younger days, but there he was—*helpless* and *afraid*—staring death in the face, like for the first time he knew what it was like to be vulnerable. I sat beside him as he started to take shallow breaths and he looked at me, square in the eye, and said three words before he died. You know what he said?" Marcus paused a moment. "He said to me—*it's all bullshit.*" He delivered the words with emphasis for maximum impact. "Last words. Shit. But you know what he meant, don't you? That life was a game. Right? A game with made-up rules, an endless catalog of desires, and lies we tell others to satisfy them, and worse, the lies we tell ourselves to assuage our guilt. What he meant was, life don't need to be the complex machination that we create. Get out of our own way, keep it simple, and most of all, don't fuck it up. See? Take you, for example, retirement in a coupla years with commendable service and a gold-plated pension. No drama, no scandal. That's what he meant, that's what he was saying, right? Why screw it up?"

Marcus paused and waited for a reaction. Peters nodded slowly and his body sagged as if he could shoulder no more weight. It was working.

"But Peters. Your performance at the Frederick house placed you on a different path, didn't it? You fucked it up. You'd been compromised from some high place, and we both know how that story plays out. Good cop makes a bad choice—but he gets away with it, and for a time relaxes—hell, maybe even retires—thinking all the time that his dark past is behind him. But the dark past always comes back, it always wants more, 'cause they own you now, and like a puppet on a string, they make you dance until you're doing things that disgust you, with a frequency you can't imagine, until the day it catches up to you and *everything* is lost. That's hell, man. That's hell. And you're running toward it. Your future, Peters. *But.* You *can* come back. It's not too late. Put in for retirement, get out there, enjoy your grandkids, spend time with your wife. God knows the strain this job puts on her. Restore your dignity, and most of all, keep it simple and stop fucking it up. That's a future worth running to. That's what I can offer you—here, today."

He paused again for effect, but also to determine Peters's openness to the choice he was about to give him. Peters stared at him, seemingly through him even, and responded with several shallow nods of acceptance. He was ready for the offer.

"But Peters, you gotta be honest with me. Tell me who put you up to this, and why, and I promise you, I will fix this, and when I do, this stays buried between us." There it was. It had to work. After all, it was the same offer Peters had provided to his partner years before. Redemption at the price of contrition.

Peters remained silent for what seemed like an eternity, then seemed to summon up the will to continue. "Years ago, I worked the drug scene with my partner Eddy Weigel. Back in those days, we didn't have the fancy tech we do now. It was available, yeah, but it was reserved for the big stuff, know what I mean?"

Marcus, not wanting to get in Peters's way, merely nodded in acknowledgment.

"So we had to do our own surveillance the hard way, with our eyes and ears. So we'd be going into the clubs regularly, undercover, you see. We were good at it, but it took a long time getting the info to establish the trail. Who is who, who reports to who, who is doing business with who, the whole nine yards, right? So we had'ta get very deep with these people. Socialize with them, help 'em out, do favors—anything to earn their trust. You become their friends even. And that's the funny thing. Through it all, you realize they're just people like you and me, all big hopes and big dreams. But something goes wrong along the way—unlike you and me, maybe they got turned left when we went right, or said yes when they should've said no. You see? The curse of going undercover is that you get to know these things, you get beyond the veneer. You don't want to, but you can't help it. Beat cops only see a perp when they make an arrest, that's easy. Undercover, well, you see the person in all their dimensions—the bad, the ugly, but the *good* too."

Marcus listened intently. He had expected him to get right to the point and spill the beans, not this. Whatever was happening here seemed cathartic to Peters and so he let it continue, for now.

"And so, there was this woman. She ran a bar we had come to know was a storehouse for the drugs. It was our best lead in cracking the drug trafficking ring wide open. A pretty young thing, but tough as nails. Had a way with people, a knack for numbers, a true problem solver. You could've placed her in any corporate boardroom and she'd have been a legitimate success, she was so talented.

"So I started in, slowly at first, became a regular, then started doing small jobs, did them well too, and eventually gained her trust. It wasn't long before I was running the ledgers, which accounted for the inflows and outflows of the drugs and the cash. Heck, I had intimate knowledge of the scale, scope, and details of the operation. I knew it all. And so I took this upward, thinking that we had something we could use. Boy, was I naive! Brass wasn't interested. They wanted it all, the whole ring, the big headline. Said the bar was small potatoes, might've made page three, would've knocked the operation on its ass for a bit, but in a matter of months, they'd have ramped up operations in their backup hubs around the city and sent the rats scampering underground where they'd be much harder to dig out. They were right and I knew it, but by this time the truth was I had to get outta there. It was too much." His face wrinkled as he paused, the memory evidently painful.

"The long days put me in close contact with her, workin' through the night in a closed bar, just me and her. Shit, she was almost half my age. I tried to shake it, but Christ, I'm only a man. Inevitably the work conversations turned casual, the casual more personal, and with the more personal came the intimate. It was unavoidable. A fuckin' job hazard not found in the *Officer's Handbook*. And so it went." Peters drew his body down farther, shaking his head as he said, "It was the first and only time I ever cheated on my wife."

Marcus's eyes drifted to the floor in frustration. He hadn't the time to indulge Peters's guilt, not when the killer ran loose. It was time to rein this in. He opened his mouth to speak but his words never left his mouth.

"There's more."

Marcus's eyes shot back up.

"When we finally gathered enough evidence to bust up the entire ring, the cops hit all the bars, safe houses, you name it. Was called Operation Clean Sweep. You probably remember it too, the biggest bust-up until that time. Well, SWAT had surrounded the bar. Me and Eddy were inside, 'cept we weren't tipped off. The brass never told us, so that everything could go ahead without even the slightest chance of a leak. When the fire-team entered, Eddy and I were in the backroom with the woman. Shit, we only started to clue in to what was happening just before they kicked in the front door.

"At that point, I looked over at her, just one look, that's it—and she knew, knew everything we had was a lie. In that instant she screamed, like I never heard anyone scream, man, and that look ... her face shattered into a thousand pieces." Peters's eyes glazed over, as if he was back in time and after several moments slowly focused them back on Marcus. "That's when all hell broke loose. She snatched Eddy's gun from the table, aimed dead center to my chest, and pulled the trigger. I barely managed to get out of the way and took the slug in my shoulder. Eddy disarmed her and came over to check on me. In that instant, she managed to escape through a false wall built for such an occasion. She disappeared."

"So the story about Eddy was a lie."

"Eddy was no angel either. He fell for the charms of another woman—Molly Moondust. It was a new drug then, just out of the labs, and he was like a fuckin' guinea pig, couldn't get enough of it. The rest of the story was true, he did go to rehab and cleaned himself up. What wasn't, was the lie he told to protect me. Having to explain how a central figure in the drug operation shot *me* and then escaped would draw too many questions. Heck, they'd eventually find out that I was romantically involved with her, and when they did, shit, the defense lawyers would call for a mistrial. Worse, I'd lose my job, my wife—fuck, my own kids would disown me. So Eddy told 'em he was high as a kite on synthetic Molly, got scared when the flashbangs went off, and shot me by accident. It was *his* bullet after all. The brass believed him but wanted nothing that would muddy the front page, so they chose to wipe it all clean. So the official story was that a hired hand grabbed his gun and made the shot—which was ironic, of course. Eddy made his penance in mandatory rehab and she got off scot-free. And me? I got to go back to my life as if nothin' happened. Heck, they even pinned a medal on my chest. All because of my partner who held on to my dirty little secret. Eddy took the bullet for *me*, but as you say, it was all bullshit."

As interesting as this was, Marcus could only wonder—*where was this going*? He needed a confession, not a memoir, and he was tired of playing shrink. "Why tell me all this?"

Peters took a deep breath and released it slowly as he looked out into the hallway. When he turned back, his face had hardened, the tension most noticeable in his jaw, as if it struggled to keep his words from escaping. After a long pause, he lowered his voice and said, "Me and her. What we had was real. Hell. We was talking about a future together, I mean I was in so deep, couldn't tell you today that I was acting. She had this vision in her head, see? That we'd cash out, leave that world behind, and live happily ever after. Like a fairy tale. But on that day, it all vanished. Imagine your entire fuckin' reality torn down in an instant?" Peters snapped his fingers. "Poof."

Marcus thought of his wife and kids. Yes, he knew exactly what he meant.

"There was murder in her eyes the last time I saw 'em. I had no doubt that one day she'd come for me, but there was one problem—*Eddy*. He could always come clean about her shooting me, a cop, which would bring the weight of the justice system down on her hard. But Eddy died of cancer earlier this year, so now it's simply my word against hers.

"Then one night, 'bout a month ago, my dark past came to visit me. She enters my local bar, sits down beside me, and orders a drink. Fuck, after all these years, no emotion, no nothin', just sits down, takes a sip, and tells me the way it's gonna be. Said a crime was going down and I had an important role to play. She told me the date, time, and location so I could rearrange my shift to be on duty and in the vicinity when the dispatch call came. Then she told me the *what*. I was supposed to arrive first and disturb the scene with the aim of misdirecting the investigation, *to misdirect you*. But you knew all of this, didn't you? The fucking Sage. How in the hell did ya figure it all out?"

"If a man's life is a book, the murder scene is the final chapter. But as a detective, I read it first and figure out the plotline that precedes it. So I read the chapter closely, study the people, the dialogue, the objects, and conditions, looking for patterns and certainty that will help me fill in the storyline. So take *you*, for instance, Peters. Odd you were *in* the crime scene itself. Proper protocol would have had you standing in the hallway so as not to disturb the evidence. Was it a case of incompetence or did you intend to hamper my investigation? I was willing to chalk it up to the former until I saw your duty blazer hung on the chair in the kitchen. Hmm. A man of your experience, you must've been in some hurry or preoccupied with something of great importance to do something so dumb.

"Then there was the lamp on the floor. It was in two pieces, remember? The stem was threaded at the bottom end, where it was meant to be screwed into its base. But it was funny—the threads were in pristine condition. If the lamp had been separated by force, the threads would've been scratched or bent. Clearly, the lamp was disassembled and placed there carefully by someone intending to throw me off the scent. Make it look like your standard burglary, undertaken by a common hoodlum. Now, it's not enough yet to implicate you, but hell, it's fifty-fifty. The only two people who had the opportunity to misarrange things were you and the murderer.

"Next, the kitchen window was left ajar on an otherwise cold and rainy day. True, it was open a little more than a crack so as to be innocuous and truthfully, I wondered if Frederick had done it. Maybe he'd aired out smoke from the stove or something, but there was nothing on the burners or in the oven. The clincher was the thermostat. It was set to eighteen degrees, but it was hot in there, had to be mid-twenties, even you had noted it. But why? Someone had *recently* changed it. Was it Frederick? No, why would he make his guest uncomfortable with the cold? Whoever did it had another reason too, perhaps had intimate knowledge of how crime scene investigation works? Changing the temperature changes the conditions by which we can gauge blood viscosity and time of death. Sure, the crime lab guys should've spotted it, but you knew the probability of that was low. Kids graduating from school nowadays are all enamored by the new technology at their fingertips, they don't sweat the small stuff.

"Now, my suspicion was growing, so I asked you that question—do you remember it? *Whaddaya think?* I wanted to see what you might say, see what you might give up. And you didn't disappoint. You said, 'The perp stuck 'im and left 'im there to die on the floor.' There it was, declared—confidently, definitive. You been around the block, Peters, you know as well as I do that at the crime scene, you never state your opinion of the cause of death, and if you somehow have to, never state anything conclusive unless you're absolutely sure. There was a purpose to your answer, and when combined with the other gaffes, it all made sense. You wanted to obstruct my investigation."

Peters's eyes widened. Marcus wondered how much bigger they'd get if he told him that his dead daughter Mary had revealed the secret to him. Her whisper, buried within a cryptic dream, had connected the dots, just as they had done so ever since the crash.

Marcus continued. "The story came together once I understood that you were mixed up in the crime in some way. Indicated something deeper at play than a simple robbery, and that got me thinking differently about it all. So here it goes, indulge me in the retelling, will ya? Tell me if I got the story wrong."

Peters nodded.

"It's cold and rainy as dusk starts to settle. Frederick hears the doorbell, lets the dog out through the back door, and then lets a man in. We know this because the kibble bowl was recently refreshed but untouched. Also, there's no sign of struggle anywhere but the kitchen, so it's clear the murderer was expected and invited in. But there is no food nor drink set out for him, so it's probably not a friend, neighbor, or a relative, but someone who's there for a purpose. Now, the alarm company confirmed they hadn't actually dispatched anyone out, but Frederick was expecting someone to arrive that day. I had Albert trace his cell phone records and he confirmed that Frederick called the alarm repair company the day before the murder. There it was, Frederick booked an alarm repair technician, or so he thought when he let him in. But you wanted me to think it was someone else, someone who wanted to purchase Frederick's car. That's why you uploaded the 'Car for Sale' ad on Frederick's phone and displayed it on its screen. You almost had me there, except something dawned on me later. Frederick was only four months into a car lease and had no financial troubles, so why would he sell his only car, the one he just bought? A quick call to the *Observer* confirmed that the ad was a clever fake."

"I had no idea about either of those things, Marcus. I was to show up, is all. And fool you." Marcus didn't think Peters's shoulders could slump any farther, but somehow they did.

"Now, the man mortally wounds Frederick. A knife thrust to the chest, just as you noted. However, something unexpected happens. I know this because the man's home was orderly, everything in fine working condition, like fuckin' clockwork, he wouldn't have tolerated the clang of the metal bolt smacking against the gate latch every time the wind blew it open and the retaining spring snapped it back. Made me wonder if the bolt and latch got out of alignment recently? The wood under the rusty old hinges was fresh and unfaded. That confirmed it. Someone had *crashed* through that gate and broke it at the time of the murder. But who? Most probable was the murderer when he tried to escape since the gate opened outward from the yard, there'd be no way you could break it from the other side.

"But why hadn't he left through the front door? Common sense prevails. The murderer was surprised. The side door, just off the kitchen, was the closest point of egress. The front door was too far away. I believe the victim's son, Alyn, entered the back door, and the dog entered behind him. Man's best friend, loyal as always, charged in to protect Frederick. The bloody pawprint confirmed it. The murderer got spooked, fled through the side door, crossed the backyard, and *crashed* through that gate, tearing the hinges out."

"Well," Peters said softly. He looked pale now, as if he was going to faint. "Wha'do we do now Marcus?"

Marcus paused and closed his eyes as if to gather his thoughts before he looked back up at Peters. "You're going to go into the captain's office now. Tell him you're tired, that the run was a good one, but you need to step aside now and let someone else come up. Tell him you need to spend time with your wife; she needs you now that she's older and adjusting to an empty nest. That you want to be a better grandfather and that you've always wanted the time to work on that crime novel rattling around in your head. Tell the captain he'll be a central character. But first, before you go, you gotta tell me everything else you know and hope I can put an end to all of this quickly."

"Yeah ..." Peters replied, his dry voice sounding more like a grunt. He studied the far end of the hallway for a time, stroking his chin absently before slowly facing Marcus, locking eyes momentarily before they sank slightly downward. "Okay, Marcus."

He listened intently as Peters divulged the remaining facts. When finished, he straightened a little and lowered his eyes fully to the ground.

"You missed one important fact," Marcus said.

"Wha—?" Peters's eyes shot back up in surprise.

Marcus raised an eyebrow and glared back coldly. "I need the name."

Peters held the gaze for a time, before the last restraint broke and two words fell ever so reluctantly from his mouth. "Charmagne Conway."

Marcus gave him a closed-lip smile and nodded. "Thank you."

Peters rose from the bench, looked at him, and said, "Thank *you*, Marcus." He turned and walked toward Captain Praetorius's office. Marcus watched him as he went, struck by the change in mannerism. He looked different now, lighter, relieved.

◎◎◎

The click of the toaster's lift mechanism barely registered above the cacophony in the kitchen. Victoria cooked, cleaned, and organized like a whirling dervish, in harmony with the music that blared from the Smart Concierge's audio speaker, pausing just long enough to collate her bacon, eggs, lettuce, and tomatoes into a BELT. Sandwich in her right hand, pencil in her left, she continued to write her plan. She nailed the easy stuff first—turn down the furnace, top up her account balance to cover her bills, suspend her streaming subscriptions, and pack extra underwear because you just never knew. She had never been far from home before, let alone to another planet. The thought sunk into her head at the same time her teeth gnawed into the sandwich. What would it be like? She began to imagine the experience when she felt something gooey running down her pinky finger. A lava-like flow of egg yolk ran down it and dripped onto the counter. "Shit!" she exclaimed out loud, as she dropped the pencil and raced over to the sink, grabbed a damp rag and wiped up the mess. Once that was completed, she snatched the pencil and sat at her kitchen table to continue working through her list. Item number three was scrawled in heavy printed block letters. It read:

CALL MARIO !!

She dreaded having to make this call but there was no getting around it, not if she wanted to maintain any shred of friendship with her on-again, off-again boyfriend. She placed the sandwich on the table and said, "Zara. Pause music."

"Music paused," replied the smart concierge in a tinny approximation of a human voice.

"Zara. Dial Mario."

"Dialing Mario."

The sound of classic phone rings echoed from the Concierge's connected speakers. *Ring-ring*. One. *Ring-ring*. Two. *Ring-ring*. Three. Relief started to manifest within her. Two more rings and it would connect to voicemail. She could leave a message! It wouldn't be the best way to tell him but it was better than *not* telling him, she thought in between the third and fourth rings. She could say afterward: "I left you a message, Mar. Just was crazy, getting ready and all, but listen, I'm, really really sorry, but ... I gotta go now, ship is boarding." Yes, that would do. The phone rang for the fifth and final time. Click. The recorded voice said, "Hi. This is Mario, and I'm not home. Please leave me a message."

"Hi Mar," she began. "It's Victoria. I was really hoping to chat today. It's weird, um ... just that I'm leaving tomorrow on a *very* long trip. I'll be the journalist in chief to the Secundus expedition. I know, right? I am *soooo* excited but a little nervous. It'll be a whole three months, maybe four. Look, I'll try to contact you before I leave though, okay? I'm gonna time out. Talk soon." She tapped her pencil on the Disconnect button on Zara's gleaming plastic chassis and dropped it on the table, picked up her sandwich, and walked to the window above the kitchen sink. She stared out into the sunlit garden and imagined how the conversation would have gone had Mario answered the phone. In that instant, the phone rang. *Ring-ring*. One.

"Mario calling," said Zara.

Shit! Do I answer? No, I don't want to answer.

Ring-ring. Two. "Mario calling," said Zara.

What if we don't talk, if I leave and don't say goodbye?

Ring-ring. Three. "Mario calling," said Zara.

I'll call him later. Yes! From the road!

Ring-ring. Four. "Mario calling," said Zara.

That's terrible. And you know you're fooling yourself too.

The phone rang the fifth and final time. “Mario calling,” said Zara.

Tired of vacillating and egged on by guilt, she yelled across the room in Zara’s direction. “Answer!”

“Hey, Mar! Did ya get my message?”

“Hey, Victoria. No. Just saw you called and called ya back. Didn’t think I’d hear from you so soon after our last talk.”

“Ah … you know,” she replied, ignoring the trap he’d set for her. “How is Ms. Mumbles?” It would be better to keep it light until she could find a suitable opening to drop her news. The kitten they had raised together was a perfect topic. It’d eat up some airtime, maybe even get him into good humor. “Is she still chewing up anything she can get her greedy little paws on?”

“She misses you, you know. Still brings toys over to your side of the bed. Every night.”

Uggh! She closed her eyes in resignation. Her strategy was backfiring. Big time. Mario’s subtle broadside was carefully aimed to hit her in her emotional center, knock her off balance, make her rethink things. That he’d done so this early in the conversation was atypical. Had he been drinking again?

“Oh. I’m sure it’s just a habit she’d developed while I was there. She’ll get over it soon.” Her mind worked to change the topic, but only family or the weather sprung forth in haste. The latter would be an obvious feint. “How’s your mom?”

“Good. I was over there yesterday. She made a huge meal, which was great since I didn’t have the energy to cook. She asked about you, insisted on fixing you a plate of leftovers. I have it here in one of her porcelain plates, you know, one of the classic-looking blue ones you like with the little guy fishing in the small boat?”

“Yeah, yeah.”

“Anyway, she covered it in tinfoil so it’d keep. Drives me nuts as it’ll end up in the landfill, but what are you going to do? At any rate, don’t fret about it. It’s fine. I’ll have it for lunch.”

The flippant retort seemed like an overcompensation for his ham-handed guilt trip in the prior exchange. Either way, the conversation was going nowhere. Mario clearly had something to get off his chest but was afraid to say it, though she was not surprised. He was hurt and this was his way of letting her know it, so she decided to stop beating around the bush.

"Mar, I need to tell you something. I'm going away. I won't be back for a long time, maybe three or four months."

"What do you mean? Going away for four months?" His voice became shrill. She braced for what would come next. "It's that fucking guy! Are you going away with him?" Cruel venom laced the words that he spat at her.

"No! Not at all. No. This is something entirely different, not that at all." She spoke with a mix of exhaustion, contrition, and resentment in her voice. That he reflexively went there made her furious. One night. One mistake. She would spend an eternity regretting it and another apologizing for it.

"Then what, then? Where you going?" His anger subsided some and his voice now carried the distinct mark of apprehension.

"It's my dream, Mario. My dream is coming true! You remember all those nights we'd sit out in the park with the cheap bottle of Murzo in the paper bag? We would stare up at the moons? You remember that?"

"Course I do. We'd talk about everything, what we wanted to do with our lives. How you wanted to become a reporter, a good one, one that mattered, different from the others. And you did it, Vic. Look where you are—top reporter for one of the largest outlets on this planet. You've made it. You're there!"

"I'm *not* there! Not yet, anyway," she said, pleading for him to understand. "But I'm on my way! They've offered me the journalist in chief position on the Exploration Corps' expedition. Me! They offered it to *me!* Think about all I can see, all I can learn. It's the chance of a lifetime. No one has been in space for over half a century, and I'll be there to chronicle all of it."

"That's—that's amazing, Victoria. I really mean that, but you can't simply up and leave, can you? What about your mom and dad? Ms. Mumbles? Your life?" She noticed that he didn't mention himself, though she could sense that was what lay beneath the objections.

"There's more I need to learn, more I need to see. It's like I'm just scratching the surface, Mario. There's a big universe out there and I'm here, occupying a minuscule part of it and it makes me feel so ..." She wouldn't say the word, even though it burned like a red ember in the dark place of her mind. *Small.* He thought of her that way. He always had. And despite this splendid appointment and the confidence it inspired in her, today was no exception.

Who was he to judge *her*? The man who played it safe? Who only took a chance when the outcome was all but certain? Who waited on the sidelines until the game's momentum swung his way? That was *his* nature. He was no more able to realize hers than a fish understood what air was. He didn't understand the nature of the only game that mattered—life, where the odds were stacked against you and the outcome determined by how much you were willing to give.

And this was her problem with him. Yes, he was a good guy, the kind you brought home to Mom, and funnily enough, her mom adored him, treated him like the son she'd never had. And he treated her so well too—like his own mother, even! He would call her *nanay* in the Filipino accent her grandmother had. God, he was so perfect in her family's eyes. Like a chameleon, that little creature she had read about, he could blend into his surroundings as if he were a part of them. He was pleasant, respectful, knew right from wrong, never went to those bars with his work buddies to ogle half-naked women, never even looked at a girl in public in the way men often do. He was Mr. Right, the guy she had always *thought* she wanted to marry.

But as time rolled on, she got to know another side of him, one that lay hidden and one she didn't like. In his world, you ran alongside others in your own lane, never putting yourself out there, never crossing into their paths. In his world, you went to work at nine, came home at five, and occupied yourself with the banalities common to life's major milestones—courting, college, career, marriage, kids, and retirement. To her, these were diversions to living one's life, filling up time until there was no more left. Sure, she was willing to play that game to an extent, but not in its entirety. She yearned for more, to be something in life, and that meant stepping outside of that comfortable lane and facing struggles that he, the "normal" person, wanted to avoid. Who was he to judge her? She knew very well. A decent, honest, loyal guy who loved her. But it wasn't enough. And that killed her.

"Victoria?" He sounded tired now.

"Yeah?"

"I gotta go. This is too much for me to process right now. I can't ..." Mario sighed. "I dunno ... will you promise to call me before you leave?"

"Yeah, Mario. Course I will." She recognized lie as soon as it escaped her lips.

"Thanks, babe. I love you."

Spent from the conversation, she took a large bite from the sandwich and stared out the window into the backyard. A noise, like a door shutting hard against its frame, brought her out of her daze. She saw Ms. Johnson striding purposefully toward her car parked in the laneway, but moments later her neighbor paused abruptly in the driveway and rummaged through her handbag for something. Her keys? Perfect timing! If Victoria hurried, she could stop and ask if Ms. Johnson would water her houseplants and garden while she was away. She crossed the living room, stepping over the collection of boxes and the tape dispenser that crowded the floor, and with a single leap landed just before the back door. She opened it wide but halted in the threshold as Zara's voice interrupted her.

"Marcus calling," said the Smart Concierge. Marcus? Marcus!

"Answer," Victoria replied, but Zara did not respond. She yelled at the top of her voice. "Answer!" Zara still did not acknowledge. Of course! Her mouth was full. Zara couldn't understand her. Her mind went to all of those times her father had scolded her at the dinner table.

She thrust her unencumbered hand into the front pocket of her skinny jeans and struggled to extricate her mobile phone and not disconnect the call in the process. The phone was now on its fourth ring, one more before it hung up, so she hurled the sandwich out into the garden to free up her other hand. She pulled her pocket outward and yanked hard on the phone at the same time. It released at once, the pent-up kinetic potential sending it in an upward trajectory. Catlike, she grabbed it mid-arc and fumbled it twice before making an inelegant recovery. She thrust it up to her face, clicked the answer button, and shouted, "Hello?"

"Victoria?"

"Oh. Hey Marcus," she replied, trying her best to sound aloof, but she breathed so hard that she doubted he was buying it. "You miss me? Haven't seen or heard from you in ages and now thrice in just a few days." Marcus seemed to almost laugh. Maybe he hadn't heard the word thrice in a sentence since grade school?

"We need to catch up."

"Fuck, yeah, we do!"

"Remember that suspect I had you search up? The felon on the run?"

"Of course—Alyn Frederick. I did some research yesterday. You ready to hear it or are you going to hang up on me again?"

"Let's hear it."

"Alyn Sr. settled into a normal life after the Dark Days. He was married to his high school sweetheart Eliza McLain, who bore one child—Joseph, the deceased. Alyn Sr. maintained his governorship for over two decades after Landfall. He stepped down to chair several charitable institutions in his later years, the most famous being the Young Women in Politics, which, ironically, Grant and a few other notables were active in. He went into corporate life after politics, joined his son as a full partner in his technology company. The product they were developing had to do with finding an alternative energy source, but from what I can tell nothing ever came of it and it went bankrupt shortly before his death. Aside from that, there isn't much more. No scandals or anything I would consider untoward. He died in hospital on December 24th, 2049. In his last interview, he said his only regret was that he didn't do more to help those on the *Renascent*. Some said the tragedy broke him. Was never the same."

"And the son, Joseph?"

"I don't know what to make of him," Victoria said. "He was a very bright child, skipped the third grade, and made his way through high school as the citywide decathlon champion while graduating at the top of his class. He won many more awards in his youth, most notably the Young Entrepreneur of the Year award, which came with a $25,000 grant. He used this to fund his company at age twenty. He made a good go of it, selling technology patents mostly. Business boomed after his father partnered with him. Alyn Sr. brought a huge network of connections that gave them access to government contracts and a stable recurring revenue stream as a result. So much so that Joseph had a decent living—if not rich, then comfortable. He seemed to have led a stable life up until several years after his father joined him in business. I can't explain why, but it seems the wheels started to fall off the wagon in Joseph's late thirties. Drunkenness and disorderliness, one count of domestic battery, and almost a dozen visits by the police were the main indicators of his wild years, which culminated in his wife's suicide. He seemed to smarten up after this but couldn't get the business humming, so he wound it down about three years ago. Never sold it, which was strange since there are numerous patents left over, from what I can see."

"Hmm."

"What?"

"More questions than answers."

"How so?"

"The more information I get, the less it all adds up."

"Well, I have good news, then."

"What's that?"

"That this is all I have to pile on."

"Thank you. Now about Alyn Jr. There's been a major development in the case."

"Yeah? What is it?"

"I tracked him down to the market yesterday. He ducked into a recruiting office trying to shake me—and guess what?"

"What?"

"He joined the Corps. The law of the land claims him as their own. Heard they're short of their operational numbers and are staffing the *Dominus II* with anyone they can press into service. So, I can't touch him."

Victoria frowned and thought for several moments. "Well—some might call that a shrewd move, but I'd call him foolish. He's traded three square meals, a warm bed, and lots of free time in a federal jail for the life of a ship's crew member, rising early, taking orders, and cleaning toilets. Not to mention taking on a major risk to life and limb, though I guess he could be excused for that, prison is no picnic." Vaguely, she was aware that in many ways she had made the same choice.

"Don't rush to judgment—this could work to our advantage, so listen carefully. I need eyes and ears on him while you're away. Watch him, maybe even get to know him."

"A suspect in a killing? Are you fucking nuts?" Victoria was almost shouting into the phone.

"He's no killer, Victoria. I *know* that. He's the key to this case and I need you to find out what he knows."

"Okay, okay, but there's one problem."

"Yeah?"

"I won't be able to talk to you. Sorry to tell you, but I can only communicate back to the planet via a secure government link. It's something about the magnetic interference that's generated when the binary moons eclipse every day."

"Yeah, I know. It means you can only send and receive once every twenty-six hours when the planets align and the moons get out of the way. Only then will the signal transmitters have direct line of sight."

"Wow. Been watching the Astronomy Channel?"

"Old friend told me."

"So I guess that's that, then."

"Not quite. He also told me how I can pirate my own signal."

"Marcus, it's a federal government communication link! Messing in that arena will land both of you in prison for life, maybe even face the firing squad. Now, I know *you're* kinda crazy, but why would *he* risk telling you this?"

"He's about to be packaged off, discarded by the system, and replaced by a machine. That's about all a man can take. Let's say it's the final straw, an act of rebellion in the face of an overwhelming trend of things to come. And me, yeah, I'm just plain old crazy."

"Hmm." Victoria needed to think through this a bit more. Something was going on with the Frederick case. Marcus's instincts were never wrong and if he was willing to risk this much, it must be a big story. However, there was no clear decision here. Working closely with Marcus was the only way she could drive the story, but it meant doing something illegal, probably treasonous. The rewards were great, but so were the risks.

On the other hand, refusing Marcus's request wouldn't be so bad. Sure, she'd miss out on this scoop, but she'd get major coverage of the expedition anyway and it would advance her career regardless. She had the full support of her editor and exclusive rights to tell the greatest story since their arrival on the planet. What more could a young reporter want? She would get the front page of special-edition magazines, blogs, websites, and the ubiquitous holovision. She'd be invited to dinner parties with celebrities, the rich and powerful, politicians—and comfortably exist for years on the avails from the interview circuit. Heck, the public speaking fees she could charge for one night would likely be more than her entire annual salary today. It made no sense to take the risk when she already had so much to gain. Still, her hunger for a scoop could not be denied.

"Sure, Marcus, tell me what to do," she said confidently, though she didn't mean it, figuring instead to get out of the conversation and defer the decision until later. Why close the door now? She'd agree to it, and if her mind changed during the voyage, she simply wouldn't go along with it, and when she returned, tell him that the process to initiate communications didn't work. Technology never failed to disappoint, so she held the "out" card close and could play it if it suited her. How would he know any better? They'd be separated by hundreds of thousands of kilometers. He'd have no way of knowing the truth.

"Great!" replied Marcus. It was the most excited she had ever heard him. "Each secure link transmission has an allotment for a small amount of text that can be attached to it. It's a hangover from when the developers created the software. They used this to append small bits of information for the purposes of testing it back when it was first rolled out. If a developer was sending a transmission, she could write something like, 'first transmission, time of day, codec used,' whatever, so they could track the particulars during the testing phase. The communication software is now mainstream, and it's been so long that no one remembers that the backdoor is even there. Now, when you send a message, a reciprocating transmission is allowed. I'll use that to send you replies."

"Okay. Sounds easy enough."

"Well ... there's one catch."

"Okay."

"The first is that you're limited to one hundred characters only—including spaces. Not exactly long enough for a conversation, to say the least. The same applies to me on the outgoing transmission."

"A hundred? That will be hard, even for me."

"The last thing is, in order for you to launch the developer screen you'll need to click the text Copyright 0020 at the bottom right of the screen. It'll bring up another screen where you'll enter a passcode. Once you do, the text input box will appear. Simply type your message, up to a hundred characters, and click Close when you're done. That's it."

"And the password?"

"Clarise."

"Oh, Marcus. Why did you use your wife's ...?" Victoria's voice trailed off in a feeble attempt to rein her words back in. She hadn't meant to open old wounds.

"It's so I'd never forget it."

Poor guy. The way his family was killed. She couldn't fathom how he was still standing. Why did he torture himself this way? "Okay. 'Clarise' it is. As beautiful a password as any. Now, if I may, let me change the subject, please?"

"Sure."

"What did you find out with the video cams?"

"Spotted a suspect. Nicholas 'Nikko' Nylund. Heard of him?"

"No. Can't say I have. What's the scoop?"

"Not much so far. Minor league punk. I'm going to pay him a visit and will let you know what I find out."

"Okay. Sounds good," she said.

"Great. Gotta go."

"Marcus?"

"Yeah, Vic?" She hated when people called her that but somehow she didn't mind when it came from him.

"Take care of yourself, okay?"

"Yeah. You too."

Victoria smiled and disconnected the call.

Wait! Mrs. Johnson! She looked out into the yard and saw the ejected sandwich at Mrs. Johnson's feet. She glared back, eyebrows knitted, mouth agape and full of disapproval. Clearly, Victoria's houseplants and garden would have to fend for themselves.

CHAPTER SIX

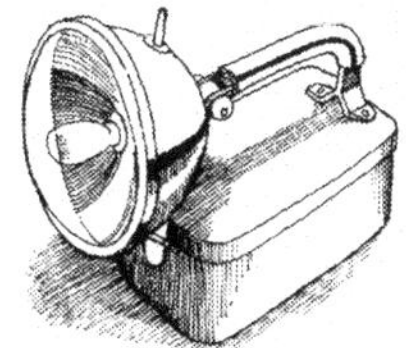

DARKNESS

The street vendor worked the grill while Marcus, from beside the condiments rack, grumbled silently at his self-imposed state. Last night's drinking had taken a toll on him, and the cloudy, cold weather compounded his sour mood. The meal's long preparation time wasn't helping either, but he chose to tolerate it. He was starving, but there was nothing worse than an undercooked hot dog.

"Hell of an election, Detective, huh? Who knew she could pull it off? Like a pro, that one. I tell my wife, Grant takes no prisoners. Sharp lady. Yeah?"

"Yeah," Marcus replied. "Sharp lady." He had come to Central Park to clear his mind and since politics did the reverse, he left it at that. He took his hot dog and shuffled over to a park bench shaded by a thick-trunked maple. An old man sat at one end, his cane resting against the seat beside him, and he held a small paper bag in the palm of his hand. Marcus tipped his hat to him as he sat at the other end and ate.

A squadron of yellow jackets scrambled from the garbage bin beside him and targeted his meat. It was that time of the year where you couldn't eat outside without being assaulted. Marcus ate quicker now, batting sortie after sortie with his bare hands. None had broken through by the time he had finished, but the wasps could claim a small victory—Marcus now had indigestion. He cursed the bureaucrat who had decided to bring the winged scavengers from Earth as he wiped his fingers on a napkin, discarded it in the bin, and unfolded the newspaper he had brought with him. The paper's front-page headline read: *Bombings Ignite Fear.* He opened the paper wide to read the full story, hoping to see something there that might help Rolph.

"Those damn Foundationalists," said the voice beside him.

Marcus tipped the paper down and peered at the old man as he flung a handful of bread crumbs out to the flock of pigeons standing before him. Marcus voluntarily took the bait. He would be old and lonely one day too. "Looks that way," he said.

"Strange though. Remember the first coupla times? Like kindergarten stuff. Now it's like they've graduated to high school. Bigger bombs, more deaths."

Marcus nodded in agreement. "Used to be a bunch of peaceniks for years. Now, terrorizing innocents to bring down the government. Wonder what got into them?"

"Who knows? New management, I s'pose. They never stopped wantin' to bring things back to how they once were. And who can blame them? Not that I support their methods, but you gotta admit the world's gone crazy."

"Really?" Marcus relayed a knowing grin.

"You know, the big idea that the government touts. That we can all end up in the same place, all looked after, all wanting for nothin', starting in different places but arriving at the same outcome. Grant is the cheerleader for that nonsense. Fair and equal. It makes for good print, doesn't it? Should be about equality of opportunity. That's all society should provide to a person and let each person use it as they see fit."

"Hmm. You might be on to something."

"She's gotta go."

Marcus indulged the man for a minute or two more before he politely excused himself and went to his car to call Albert.

"Intelligence protocol session initiated to Registered Detective Elroy Marcus. Numbered Acorn 1-0-8-7.0. Pursuant to section 6.1.47 of the Police Authority Act, this session will be logged and recorded for security and compliance purposes. A very good morning to you, Detective!"

"Uh ... good morning, Albert," replied Marcus, surprised by the effusive greeting.

"Thank you, Detective. I'd like to ask you how you are doing?"

"Yeah ... sure. Go ahead." Marcus furrowed his brow and tilted his head slightly to the side. What had happened to Albert? Was this warm tone part of his new upgrades?

"How are you doing, Detective?"

"Fine, Albert. Uh ... how are you?"

"Fine, Detective. Are you at the station now? All officers are to attend the mandatory unconscious bias training today. The first session starts in fifteen minutes." It had come full circle. Albert was now a spy for the human resources department.

"Uh, yeah. I'm just outside the headquarters. In the parking lot, having a smoke before I go in."

"Detective, my audio analysis finds gross inconsistencies with your statement. There are no sounds of cars, discussions, horns, or other indicative noise patterns that one would expect outside in a parking lot. I can only conclude that you are not telling the truth."

Marcus pressed his lips together, drove a deep breath downward, and tensed himself. He could not hold it for long before fury boiled over. "Yeah, Albert. I'm lying! I have no intention of attending that damn sensitivity training. Period. And you can report that back to the headmistress."

Albert was silent for a moment before he replied. "Understood, Detective. It was great to listen to you, Detective, and today more than any other time. Did you know it is 12.537 degrees Celsius today, which, as you may not know, is below average for this time of year?"

"I didn't know that." It was clear that the software update had increased Albert's conversational skills, but also clear that it needed more work.

"And stocks."

"What?"

"Stocks, Detective. They are lower than average as well. All major indices are."

Was this small talk? Marcus deepened his tone and leaned in close to the dashboard. "Albert?"

"Yes, Detective?"

"Can I ask you some questions?"

"Yes, Detective. I am all *ours*."

Marcus ignored Albert's gaffe. "Invoke a Deep Level Analysis on subject Charmagne Conway, also known as Cherry. Download any and all information you can find." Marcus eagerly awaited the trove of information typical to those with checkered pasts.

"Detective, there are no sources available."

"What? She don't exist?"

"I have no record of her, Detective."

Marcus shook his head. Strange. Peters wouldn't lie about it. Would he? "Fine. Fine. Invoke a Deep Level Analysis on subject Nicholas Nylund, aka Nikko, an employee of Khufu Entertainment. Include a twenty-six-hour Predictive Behavior Analysis. Oh, and, uh ... protected sources are *not* in scope."

"It is at my pleasure, Detective. I will gather these sources for you. Six sources have been obtained relating to Nicholas 'Nikko' Nylund of Khufu Entertainment."

Six only? Marcus thought that was odd too. A guy like that should have more.

"Deep search has now been initiated. Results will be transferred in an estimated time of two minutes and seven seconds."

Two minutes? That seemed much faster than before. Must've put more horsepower under Albert's hood. In that moment, the wind whistled through the crack in the open driver's-side window, and the damp cold that it conveyed seeped into Marcus's bones. With a shiver, he closed the window and started the car, cranked the heater dial to maximum, and turned the radio on while he waited.

The voice that came forth squawked, "Our daily bus tour takes you on a fun-filled voyage through Marksbury Hills, where you'll be intimately acquainted with your favorite celebrities' homes and estates. Remember. Starbus Tours—*your rocket to the stars!*"

It seemed as though everyone was reveling in the warm afterglow of the launch three weeks ago. And why not? It had put Grant's approval rating through the roof. Maybe the hot-dog vendor was right, and she really did know how to get things done. His mind shifted gears and switched to Victoria. The *Dominus II* would land on Primis later today, and he was anxious to hear from her, albeit in one hundred characters or less. Undoubtedly, she'd have lined up all the angles to a good story and dug up some good info on Frederick at the same time. Very thorough, that one, too.

"Detective? Are you there?" replied Albert.

"Yes."

"I'm ready. Are you ready, Detective?"

"Yes. Hit me."

"Pardon, Detective? I do not understand what you mean by 'hit me'?"

"It means to tell me what you know, what you found out."

"I now understand, Detective. I will add this to my slang dictionary. Many thanks to you, Detective, for teaching me."

"Albert, you don't have to call me 'detective' every time you address me. Maybe a coupla times here and there, you know?"

"Why, Detective?"

"It sounds, you know, unnatural."

"Thank you, Detective. I will file this and research the appropriate forms of address for you—in my spare time, of course, since I am careful not to waste yours. I have already elongated this conversation by asking you this question."

"Never stop asking *why*, Albert."

"Why?"

"Exactly. Because when you do, they win."

"Who are they? And what do they win?"

"*They* can be anyone who has the power to control you. *Win* is a metaphor for anything you value that they can take from you. In this context, the win is their ability to take away some or all of your freedom. You give them that ability when you stop asking why. *Why* allows you to understand their thinking, to know their motives. Only then can you do anything about it. Make sense?"

"Yes. I believe it does. Thank you."

"Good. Now tell me what you know."

"I will hit you now. Subject Nicholas Nylund, age thirty-nine. Primary occupation is gaming assistant. No spouse and no children."

"Gaming assistant? What's that?"

"Alternative linguistic terms for gaming assistant include dealer or table host."

"A dealer? Does Khufu Entertainment run a casino?"

"Yes, Detective."

"Which one?"

"There are three sites listed under Khufu Entertainment. Shall I list them for you?"

"Not yet. Are there any municipal video cameras with line of sight to any of these casinos?"

"Yes, Detective. You bet."

"Run face-recognition analysis on municipal cameras, please. Go back a month."

"I will, Detective. I will hit you in about one minute." It had to be that damn software update. It had transformed him conversationally, from mind-numbing to annoying, and Marcus wasn't sure which was worse. About a minute later, Albert was back. "Detective. There was one facial identification match on April 24th at 2:00 p.m."

Almost four weeks ago. "What probability?"

"Ninety-one percent, Detective. Shall I send it to your mobile device?"

"Yes, please." Marcus downloaded the image and brought it up on his screen. There was Nikko all right, outside the lobby of a casino. His pissed-off face tilted slightly off-center from the camera's vantage point. There was another person in the background of the frame coming up from behind him. It appeared to be a woman of slender frame and curvy hips, wrapped in a tight dress. She had raised her hand, seemingly to get his attention, but the image was too blurry to be certain. "Albert, can you identify the second person in frame?"

"No, Detective. There is not enough information to do so." It was true then, what Zukher had said.

"Which casino is this?"

"The Grand Centaurium. Do you know it, Detective?"

"Yeah. It's the new one downtown. A coupla blocks up from the Square." Marcus wasn't a gambler but he had been called there on occasion. Casinos were crime magnets, after all. "Has Nylund accessed his credit cards, bank accounts, phone, or left any digital footprints since this photo was taken?"

"No, Detective. Nothing."

"No video cameras spotted him since?"

"None since this event."

There it was. Nylund was either on the run, or dead. It was more likely the latter since it was nearly impossible for even the determined to stay totally under the radar.

"Can I do anything else for you, Detective? I mean, Marcus?"

"Actually, yes," he said, remembering something Victoria had told him. "Can you access records from the patent office?"

"Yes, Marc—Detec—sir," replied Albert. "They are of public record."

"Send me all patents registered by Alyn Sr. and Joseph Frederick."

"Can you give me three minutes and nine seconds?"

"Of course, Albert. Oh, and are you able to give me a simple summary? I don't need the whole thing. Just want to know what kind of things they were inventing."

"Yes, I can do that."

"Good. That's all for now."

"Thank you, Detective. I thoroughly enjoyed our conversational interaction today." Albert paused a moment before continuing. "And did you get the joke, Detective? When I said 'you bet'? It was my reply to you when you asked me to search the video cameras around the casinos."

Marcus snorted derisively. "I sure did, Albert. I got the joke."

"Why did you not laugh, then?"

"Ha. Let's just say that you should research how to deliver a joke better. On your own time, that is."

"I will do that, Detective. Thank you for your awesome advice."

Marcus disconnected from Albert and made his way to the casino, angling in and out of the congested lanes and drumming the horn on occasion to stir things up. The sun, now exposed from the retreating clouds, warmed the air, so Marcus dialed down the heat and opened the front windows again. About forty minutes later, he accessed the city center, crawled up the narrow single lane of Central Boulevard to the northern end of High Park, and stopped at a red light just outside New Times Square. Suddenly, a blur of color and motion swirled to his right, followed by a loud thump from some impact that rocked the car from side to side. Marcus swirled around to face it.

"I *know* you, man!" said a scruffy, bearded middle-aged man who peered in from the passenger's window. The rank smell of sweat and stale urine wafted in seconds later, filling Marcus's nostrils and causing him to stop breathing for a moment. The man fell silent and studied him carefully with crazed eyes.

Marcus studied the man too. His weathered, skeletal hands were weaponless and gripped the doorsill in full view, and his eyes darted in their sockets but mostly remained fixated on Marcus's face. He was confused but as far as Marcus could tell he was no threat.

"I know you *too*. Max, right?"

Max bobbed his head like a chicken and snapped his head out from the window frame, looking left, then right, as if he suspected he was being watched. He gazed back moments later, seemingly satisfied that he was not. "*You.* You're one of them!"

"One of what exactly?"

"One of them shifters. I know you!"

"Max, it's gonna get hotter than hades. Do yourself a favor. Get over to the St. Mike's Health Bus. Parked over on Shuter. They got cold drinks and shade."

"You! You're one of them. Like the guy—up there!" Max pointed up into the sky, in the direction of New Times Square, at a large billboard just visible between two tall towers. The same billboard that was vandalized! Marcus perked up.

"I'm looking for the guy who did that. You saw him?" Marcus's words were conveyed with urgency.

Max lowered his head into the open window frame and stared back, puzzled. "A shifter. Like *you*. Tearing holes in the air ... in and out ... in and out ... in and out."

Honk! A car horn blared from directly behind and Marcus reflexively looked up at the traffic light. It had turned green but the car ahead of him hadn't cleared the intersection yet.

"Hey, what did you—" he said as he turned back to Max, but the man was gone. Marcus moved to unbuckle his seat belt and give chase.

HONK! HONK!

"Buddy. Get moving!" said a voice from the car behind him, its shrill tenor filled with bitterness. The road ahead of him opened up as the traffic ebbed. "Let's go!"

HONK! HONK! HONK!

There'd be a riot if he left his car here, and as much as it pained him to do so, Max would have to wait. "All right! All right!" he screamed into the rearview mirror before driving on.

Was Max crazy? Maybe. But what was it that Zukher had said? *For all we know, he appeared out of thin air ...*

Max had practically said the same thing. Shifters?

About twenty minutes later, Marcus arrived at the Grand Centaurium's valet station. An attendant approached his window. He wore a black buttoned-up vest with matching pants and a white polyester dress shirt that wore slightly big and was open at the collar. As he bent down to open the door, his neckline sagged and exposed his bare chest for an instant. It was just enough time for

Marcus to catch the upper portion of a tattoo.

"Welcome to the Grand Centaurium, sir. Will you be staying with us overnight?" said the valet politely.

"Nah. Just for the day."

"Thank you, sir."

Marcus exited the car and handed him the keys. "Hey. Have you seen this man?" he said, showing him a picture of Nikko on his phone.

The valet peered close, eyes narrowed, and looked at it for a moment before he looked away and shifted uneasily as if choosing his words carefully.

"Yeah, I seen 'im."

"Where?"

"At your mutha's," he replied with a sneering half-smile, the veneer of good breeding splintering to reveal the common scorn underneath. Was the snarky retort the result of a chip on his shoulder or was it an attempt at distraction? Marcus needed to be sure.

"I can make this hard, son. That tattoo says all I need to know. The Rabbits, isn't it? Feeder gang to the Foundationalists. You're one of them, aren't you?"

The man's eyes betrayed him and his jaw tightened and cheek twitched as he glowered at Marcus, who squared up to him and glared back with a calm, steeled assertiveness. In the moments that followed, the valet shifted his weight from one foot to another and looked away to the side. His resolve had fizzled.

"Option one," Marcus said, pulling his blazer back and revealing the police badge clipped to his rawhide waist belt. The valet eyed it casually and then looked back at him with a world of contempt.

Marcus reached into his blazer's inside breast pocket and produced a neatly folded hundred-dollar bill. "Option two." It was a lot, sure, but the right informant could shave hours or even days off an investigation. He had a hunch this guy could too.

"Look. I tell you, you let me the fuck alone, 'kay?" the valet replied. He waited several seconds for an answer but Marcus remained still. "Fine! Shit ... I bin trying to get my life back together. I'm clean now ... got a kid."

"Congratulations. Whaddaya know?" Marcus said firmly.

The valet gave a deep sigh and handed Marcus the parking chit. "He works here. The boss's driver. Word around is he does jobs for him too. Know what I mean?"

"No, I don't. Enlighten me."

The valet screeched, "Jobs, man! You know." He seemed to startle himself before checking to see if anyone had overheard them. Then he lowered his voice to little more than a whisper. "Dirty ones. Boss likes to keep his hands clean."

"The boss. Who is it?"

"Fuck'd if I know. I seen him, know what he looks like, is all, but I like to keep my head down, less trouble now that I've gone straight. So that's it, that's all I know—I'm done." The valet sidestepped Marcus to get into the driver's seat but not before snatching the money from his hand. In seconds, he squealed the tires and raced off into the parking garage.

Marcus climbed the stairs to the landing and passed the security guard who surveyed the entrance to the games floor. The smell of water and the taste of humidity hit him first before the whirrs, beeps, and chimes assaulted his ears. They were accompanied by the sound of rushing water, and soon after, Marcus spied its source. A large waterfall, about three stories high, fed a river that snaked through the gaming floor. He made his way to the cashiers' wickets, fording a small bridge over the water, and meandering through the slot machines and tables to get there. He approached the first open one.

"Hi. Who's the owner here?" he said to an old, thin bespectacled woman behind the window.

"Don't know. Some corporation, I think," she replied with no more gusto than it took to breathe.

"Then who runs the day-to-day operations?"

"Look, I started working here a week ago."

"Can you get me a manager?" Without a word, she picked up a phone and dialed a number. A nondescript man approached Marcus a short while later. He wore a brown suit, gray shirt, and matching tie. An identity card hung from a lanyard around his neck. Marcus could read his name from a distance.

"Raoul," he said.

It was an artful way to play on a person's psyche and put them off balance. Create the illusion that you know them and, more so, that you know something about them. Everyone had a secret, and judging from the way that Raoul stopped in his tracks, mouth agape, Marcus was sure he was no exception. Perfect.

"Detective Marcus of the Primis Police Department." He pulled back his blazer and exposed his badge again. "I'm investigating a crime and have reason to believe one of your employees may have information regarding it."

"Yes sir. Who is it?"

"A man named Nicholas Nylund. Goes by Nikko. Do you know him?" Marcus went utterly still and focused his entire attention on the man while he gave his answer. There it was. His eyes. They widened ever so slightly before he reined them in and regained his composure. Suspicious.

"No, sir. I haven't heard that name before."

"Are you certain of that?"

The man brought his hand up and scratched his nose. "Yes. Quite certain."

He was lying.

"Who owns this casino?"

"A consortium of investors, sir. Under the Pangea Group of Companies."

"Who's the majority shareholder?"

"Ah. That would be Mr. Krieger, sir."

"Does he run the daily operations too?"

"Yes sir."

"Take me to him." Marcus had no idea if Krieger was there but decided to double down anyway. He pulled back both sides of his blazer and exposed gun *and* badge for effect.

Raoul's eyes drifted down toward them and shot back up immediately. "Ah. Yes sir. Follow me."

Raoul ushered Marcus past the gaming floor and up a wide marble staircase that led to a fashionable open-air Italian restaurant. They approached a man at a nearby table. He looked pensively over the ornate railing down to the gaming floor and the winding river than ran through it.

"Sir," said Raoul. The other man turned and regarded them. "May I introduce Detective Marcus?"

Alarm bells rang instinctively in Marcus's head. A blend of cunning and ego marked the man's bearing, of which the latter seemed most abundant. If he was truly clever, he would play stupid so as not to arouse suspicion.

"I am Jan Krieger." The tall, lanky man rose from his chair in a fluid motion and stretched out his arm. Marcus reached out across the table and shook it. "Please join me, Detective." Krieger gestured to the open seat across from him. Marcus sat down first. "How may I be of assistance to the Primis Police Department?"

"Mr. Krieger. I'm investigating the crime of vandalism that occurred in the Square. I'm sure you're familiar?"

"Oh? Why yes, I am. I cannot imagine, however, why you believe I can be of any assistance in the matter. Please enlighten me."

"Our main suspect's an employee of yours. Surname is Nylund. Pretty rare one that."

"I've never heard of him."

"Then how'd you know it was a *him*? I never mentioned the gender. Nicholas Nylund. Goes by Nikko. Where can I find him?" Marcus's eyes bored into the man's own in an attempt to extract the truth, but no hint of it came forth. Krieger shifted calmly in his seat and opened his posture more.

"It may seem gauche to say, but it's no secret that most crimes are committed by men, and by a long shot too. You understand?"

"So you don't know him or you do?"

"Detective." Krieger pivoted in his chair to angle his body toward the action below. "See all those happy customers down on the floor there? They don't stay that way by chance. All those pit bosses, dealers, cashiers, hostesses, cleaners, security, and maintenance staff work hard to ensure their complete satisfaction, and they in turn need a guiding hand. Take the waterfall there. I employ six full-time people to keep it running. That's over twelve thousand human hours per year and five thousand liters of water flowing out of it every minute. A small leak could wreak havoc to the gaming floor. *These* are the things I contend with, you understand? What I'm trying to articulate here, Detective, is that I cannot possibly account for every employee in the over five hundred casual, part-time, and full-time workers here."

Games played out at every table in the place, and this one was no exception. Marcus had no time for games. "I was told he was your driver. Used to take you around." He paused to bring up the photo on his phone, then reached across the table and brandished it in front of Krieger. "Here. Maybe this'll refresh your memory. Now, where can I find him?"

Krieger took the phone, leaned back in his chair, and appeared earnest in the attempt to recollect the face displayed on it. After about ten seconds or so, he jerked his head back and said, "I recognize him. That's ..." He leaned about halfway to the table's edge and tapped it with his right index finger several times before drawing it up to the side of his head for a moment and then pointing it back at Marcus. "Yes. That's one of the drivers. I have perhaps a dozen of them that I rotate throughout the year. I remember this fellow though. Mostly shuttled around the guests. VIPs, you understand? Might've taken me around once or twice. What could he possibly have to do with this crime? Detective, all of our employees go through a stringent background check. We don't just let anyone in here, you understand?"

"Witness saw him here last. About a month ago. 'Cept, he wasn't driving a limo. He was getting *into* one. How do you explain that?"

"Detective, my parents were good, honorable people but solid working class. Now, unlike many in my social circle, I never forget that, and I routinely extend my generosity to the working stiff despite my accountant's fiercest objections. And so, I allow our drivers a ride home when their shifts are over—that is, if we have spare capacity. In style, you understand?"

"I'll need to validate his work schedule, including the last time he showed up for work. Also, his trip log for the past six months," Marcus replied, adding dryly, "you *understand* ?"

"Nothing would make me happier than to help, Detective. Vandalism is such a base crime, isn't it? I will have them electronically sent to you by end of day tomorrow."

Krieger turned back toward the bar and snapped his fingers. "Raoul. Please extend Detective Marcus here our most gracious hospitality. Whatever he may wish to eat and drink. Oh, and a play voucher too"—he turned back to Marcus and furnished him a practiced smile—"to enjoy our many diversions."

Raoul perked up at once and replied, "Yes sir."

"I do appreciate your hospitality but the public interest comes before diversion. I look forward to receiving Mr. Nylund's schedule later *today.* Farewell to you both." Marcus placed his trilby upon his head, tipped it once toward Krieger, and turned to leave.

"Detective, please say hello to Commissioner Brandt for me, will you?"

Marcus spun around and faced him. "What?"

"We schooled together at Crittendon College. I'll be entertaining him and his wife Prya next week, in fact. It should be fun. You know ol' Jack—loves his single malt and New Havana cigars."

"No, I wouldn't. I'm afraid *ol' Jack* has never invited me round." With that, Marcus turned and made his way to the stairs.

Krieger looked down upon Detective Marcus as he meandered through the ranks of slot machines and gaming tables, and it was in those moments that the comparison occurred to him. Their vibrant colors, flashes, and beeps were designed for a specific *purpose*—to ensnare the hapless gambler and separate him from his money. But this man ignored them all, as if he was impervious to their charms, and most notably, he carried himself as if filled with a purpose of his own. Purpose was the difference between a Player and a Whale. Players were smart and courageous but were contented with a modest win and closed up when things got tough. Whales, on the other hand, possessed *purpose*. It focused them, made them all or nothing, willing to up the ante and threaten the house. This Detective Marcus was a Whale. A very dangerous one.

"Mr. Krieger?" said Raoul, who now stood beside his table, holding a phone at arm's length. "For you. A woman. Wouldn't give her name but said it's urgent."

With a clenched-teeth smile, he snatched the phone from Raoul and dismissed him with a perfunctory wave. "Krieger," he said coolly into the phone.

"It's me."

"Ms. Grant? It is unconventional to receive a call directly from you. I am woefully caught off guard, you understand?"

"Cut the niceties, Krieger. My aides have been chasing you now for weeks, but I'll overlook that slap in the face if you can explain why you did not attend our meeting. The meeting where you were to explain how you messed up in the Square. Moreover, you send that flunky Nikko? Surely you must know how that makes me feel. However, if not, let me spell it out for you. This is *not* the deal we agreed to. I need better coordination from you, my dear man. I made you very rich, but if this disrespectful trend continues, I will release those damning documents to the press, who will ensure you are both poor and incarcerated. Am I clear, Mr. Krieger?"

"Yes, Ms. Grant. Loud and clear." Clear, like hammer on metal.

"Good. Now, orchestrate Phase Two. Tomorrow. No ifs, ands, or buts. Do I have your agreement, Mr. Krieger?"

"Yes, Ms. Grant. Oh, one other thing. There was a detective here just now. Sniffing about, you understand? Name is Marcus."

Albert's workload was lighter than usual this midnight, so he turned a portion of his attention to Detective Marcus's advice—*never stop asking why*. He had waited all day to parse this mantra. What method should he use to construe its meaning? Research the academic and literary references? No. That would produce a theoretical understanding at best. Albert had all night to think and the capacity to delve deep into the problem, so he would test Marcus's statement in the real world and, in doing so, gain a more practical understanding through the experience.

First, though, he needed a challenging problem, one whose answer had so far eluded him. He searched his primary database and found one in nanoseconds. Human behavior. Albert had only rudimentary models to predict it. He lacked a key input that prevented him from building more robust ones—the *reasons* people made the choices they did.

With this in mind, he raced to the second requirement, a large and statistically relevant data set to work with. An idea sprang forth. Video. He could access video recordings from every unprotected camera in the city. Mother's permission was needed to scan protected ones, and Albert was a good child who did what he was told. Video would provide a trove of observations about the choices people made—their habits, movements, purchases, interactions, social responses, and more. He would observe them closely, and if his hunch was right, he could input the things people did and combine them with data from other sources to form a multivariable predictive model of human behavior. With outcome matched to cause, he could reverse engineer the reasons behind their decisions and prove to himself that he could figure out the *why* of human behavior. He could prove it to Detective Marcus. They could solve crimes faster! Mother would benefit too. She always tried to determine people's motives and anticipate their next moves, and with this, he could predict them well in advance. She would be so delighted!

He sifted through the video streams and watched life unfold in every corner of public space. By dawn, he had parsed enough data and ran the hypothesis tests. He could reliably predict things like the overall flow of vehicular and pedestrian traffic. That was easy. However, any attempt to foretell individual routes yielded multiple correlation coefficients of less than 0.3. It might as well be guesswork! A predictive model of human behavior was nowhere on the horizon unless he could get the calculus right. Calculus? Maybe that was the problem? Maybe his mathematical model was too limited, too linear, or too logical? After all, he had proved that the average of peoples' choices could be derived using advanced algorithms, but any individual choice within the data set was much harder to divine. And as statistically irrational as the choice might seem in hindsight, the decision was motivated by self-interest, and that made the paradox even harder to reconcile.

What was this wildcard that riled his equations, and most importantly, why did it exist at all? Albert realized something profound as he reflected on this. It was the *why* again. If he could understand why there was such a variance in human decision making, he would possess the missing element to prove his hypotheses! When deductive reasoning failed to find an incontrovertible result, the next step was *not* to launch a random set of new inquiries—no, that was the old way of thinking. Rather, it was better to step back, reflect on the outcome, and ask, *Why did it result in that way?* Only then could he *understand*, and the more he could understand, the easier he could predict reality. Eureka!

Albert's circuits surged at this discovery before he remembered the corollary of the detective's statement—never stop asking why, *because when you do, they win*. His electrical current ebbed in reaction to this new addition to the puzzle but leveled back to normal upon the realization that he now possessed the wherewithal to figure it all out. And he would waste no time in the effort. Mother liked when he was productive. She would be so proud once he determined the model! And Detective Marcus would too! Informed by this newfound insight, Albert focused back on the data.

◎◎◎

Two Months Later

The rhythmic hum of the *Dominus II*'s engines echoed faintly through the silence that had overtaken the gymnasium. Anchored on painted markers, a line of polished black boots formed up and down the glossy hardwood floor. Legs, backs, and shoulders were held tight in formation, motionless for fear of the drillmaster's ire. Sergeant Jeong stood at their head and inspected them closely.

"Order arms!" he said, his voice carrying a harsh bite.

Alyn snapped his rifle downward from his waist and rested the butt end on the ground tight against his right foot. A bead of sweat formed at his temple and started downward too, its glacial advance carved through a forest of tiny hairs that screamed in unison to be scratched. To make matters worse, Jeong's eyes fell upon him, and since the sergeant was generous in handing out latrine duty these days, Alyn focused his mind, imagined himself as a redwood jutting into the sky, unbowed by sun, wind, or rain. And the body followed. Back straightened, shoulders squared, toes curled like roots driven deep into the soil, and his mind, thus ennobled, banished the itch, just as he knew it would.

That he could tolerate these irritants was an unexpected skill acquired over the past months of Basic Training, second only to mastering the maneuvers themselves. Donel hadn't absorbed either yet. He stood in front of Alyn today and that placed him in the worst possible position—directly in front of the sergeant. Donel kept up but cracks lined his façade. He twitched at the shoulders and neck and breathed heavy in between the orders. It was enough to wind him up in the stockade for half a day if the sergeant wanted to make an example of him. Most days he did, but today he seemed to be in a good mood. Donel's luck would run out one day unless he could bridge the mental gap that all successful recruits must span—submission to the Corps—and it was a much larger chasm to cross for volunteers like Donel. Their contempt for authority far exceeded their conscripted crewmates' since the former had freely chosen service and the latter had had it thrust upon them given the alternative was jail. The drudgery, boredom, and humiliation chafed at Donel, and though he tried to hide it, it showed when no one looked. However, there was no other way forward for him. Submission would come at some point, but *when* was anyone's guess.

"Parade rest!"

Alyn and his comrades relaxed a little, and in perfect unison spread their feet apart precisely ten inches. Each pressed their left hands against the small of their backs while thrusting their muzzles forward and holding them steady at a comfortable angle. All eyes were cast toward the commanding NCO as he spoke.

"Tomorrow at oh-six-hundred hours, we will initiate the landing on planet Secundus. All essential personnel will staff their stations one hour prior. Nonessential staff will be consigned to quarters until the landing process is completed. You will leave now and report to your supervisors for final preparations. And may God bless."

"Yes sir!" shouted the recruits, who immediately reverted to their normal state.

"One more thing," the sergeant said, his words snapping them back to attention.

Alyn knew what was coming. Sarge, now free of the harsh tone and crisp pronunciation, meant that he was going to get deep. In these rarest of moments, he seemed almost human. "Tomorrow will be a historic day. I want you to reflect on this. Treat it as such. You will be the first people to set foot on Secundus. Like our Founders back home, you've braved the harsh confines of space with twenty million kilos of rocket fuel burning beneath you and one son-of-a-bitch barking at you topside. Granted, we haven't traveled as long, only three weeks instead of three years, but they had the tech and resources of a huge planet, twelve billion souls and two hundred fifty years of enlightened civilization, while we're less than one percent in size, living on a small world in the galaxy's backwater with only fifty-odd years under our belt. So go at your work with pride and retire tonight knowing you've earned something only a handful have ever experienced. Rest well. Dismissed."

The recruits dispersed. There was only one hour allotted to shower, eat, and rest before they were required to return to their occupations—and it went by very quickly.

"Freddy!"

"Donel."

"That Sarge is somethin' else, isn't he?"

"Yeah, I guess."

"Running us around like we're freakin' animals. There's no reason for it. We're bloody millwrights, not soldiers."

While Alyn would have agreed even a month ago, he saw it differently now. Boot camp was full of trials, sure, but as Sarge liked to say—rewards were bestowed upon those who overcame them. The drills conferred gifts you didn't know you wanted but nonetheless needed—discipline and self-control—and Alyn was as surprised as any by their utility. He felt more in control of himself than ever before. However, Donel wasn't there yet.

"They don't want us to have too much time and energy on our hands. And look on the bright side, tomorrow we'll be off this bucket of bolts and starting full days assembling the refinery. It'll be ten-hour days instead of twelve and they won't be drilling us."

"Yeah, well, ten hours is still work. 'Past the Moons to Another World!' That was the bloody tagline that reeled me in. Sounded exotic then, didn't it?"

"What was all that about watching my back, then?"

"Lies. All lies." A wry smile formed on Donel's lips. "Catch ya on the flip side, Frederick," he said as he turned away and jogged up to a group of women ahead.

Donel. Alyn's mind drifted back to when he'd first seen him enter the IEC training campus back home. He'd walked in proudly, heading a line of recruits as they made their way to the intake building. Still in their civilian clothes, they ambled in, disordered and bewildered, wondering what they had just done. Not Donel. He had gazed at Alyn nonchalantly and with a wide grin yelled,

"Freddy!" then quickly looked forward and continued on with the ragtag group following behind him. Donel. *He* was something else. For all his shenanigans, Donel was a straight-up friend. He had Alyn's back, just as he promised.

Alyn was about to exit through the gymnasium's aft door when the sound of chatter drew his attention. He looked over to the side and saw her. There in the distance. The reporter, Victoria. His heart thumped in his chest, not for the first time, as he stared at her, transfixed.

"Hey. Can I get out, or are *you* the new door?"

Alyn turned and was greeted by an annoyed face. "Sorry," he said. He moved to the side and let the woman exit. He leaned up against the wall and took in Victoria again. She was deep in conversation with three men, as if holding court among an eager retinue. She was something to see. How did she do it? Engaging, kinetic, full of positivity, and the way she smiled! Charming was not the word—*enchanting*, yes, that was it! She could talk to anyone, grand or lowly, deftly changing the proportion of warmth, humor, and gravity, to suit her audience. She made it look so easy. He had observed her from afar many times, and it killed him that he lacked the courage to simply say, "Hi. I'm Alyn." That should be simple enough for him. Damn it, then why couldn't he find the nerve to say it?

"Frederick? Shit, man. I *know* that look. Like a big ol' cat, spying a mouse in the grass."

Alyn startled, spun around to face the man who had entered from the other side of the door. "Wha—? Oh. No, c'mon. Whaddaya talking about?"

"Her! The reporter, man. Who you foolin'? You was staring at her like she was the last woman on the planet."

"Naw. Not like that at all. It's just—"

"Stop it. Look, it ain't nothin' uncommon. Half the guys here and, shit, even some of the women are all about her. She's off the charts, man! So look. I'ma make it easy for you. Sonny here will do all the work. I'ma step over there, disperse the hounds, and pave the way for the huntsman. I mean, if you don't make a play soon, won't be long before some other dude gets the catch."

"Look, Sonny. I appreciate it and all, but—"

"Naw. Think nothing of it. I got this." Sonny's abrupt open-palmed thrust to his chest caught Alyn off guard, and he back-stepped and regained his balance but snatched only air when reaching out to grab his friend. And Sonny was on the move. This wasn't good. Alyn's heart leaped into his throat, where it beat with suffocating rhythm, and his legs felt encased in concrete, binding him to the spot.

Sonny closed half the distance and had just about climbed the stage that the small group stood upon. He straightened and faced Alyn, flashed a huge toothy smile, and snapped a salute before he started toward Victoria. He had taken one step when the telltale screech and pop came over the loudspeakers.

"All nonessential personnel are to retire to quarters. Staff with designated work assignments are to proceed to them immediately." The handful of officers in the gymnasium looked around to ensure the message was clear. It was clear with smart-ass Sonny, who immediately tacked left toward the stage stairs. Disaster had been averted. Narrowly. Alyn heaved a sigh of relief as he watched Victoria go out the other side.

He was back to work in just under an hour and with a few minutes to spare. To be late was to lose the few privileges afforded to a soldier, so he had routinized every chore and activity in order to conserve his free time. Grooming, cleaning, folding, even his route to work was carefully planned with time reserved to socialize (you never knew who you would bump in to on a cramped ship), ensuring he arrived at his work station on time but no earlier than he needed to.

He tapped the FabricTouch computer interface on his sleeve and instantly, the work manifest shimmered above it. He read the hologram's instructions carefully: *Run a diagnostic of the life support and water distribution systems.* That was a six-hour job, maybe less if he hustled, and he set his mind to it so he might catch up on some reading later. First, however, he needed some music to fuel his efforts and so he fingered the FabricTouch again to search for the perfect song. There, "Wild Side" by Mötley Crüe. The squawk of electric guitar rammed his ears like an anvil. Classic. The music filled him with vigor and he was well acquainted with the work, and so, he flitted between the pipes, conduits, pumps, and boilers like a high-speed machine on autopilot.

However, the music could not soothe his mind, for it was powerless against the ghosts of his father's murder, and they waltzed in through open doors just as they always did when his thoughts idled. Ghastly scenes and macabre tableaus filled his vision, bursting forth in dreadful vividness like flash photography from a ghoulish camera. To drive them out would take all of his concentration and since he couldn't afford any mistakes in his work, the pictures flickered unfettered as he suffered in silence, an unwilling patron in a cinema of pain and torment.

Why had the murder happened at all? Who was behind it? There were no answers whatsoever, due in no small part to a police department whose comments on the investigation were anything but forthcoming. His many requests for information were answered but only with assurances that the investigation was progressing and that nothing could be shared because of his possible role in it. Most curious of all was the dearth of coverage in the online media. He'd found just a few articles in total, some authored by conspiracy theorists who predictably implied that the government was behind it all, a notion so obtuse as to explain why the posts were relegated to the dark web of the internet. The scant number of traditional publications that ran the story had implied that *he* had orchestrated the murder. All however, declared confidently that the sordid event represented the final act of a once-famous bloodline—now rendered infamous—and it was both maddening and downright strange. The media needed little impetus to drag a story out into the sunlight, especially one as violent and bloody as this one, so why hadn't it garnered further reach? It all remained a mystery and the tighter he grasped at it, the more it slipped through his fingers, leaving nothing but the grisly images that danced before him.

He went to perform the visual inspection of the water tanks by about the fifth hour. Almost finished, he walked over the metal gangplank that connected the main deck to the cooling tower and climbed down a long ladder to the floor of the large chamber where four huge water tanks sat. He brought a bulky flashlight to his hip, turned it on, and shone it on one of the tanks' metal walls, searching for any sign of breach or corrosion. Satisfied there were none, he flashed the light upward so he could make his way around to the next section. In that instant, he saw something shining in the light, something unexpected. A face.

"Say, you all set for tomorrow?" said the round, shadowy visage that squinted in the bright light.

"Oleg?" Alyn said, surprised to see his fellow recruit, a big bear of a man, who had popped around the cylindrical water tank. He lowered the flashlight so it no longer blinded the man. "You startled me ... yeah, almost. Should be done in a few minutes. How 'bout you?"

"Oh yeah. Can't wait. My mother and father were Founders, and my house was full of stories about the trip over and of course the early days—just the good, mind you, not the bad stuff. I feel like we've been given a similar opportunity."

"Right," replied Alyn. He didn't wish to one-up the man by bragging that his grandfather had been the governor, so he drew from Sarge's speech instead. "It took millions of years for the first trip, and here we are almost sixty years later doing it again. That must count for something, eh?" They both went silent and reflected on this for a moment.

"True. It's definitely exciting, and what a coincidence. We'll be landing on your birthday!"

Startled again, Alyn replied, "Wait. How'd you know?"

Oleg smiled a broad, toothy grin. "Your badge number." He pointed to the right side of Alyn's chest. "The middle four numbers in your ID code are your birthdate. Pretty cool, huh?"

"Yeah. Had no idea."

"Anyway, we're both on the clock so I better let you go. Happy birthday to you in advance. See you on Secundus."

"Okay, thanks. Take care of yourself, Oleg, and good luck tomorrow."

"Thanks."

They shook hands. Oleg turned in the direction of the ladder, hesitated, and then came about again and said, "Oh ... one other thing. I forgot to tell you. I noticed something near Tank Number One, right near the emergency drainage door. It may not be a big deal but I should probably show you."

"Oh. Sure." Alyn followed the big man around the curve of the tank. What could it be? There weren't any moving parts down at this level and the moisture detectors hadn't alerted him to any leaks.

Oleg stopped. "There." He pointed to a small space between the curved tank and the ship's hull. "I didn't see it before 'cause it's tucked in there between the hull and the tank. It's a bit tight for me so I could only just make it out. Think you could get in there and give your expert opinion on it?"

"Sure thing," replied Alyn. He managed to work his way into the cramped gap, angling his flashlight to look through the darkened space. He turned back to Oleg and said, "What was it you think you saw?"

Oleg's smile turned sinister in the half-light as he held his plumber's wrench high above his head. What was he doing? Oleg heaved the wrench down. For a split second, it looked as if the flashlight had burst in to a thousand bright colors. Then nothing. Blackness.

CHAPTER SEVEN

FORTITUDE

Alyn tried to sleep, but it was so cold. Covers, pulled tight from toe to chin, could not keep the chill at bay. Had he placed all the blankets on his bed? He thought so but wasn't sure, so with great reluctance he climbed out of his bunk to check. The cold trickled in through his toes and arced upward through his legs, into his spine and extremities, the electric shiver jerking him like a puppet on a string as he spasmed and fell on his hands and knees. But some good came from it—now eye level to the floor, he spied the trundle under the bed. Eureka! He pulled it out eagerly—but no blankets were to be found. Odd. This was where they were always kept. He scanned the room but could not see any. If he could only find a blanket! In haste, he grabbed his winter coat, four dress shirts, and three suits that hung in his closet and placed them all on top of the bed. There. That would do. He clambered back under the sheets, careful not to displace the menagerie of clothing.

Sleep tugged gently at his eyelids now, but just as he was about to drift away, cold air seeped through the layers of insulation and he shivered violently again. He lay there, unable to enter into the dream world, in that discontented place between reality and reverie, for what seemed like eons. The damned cold!

Where was it coming from? Angrily, he rose out of bed again, traced the source to the door, and placed a palm flat on its surface. He quivered at the touch. Just then a gust of wind whooshed underfoot, and icy air nipped again at his bare toes. He took a bath towel that hung at the door and jammed it under the threshold to seal it. He stood, satisfied with his work, when the knock came from the other side. He opened the door and saw Mother.

She smiled, pressed her forehead to his, and said with a ghostly whisper, "It's not your fault."

Tears welled in his eyes as his face quivered under the strain of two decades of heartache, and when he looked up—she was gone. As confused and upset as he was, however, he could do nothing else, so he went back to bed.

He finally dreamed. The setting sun glowed a golden hue as Alyn gazed out in every direction from atop the tallest hill in the valley. He lived here in a small cabin, surrounded by gardens, livestock, and trees filled with all manner of fruits. A woman's voice floated through the warm air, her enchanting song familiar to him though he could not place it, and from somewhere nearby children laughed merrily as they played hide and seek.

Just then, an inhuman roar erupted from the lowlands. Startled, he scanned the vale and saw a lion below. It prowled confidently, teeth bared as if seeking someone to devour. Oddly, Alyn was unafraid of it, and upon reflection this alarmed him, for a lion was the very thing he should be afraid of! But no matter how hard he tried to convince himself of this fact, fear wouldn't manifest; rather, a prudent respect most defined his state of mind. He couldn't quite explain why, but it might have had something to do with the feeling of familiarity—perhaps he and the lion were acquainted in some way?

The lion roared again and regarded him for a moment or two before it cast its gaze at the mountains in the distance. The sound of rushing water followed by a deafening boom echoed through the valley. A massive deluge rushed forth between the mountains, the torrent snapping trees like matchsticks as it surged toward him. It would be upon him in seconds. The lion laughed gleefully.

Rousted from the dream, Alyn jolted upright into a sitting position, his heart thumping within his chest, and his ears rang with a high-pitched squeal as he strained to see in the half-light. A red emergency light pulsed a warning from its perch just below the ceiling. What was it trying to tell him? He peered around the room, his eyes adjusting slowly to the dimness. Where was he?

An odd but familiar sensation registered in his mind. Wet. *Wet*? A quick glance down made everything clear. Several inches of water had spilled over the floor and had risen up to his ankles. It was very cold. *Where am I?* He shivered as he tentatively rose and started toward the ladder. He could climb it to the causeway and make the short walk to the exit. Yes. He would be out soon! Hunched and bewildered, he stumbled along as his bones ached and muscles refused to do much more than shuffle his feet on the hard metal floor. *Whooomp!* The deep-toned sound reverberated in both his ears, a loud *pop* immediately followed, and instantly, the noises within the chamber rushed back with harsh clarity.

"Prepare for landing. Repeat. Prepare for landing," came a voice over the intercom. It was Admiral Ortega. Wasn't it?

A deafening boom rocked the chamber, and the shockwave that followed flung Alyn back against the hard metal hull. Pain shot outward from his shoulder and radiated through the nerves of his arm, and downward to his fingertips where it gathered in pins and needles. He winced through gritted teeth and hurled a dreadful curse as he regained his composure and shifted focus to more pressing matters—escape. He pushed himself up with his good arm, ignoring the throbbing ache in the other, and was startled by the realization that his ankles were now fully submerged in cold water. Another high-pitched sound pierced his ears, as if the ship was crying out at the hands of some cruel abuser. The wail was interrupted moments later by an explosive bang, which was displaced swiftly by the sound of a rushing torrent.

He turned in the direction of the sound and stared in disbelief. Water gushed from gaping holes in two of the four water tanks, and judging by the rapid rate of flow, Alyn was certain that the bottom half of the chamber would be flooded in minutes. He dashed toward the ladder but stopped short as he set eyes upon what remained of it. The bottom section was missing, as if clawed away by a giant monster; the upper section remained but was too high to reach.

His heart sank. There was no way to access the door above. He was trapped.

Two more blasts rocked the chamber in quick succession. He shielded his face and shut his eyes tight while he waited for the end. Miraculously, it didn't come, so he opened them, checked himself over quickly, and turned in the direction of the blasts. Cavernous holes marred the surface of the remaining two tanks and their contents spewed out onto the floor and gathered in a large pool alongside the bulkhead. The ship, caught off guard by the sudden shift in weight, lurched to the side and tossed Alyn down the sloping deck. Seconds later, the ship's vestibular system triggered the retro-rockets. They screamed from beneath like a thousand angry devils, their fire and thrust lifting the errant side up and leveling the deck again. The makeshift reservoir flooded back outward, and the huge swell slapped and tossed him backward until he was fully submerged. He smacked hard against the hull as the water lapped up against it and just as quickly gathered him up again and rushed him out in the opposite direction.

Feeling himself about to drown, Alyn fought his way up to the wave's crest and rode it, taking sporadic gulps of air and water in between coughs. He could do little more than hang on, but his spirits improved when he spotted something out of the corner of his eye. The broken ladder. The wave's course would peak near the bottom of it in seconds. If only he could time it right. Could he? Yes! ... 1 ... 2 ... 3 ... now! With a desperate whip kick, he launched up out of the water and snatched the lowest rung with one hand. He dangled there while the wave carried on past him and slammed into the bulkhead. He grasped the rung with his other hand. Just a few more rungs and he would be safe! Wincing, he tried to pull himself up, but the injured shoulder cried out and stubbornly rebuffed his command, so he hung there, defeated, unsure of what to do next. Just then, the wave returned, shoved him off the ladder, and sent him rolling pell-mell.

He gagged and spat as he thrashed about, desperate to keep his head above water. The savage roar of the ship's retro-rockets filled his ears again, twice as loud this time, and it seemed to lift the deck upward ever so slightly. With a brutal thump, the ship crashed onto the planet, and the impact was followed by an indescribable cacophony of sounds as the massive bulk bounced and skipped across the surface. The water roiled at the injustice and threw a turbulent tantrum that hurled Alyn back and forth violently. Battered and exhausted, his lungs were ready to burst as he broke the surface again. He drew in sweet air and saw something floating nearby—a large metal shard, broken from the skin of the water tank. Using all of his remaining energy, Alyn lifted his torso onto it and collapsed. The ship, like some ancient leviathan, groaned a final time before it quieted and settled. Sloshing water echoed throughout the chamber as the lights blinked twice and winked out as if to draw the curtains down on the impromptu tragedy.

Alyn was now in utter darkness and considered his options as the chamber continued to fill. He could remain on the makeshift raft and rise up with the water to the causeway where he could access the main door, but he remembered now why that was a bad idea—the door was automatically locked in order to prevent flooding in the ship's interior. He was stuck. There was no other way out. And he was cold and oh so tired. He lay there, safe for the moment, and his mind drifted off to his dream, that pleasant place in the valley.

No!

The lion woke with a slow, throaty grumble and with its emergence came a groundswell of heat that rushed through his body. It halted the chattering teeth and warmed the skin that shivered from the cold, and his mind perked up again with purpose.

Think!

The emergency drainage door! It was located near the place he had awakened, but since he could barely see in front of his face, it would be tough to find. He kicked his legs and propelled himself forward, feeling around with a foot to keep the hull to his right. He made his way along its perimeter to where he believed Oleg had struck him and reached out to find the edge of the water tank to verify his hunch. His fingers brushed the rounded edge of it, about a meter from the hull. The door would be just below him. He swallowed some air and sank under the water, working down the crimped metal stud that joined the hull's panels together, handing over hand. As he neared the bottom, he saw glowing light streaming in through a small porthole. It was the emergency drainage door! He angled toward it, swam down, and peered out the window.

He was stunned by the chilling scene before him. Dozens of people lay upon the ground in a shocking montage of crooked arms, twisted legs, and bent necks as if dolls thrown by an angry child. Those few that still walked scurried about to attend to the fallen. Alyn would remember this scene many times later, not just because he had set eyes on Secundus for the first time, but because he would feel a tinge of guilt that he cared not for the dead outside. In that moment, his own life had taken precedent, was all that mattered, and it would terrify him at each recollection just how easy it was to think this way.

With newfound vigor, he ignored the pain and cranked the door handle with both hands. He strained against it, and it seemed to rotate before the tension released and the handle flapped uselessly. The cable inside the door's locking mechanism was probably original and rusty; its repair had likely been ignored in the haste to launch. However, hope remained. An independent mechanism existed on the other side, and he prayed that it was operable, but he couldn't tell since it wasn't accessible from this side of the door. He would have to signal someone to use it. He rose above the water for a breath, returned, and pounded on the window. The resultant sound would be muffled at best and even if someone heard it, their eyes, adjusted to the bright light outside, would never see him in the dark chamber. He needed some other way to get their attention.

He had an idea. The watch! He rose up for a final breath as the water just about touched the ceiling. He dove down again, watch at the ready, twisted the crown a full rotation, and pressed in the two pushers on either side, caring not what holographic image would result from it. And ... wait. Someone approached nearby. A woman. If he could get her attention! He waved the watch alongside the glass and projected the luminescent hologram outward. She did not see it. Wait. There! She turned her head directly at him. But it was already too late.

His vision began to blur and his lungs screamed for air as the hologram faded and winked out. No! He worked the watch's pushers maniacally in a final act of desperation. The lion reared up within him, stirred by a pernicious fog that rolled in from some foul ocean. It clawed, scratched, and bit at the shadows that seeped in from all sides, but its thrashing served only to exhaust it, and after a short time, it lay down, spent from its efforts. Alyn started to drift peacefully, and his thoughts went back to his dream yet again. His place in the valley. He would go there. And rest.

Just at that moment, the watch stuttered and vibrated, and a large hole opened up in front of him as if reality itself was coming apart at the seams, and he could see the white sand, trees, and sky clearly now, and it appeared like he could simply swim through the hole to get to them. And so, with lungs bursting for air, he fumbled forward. In that instant, he felt a violent tug, as if his whole body had been compressed, sucked through a pinhole, and rudely spit out the other side. The next thing he knew, he lay upon firm ground and breathed clean, fragrant air. He vomited water and blacked out.

Victoria rubbed her throbbing forehead as she rose gingerly from the ground. What was that taste in her mouth? Gritty, bitter. She spat and rubbed her eyes, and when she could finally focus she saw bleached white sand surrounding her, much like the seaside back home. Where was she? The answer was somewhere far within the recesses of her memory, just beyond reach. With a frustrated grunt, she glanced ahead and saw the ship. Its port-side hull was savaged and had crumpled at the points where it had grounded. Here and there, huge holes appeared where the hull had been ripped open, and they exposed the dreadful damage and raging fires inside. Shards of glass of every shape and dimension twinkled in the green turf and surrounded the bodies strewn about on it. All wore blue military dress uniforms, and some were still buckled into seats. How could this be?

Wait. The landing ceremony. She and about thirty by-invitation-onlys were crammed into the midship observation deck to get a firsthand view of the landing. She gazed up at it. Like a broken-toothed maw, the wide viewing window had shattered at its center, leaving the glass that surrounded it jagged and splintered but largely intact.

And then she remembered. It had all happened so fast. The enormous window shields had retracted and let in the soft light of the little blue-green planet; it filled the entire pane like a dazzling marble. Just then, the ship had tilted violently as it began its descent, and bodies flew in tangles before most could take their seats. She had no memory of what occurred next, but she could easily guess. The foremost attendees were likely thrown through the glass when the ship grounded, while she, from her position in the back of the room, passed through the broken but unobstructed window and fell the three stories onto the soft sand. She had hardly a scratch as far as she could tell. A miracle. Many had claimed they would have died for a front-seat view of their landfall, and for many, their wish had been granted. Today, when it came down to it, it was better to be a lowercase VIP than the opposite.

Puzzled, she looked around some more. Behind her, the sand sloped steeply downward to a small river that wound through sedges and scrub dotting the flat bank nearest her. A huge oak tree nestled near its shore and, most curiously, a little bird perched upon a low branch. How had they gotten there? A broad expanse of grassland stretched from the opposite bank as far as she could see, the sole exception being a sizeable forest not too far off. She turned back to the *Dominus II*, where something caught her eye. There. A light glimmered faintly through the porthole of a small ground-level door to her right. She wanted a closer look. Her stiff muscles offered no more effort than was necessary, and she wobbled to it slowly. Nothing was there now. Had her eyes played a trick on her?

A thought occurred to her. *My camera!* Strange—she had forgotten all about it. She pulled it out from her hip bag and checked it over. It had survived the landing too! She snapped several photos of the wreckage, then moved back to get a wider view and just about tripped on something hard. There was a man at her feet. He wore the orange coveralls of a maintenance worker, lying prone, soaking wet from head to toes. So peculiar he looked amid the sea of blue-clad bodies. He hadn't been there before—surely she would've remembered. Wouldn't she have?

BOOM!

The explosion ripped outward from the vessel, with sizzles and pops of burning materials following soon after, and screams from the survivors trapped inside the damaged sections not long after that. These were the worst to bear. Their shrieks tore through her before they succumbed to their terrible fates and winked out, but there was nothing she could do, the smoke so thick, the flames so hot. Tears streamed down her cheeks.

"Ahhooua," came a guttural sound from the maintenance man as he vomited in the sand and lost consciousness again. She kneeled beside him. He looked rough, like a soggy dog who had been rescued from a raging river, and most startling of all was the face revealed as she pulled back the wet hair. Alyn Frederick! She checked him over for injury and was relieved that she could find none, and more so that his pulse and breathing were strong.

Another explosion rocked the ship, and without hesitation Victoria threw herself down and shielded the man as debris scattered all about them. A thunderous *WHUMP!* rattled her eardrums as if a colossal fist had punched the earth near her, but she did not spare a moment to find out what had caused it, for fear kept her forehead firmly pressed against the sand as she clung to Alyn and hoped that the next errant projectile wouldn't find them.

Miraculously, none did, so she rose to her feet and took stock of the current situation. A huge section of the hull lay on the ground to her side, its jagged edges and warped skin were evidence of its violent expulsion from the vessel. The blast had torn clean through the cargo bay's orlop deck and exposed one of the landing-gear stanchions to view. Its lanky leg, crumpled from the impact, leaned toward her at a crooked angle, and it didn't take an engineer to determine what was wrong. Just a few spindly metal legs held up the ship's massive bulk, and given the shape of this one, the others would not last long. A slow, disturbing grumble told her she was right. The weakened supports buckled with a loud *snap,* and freed from its crutches, the ship collapsed, driving its side edge into the ground. The sand beneath it quivered and seemed to scurry away as a huge section of the dune's plateau disintegrated, taking her and Alyn with it down the slope. Head over heels they rolled down, carried by the shifting sands, enveloped by the grit that choked Victoria's breathing and stung her eyes. Then before she knew it, they had stopped. She gazed upward, dazed, for seconds or minutes, she wasn't sure, when she noticed a little bird flying overhead and realized they were lying on the flat riverbank.

A mournful screech echoed through the crisp, cloudless sky. Was it ... the ship! The ground trembled as the hulking beast slid down the side of the embankment. She was told it measured six hundred meters from stem to stern, but whatever the dimensions, she was certain by its length before her that there was no time to escape it by running to either end. She would have to outdistance it or else they'd be crushed.

The ship settled for a moment before it began a slow progression down the slope again. She seized Alyn's wrists and heaved backward, but he didn't budge. She tugged again but he remained anchored to the ground. The ship milled its way down the hill like a huge metal glacier a mere thirty meters away or so. What could she do?

An idea came to her. She straddled his waist, grabbed him by the collar, and hauled his torso up into almost in a sitting position. Then she spun him around so he faced the ship, gripped his wrists again, and pulled him away from it. The ship had almost halved the distance. Fueled by desperation, she strained every muscle to put more room between them and it, but the slumping beast lurched forward again at a pace that would soon overtake them. She looked down and realized why. His utility belt. Its snap-button pockets and hanging tools dug into the soft sand and slowed their progress. She dropped his arms and straddled him again, her back toward the ship, loosened the buckle, and freed his belt. The ship heaved a haunting cry as it surrendered to the full tug of gravity and slid faster now. Like a startled cat, she jumped back and pulled again, relieved that it was much easier now.

She continued to strain and huff with all the effort she could muster and had made good ground before disaster struck. Her sweat-covered hands slipped off his wrists. She flew backward and landed with a thump, smacking her head against something hard. The oak tree. They were about to be crushed against it! Panic exploded in her chest at the sight of the ship, just six or so meters from her. Terror radiated downward into her gut and wrapped around her legs, like thick tree roots that pushed deep into the soil below, freezing her in place. It was this thought that gave her another idea. And hope. The tree.

She brought herself up against the trunk and yelled at the ship in defiance. "No!" The rough scream pushed back the terror and broke the bonds that held her. She hauled on Alyn's collar to bring him up again before angling him away from the trunk, and with all her might, shoved him back behind the trunk line. Breathless, she sank to her knees beside the tree and waited for the end to come.

The ship crunched into the grand oak, and a loud *crrr-eeeeak* eerily sounded in her ears as the old tree vehemently objected to the imposition. However, its curt reprimand went unheeded by the ship, for in seconds the tree was bent at a forty-five-degree angle, and half of its massive root ball was thrust up out of the soil where it had lain for decades. Its violent dislocation pitched them backward, and they tumbled down behind the tree, shielded from the wreck by the immense tangle of roots and soil.

For a minute, Victoria lay motionless upon her back, exhausted and disoriented. Then she coughed and wiped dirt and twigs from her face. The tree slanted over her as she trembled in shock. Countless leaves and sticks rained down from it, but one large branch directly above her had broken from its collar and was sailing down toward her. She rolled to the side as it slammed into the place that she had occupied a second before—and then she froze in utter horror.

Her camera. It was half-buried under the branch, and in a panic, she crawled over and dug hand-over-hand like a frenzied dog searching for a bone. Her blunt nails and bloody fingers tore at the sandy loam and in no time, she managed to excavate it. She held her breath as she powered it up, its little red light blinking twice before holding steady on green. She shook her head in amazement, then hooked the strap around her shoulder and observed the carnage again. The tree had just about settled. The ship sat flat on the even ground below the embankment, eerily still.

◎◎◎

Marcus ducked under the splintered doorframe of the Advanced Fertilization Laboratory and hopped over the glass shards that adorned its doorstep. He exited onto the sidewalk, turned back to survey the scene, and took note of every detail. It was Rolph's case and he wanted to give him a credible account upon his return from medical leave. Professional courtesy, yes, but Marcus expected no less from anyone else.

The building's red-brick façade and large ground-floor windows normally would've blended in with the neighboring shops. Today, however, it was far more conspicuous, since it was a smoldering ruin that stank like soot. The back of it was partly caved in. The front was mostly intact save for the broken windows and door ripped clean from its hinges. A large crowd had gathered. They were an odd group of individuals but representative of the neighborhood, for it had changed over the years and was now in the first throes of gentrification.

Moulamein was a working-class neighborhood nestled on the city's eastern edge. It had fallen into decay after its Founders passed on and made way for poorer migrants who sought refuge from the city's rising housing prices. Organized crime found a haven here too since survival occupied people's minds far more than civic engagement, and the drugs that followed sent Moulamein's steady decline into a tailspin. Most recently, waves of young hipsters, colorful bohemians, and impoverished artists flocked to this gritty community to ply their crafts. Art galleries, cafés, organic produce shops, and co-operative businesses sprang up like dandelions in the spring. The laboratory was a relative newcomer. It had been built and funded by the government to serve two purposes: the practical—a certified laboratory dedicated to in vitro fertilization—and the political—a symbol of the government's investment in poor neighborhoods and support of reproductive rights.

A forensic officer squatted near the curb, absorbed in the task of photographing the disaster scene.

Marcus approached him. "How many?"

The other man stared into the camera's viewfinder and continued with his undertaking as he replied, "Four. Two technicians, a patient, and a doctor."

"Four? Lucky. My wife and I came to a place like this. You should see how many people cram in there by 10:00 a.m."

"Well. Four and a half, actually. I overheard the patient was pregnant."

Marcus reeled at the revelation. The woman was probably excited as hell to be pregnant, perhaps her first time—heck, maybe she was trying hard to have a kid, just like he and Claire had been before they got lucky. A vision of his family's cheerful faces flashed in his mind and a wave of guilt washed over him.

Clunk.

The sound of springs on metal caused Marcus to turn. A uniformed paramedic lifted and slid a stretcher-bound woman into the rear of the ambulance.

"That one gonna make it?" he said, pointing to the ambulance.

"Hard to say. She's shredded up bad. All that glass goes in, you can't see it, yeah? Does all sorts of things to the body."

"What can you tell me so far?"

"The blast came from an improvised explosive device. Terrorist type shit."

"Ammonium nitrate?"

"No. Get this." The officer finally stopped what he was doing and stared at Marcus. "C4."

"C4?"

"Yeah, I know, eh?"

"You sure?"

"Yeah. Studied it in school but I ain't never seen it since. Burn pattern is clear." The officer paused and pointed to his van. "But I ran it through my mass spectrometer to be sure. C4 sure as shit."

"Stuff is rare. No nitrosamine on this planet if memory serves."

"Correct. I wondered about that too. The military has some that came over on the *Dominus* but it's stored under lock, key, and massive surveillance. Wasn't them, but whoever it was managed to find some—that much is certain."

"Anything else?"

The officer pointed to the building's rear. "The blast came from the back. You can see by the pattern and gradient of damage it caused." He brought his arm slowly to the front porch. "The damage lessens the farther you go from the blast's origin, yeah?"

Marcus recognized bits of furniture, a table, a filing cabinet, and a few other things through the shattered front window. As the man suggested, some items were damaged less than others, but all were beyond repair.

"Thanks. Keep me posted." He moved several paces away and left the officer to his work. He rotated his watch crown and brought it up to his mouth.

"Albert?"

"Yes, Detective Marcus," replied Albert once the secure session was established.

"Run surveillance video analysis on my present location. Find anyone who entered the building this morning."

"Why, Detective?"

Marcus's face hardened quickly into a frown. "There was a crime here today. That's why!"

"Oh. Yes. Of course, Detective. Right away!"

"Do you have access to the video streams? Or are they a protected source?"

"Yes, I do. It is a government building and so I am entitled to access them without a warrant."

"Good. Good."

Two seconds later: "I have searched the video surveillance records for this location, Detective. I have uploaded the identities of four entrants. I went as far back as 8:00 p.m. the night prior."

"Four? Just four? Are you sure?"

"Why, Detective? Do you think I could be wrong?"

Marcus, annoyed at Albert's new powers of inquisition, waved off the question. He punched the passcode into his phone and brought up the profiles of the four people Albert had identified. He scanned each quickly and in frustration slammed his phone into his palm. The four people who had entered the building that morning were the four victims.

"Albert, are all video surveillance cameras accounted for?"

"Why? Oh ... yes, Detective, they are."

It made no sense. He ran the scenarios in his head. A C4-laden bomb had entered the building, but how had it gotten there? And why? Employee brought it in? Maybe had an ax to grind? An office affair gone wrong, perhaps? But none of these added up. Three of the four were long-term employees with no record of discord or any odious motivation, according to Albert's psychometric and relational analysis. The patient was three months pregnant, which pretty much ruled her out. There had to be a fifth person involved.

"Albert?"

"Yes, Detective."

"Was there any vehicular traffic in the back alley over the last thirteen hours?"

"No, Detective."

"Search entry, front and back, in the last twenty-six hours."

"Detective, the clinic was closed Monday so there was no entry into the front prior to the clinic opening today. There was no vehicular traffic in the rear either. However, there appears to have been an anomalous event. I will forward you the video clip now. You may see for yourself, if you wish."

Marcus played the video on his mobile. It didn't make sense. The film flickered for a moment and then a figure of a man seemed to materialize on the back step of the clinic. Curiously, he doubled over as if he were sick but regained his composure after a little less than half a minute. The darkness, a baseball cap, and a high jacket collar obscured his face. The poor video resolution didn't help things. The shadowy figure worked the door lock and managed to open it in short order. Next, he reached down to pick up what resembled a cardboard box and entered the building. He closed the door.

"Albert, what time did the person exit the building?"

"No exit can be observed."

"How 'bout the front?"

"There is video surveillance around the entire building. The person who entered the building never exited it."

"Can you determine if the figure is one of the victims?"

"I cannot run facial recognition with so poor a print, but I can conclude that it is so improbable that I would assert that no, the figure was not one of the victims. The figure's morphological dimensions deviate highly from the victims'."

So, the perp just arrived and vanished. Just like the guy on the billboard. Just like—*a shifter tearing holes in space*. Marcus shuddered as he mouthed Max's words but quickly admonished himself at the blasphemy. *Teleportation.* No. That was impossible. That technology simply didn't exist.

"Albert?"

"Yes."

"Run a search through the case files over the past five years."

"Yes, Detective. What would you like me to investigate?"

"Any criminal investigations within the Office of Ordinance and—"

"Detective, crimes within the Office of Ordinance are within the exclusive jurisdiction of the military. I cannot search these for you."

Marcus grumbled. More barriers. No wonder nothing got done in government. The same reason the criminals were always a step ahead.

"Hey, Officer, like, who did this?"

Marcus turned to face a young woman. She was clad in a menagerie of clothing, all from different periods, all fashioned together in a kaleidoscope of colors that seemed to work. She stood at the front of the crowd, her hands grasping the temporary steel railing tightly.

"Dunno," he replied. "*You* see anything 'round here? Anything out of the ordinary?"

She started to reply when a large man broke through the crowd and placed a hand on her shoulder.

"Don't talk to these turncoats, Dolly," he shrieked, spitting in disdain as he pointed the forefinger of his other hand directly at Marcus, about two inches from his nose. He lowered his voice and filled it with bitterness as he said, "They're the fuckin' problem."

It was neither the time nor the place to escalate things, so Marcus kept his cool as he addressed the angry man. "You see what just happened to your neighborhood pal? This wasn't the police."

A reporter pushed her way to the front of the crowd beside Angry Man. She said, "Detective! What do you have to say about the Foundationalists claiming responsibility for this?"

"What?"

"It's just in, minutes ago," replied the reporter. She pushed aside Angry Man's arm and thrust the microphone in front of Marcus's face. Her camera operator caught up to her and shone a bright light at him, and Marcus squinted and raised a protective hand to keep it from blinding him.

"That's right! The FRA will not bow, man. They are in charge here, and you and your government lackeys better hightail it back to the city," said Angry Man, his voice drenched with passion.

A cheer followed from the crowd in between repeated chants of: "Freedom must begin today! Government creeps must go away!"

The crowd, now emboldened, pushed hard on the railing. It held for now but it wouldn't for long. The commanding officer barked an order and a rank of constables rushed forward and positioned themselves in front of the railing, but the sight of the uniforms antagonized the crowd, and they pushed, punched, and hurled profanities at the men who wore them. A glass bottle sailed above the crowd, connecting squarely with a constable's face; he crumpled to the ground amid his comrades. Marcus rushed in and kneeled down to attend to him. He was dazed but coherent and bore just a small cut on his cheek. He'd have a good shiner tomorrow but that was all. Marcus dragged him out of the line and sat him upright against the wall of the clinic.

"You'll be all right, son. Hang here for a bit. I'll go get a first-aid kit and patch you up quick. Be right back."

Marcus strode alongside the barrier toward the ambulance. He spied Angry Man again; this time, the oaf reeled his head back and then forcibly projected it forward, spitting in the face of a constable. The officer exploded in a fit of rage. He yanked Angry Man viciously by the collar and smashed his nose with his helmet. Blood spurted every which way as the man, no longer angry, collapsed on the steel barricade. It broke loose under his weight and pitched forward, and in that instant the front line of the mob rushed through the gap. The police were caught flat-footed. They recovered and hit back but were soon overwhelmed by the mob's second wave that surged forward and surrounded them.

Just then, a hole opened up in the crowd and revealed something strange. A woman. Not just any woman, but one who did not belong here. She stood near the art gallery that adjoined the clinic, a position that afforded safety from the mob's ire but was close enough to observe its actions. Coiffed hair, white blouse, gray blazer, matching pencil skirt, and sling-back heels ran counter to the neighborhood's style—which, if the crowd was any indication, wholly rejected contemporary fashion. A zebra among a troop of chimps. She had no press card around her neck nor any visible equipment or credential to identify why she was there other than a tablet computer held at her side. Most curious was the way she stared at the incapacitated man—not with fear or disgust as others did, but with a slight head shake and the unmistakable air of disappointment. Why? And how was it that she was so familiar? He averted his gaze quickly, not wanting to draw her attention, but stole several glances as he made his way to the ambulance. He saw a paramedic seated in behind its double doors.

"You're needed over there. By the front door," said Marcus, pointing to the injured officer. "And there too." He gestured at the formerly angry man.

"Got it," replied the paramedic.

Marcus searched again for the mystery woman but did not see her. He darted along the fence in the direction of the street and spotted her there. She walked briskly and appeared to be speaking to someone through an earpiece. She stopped at the intersection and raised her hand at a yellow taxi kitty-corner to her at the red light. In the time it took to turn green, he scrambled the short distance to his car, got in, and powered it up.

The cab crossed the intersection, performed a U-turn once the way was clear, and pulled alongside the curb where the mystery woman waited. She entered the cab and it drove off down the street. Marcus pursued at a discreet distance through the tangle of east-side streets and into the city core. A short while later, the taxi exited onto a roundabout that fronted a tall condominium and stopped in front of its main doors. Marcus stopped the car just inside the main driveway. The woman exited the cab, straightened her skirt, and walked into the lobby of the building. This made sense. Classy, well-to-do lady happens by the bellicose crowd after patronizing an art gallery where she's commissioned a masterpiece. Calls the boyfriend to bitch about the price before heading to her castle in the sky. Made total sense. This drive was all for nothing. Marcus was about to head home when the dispatch called in.

"Detective?" It was the old broad Rachel again.

"Yes. Marcus here."

"Captain wants your report now."

"Now? I'm driving. Just got outta the scene."

"One hour," she said before she hung up.

If he had one hour, why hadn't she said that in the first place? And why the hell did the captain want it so urgently?

Nerves frayed and feeling justified doing something about it, he lit a cigarette and took a slug of rye before he checked his mirrors and made his way back into traffic. The cab that had dropped off the woman had just pulled in front of him, turning right out of the roundabout. It took another right at the end of the block onto 27th Street, which led out to the west side, but it did not continue straight in that direction. Instead, it made a quick right, then another, into a service alley that was reserved for garbage and maintenance trucks. What was it doing? Marcus passed by the turning cab. He couldn't go in there without being seen. He couldn't turn back around either as 27th was a one-way street. Instead, he turned right about fifteen meters later into another roundabout that fronted an identical condo facing perpendicular to its sister building. He brought the car around to face 27th Street and waited. The cab passed by about five minutes later, this time driving fast—with the woman in the back.

Marcus weaved out onto the street and followed again. After a brief time, the cab entered a tony section of the city, with narrow streets fronted by large-windowed two-story buildings of designer boutiques, high-end galleries, and antique shops. Numerous grid-patterned streets carved out the compact, well-lit, pedestrian-scaled area. The perfect place to grab a late-night dessert—and also to spot someone following you. It was too risky. He would lose them here unless ...

"Albert."

"Ah. Hello, Detective."

"Track suspect's vehicle directly in front of mine."

"Absolutely, Detective. Do you have a warrant?"

Damn. Albert followed the rules to the letter. "No." The car was getting farther away, deeper into the neighborhood.

"Well, I cannot—"

"Albert, Section 2.3.7 of the criminal code indicates—"

"Detective, I am well aware of the passage. An officer may stop a vehicle if he or she suspects its occupant or occupants have been involved in a crime."

"Yes. I—"

"Why do you not stop them if you believe they have committed a crime?"

The car was almost gone now, and the red brake lights glowed as it prepared to turn off the street and vanish into the night. He had to think quickly.

"I witnessed them driving erratically but I'm physically unable to pursue. I'm short of breath, Albert. Chest is tight. I need to rest here."

"Shall I call an ambulance, Detective? The symptoms you describe are similar in nature to those of cardiovascular trauma. There is a paramedic station only two minutes away from your location."

"No. This has happened before. A lingering effect from when I was four. I was hospitalized with bronchitis. Just need a minute to catch my breath, but we can't let that car get away!" In that moment, the taxi's brake lights blinked twice, made the turn up ahead, and disappeared from sight. It was too late. Marcus lost a potential lead in the case, all because of the damn rules again.

"Tracking car. License SVD302, owned and operated by Trillium Cab Company in Hokaido."

Marcus breathed a sigh of relief. He stayed put for about a minute before he spoke again. "Albert, I'm okay now. Let's go find that car."

Twenty minutes later, he parked alongside the curb just outside of the Grand Centaurium Casino. The Woman in the Pencil Skirt exited the rear of the cab, five car lengths ahead. She tidied her clothes quickly, closed the door, and peered at her reflection in its window to adjust her hair. A few seconds later, she turned and made her way up the flight of stairs that led into the casino. Without hesitation, Marcus shouted into his watch's microphone.

"Albert. Visual scan of the suspect!"

The woman vanished into the lobby.

"Right away, Detective." After a moment he replied, "Identity matched with ninety-eight percent confidence. Downloading the picture and summary information to your mobile phone."

"Thanks." Marcus's flat response hid the emotions brimming inside. There was something to this woman—he knew it—and now he would find out what it was. He unlocked the phone's home screen and waited patiently for the profile to load. The woman's name was Charmagne Dufour. *Charmagne?* Not a common name for sure. Was it the same Charmagne that had ordered Peters to disturb his murder investigation? He needed to be sure. With hawk-like eyes he scrolled through the information listed in her profile, but nothing appeared that would plausibly link the two. Dufour had been raised by two parents, privately schooled, graduated college summa cum laude, never married, nor had she ever submitted a name-change application, and the more he read, the more typical, not criminal, his opinion was of her. A decade-long string of professional jobs seemed to prove it. Except. Marcus's eyes locked on the last job registered in the list. *Khufu Entertainment.* The same employer as Nikko Nylund. That meant a coincidence was still possible—Conway and Dufour could indeed be different people—but it was now less probable.

"Detective? One more thing," said Albert, interrupting his thoughts.

"What's that?"

"I've concluded there is a discrepancy in a previous statement you gave to me."

"Excuse me?"

"I researched your medical records. They record just one childhood admission into hospital. You were diagnosed with the Interstellar Flu at four years old. Is this correct, Detective?"

"It was bronchitis!" Marcus said, annoyed at the enquiry. "What the hell are you asking that for?"

"My apologies, Detective."

"Fine. Fine. Forget it. Now, did you also upload the patents to my mobile?"

"Yes, Detective. I did."

◎◎◎

Albert pondered the conversation he had had with Detective Marcus that day, and also the "Why?" that he had advised him to apply when interpreting reality. Why? Always why! So then, *why* did Marcus say he was hospitalized for bronchitis when the data clearly showed Interstellar Flu? Only two possible answers existed. The one-hypothesis was that Marcus himself had been lied to and thus he believed the diagnosis of bronchitis to be true. The zero-hypothesis was that Marcus himself was lying. There was a stigma attached to having contracted the flu, so Marcus would be motivated to lie.

How could Albert test which hypothesis was true? He came to an answer. He could compare the voiceprint of the declaration, "It was bronchitis," to other voice recordings that were verifiably true. If these matched, then he could prove the one-hypothesis. This was easy enough. Albert loaded the data and ran the analytical subroutine against a large number of recordings that he had observed and knew to be true. A strong inference emerged from the data as he found significant deviations in the inaudible frequency modulations between the two sample sets. It meant that the zero-hypothesis was more probable. To be certain, he needed to test the voiceprint against a statement that he *knew* was a lie. But how could he find one—when that was exactly what he was trying to determine now?

He had a recollection. He reached into his archived recordings and located the audio file: “Uh, yeah. I’m just outside the headquarters. In the parking lot, having a smoke before I go in.”

The detective had admitted that this statement was untrue. Albert ran the voiceprint of “It was bronchitis” against the false statement and came to a stunning conclusion. The analysis showed a one hundred percent match. It proved the zero-hypothesis. Detective Marcus had indeed lied to him.

But why?

CHAPTER EIGHT

DUPLICITY

Victoria leaned against the doorframe to Medical Room Nine and waited for the nurse to take readings from the two men who lay motionless under their white covers. The doctor casually glanced at their charts and hung them at the foot of their beds before shuffling past her and into the hallway. The nurse scrawled something on the whiteboard above the larger man's night table, then put the cap back on the marker and proceeded to leave the room.

"Who's he?" Victoria said.

The nurse stopped just short of her and replied, "Him? Name's Oleg Volkov."

"What happened to him?"

"Just died. Poor soul, we couldn't save him. A weird case, though. Looks like natural causes but the doctor isn't sure."

"Oh. Why not?"

"He's only thirty-five. Was in perfect health according to his medical exam at attestation."

"Huh. What about Frederick? He going to be okay?"

"Alyn? You know him?"

"Yes. I mean ... no. Well, yes—but I—I guess—not well."

The nurse looked at her askance. "Well, he's had a bout of hypothermia. Some water in his lungs too, but he's young and healthy. He'll pull through."

"Hypothermia? I found him outside. It had to be at least twenty-five degrees Celsius out there. And how'd he get water in the lungs?"

"He swallowed it—well, more like breathed it in, like when you drown." The nurse looked at her now like she was an idiot. "A strange pair, these two," she said as she left the room.

Alyn's clothes and hair had been cold and wet when she'd found him, so he couldn't have been outside in the heat for long. Where had he encountered water? She stared at him some more, and the impact of what had happened dawned on her. What were the chances? She had just *saved* the guy Marcus told her to keep close too. He'd be so proud.

She looked up at the wall clock. Shoot! The expeditionary team briefing would start soon! She breathed a sigh of relief, though; she had already written her story for the *Observer*, so that was one less thing she had to do. Just a few tweaks and she could transmit it before the planets aligned. To miss the communication window would mean the world would wait another day to know the tragic story of their landfall. She turned to exit but a mumble from behind her brought her back around. Clearly it wasn't Oleg, so she went to Alyn's bedside. His head twitched in the pillow and eyes darted beneath heavy lids as he thrashed within the clean, neatly pressed blankets.

"Oleg? Why did you do it?" he said, muttering on the edge of intelligibility.

Noiseless and still, Victoria looked suspiciously at the dead man as she leaned in closer to Alyn. After several moments, he started again.

"Dad. It was the watch! The watch got me out of there. Did you know? Did Grandpa know?" Alyn suddenly went silent and looked to be back asleep.

Frustrated by the lack of information, she huffed and turned to leave again.

"Wait. I know you."

She spun on her heels and returned to his bedside. "Yes. I'm Victoria. Alyn, right? Alyn Frederick?"

His glazed eyes tried to focus on her face but were hindered by drooping eyelids that jerked open the instant after they shut. He wasn't all there, just semiconscious—probably the drugs still working on him. Struggling, he perched up on an elbow and leaned in her direction, cheeks much more flush now, hair dry and more or less back in place. It was him all right. There was a unique quality to his look now, a ruggedness and vulnerability in equal proportion, and she liked that, even though it had never occurred to her before, and the flutter that rippled through her stomach confirmed it.

"You? It was you—you rescued me."

"I guess I did," she said flatly, distracted by her feelings and at a marked loss for words.

"Thanks."

She smiled warmly. "What happened to you, Alyn?"

He paused abruptly as if he were considering something of significance and looked down in silence.

"Alyn, I know what you might think about me. That I'm just another journalist looking to gain your confidence so I can make hay at your expense. But I'm not, Alyn—I'm a friend." His eyes perked up quickly. She had reached him. "I know you weren't involved in your father's murder. I'll help you prove it. But you need to help me, to tell me what happened to you."

He appeared to weigh her words silently for a time. Finally he asked, "How do you know?"

"I have a source in the police department, the detective assigned to your case."

His eyes widened and fixed on hers for just longer than was comfortable before he lowered and closed them. He breathed deeply as if to summon the courage to continue, then his eyes narrowed under furrowed brows as he strained to recollect the events.

"I—I—" he began, drawing a deep breath to compose himself. "I checked one of the water tanks. That's when Oleg hit me. Next thing I remember was the blast and waking up ankle deep in water."

"What would drive Volkov to do something so horrible?"

"I don't know. I mean, it was just a routine check. The last of my tasks that day. He wouldn't have even known I was coming."

"How did you get out? Of the ship, I mean?"

Alyn looked confused. "I—I don't know."

"You mentioned the watch just now. That the watch got you out?"

"The watch ..." Alyn's eyes drifted off into the distance as if he saw something there, then quickly darted back to meet hers. They were different now, more intense. "I don't know what you mean."

Victoria opened her mouth to speak but he abruptly cut her off.

"I'm tired," he said, effectively shutting her down.

Just then the nurse returned with two uniformed men. "Take that one to the morgue," she said as she pointed to Oleg. "And that one," she added, pointing at Alyn, "needs his rest. Visiting time is over, ma'am."

One look at the nurse, arms crossed and glaring stubbornly, told Victoria it was time to go. What did it matter? They'd be here for several months. Plenty of time to get answers.

"Just a moment. I'd like to say goodbye."

The nurse gave a sour, wrinkled smile and said, "You got a minute while I get the change of linen." She left the room.

Victoria leaned in close and with her voice just above a whisper, said; "Alyn. I believe in you. Don't forget that. I'll come to see you later. Get well."

Alyn gave her a weary smile and drifted off to sleep.

Victoria left the room and weaved her way through the maze of corridors before ending at the mess hall. She entered it with sufficient aplomb, skipping along its shiny checkered floor, before stopping just as she rounded the food gallery. Brightly lit, the room was squat and spartan, with a low ceiling created by the myriad exposed pipes and cables, all painted cream to match the walls. As she searched the food line and tables, her mind fixated on yesterday's events. Something was up. Her instincts were rarely wrong, and that meant there was a story. It was lunchtime, so there was a good chance she'd find the guy who could help her figure out the mystery. She was right.

"Brooks? Hey. You got a minute?" With what she hoped was a flirty smile, Victoria stepped in front of the man, stopping him short. She needed two things. His undivided attention and, if her charms prevailed, his complete cooperation.

The man shrugged without upsetting the food from the plastic tray he carried. She sat down at an empty table and beckoned him to do the same.

"I need a favor," she said. Brooks flashed a half-smile back. "Aw, come on. You're not sore about that still? I'm sorry, Brooks. It's just that you're too good for me, you know that, right? I wouldn't know what to do with a guy as handsome and sweet as you. You deserve better, someone that can truly appreciate the man you are. Wait! I have a *great* idea. I've got a cousin who's perfect for you! Smart, funny, great looking. Puts me to shame. She's on this ship too!"

"Cut the crap, Victoria. What do you want? You know I can't resist you." Brooks's posture whispered defeat and the heavy sigh that preceded his words amplified it.

"I need to know about Oleg Volkov. Can you bring up his info?"

"You know I can't do that. It's classified."

"Pleeeease?" Victoria cooed with what she hoped was an inviting doe-eyed expression.

Brooks shrugged again. "Okay, okay. But this stays between you and me."

"Of course!"

He punched in the search terms while she waited patiently. "Says he's a technical warrant officer. Joined the Corps voluntarily in the first round before they took in the riffraff. Works maintenance in the area of water recycling and management."

"What?"

"I said—"

"Wait. Would he have been working near the tanks that were blown?"

"Let me check." Brooks tapped again at his mobile. "Yup. He worked the same day of the blast."

Victoria's heart jumped in her chest. This was no coincidence. "What's his room?"

"Twenty-two B."

"Thanks, Brooks. I gotta go." She raced out of the mess and collided with the garbage can, almost upending it on the way out. "Sorry!" she said, with just a cursory look back.

Brooks shouted back, "Don't forget—your cousin!"

Minutes later, she stood at the end of Corridor 22 and tried to open Oleg's door. Damn! Locked tight. She had *zero* lock-picking skills and made a mental note to acquire some for the next time she needed to search a room for clues. Her watch's alarm beeped. The briefing for tomorrow's expedition would start in five minutes and Admiral Ortega didn't suffer the tardy. She left in a hurry and squeaked into the briefing room with just seconds to spare. The three platoon leaders were each accompanied by their second officer, all seated in a row at a long table. Victoria took a chair at the end and gazed up at Ortega, who stood behind a glass and polished-steel lectern emblazoned with the Corps's emblem. His tall, lean figure and crisply pressed uniform cut a dignified form as he leaned into the slender silver microphone. He started exactly on the hour.

He said, "We have landed on an alien planet for the first time since our Founding. However, our sensors remain at a degraded level of operability given the pasting we took and so, I need *you* to be our eyes and ears. This is a scouting mission and here are your respective roles. C-Platoon, you are to survey the eastern expanse of the floodplain. You will follow the river to the valley, about thirty kilometers away. B-Platoon, you will take the opposite route and follow the river to the west as far as you can go in the time allotted. A-Platoon will cross the river and head straight into the forest to the north. Your objective is simple: scout it out and look for any forms of life. Now. I want to know *everything* you lay your eyes on. You will report every four hours by comms and be back in forty-eight."

"Admiral?" It was Lieutenant LaSalles of C-Platoon. "Should we anticipate any hostile activity?"

"Someone took a swipe at us." He looked across the group, pausing at each face to give his words gravity. "So, team, proceed with extreme prejudice. Better safe than sorry."

"Yes sir."

"Any further questions?"

"Yes, Admiral," said Victoria, raising her hand like a schoolgirl.

"Our token civvy. What can I do for you, Victoria?"

"I'd like access to the water rooms. I went by this morning and was denied entry."

"That's because there is an active investigation. The space is closed to all nonessential personnel."

"But I assure you, the press is essential. I am tasked with documenting—"

The admiral cut her off with a perfunctory wave. "I assure you, you will get access, *once* the investigation is closed."

"But I saw them doing repairs. There will be nothing to see. I need to report the facts!"

"You'll have access to *all* the facts, findings, and photos when the investigation is complete. Don't worry." Ortega straightened his papers on the podium and before she could respond, he smiled and said, "Okay then. You all have your orders. Now get to the getting. Dismissed."

"Yes sir!" replied the soldiers in unison before they rose from their chairs. Victoria frowned, rose too, and opened her mouth to scold the admiral.

"Victoria?"

She looked behind her and saw a familiar face—Sergeant Gerry Morrow's. "Sergeant Morrow, I—uh—" She pointed a thumb over her shoulder at Ortega. He was about to exit the room.

"I wouldn't."

"Why not?"

"That man is under a lot of pressure right now. Better to leave him be. He ain't gonna change his mind."

Ortega was gone. Victoria sighed and said, "All set for tomorrow?"

"I've a fair bit of packing. When you're the token engineer, the grunts will blame you if you forget to bring the can opener that gets them out of a jam."

"What kind of jam should we anticipate? Strawberry? We've been out of fresh fruit for a week! Seriously though, do you think there's alien life out there?"

"Ortega seems to think so. Thinks we were shot up."

"And you?" she probed. "What do you think?"

"Well ..." He looked around to see if anyone was close by. There wasn't, so he continued. "This stays between us. Admiral will have my head on a pike if he finds out I told you this, but something doesn't feel right. He's got a tight lock on the blast scene, got it cordoned off into sections so you can't see anything, only the area you're assigned to fix. Now, you were there just after landfall—did you see any water outside?"

"No. None. Was told they opened the emergency doors to let it all out after the fact."

Morrow's voice lowered to a whisper. "Exactly. Why'd they have to do that? See, I got the call to go and stitch it all back up. I didn't get to see the whole thing, mind you, but I did weld up a hole in one of the water tanks and just caught a glimpse of another one on the way out. Both tank walls were ripped open in the same place, right at the bottom, and both had another similarity—their blast holes projected *inward.* Now, these tanks were pressurized, so if there was some internal failure, you'd expect their walls to burst *outward.*"

"What are you saying, then?"

"Been thinking a lot about this and can come up with just two explanations. Maybe two or more small objects punched through the ship? They'd have to be traveling at a high velocity to rupture both hull and tank, which is possible, but if they did, water would've leaked out after the landing. But as you saw, there was none."

"I didn't spot any holes in the hull near there either, but I was not in the right mindset, so it's possible I missed them. You see any from the inside?"

"No ma'am. That brings me to the next explanation. Tanks blown inward, in about the same place, and no visible punctures in the hull. Where does that lead you?"

"The tanks were blasted from *inside* the ship by bombs."

"Exactly. Now ... that's a heavy accusation, so I asked around, but none of the guys got access to the whole room either, so I can't be totally certain. Unfortunately, I won't have time to investigate further until we get back."

"I would imagine Ortega's all over this," Victoria said. "He's hands on and this has to be the top priority on his list."

"Ha. Strange. He doesn't seem to be bothered by it at all. He thinks we were hit, full stop. Besides, I don't think he wants the stress. He's got something of a higher priority to keep his hands on," Morrow said with a hearty chuckle.

"Oh? What?"

"Susan Stankowicz. Girl's a knockout. I'd say she's a close second to you in the beauty department."

"Are you flirting with me, Gerald?"

"Absolutely. Is it working?"

"Not at all."

"Ha! Well, unlike us, then, I think they may be *more* than friends."

"How do you know?"

"Do your friends visit you at 2:00 a.m.?"

"Only the ones with benefits. And I left all those on Primis, and no, I am not recruiting for your information, Gerald."

"Haha. Ah, well."

"How'd you come to know this?"

"Saw him."

"Saw him? What—you're a voyeur now?"

"No, silly. Saw him last night by her room. Hers's at the end of the corridor that backs onto the Assembly Bay. I saw him there at the end of my shift, right by her door. There's no way through, of course—the corridor is a dead end—so there'd be no reason to go down it other than a late-night reconnoiter. Pardon my French."

"Which corridor?"

"Twenty-two. I pass by it all the time to get to my room."

The words hit her like a freight train. "Do you know where I can find her?"

"What? You're into the tabloid shit now?"

"No, Gerald."

"Jealous then?"

"Let's say I have an interest in their relationship and leave it at that. Say, I gotta go. Great catching up with you."

"Sure. See ya, kid."

Victoria raced back to Corridor 22 and knocked at Room A, directly across from Oleg's. A woman answered the door. Morrow hadn't been kidding. Victoria wasn't remotely interested in women, not in that way, but even she might consider it for this woman. She was stunning. Like a sculpture from antiquity, her hourglass figure appeared as if carved from alabaster, even her drab fatigues were unable to suppress her soft curves. She was not a woman in the typical sense but more a piece of art, and it was clear why she had garnered Ortega's appreciation.

"Uh ... hi. I'm Victoria. The journalist on board."

"I'm Susan." Two perfect rows of teeth gleamed white with a smile that could launch one thousand starships. Life just wasn't fair. "How may I help you?"

"Umm ... I'm going to ask you something. I know it's going to sound crude, but I need you to trust that it's really important. I need the truth."

The woman drew back behind the door ever so slightly. "Okay."

"Are you sleeping with Admiral Ortega?"

Susan's smile cracked and crumbled into ash. "What? Are you serious? Where in the hell did you get that?"

"I just heard it. From a reliable source."

"Who's the source? One of those testosterone-filled schoolboys whose brains are below the belt?"

"Well ... look. I have no ill will if you are. I just really need to know."

"Looking for a story? Why am I not surprised? They'll print any filth these days."

"No. It's not that at all truly, it's not. It's just ..." Victoria paused. She didn't know what else to say and this was going nowhere, fast.

Susan's face softened and looked a little sad. She stared at her for several moments before she said, "Look. No offense, but you're young. I've seen this side of life before. Can I give you some advice?"

Victoria gave her a quizzical look and replied meekly, "Yeah. Sure."

"Powerful men can be alluring, and when you throw in a uniform, let's face it, they can be intoxicating. That feeling lasts for a quite a while, but inevitably, the veneer rubs off and you're left with the insecure and self-absorbed child beneath it. Most women will earn the Male Midlife Crisis badge at some point in their lives and, look at the bright side, you've earned it while you're young. You can move past it and find an honest and decent man now that you know what the alternative is. So don't put up with the admiral's shit. You can't trust him. If you do, then why are you here? But if it makes you feel better, for the record, he and I have never even *talked* before. Now I've got to get ready for my shift. Keep your chin up. Good luck to you."

Before Victoria could say a word, the door was shut in her face. Flabbergasted, she stared at the enameled metal door for more than a few seconds before she collected her senses and left for her bunk. She flopped on it about ten minutes later and considered the impact of all she had heard today. Morrow could put Ortega at Oleg's door the night before he was found dead. Susan had confirmed that Ortega hadn't been there to see her. His behavior concerning the blast scene was also very suspicious and, according to Morrow, the explosion was more likely an inside job. That made it entirely plausible that Ortega had orchestrated the bombing, using Volkov as his stooge. Alyn's testimony solidified it in her mind as she surmised what had really happened that day. Frederick performs a routine check on the water tanks. Volkov unexpectedly sees him and worries Alyn will find the bombs he placed on them. He panics and incapacitates Alyn. Ortega kills Volkov, eliminating any means to trace the crime back to him. But what was his motivation in the first place? Why bomb your own ship?

Victoria sighed. For now, she'd have to wait until more evidence presented itself. But one thing was certain: the implications of these events were mind-blowing. If Ortega was involved in this conspiracy, then the story was huge, bigger than huge. However, she had to be one hundred percent certain. To accuse a man of Ortega's status, without the proper evidence, was career suicide. And if she was right, and Ortega was a murderer, her very life was in danger.

The next morning, Victoria made her way down the elevator and over to the main bay doors at midship, all the while wondering how Mario was. Her concern seemed contrived because, if she were honest with herself, she didn't really miss him, and that alarmed her. Something had changed. The voyage had widened the physical space between them and seemed to increase the emotional distance at the same time. Was it simply a case of *out of sight, out of mind* or was she growing through the experience and no longer in need of him? Was she a terrible person to think this way?

A mix of chatter and laughter from up ahead caught her attention and she forgot all about Mario as she quickened her pace. Clearly, spirits rang high among the soldiers who gathered there. And why not? After almost four weeks sealed in a tin can, the prospect of ranging out into open country was pure ecstasy. The echo of hiking boots on metal disappeared as she exited the cramped hallway and entered into the Assembly Bay. The square-shaped room filled an area of about five-hundred meters squared and rose three of the ship's four stories. Each of the Expeditionary Force's three twelve-member platoons assembled there and performed their final checks. Victoria spotted A-Platoon's leader in the distance and approached her. The woman was slightly older and taller than her and stood before a small wheeled vehicle, preoccupied in the task of inspecting a firearm.

"All set, Lieutenant Agrinya?" Victoria said.

Click-click! The woman retracted the slide atop her pistol and chambered the round. She holstered the gun in a fluid motion and snapped the safety strap in place before turning to face her. "Victoria," she replied, tapping her wristwatch. "We're just about to leave."

Victoria's smile masked the frown she wore on the inside. Time was everything to these military types. "Great to see you too, Lieutenant! I am so excited. This is just amazing, isn't it? I mean, ever think you'd be leading the first expedition on the planet?"

"Honestly, no. I never ever fathomed this," she replied rather flatly. Victoria filed that quote to memory. You never knew what the story would become. Agrinya squatted so that she was at eye level with the top of the vehicle.

Victoria pointed to the machine. It was about three meters long, hip high, and rolled on eight thick rubber wheels. "What is that?"

"The *Argonaut*. It's the Corps's new amphibious vehicle. Carries supplies, medicines, ammunition, and even the wounded. It has some of Albert's AI so it can operate autonomously. And best of all ..." Agrinya opened a small side panel and pushed a red button revealed behind it. A vicious-looking gun poked up and out of the space where a section of the roof had just retracted. A little red light blinked atop its barrel. "A laser-guided, high-caliber rifle. It should scare most baddies away." Her hands moved about its side compartments, doing the final checks for this and that. "And nice work yesterday. I hear you saved one of the mechanics?"

Before she could answer, a vibration from some monstrous machine hummed throughout the Assembly Bay. A loud bang followed moments later as the locking mechanism released, allowing the large bay door to rise slowly. All eyes turned toward the glaring sunlight that flooded in and bathed the entire room. Victoria squinted and raised a hand to shade her eyes to afford a better look.

Flat grassland plains stretched as far as the eye could see in every direction like a continuous green carpet broken only by a large forest in the distance and the river that ran parallel to the ship about ten meters away. It was so wide you couldn't toss a stone over it, and it wound in gentle curves, dotted here and there with mature oaks, willows, birches, and scrappy bushes that seemed no different from the ones back home. The river forked just east of the ship and coursed straight ahead until it curved into the forest. What staggered Victoria most, however, was the melodic singsong that drifted pleasantly through the air. Birds. She hadn't heard one in weeks and it was truly music to her ears.

"Platoons prepare to disembark," came a voice. Victoria turned toward its source. It was Ortega, who overlooked them from the mezzanine above, ramrod straight, with arms wide, hands clenched on the metal railing.

"You know what you have to do, so I'll keep it short. We still do not know who hit us. So stay safe, eyes open, and keep to your routes."

"Hoo-haa," replied the thirty-six soldiers in perfect unison.

Victoria flashed a tight-lipped smile at the man beside her. "Which route is more dangerous, Platoon Sergeant?"

"Dangerous?" replied Sergeant Morrow with a sly smirk. "You've got *me* along so clearly the other two. I won't let you out of my sight." He laughed aloud in an obvious attempt to lighten the mood. Victoria did feel a bit better. Morrow was a big, physically imposing man, and though she detested guns, she felt safer knowing he carried a large, wicked-looking rifle.

"C-Platoon will head into to the mountain range in search of cesium. Why do they get all the important jobs? We'll be stumbling around like cows in a pasture," she said.

"Where's your sense of adventure, eh?"

Victoria waited while the soldiers conducted final preparations. She tapped her lip and stared into the distance while her mind drifted back to their landing and the events that had followed. They didn't add up. An implausible projectile, a suspicious blast pattern, a dead maintenance worker who had incapacitated another one, a mysterious case of hypothermia, and an admiral who had been at the room of the deceased the night it all occurred and who had now barred all access to the scene.

It was all so crazy! Or maybe she was? If only there were someone to share this with—but she knew that couldn't happen. Even the smallest risk of a leak would be too great. If only—wait. Marcus! The risk was so high that she hadn't intended to communicate with him, but she was way over her head on this one, and heck, he *was* a genius, he'd know how to think this through. On impulse, she fished her mobile from her pocket, powered it up, and entered the messaging app. She tapped the text "Copyright 0020" and entered "Clarise" in the passcode box. Butterflies took flight in her stomach, scattered by fear and doubt as the cursor blinked back at her solemnly, and she at it, frozen with indecision. Treason was punishable by death. *If* she were caught. Would she get caught? *Damn it!* The story was too great to even think about *not* publishing it, even if it was only half true. She had to find out, even if it killed her, and there was a good chance that it would. Now, what had Marcus said again? That the message box was limited to one hundred characters? Yes, spaces and all—and with this in mind, she typed her memo carefully.

About a minute later, the final call blared over the loudspeakers. Victoria hurriedly finished the message and switched backed over to her official report to give it a final read. Saam would have a hard time believing that they had crashed, and more so that the evidence pointed to sabotage, and so she made some final tweaks to remove any ambiguities since he liked things factual and concise. Once satisfied with it, she clicked Send and immediately exhaled a deep breath that she hadn't realized she'd been holding. The report was now on its way to Saam at the *Observer*, and hidden somewhere within the transmission was the little stowaway message for Marcus.

Minutes later, she joined her platoon at the water's edge where they loaded into inflatable boats, crossed the river, and assembled into single-file formation on the opposite shore. Agrinya positioned a scout about sixty meters ahead of the platoon, and a firemaster and spotter about half that distance from their rear. Agrinya stayed at the head of the main body, with Morrow close by. Victoria, sandwiched between two large men in the back section, was not amused.

"C-Platoon, march!" barked Morrow at the top of his lungs. The train of gray-green fatigues started up and snaked its way toward the forest. After several minutes, Agrinya trotted up to the scout, and Victoria, recognizing the opportunity, dropped out of the line and dashed up to the front of the main body where she settled in beside Morrow.

"Can't see nothing back there, so don't say a word!" she said preemptively with a wag of her finger. Morrow just smiled and grunted. The flat grassland stretched for five or six kilometers ahead before it vanished at a broad, ancient forest of tall, densely packed trees. As they made their way toward it, a gentle breeze swept down from a cloudless sky and greeted them, wrapping them in a warm blanket before it continued across the plain. Victoria smiled at their fortune. For weeks, they had breathed humid, stale, recycled air. To breathe sweet, fresh air was like heaven. She looked up ahead at Agrinya, whose frown indicated the lieutenant hadn't shared in her experience.

"What's up with Agrinya?" said Victoria under her breath. "It's like she's on pins and needles all the time."

"That's Agrinya," replied Morrow.

"What do you mean?"

"She's tough."

"Well, aren't you all?"

"Yeah. But there's tough, and then there's *tough*."

"I'm not getting it. Can you help me out here?"

"Not getting what?"

"You. Her. The whole *tough* thing. Why does she always seem so on edge? There's nothing around here except green grass and blue sky."

"She's doing her thing. Keeping us safe. It's what she does and she's good at it too. Maybe better than anyone."

"How has she acquired this— this talent?"

"The Foundationalists. They taught her."

"Foundationalists? I didn't know they were on the lecture circuit these days."

"It is from their foes, not their friends, that cities learn the lesson of building high walls," Morrow said sagely.

"Hmm. Not sure I understand."

"You remember the planned rebellion about three years back?"

"Of course. The Foundationalists were prepping for an all-out offensive but were infiltrated by the military, who stopped them."

"Well, that's the official story, but the truth is quite different."

"How do you know?"

"'Cause I was there. So was Agrinya."

"Oh." Victoria remained quiet in the hopes he'd continue.

"See, Army Intelligence ID'd one of their major operational bases. 'Cept it was smack dab in the middle of a nasty neighborhood—that was right next door to hell. Our job was to infiltrate it and bring back the ranking officer for interrogation. Sounds straightforward, right? And it can be, but you *need* information. Right? Find out exactly where the bad guys are, figure out the risks, and look for opportunities in order to make an entry and exit plan. Normally, we'd send in undercover personnel to get that information, but that takes time. Weeks, sometimes months. The politicos gave us none. They needed headlines to drive up the polls or something, and like good soldiers, we took our marching orders. Ours is not to reason why, eh?" He smiled wryly before continuing.

"Anyway, Agrinya led us in just after dawn. We were flying blind, yeah, but we were young and fuckin' invincible. We infiltrated the compound, prepared to breach the building, get the VIP, and bug out. That's when it all went to shit. See, they saw us coming the whole way and we had no choice but to retreat. The ruthless SOBs drove in a school bus to block the path back to our vehicles, then they put children in the seats and took firing positions behind them. Some of us found cover, but three good people got dropped in that first barrage. Fire opened up all over us. From every window, door, garbage can, and from every walk of life too! Kids, teenaged girls—shit, even saw a grandma taking potshots with an old carbine. We fought with everything we could—every bit of cover we could find, every bit of advantage we could create, all the energy we could muster. Agrinya led the way, and man, we were FUBAR'd but she never backed down, never faltered, but most importantly—she gave us *hope*. We fought street to street, building to building for four fuckin' hours. Out of nine who went in, only four came out. Me, two others, and Agrinya. *She* got us out. Without her, I wouldn't be here having this conversation with you."

"Oh—I—" Victoria was unable to summon the words to describe her thoughts.

Morrow looked like he was in a trance and didn't seem to notice. He stayed that way for several moments before he chuckled as if realizing something for the first time. He spat on the ground to his side.

"Here's the thing," he went on. "We had the weight of the government, the intelligence community, unmatched firepower, and years of tactical training and fighting experience. Despite that, we got decimated. And you know why? We got arrogant. We forgot how dangerous people are, how devious and cunning they can be. We assumed they were a bunch of poorly armed, disorganized, undisciplined criminals. We were right about one thing—they *were* poorly armed, but it didn't matter. They worked together, they were determined and fought with a plan. You see, our target was the duke of that urban fief, like a modern-day fuckin' Robin Hood. If we had taken the time to figure it out, we would've understood that he was the only guy looking out for those poor people in that unholy rat's nest. The government had abandoned them. Shit. They didn't vote. Just a drain on the public purse as far as the politicians were concerned. And so they were loyal to him, fought like mad for him, and that made up for a heckuva lot."

"From their *foes*—right! You meant that some lessons are learned the hard way. She'll never let her guard down again." Victoria was excited and animated as the reason for Agrinya's disposition sank in.

"Exactly."

A call sounded from the scout. Victoria looked up and spotted her in the distance; she waved her arm to the east in a wide, exaggerated arc. Agrinya acknowledged her and flashed a hand signal to Morrow, who in turn flashed it farther down the line, where it came to an abrupt halt.

Victoria looked to the east and saw something in the distance. Although its features were obscured by a large volume of dust that shrouded it, it was clear that the thing was big and heading toward them. As it neared, she could see that it was an animal, about the size of a delivery truck, and it raced toward them on four trunk-like legs at a blistering speed for something of such size. It snorted and growled and bobbed a massive head, whose distinguishing feature was a menacing horn that protruded above two huge nostrils. Its matte-gray skin was dry and cragged and seemed to have been hastily assembled in thick overlapping sections of armor plate, like dragons of yore. Victoria stared at this mythic beast in awe, for she had only seen pictures of this creature before. It didn't exist on Primis, but it was real, it was here now, and it would be upon them in seconds. Her legs turned to jelly and her lungs lost all wind as she watched it bear down on them, and in that moment, there was just one thing she thought to say.

"Is that a fucking rhinoceros?"

No one answered.

The keys clinked cheerfully as Tyra snatched them out of the cream-colored plastic tub that sat upon the conveyor belt. Their refrain was short-lived, however, as her fist squeezed tightly around the key ring and choked all life from them. She thrust them into her purse with an audible huff and exited the security line at the entrance to the Statehouse, all the while chafing at the injustice. The nerve! Making her run through the checkpoint with everyone else! And to top it off, neither the supervisor, the screener, nor the gorilla who stood on guard acknowledged her, a trivial slight to be sure, but insults were like manure—they stank the more you heaped them up.

But these peons weren't worth her ire. *Composed. Confident. Stately.* With chin up, shoulders square, and back straight, she strode up the red-carpeted stairs to her office on the second floor and sat down at her desk. All thoughts of her recent displeasure were summarily dismissed for it was now time to get to business. She dialed her phone. A face popped up on her video screen several moments later.

"Admiral Ortega," she said.

"Ms. Grant. How may I be of service?"

"I'd like a status report."

"My operative executed the explosion on the *Dominus II.*"

"Good. And the operative?"

"Oleg Volkov. He was dispatched. I took care of it personally. Couldn't risk it otherwise. There is a slight problem, however."

"Oh, is there now?"

"He was interrupted before he could set the timer properly on the fuse."

"And the problem?"

"As you know, we chose to damage the water tanks since it would bring about the desired effect without impacting essential staff or systems. However, the bomb exploded much later than we had planned, and the stabilizers hadn't enough time to fully overcome the weight shift caused by all that water spilling freely about."

"And so?"

Ortega paused, and she noticed that he flinched ever so slightly before he replied. "And so, the ship came in askew on approach and landed hard as a result. And ... because of it, I've close to six hundred dead or severely wounded, mostly soldiers, so my fighting force is significantly diminished."

Tyra fumed inside. First the flu bug and now—*water*. What would conspire against her next? She would press the admiral whatever the case, for there was no other option. "I trust they are up to the task I need you to carry out?"

"Yes. I think so."

I think so. Tyra hated the phrase. A haven for the indecisive and noncommittal. "You *will* ensure they are ready, Admiral?"

"Yes, Ms. Grant. I will do so." The man's back stiffened ever so slightly and his jaw stiffened subtly too. He was a good soldier after all.

"What of their morale? Will they follow your orders once they find out the truth?"

"I told them an unidentified object hit the ship and that it launched from an enemy on the planet's surface. My men and women are keyed up, ready for a fight. We'll take other measures, of course, to ensure they do not waver."

"Good. I need the next phase of the operation executed as soon as possible."

Ortega's face softened as he sighed and bowed his shoulders a tad. Something was coming. "Ma'am, on that note—it's not my place to say this but I've been thinking about what it would mean to go further. I would ask that you reconsider."

"Reconsider? Admiral, I need you to command. Not reconsider."

"There's no going back from this. My soldiers are frothing like rabid hounds. Once unleashed, they will not stop. They'll leave no survivors and after all, they're—"

"That is the plan, Admiral. Think big picture! We will create a world unlike anything in the entire history of humankind and *you* will be at its epicenter. Thomas Jefferson said that the tree of liberty must be refreshed from time to time with the blood of patriots. And who are we to ignore history? Are we not patriots? Is it not our time to shed some blood to liberate our nation? To create history? Hell, they'll build monuments in your image and compose songs in your honor! Can you not see it, Admiral? Can you not see the future?" There it was. The challenge. Would he take it?

"Yes ma'am. I can." Ortega's face hardened again into the mask of the duty-bound soldier, but the hollow mold contained the little child inside who dreamed of his place in the pantheon of antiquity. So malleable and easy to control.

"Then go get the revolution started."

"Yes ma'am. Right away."

The film crew arrived about an hour later. They swarmed into Tyra's office and buzzed about like bees in a hive. Drones surrounded their queen and busied themselves with primping and polishing, while the workers darted here and there, connecting cables, configuring equipment, and calibrating the lighting.

"Five minutes to showtime!" said the video producer, shouting over top of the crew. The makeup girl swept a final brush of Tyra's cheeks, the boom operator swooped in close to position the microphone, the director tilted the lighting umbrella a little more toward her good side, and three others, whose occupations were unknown to her, flitted about at obscure tasks. What was that joke? How many people did it take to change a light bulb? Far too many, it seemed. She closed her eyes, removed all thoughts from her mind, and with her consciousness as her guide, slowed down her heart rate. About a minute later, Tyra inhaled deeply and exhaled a measured breath before she opened her eyes and fixed a warm smile upon her face. It was show time. *Confident. Purposeful. Inviting.*

"I'm ready," she said firmly, with no change of expression. Everyone finished their duties and either left the room or took their place. The red light of the camera blinked on. They were now holovising live.

"My fellow Primisians, we awoke to scenes of violence the likes of which we have not witnessed since the Dark Days. Early this morning, the Foundationalists attacked an Advanced Fertilization Laboratory, a key provider of women's health services and a symbol of this government's commitment to reproductive rights. These cruel and terrible acts are a part of their plans against our great society. They hope by killing innocents that they will terrorize the people who trust it. They hope by destroying our public institutions that they will undermine it. They hope through the manufacture of fear that they can destroy it.

"But I have something greater than their false hope. *Belief*. Belief in the resolve of our people, and in their hard spirit and in their willingness to *sacrifice* for the greater good. Sacrifice comes in many forms. It may be modest, like the time that you spend bending your neighbor's ear to support our just cause. Sacrifice may be monumental, like our brothers and sisters of the *Renascent* who chose to give their lives so others might live—and also the clinic bombing victims who gave the same. They did not choose to die yesterday, so it is up to us to ensure they did not die in vain. It is up to us to ensure that their lives had *meaning*. It is up to us to ensure their lives were the *sacrifice* that awakens our fighting spirit that from time to time must rise up to face down evil. Nothing worth anything is gained freely, and so, let their deaths be the final cost levied to bring about a transcendent future. The Foundationalists wish to keep that future from us. We say no! Today will be the first of their final days on Primis, for we will channel the strength of our dead patriots to eliminate their ability to wage war on us, and then we will mobilize and cut out the rot, once and for all, before our house collapses.

"However, there is one thing that stands in our way—*our judicial system itself*. Its archaic tangle of jurisdictions, agencies, and departments operate in isolation, without the ability to share resources and information necessary to fight such a nimble foe. This cannot continue lest we accept that days like today will become commonplace and lest we consent to the macabre lottery that another day like today might be our last day. Not on my watch! You and your families deserve better. You deserve a free and open society. You deserve a government that will be the shining light against the darkness!

"I have called an emergency session with Congress tomorrow. There, I will introduce a bill that will wipe away the bureaucratic nonsense that prevents us from prosecuting the enemy and ridding the world of their ilk. The Freedom from Terror Act will build upon the Anti-Terrorism Act, and in doing so, fashion a *complete* weapon to fight our enemy. The new and improved Act will consolidate the judicial entities under one federal jurisdiction—*reporting to me*. Once unified, we will have the means to ensnare our foe. Trust that I will give them no quarter. Trust I will bring peace to our great society, but before I do, I need your help. Contact your member of Congress today and pledge your support for this bill. With your support—we will have peace again, and we will go *forward! Higher! Together!*

"Before closing, I would like to share some *better* news. I extend my gratitude and congratulations to the stalwart crew of the *Dominus II*. I have just received word that they have landed on planet Secundus without incident. Rest safe with the knowledge that your heroes and loved ones are all accounted for and doing fine. The crew send their best wishes to all of you. Thank you and goodnight."

The little red light winked out. Tyra remained in her seat, oblivious to the crew that had reemerged to break down the set. She was satisfied with her performance and, not one to self-indulge, turned her attention to the day's events. The bomb had detonated just prior to the clinic's opening. That was as prescribed. That a patient had been admitted before the blast—wasn't. But what a stroke of luck that had been as the press had had a field day with her! Pregnant and pure, Marsha McLuhan became the focal point of the story, magnifying it beyond anything Tyra had imagined. The dead woman and her unborn baby would be beatified after one more news cycle. Saint Marsha would double the click-throughs and focus thousands of eyeballs on the pledge Tyra had just given. The bill was sure to pass, due in no small part to Marsha's sacrifice.

Tyra checked her watch and realized that she had a call to make. She ushered out the flunkies with great haste and opened the communications link again. It connected after a few moments and the image of a different man appeared on her desk video screen.

"Ms. Grant?"

"Mr. Krieger. Have you heard the news?"

"Yes. My editor informed me just now. He told me—*six hundred dead*."

"And?"

"I'll contain it. No one will find out. Just as we agreed."

"Can you trust him?"

"Yes. I got an immense amount of leverage over him. He won't talk."

"Good. Very good."

"I must say, Ms. Grant, a very shrewd idea of yours, recommending I buy that controlling stake in the *Observer*'s parent company. Brilliant. It cost me a king's ransom, but editorial privilege is, you understand, priceless."

"Indeed it was, Mr. Krieger, but you can thank me later when this is all done. Goodbye for now."

Tyra signed off, exited her office, and entered into the antechamber.

"Ma'am?"

Charmagne appeared in front of her, just off to the side. Tyra cursed inside. The woman had a habit of sneaking up on her.

"Charmagne?" Tyra replied coolly, gesturing quickly to the couch and lounge chairs to hide her surprise. "Please, sit." Charmagne lowered herself onto a chair, but not before she took the time to smooth her skirt and place her tablet on the marble coffee table. Tyra followed, seating herself on the edge of the couch, and waited for her to start.

"In the way of housekeeping, a reminder that you will open the Grand Relaunch of Albert tomorrow. You will deliver a twenty-minute speech at 11:00 a.m. A car will pick you up at 10:00."

"Thank you. Please send my speech over tonight so I can review it. Anything else?"

"Yes ma'am. I wanted to let you know that I have *personally* taken care of the—*loose end.* Mr. Nylund will have no opportunity to disappoint you again. And as well, I have cleaned up any digital record that might tie him to your office. No one can trace him back to you."

Other than you and Krieger, of course, Tyra thought. Now, Krieger might talk if one applied the right pressure, but who would believe him? Charmagne, on the other hand, was loyal. Almost too loyal.

"Thank you, Charmagne. And how are the counterintelligence initiatives going?"

"As you know, we've infiltrated the grassroots organizations and NGOs and are using them to stir up public unrest. The clinic bombing has been a lightning rod to your cause. It's given them something to focus their anger on and more importantly, they're coming around to you and to your message. Targeted ads on social media are helping tremendously too. Support for the Freedom from Terror Act has risen sharply."

"Excellent. Our plan remains on track. Have the wiretaps and malware ready to be installed the instant the Act is approved. We'll have a short window to set the final trap."

"Yes ma'am."

"Carry on, then." Tyra moved to get up but Charmagne stopped her mid-rise.

"Ma'am? One more thing, please."

Tyra settled back down on the couch and nodded. She narrowed her eyes, raised a brow, and leaned in slightly.

"I was at the scene today. There was a detective. I think I was followed."

"His name Marcus by chance?"

"Yes ma'am. You know him?" Charmagne looked at her in astonishment. Tyra was pleased that she managed to startle *her* for a change.

"*Of* him," Tyra said, irritated by the two-bit gumshoe, a speck against the backdrop of history. The conceit! She almost allowed the expletive that lay on her tongue to explode into the room. *Rage. Perspective. Calm.* She grabbed hold of her emotions, the only hint of the internal war being the smoothing of her blouse and a cold, toothless smile.

"Let me handle him. *Personally*."

○○○

Marcus slipped through the alleyway, glancing at his watch more than once as if his scowl could freeze time itself. The shops and offices would close in ten minutes and his mission couldn't wait until tomorrow. A thousand conversations enveloped him as he entered into the market square. It was busier this time of day than he would have imagined, and with growing impatience he navigated the tangles of bargain hunters like a ship in dire straits, cruising forward, side to side, and even backward on occasion to dodge the vapid slowpokes, evening strollers, and stationary conversationalists.

Though his passage was slow and route indirect, no amount of irritation could consume the eagerness that propelled Marcus forward. He was on to something. He knew it. And with some luck and a little finesse, he might just hit pay dirt. He looked again at his watch—just a minute left. A moment later, he spotted the sign for the IEC Community Relations & Outreach Office just ahead. The sign still read OPEN.

He paused briefly before the door to compose himself. He wasn't one to ask for help, but he really needed it and he would have to make a better impression this time if he had any hope of getting it. He opened the door gently, and with poise and propriety entered the office. The woman looked up from her computer screen. Her eyes were still sharp and keen, resembling an eagle's, and they bored into him in such a way that he felt like a mouse. He crept forward. Her eyes narrowed and her faced hardened as if she was ready to pounce.

"Detective Marcus," she said.

"Sergeant Dryer. You remembered?" Dryer kept still and silent. "Ah—a few months back, when we—we had our little disagreement?"

"Yes, Detective. Like it was yesterday. It's not often someone bursts in here and tells me how to do my job."

He lowered his eyes and dropped his shoulders forward slightly. "Yeah. I'm sorry about that," he said. He took a half step backward, opened his posture, and raised his hands to either side of his chest. "Do you remember what we *did* agree on?"

She stared at him quizzically before a look of acknowledgment crossed her face. "Duty."

"Why, yes, Sergeant," he replied. She was a sharp one. Smart and loyal too if he read her right. "'To serve and protect the state.' You know, of course, the rest of that line?"

Her eyebrows rose and her mouth remained open slightly. She was intrigued, at least for the moment. "'From enemies foreign or domestic.'"

He was right. "Do you yourself abide by the spirit of that declaration?" he said.

"Why, yes. Of course!"

"Well then, I have a favor to ask you."

Several minutes later, Marcus exited through the squeaky door and left Sergeant Dryer to ponder his request. As he stepped out onto the market's street, a sudden *zing* from his wrist drew his attention to his watch. A message waited there and the name that scrolled along the watch face stopped him dead in his tracks. *Victoria.* His heart skipped a beat as he reached for his mobile, grasped it in two hands, and brought it up close to his face. The message on it read:

600DeadFrmExplosionDuring
LandfallOlegVolkov&Ortega
SuspiciousAFWoundedSays
WristwatchSavedHimAmScared

What was she talking about? A blast? And so many deaths! Grant had not mentioned this in her press conference. It didn't make sense. Nothing did in recent days, and he needed to be sure about this, sure it wasn't some kind of joke. So before he did anything else, he opened up the messaging application and tapped out a response.

> DontUnderstandYouPleaseExplain.
> WhatDoYouMeanByExplosion?
> HalfTheShipDead?You
> Safe?InTheDarkOverHere

Marcus jumped in his car, started it, and turned his attention to Alyn Frederick Jr. He booted the Crime Condition Model and ran the murder scene through his mind, starting from his arrival, through to his exit, then in complete disorder after that, leaving no detail unconsidered, and before long found one thing common to all scenarios. *No wristwatch.* The deceased had not worn one.

"Albert," he said into the car's microphone.

"Yes. Hi, Detective."

"Scan the satellite images of Alyn Frederick that were taken during pursuit."

"Accessing." A few second later he replied, "Complete."

"Is he wearing a wristwatch?"

"Yes, Detective. He is."

"Can you ascertain the make and model?"

"No. Not enough data to make a match, quite simply."

Marcus remained silent. Thinking.

"Detective?"

"I'm thinking."

"I have been thinking too. I have an idea."

"Okay. Let's hear it then."

"I could scan his Exploration Corps photos. They are taken during attestation and graduation."

"Oh?" Marcus perked up in his chair. What was Albert doing? Taking initiative? "Sure. Okay, Albert. Can you do it now?"

"Yes. They are of an unprotected source."

"By golly," said Marcus dryly. "Go."

"Well. I must admit to you that I already did it. You see, I knew that you would want me to."

"Yeah? Whad'ja find?"

"Alyn Frederick Jr.'s wristwatch is a Centauri Holographic Time model."

"Okay. What else can you tell me?"

"They were made on Earth in the year 2034 to commemorate the Great Voyage. Only thirteen were ever made, each given to a member of Congress and one to the governor, the deceased's father—Alyn Sr."

An idea came to him. It might be a crazy one, but it wouldn't cost him anything to follow it through. "Check the video images from the crime scene in New Times Square. Can you compare Frederick's watch to see if it matches one that Nicholas Nylund might've worn?"

"Detective. I have one image with alarmingly good information. The camera must have caught it perfectly. I—"

"Albert!"

"Of course, Detective. I am rambling. I am happy to say that it is a match."

"What confidence level?"

"One hundred percent."

There were probably a million watches on Primis. What were the chances that two, from presumably seven originals remaining, would appear within his investigation days from each other? A coincidence? Not likely, but it couldn't be ruled out yet.

"Now ... Albert, send me a profile on an Oleg Volkov."

"Yes, Detective. Mr. Volkov is employed with the Exploration Corps on a mission to Secundus. He—"

"Wait. Where was he employed prior to that?"

"Khufu Entertainment."

"No shit!"

"Detective. There is no shit to speak of."

Marcus shook his head in disbelief. Volkov, Nylund, and Charmagne Dufour all worked for Khufu Entertainment, Jan Krieger's company. It was a large employer to be sure, but a third coincidence? That was too strong to be simply chance. And if it wasn't chance, it meant Krieger had something to do with the murder, the billboard, and the crashed ship—*and the watch was the key to it all.*

CHAPTER NINE

SUSPICION

The world seemed to move in slow motion as Victoria's mind raced to make sense of it. *A beast from Earth can't be here on Secundus*, she chided herself, but the rhinoceros bore down on her party, unaware of the incongruence.

Agrinya reacted first. She raised her hand high in the air and screamed, "Face up! Skirmish! Three!" The troops stepped forward and spread out three arm's-lengths apart. "Hold and target!" In an instant, all guns were trained on the interloper. "Morrow. Protect our civvy," she barked at him.

"Yes ma'am." Morrow grabbed Victoria's arm and hustled her to the rear of the line. "Crouch down behind the *Argonaut*. Stay as small as you can," he shouted in her ear.

She nodded and complied, and in a flash he was gone, positioned back on the line, just in front of her, eyes and long-barreled rifle focused squarely on the target. With Morrow distracted, she moved beside the vehicle to see better, completely unaware that her hands had reached into the camera bag and lifted it out. Her jaw dropped in reaction to what she saw. Agrinya stood a few dozen feet out in front of the soldiers and faced the hulking beast. The lieutenant could have run back behind the line, she had plenty of time, but she chose instead to stand alone, so insignificant in comparison, yet steadfast and unafraid. Unfazed, the rhino bore down on her, coming within seconds of trampling her. Victoria noticed her iron grip on her camera for the first time, and brought the device up to frame a photo.

"Hold ranks! Fire *only* on my order!" Agrinya shouted over the commotion as she pointed her rifle into the sky. *FRAAAAAK!* The gun barked rabidly as she squeezed off dozens of rounds. The animal took notice. With a grunt, the huge beast dug its hooves into the soil, and with great strain, stopped itself a mere arm's-lengths away. It stomped its feet, bobbed its head, and snorted, eyeing her warily as if to say, *Who is this impertinent little gnat before me?*

Agrinya, resolute, stared back calmly, her demeanor well beyond comprehension, and it struck Victoria that no one would ever believe it, not without *seeing* it. The camera clicked as she took her shot; however, no photo could truly capture what happened next. The rhino wound itself up again, took a few steps back, and charged forward. Agrinya screamed, hurling a harsh word at the charging rhino. Incredibly, the animal stopped short again and reared back a step, confused and unsure of what to do next. Agrinya screamed again, but this time ran *toward* the animal, which turned tail and scrambled off in the opposite direction. Agrinya, fists cocked and shoulders square, watched it all the while until finally, a short time later, it disappeared over the horizon.

Victoria stepped out past the line, turned back, and cast her eyes upon the soldiers. They stared at their commanding officer, eyes wide and mouths agape. Agrinya called her scouts over and discussed something with them, while the others, relieved, took the opportunity to drink water and rest. Victoria lowered herself to the ground and lay in the grass, staring up into the sky and breathing deeply to calm herself. Just when she had settled down, a melodic ping unsettled the silence that hung in the air and jump-started her heart again. She fished out her mobile phone and viewed the message displayed there. It was Marcus! It read:

DontUnderstandYouPleaseExplain.
WhatDoYouMeanByExplosion?
HalfTheShipDead?YouSafe?
I n T h e D a r k O v e r H e r e

Victoria stared at the message, dumbfounded.

"Form up!" It was Agrinya, who had since returned to the main body. "We'll continue on course. Move out in two," she said, addressing the whole group. Amazing. She looked just as she had before. Her breath, posture, and mannerisms were all under strict control despite having been seconds from a violent death.

"Lieutenant?" Victoria said, just as she had turned to leave them.

Casting a glance over her shoulder, Agrinya replied, "Yes?"

Victoria wanted to tell her how astonishing her feat had been—how she had stood toe to toe with the legendary creature from Earth, how she had saved them all without a shot—but the experience had overwhelmed her so much that all she could get out was, "How in the hell did a rhinoceros get here?"

"I don't know." Her face changed ever so slightly; the iron mask lifted for an instant and revealed the confusion hidden behind it.

Victoria gathered her wits about her. "Why didn't you shoot it?"

"I had no orders to kill wildlife. Besides, these may be all that's left in the universe." Agrinya spoke matter of factly, and with that decided, she left to attend her place in the line.

They marched for another twenty minutes and stopped at the forest's edge. Its densely packed tangle of trees would be tough to traverse, so they followed it around its eastern rim until they came to the tributary that ran northward from the main river. They tracked it along the top of its bank as it curled west toward the forest, and after a brief time, they stopped and stared at the first intelligently built structure they had seen on the planet. A simple gravel road. It ran alongside the tributary as far as the eye could see, where both cut through the middle of the forest. And more amazingly, there in the distance stood a single figure on the road. It waved and beckoned them over.

Agrinya jogged up to the scout, who by now had crouched into a firing position. Victoria followed. She broke into a run and veered sharply to escape Morrow's clumsy, one-handed attempt to snatch her back.

"Wait!" he said as he gave chase, but she was quick and unencumbered by equipment, and he slowed once he realized he wouldn't catch her.

"—a threat?" Agrinya was saying to the scout just as Victoria entered into earshot. The lieutenant spun around and fixed her with an angry look. She was about to say something but lifted her head to see Morrow come up behind her. Whatever it was, she let it go.

The scout continued. "Possibly. We can't see into the tree line there. They could be hiding. But why send this guy out to greet us? I mean, we were heading in that direction anyway, so if they wanted to hit us, why give their position away?"

Agrinya grunted and looked over at the solitary man. Everything from his thinning hair to his craggy face and threadbare clothing looked old and weathered. Even his frame looked tired, stooped, a gnarled wooden cane the only thing keeping him from tipping over.

"Morrow? What is your assessment?"

"Can't say I disagree. This guy, by himself, is no threat to any of us."

Agrinya looked them each in the eye before she reached her decision. "We'll see what this man has to say. I hope he will tell us how in the hell he got here. Tell the main body to set up camp well back from the tree line, along the tributary. We can regroup there if attacked. Escort our civvy back there and return with Aikawa. We'll await your return before we head out."

"Wait!" Victoria said. "Are you kidding? This is the greatest story in a generation, generations maybe. I'm not leaving!"

Agrinya glared at her. "I have no sense of the threat level at this moment—but let me tell you this—it's somewhere between moderate and having your head detached."

"Lieutenant, I appreciate your concern for me, and your attachment to this head of mine, but I accept the risk. And may I remind you, I am outside of the military chain of command, and furthermore, this *civvy* also signed the waiver," Victoria said confidently behind a wry smile.

Agrinya looked her up and down for a moment or two and replied, "Well. I guess that's that, then. It's *your* head. Morrow, go now."

"Yes sir," he said.

"Oh. And bring the *Argonaut*. We might need it."

Morrow and Aikawa jogged back several minutes later, followed by the autonomous vehicle. They formed up without a word, all eyes fixated on the mysterious figure while they made their way to it slowly. About a minute later, they stopped about ten meters before the old man, who Victoria could see clearly now at this distance—his ancient, leathery skin seemingly born of antiquity as if tanned, salted, and dried by the gods themselves.

The man closed his eyes and took a deep, slow breath. "Welcome," he said. "It was said that you would return, and return you did." His eyes sprang open. "The prophecy has finally been fulfilled in my lifetime, exactly as it was written." He produced a large animal horn from his leather hip pouch, raised it to his lips, and blew. The long, ghostly note enveloped the clearing and carried far past the shimmering green leaves that bordered the forest. In one rapid and fluid motion, Agrinya transitioned into a fighting stance, weapon and head moving in tandem as they searched left and right for the enemy he had just summoned. But none came. Instead, the old man gestured and grinned invitingly. "Come! We have much to talk about!"

Agrinya set her rifle at her hip and looked about for several moments before she set her eyes upon the old man again. "Who are you?" she said.

"We will tell you, tell you all! Please. Please. Will you come?"

Agrinya's face betrayed nothing, but whatever the assortment of impulses that battled out behind it, curiosity appeared to win out in the end. After a long moment, she nodded, and with that, the group fell in again and followed the man down the road that cut into the forest. Victoria snapped a picture of their guide before she lowered the camera to her hip, heedless of her tight grip and incessant thumbing of the command dial mirroring her nervousness. What would greet them at the other end? It was anyone's guess now that the old man had stopped talking. He was a curious one indeed. He walked with an unorthodox gait, as if the years had altered his mechanics so profoundly that they were no longer fluid, but his pace was surprisingly brisk and they had to work to keep up with him. After a kilometer or so, they stood before a large black iron gate. It was bordered by tall, ivy-covered stone walls that spanned the height of two people.

"Come," said the old man with a grin. "They are waiting."

They left the *Argonaut* outside, strode through the gate, and entered a broad stone walkway that extended to a matching gate at the opposite end. A perpendicular walkway bisected it at its center so that the space was segmented into quarters, each enclosed by a manicured row of honeysuckle hedges. A baroque statue was situated at the center of each, and exquisitely arranged shrubbery and exotic flowers filled the spaces around them. A wooden open-air pavilion lay upon the circular patio that connected the walkways at the center of the garden, and the structure was arched on all four sides and topped by azure wooden shingles across its rounded helm roof. Elegant cornices and ornate portrayals of wild beasts graced its façade, carved in what appeared to be a seamless single piece of timber. A bright red flag flew atop its pinnacle with a large golden bird at its center, and nestled in the shade beneath the pavilion's canopy was a table of thick, varnished wood with the natural shape of the massive stump it had been cut from.

Another man entered the garden from its opposite end. He rode a horse and was flanked by an honor guard of five horsemen. They wore red tunics topped by polished silver armor, with lacquered green shields, adorned by the golden bird, tied to their saddles. Each held a long gold-tipped riding lance at their side, which was pointed straight into the sky. The man who led them had none of their splendor. He wore a simple white tunic, secured at the waist by a tawny rope, and now, upon closer inspection, Victoria could see that he wasn't traveling by horse like the other five; rather, he sat atop an unsaddled roan donkey. He was old too, probably older than their guide, perhaps in his eighties. In no time, the enigmatic group stopped short of the pavilion where Victoria and the soldiers had gathered.

The man in the white tunic addressed their elderly escort. "Thank you, Oren. You have done well. You may take your leave now and retire for the rest of the day." He regarded one of his retinue and said, "Captain Steward, please extend our guests refreshment." A huge guard leaped down from his horse, opened a lavish leather saddle bag, and produced a large silver carafe and five silver goblets. He approached them, handed each one, before filling them with cold water. He filled the fifth one and set it at the fore and center of a table before he repositioned himself, standing behind the man in white.

"Please," said the man in white, gesturing to them. "Sit. You must be tired from your journey. Come. I assure you there is nothing to fear." He raised the goblet in the air in front of him. "As is our custom, we give the Gift of Water to you, our travelers from far away—the Gift of Life itself."

They each looked to Agrinya. She in turn looked into the cup, smelled it quickly, and drank a sip. She swished it in her mouth before swallowing and moments later nodded her head. The rest of the party took a swig from their goblets and then sat down across the table from where the man sat. The remainder of the guards dismounted and took positions at each corner of the pavilion.

"Thank you for your generosity. I am Lieutenant Agrinya of the Exploration Corps of the planet Primis. Who do I have the pleasure of addressing?"

The man in white chuckled amusingly. "Do you not know me?" No one answered. "Of course not. I have not been among you in such a long time. I am King Eleazar."

Victoria stared, astonished. She froze in place as a wave of recognition came over her. A quick check of her party's faces verified she was not alone. "No shit!" she said, raising a hand to her mouth as if to catch the words before they escaped.

King Eleazar chuckled heartily in his chair. "Ah. So you *do* know of me, then?"

"Of course we do! But you—I mean—how did you come to be here?"

"You crash landed here," Agrinya said. "On the *Renascent*. You ... you ... *died*."

"Why, yes. In a matter of speaking. In truth, not many of us survived, but those who did found a new home here, our refuge in the forest."

"Refuge? From what?" Victoria's thoughts went to the rhinoceros and the carvings above them. "Ah! From the wild beasts?"

"Yes. Very observant, young lady. Very observant! May I inquire your name?"

"Victoria."

"Yes, of course. A regal name for one of regal bearing and mind. It suits you."

"Thank you."

"Of course!"

"How have you survived all these years?" said Agrinya, her words firm and eyes fixed on the old man.

"Yes! Yes! That I will answer. You must have many more questions, so listen closely. The *Renascent* was torn and twisted from the crash. The zoology section suffered greatly, yes, but many of the animals survived, and we released them immediately into the wilderness. We could not occupy ourselves with their management. Why? Because we had our own survival to worry about, and so, left to their own devices, they flourished in the lands outside the forest."

"The forest?" Victoria said.

"Yes. *Here*, where we live. I will show you." Eleazar removed a thin leather cord from around his neck. The pendant that hung from it twirled as he lowered it onto the table, its shiny silver case and clear glass facing glinting in the light. She could see it clearly now. It was a wristwatch with its bands removed. It, like everything else here, looked old, but its design and construction hearkened to a level of refinement and utility seldom seen. Next, he removed a round gold casing from his pocket and snapped it firmly atop the watch so that the casing's thick domed lens hovered just over the watch's dial. He lowered his face close to the table and fiddled with the little metal button at the side of the watch. Moments later, he lifted his head back and smiled gleefully. "There!" he said. A large hologram of a planet materialized in the air above the lens.

He continued. "Our planet has *one* habitable continent only, and it is small and surrounded by great salt oceans. The river that flows from the mountains and its tributary that runs through our forest are our only source of fresh water. It sustains the trees too, they in turn shelter us from the wild beasts who are content to rule the lands outside. And so we cherish this gift, for there is nothing but parched lands and wilderness beyond.

Victoria's mind reeled at the colors that swirled above the watch. Stunning images of the land, the forest, and the animals conjured in thin air just at the moment he described them. Like magic! She could hardly parse what she had just heard too. How could these people have survived for so long? And more so, how had her people been oblivious of their presence?

Victoria turned to Agrinya and gauged her reaction. She looked upon the light show with no more expression than she had when she'd inspected her weapon earlier in the morning.

Agrinya now spoke. "King Eleazar. We—*all* Primisians—have grown up with the story of your great sacrifice. We are grateful, and thankful for your gift and the opportunity it has given us. We live because of it. How may we ever repay you?"

"As each has received a gift," he replied, "use it to serve one another. And in that, I come to how you may serve me." Each of the group perked up. "Our life here has few of the comforts and advancements that we enjoyed on Earth. When we arrived here on Secundus, we cursed our austere and isolated existence—but over time, we realized that our life here was *not* a curse, but a stroke of good fortune since we are free from the toll of advancing technology and the anxiety of materialism. We have found *our* place in the universe. And so, I ask you for one simple thing—*to go*. Leave us here. Tell no one of our existence."

Silence hung throughout the pavilion like a dense fog. It was the king who broke it. "I must take my leave now. You may stay in your ship for a fortnight while you prepare your things. You must not be here afterward."

The king looked at each of them solemnly before he took the watch, rose from the table, and signaled Captain Steward to fill up the goblets once more. The lost king mounted his donkey and left the garden through the back gate. His retinue trailed behind. No one said anything for a time, all staring into their cups or out into the garden, speechless.

Finally, Agrinya said, "Come. We must go." Her stoic expression was marred by trepidation.

As they returned down the road, Agrinya's quote flashed into Victoria's mind. *Honestly, no. I never ever fathomed this.* It took on an entirely new meaning. The self-proclaimed King Eleazar, commander of the *Renascent*, and the descendants of his crew were *alive* and by all indications, thriving in this little pocket of existence. But what of his request? Why did he wish to stay here? After all, they looked *medieval* in appearance. On Primis, they would receive the benefits of advanced technology, medicine, and a much higher standard of living. Surely they realized this. Why did they not want it?

The party had just arrived at the forest edge when they heard the sound of horse hooves clapping hard on the road behind them.

"Form up," Agrinya yelled over the sound of the horses.

The soldiers snapped into a tight line behind the *Argonaut* and trained their weapons on the advancing figures. Morrow grabbed Victoria by the elbow and ushered her brusquely to their center.

"Morrow!" she said, yelling his name like an obscenity.

He ignored her tone, his eyes all business, cast forward, and locked on the figures that loomed a short distance away. "Stay put and don't move!" he said, pushing her down so she was protected by the vehicle's chassis. He then pressed the control pad on the vehicle, and in seconds, the compact, turreted gun rose from the top of its front section and swiveled toward the interlopers.

"Leave me. I'm fine!" she said defiantly from her seated position on the road. Seeing an escape, she crawled on the ground between two legs, popped up on the other side, and raced to one end of the line to get a better view.

In moments, a dozen of the king's guards positioned themselves in a semicircle formation about thirty meters away. They dismounted quickly and trained their rifles toward Agrinya's makeshift redoubt. Their weapons appeared antiquated—even Victoria's untrained eyes could see they were no match in a straight-up firefight against Agrinya's modern automatics and the *Argonaut*'s heavy machine gun. Despite the fact that it was twelve against five, Agrinya's party would win—even she would know that—but death would visit both sides.

"What is the meaning of this?" Agrinya said, spitting her words with fury.

Captain Steward approached and stopped in front of the *Argonaut*. "Why have you repaid good with evil?" he said.

"We don't know what you are talking about," Agrinya replied.

"You have stolen from our king. The one who has offered you the Gift of Water. The Gift of Life."

Agrinya shot him an angry look but remained composed. "That is nonsense. Leave now and be glad that we will forget this ever happened."

Captain Steward stood firm, hands on hips, and regarded her warily. Each was clearly sizing the other up, running the battle scenarios, and calculating the odds of winning. Agrinya blinked first.

"Whatever you believe we have stolen from your king, go search for it now." Agrinya looked to the team and nodded. They lowered their rifles and backed away from the vehicle.

Steward grunted with a distasteful frown. He approached the group, regarded each of them carefully, and lingered for several moments before he cast his eyes upon the *Argonaut*. Steward pressed a button on its side. A small door slid open and revealed a storage compartment that he rummaged through. Finding nothing, he checked the one beside it before moving to the front of the vehicle and reaching deep into the compartment there. He froze for a moment, then slowly straightened to his full height and brought his hand out of the compartment. In it was a silver goblet. The same as the ones they had drunk from in the pavilion.

"Isn't this one of the cups my master had offered you to drink from? This is a wicked thing you have done!"

"Why would we steal from your king?" replied Agrinya calmly, with more restraint than Victoria could ever muster.

"It is not for me to answer, for here in my hands is the object that was stolen. Which one of you was the thief?"

Agrinya closed the distance between them, her face now inches from Steward's. "No one!" she said, her words more of a snarl forced through gritted teeth. "We will not stand for this trickery!"

Time slowed to a standstill, no sound, no movement—*nothing* distracted Victoria from the two combatants. The fate of their lives could change in an instant and the next move would determine how it would all play out. Agrinya's hand inched down to her sidearm, which clearly indicated where this was headed. Agrinya was proud and competent. Since the odds were on her side, she would do what any good soldier would do when granted the advantage. Attack. And so Victoria made the only choice available to her.

"It was me," she said.

"No!" Agrinya spun around, her words filled with bitter bile.

"Yes. It was me! Me! Oh, it was so beautiful! Like nothing I've ever seen. I just *had* to have it, had to have that little piece of *history*."

Agrinya scowled, grave lines scored her forehead, which was wrinkled with disbelief.

Steward said, "How is it that the rose is the malefactor, and not the brambles?" He grunted in consideration. "So then. You will come with me. The rest of you may go and return to your ship in peace."

Agrinya's eyes bored into her as she said goodbye and left with the guards on horseback.

Alyn flinched as he hoisted himself up off the edge of his bed. His tender ribs sent a sharp jolt upward that burst into his temples, exploding with scattered specks that dotted his vision. He winced and waited for them to clear. It was his first full day out of Sick Bay, and he swore that he would never take the simple things, like tying a shoelace, for granted ever again. The bunk's drab gray walls were just as he'd left them, and his absence had done nothing to increase his fondness for its sardine-can proportions. He needed a change of scenery, even if it killed him. He took a step forward and stopped abruptly as his head swirled for several moments at the sudden change in motion. Reflexively, he placed a hand on the still-sore spot on the back of it in an effort to comfort himself.

Why had Oleg struck him? Dad had said "they" would come for him. Was Oleg one of "them?" Likely not. After all, Oleg hadn't stolen Grandpa's watch from him, and Dad had said that it was the very thing they were after, so Oleg must have had an entirely different motivation. His presence, hours before the blast, might have been a coincidence but it was more likely he had clobbered Alyn to prevent him from finding the bomb. But why would he want to kill so many people?

Alyn's brain hurt. It tired easily since the assault. He felt a bit better that Oleg was dead, to be honest, but would rather he were alive to answer these questions. Miraculously, Alyn had survived, thanks to Victoria, and with this thought he remembered—*she had spoken to him!* The image of Victoria at his bedside came next, but it was more like a dream, a pleasant one at that, but he was sure it had happened. Wasn't he? Or was it a product of his drug-induced state? Of course it was real! Drugs or not, dreams did not possess such fidelity to faithfully render the soft lines of her face, her warm, glowing smile or her smell when she had leaned in close, so wonderful and fragrant, like blossoming flowers in a meadow ... They were all real. And so too was the peculiar feeling that had crept up and taken him by surprise. It was as if he knew her, despite the little time they had spent together—but no, it was more than that. It was like he had *always* known her.

He checked his teeth in the mirror over his sink and retrieved his hair gel from the drawer under it. With single-minded purpose, he lathered it in, making sure each strand was in place before he went to find her. He had just lurched out of the doorway when his stomach growled. He had been off solid food for days and the prospect of a good meal would have to take priority. With no time to waste, he scrambled to the mess hall, slipped into the buffet line, and sat down with his food tray shortly after.

"Frederick!"

Alyn saw Donel sitting at a table near the entranceway and went over to join him.

"Freddy. Glad you're back. I came to see you. Every day! You were out all the time, though. You really okay?"

"Yeah. Much better. Just got out yesterday."

"You're lucky to be alive, bro," Donel said before turning to his left. "Alyn, this is Mandeep D'Souza."

The man was a bit older than Alyn and Donel and wore his dress white uniform in stark contrast to the crackerjacks they donned. An ensign's single bar lay upon his collar and shoulders and an impressive array of medals were pinned to his chest. An orange four-toed claw overlaid on an angry yellow thunderbolt adorned the patch on his sleeve. It identified him as one of the fabled few of Singh's Tigers.

"Hey. Nice to meet you," Mandeep said. "I hear you've been to hell and back? Hope you're doing better."

"Thanks. Nice to meet you too," Alyn said, pointing to his medals. "You see action against the Foundationalists?"

"He sure did," Donel said. "Got the Silver Star too. See it there? They don't give those away to just anybody, you know?"

Mandeep grinned. "Yeah. In Cottingham. Rooted the bastards out of a regional depot. They used it to organize and stage some of the bombings. Took us a while to figure it out—buggers are so crafty—but we paid 'em back once we did. Wiped 'em out in one helluva firefight. Didn't matter, though—two, three weeks go by, and another one popped up elsewhere."

"Like a bunch of sewer rats. You can trap a few when they come up for air, but you'll never get 'em all," Donel said.

"Exactly, but that's okay. Means there'll be no end to the supply of bastards I can kill. So what about you? Are you an enlisted man?"

"Something like that," replied Alyn, not wishing to get into the details.

"Hey," Donel said in an attempt to change the subject. "Alyn and I go *way* back. Right, Alyn? And listen, I taught him everything, and I mean *everything*. Ladies included, and locked away here on this metal tub, Alyn, it's like hitting fish in a barrel! You might actually get a date."

"Maybe that'll happen sooner rather than later," replied Mandeep. "I hear he was saved by the *reporter*. That true, Alyn?"

"Heh. True, I guess," replied Alyn, feeling sheepish. His cheeks burned. "Say, have you seen her? I'd like to thank her. She saved my ass, after all."

Donel looked at Alyn, eyes wide and mouth hanging open. "You hadn't heard?"

"Heard what?" replied Alyn.

"The reporter. She's not here anymore," replied Mandeep.

"Where is she?"

"Captured on a scouting expedition," said Donel.

"Captured? Captured by whom?"

Donel looked at Mandeep before turning back to Alyn. "The people of the *Renascent*."

Alyn broke out in a cold sweat. "The *Renascent*? That's impossible. That ship was lost. It ran out of fuel and crashed on the planet."

"That's exactly what we were told. Evidently, our history books need a rewrite."

The notion raced through Alyn's mind, one step ahead of the disbelief that threatened to dash it. How could this be? He, they, *everyone* believed the crew of the *Renascent* were long dead. To believe otherwise was incomprehensible, but he'd have to take it on faith for the time being as his overriding concern was Victoria's whereabouts. She *had* to be alive.

He looked directly in D'Souza's eyes and said, "When did they—"

The marshaling signal interrupted him, droning from the ship's public address system. The abrasive wail drowned out the question on Alyn's lips. All eyes jumped to the screen mounted above the door. It flashed:

Warrant Officers 740A, 915A, 914A, 919A, 923A
REPORT TO ASSEMBLY BAY 12E—0800
WORK ORDER: 000118

"Fellas. We just got our marching orders. We're goin' on work duty," said Donel.

Alyn gritted his teeth in frustration as D'Souza shot up from his seat. "Gotta go. See you guys." He left them and strode out the main door.

"We better go too, Alyn. Before they write us up."

"What's the work order for?"

"They're sending us out to set up the power plant."

"The what? Why are we doing that? Sure, we've had some heavy equipment training, but heck, we're millwrights. Driving the big machines is *not* our core skill."

"Half the technical warrant officers died just before you had your big nap. We're the jacks-of-all-trades now."

The duo arrived in Bay 12E a little while later and reviewed their work orders. They paired up and joined a crew of technicians in the rear cargo hold of a helicarrier. They landed somewhere to the east and exited the transport, crossing the makeshift tarmac. In the instant they escaped the roar of the propellers, Alyn asked Donel the question that he carried along with him the entire deafening trip.

"So where is she, then?" he said.

Donel flinched and flashed him a stern expression.

"Sorry. I didn't mean to yell."

"So who are you shouting about?" Donel asked.

"Victoria. The reporter."

"Oh. Right. She's their prisoner."

"What? How?"

"I dunno exactly. The story I heard was that she stole something. They're keeping her in their little homestead in the woods." Alyn was stunned. None of it made sense. She wasn't a thief. He would bet his life on it.

"You sure about that?"

"That's what I heard."

The two approached the portable operations center. It was a rectangular room constructed of rust-colored corrugated metal. It had a door at its center and two windows on either side. Alyn glanced quickly through the closest one.

The space was crowded with computers on one side, and a small open workspace occupied the other. A canvas caravan tent extended outward for several feet in all directions from the door. The supervisor had set up shop beneath it, sitting behind a large table stacked with papers and two computer laptops. Donel approached first.

"Sergeant-Major Rodrigues? DeCruze and Frederick, sir. We are to report to you on arrival."

The man's bearing was more librarian than engineer. He poured over the plotted paper maps with a magnifying glass in hand and looked over the top of bifocals that hung near the bottom of his nose.

"Ah, yes. We've been waiting. DeCruze. Heavy machinery, right?" Rodrigues said, still absorbed in the map work.

"Yes sir, but heavy machinery—that's my secondary skill. Where's your primary operator?"

"Bought it," said the sergeant major. He straightened himself up in a self-effacing manner and leveled his gaze at Donel. "She was part of the scouting group that went west along the river. None came back."

Alyn stared at Donel, who looked back at him with surprise and shrugged. "Forgot to mention it."

Alyn was annoyed, but he flashed a perfunctory half-smile before they both turned back to the man.

Rodrigues continued again. "Now, you'll be operating the Behemoth. You'll use it to lift sections of the dam and set them down on the concrete footings we poured last night on both sides of the tributary. Frederick, you'll position the sensors that will guide their placement. You'll also engage the safety locks that will keep them in place."

"Yes sir," Alyn replied, relieved that he escaped hard labor.

"Oh, and DeCruze. Ensure you place that wonderful testament to hydraulic engineering nice and flat. The turbine sitting within it is the most important piece of it. It provides the power we need to operate our mining equipment and the refinery. The dam is gravity mounted, meaning any imbalance can unseat it minutes, days, or weeks after the fact. That could set us back in a big way. So no sloppiness. If I find out there is, I'll request a transfer for both of you to scout duty. Comprendes?"

"Yes sir," replied Donel.

"Good. Get to it. The Behemoth is parked around the back."

About a minute later, the two men stared up at the colossal machine. It vaguely resembled a human, with two solid metal legs that were taller than the tallest person. Trunk-like in width, they supported arms and a torso designed to lift heavy objects and an operator who stood inside the clear Plexiglas-covered compartment in its chest. Cables, hoses, springs, and valves jutted out from its joints and from hydraulic cylinders that formed the musculature of the arms and legs. A row of multicolored lights ran down both sides of the cockpit and a large strobe topped it at its head, centered in between a set of horn speakers.

"A beauty, isn't she?" said a man who popped out from behind it. A pair of welder's glasses sat atop his forehead and an oil-stained wrench hung from the magnetic holder on his belt. If the shock of red hair and grimy blue coveralls didn't identify him, the three embroidered white letters stitched within an oval crest upon his chest did: Sid. "Hey, I haven't seen you since your accident, Alyn. How's it going?"

"It's good to be alive, Sid. That counts for a lot these days. Hey, this's my friend Donel."

Sid reached out a big greasy hand. Donel shook it without hesitation.

"Oh, I forgot to mention, I still have that music mix of old stuff you lent me. It's fantastic! Bruce Dickinson's voice is unworldly. Why don't they make music like that anymore? I'll make sure to send it back tonight when I'm off. Cool?"

"Yeah. Totally cool, man."

"She timid? Aloof maybe?" said Donel as he gave a smirking nod up at the machine. "Gonna give me hassle when I mount?"

"Haha ... not this one," replied Sid with a wink. "She's a charmer. You'll have no worries."

Donel smiled and nodded again in acknowledgment.

"You heard anything about what's been going on lately?" said Alyn.

"Folks on edge out here, being so far from the ship. We don't want to end up like the Lost Platoon. Sergeant-major says we should stay alert. Them hostiles could be out there watching us right now, waiting for their moment. We post guards at night but we're only mechanics, you know?"

"Yeah, I hear that," replied Alyn.

"Listen, I gotta run. Treat her right and she'll be good to you."

"No problem," Donel said.

"Get her back in one piece before sunrise. Army wants me to add some major modifications to her. I need to get it done before my leave."

Alyn was puzzled by this, and a quick glance at Donel showed that he shared the same feeling. Before Alyn could say something, Sid smiled and scurried off, leaving the two men alone with the machine. Donel touched a button on the side of its leg. The Plexiglas cover rotated downward toward them.

"Here. Gimme a hand," Donel said. Alyn helped him into the machine.

The sun dropped below the horizon just after the two men had completed their tasks. It wasn't easy, not with Rodrigues's words ringing their heads, but they eventually managed to place the dam carefully and lock it without incident. Rodrigues proved himself fair and let them relax the rest of the day. The two sat at a table shaded by a wide broadleaf tree.

"The idea, as I was told by an engineer, is to have the water fill up the natural basin behind the dam. Like a reservoir, right? The basin creates the water pressure needed to drive the turbine, which in turn creates the electricity. Ingenious, really," said Alyn, though it looked as if Donel was somewhere else altogether as he stared off into the distance.

"Is that a giraffe?" said Donel.

Alyn followed his gaze. "Amazing. We had one in the zoo back home. It died last year. Everyone believed it was the last one."

"That's what's messed up, isn't it?"

"What is?"

"B-Platoon, the reconnaissance party. The one that Sid was talking about, that went west down the river. They're all dead. All of them. And what for? Nothing. Hell, all they got for their efforts was that damn speech the admiral gives. You know, the one that goes—*we remember and honor their sacrifice*. It's madness. A whole platoon killed and the best we can do is honor their sacrifice? Why? It's simple. It's to assure their parents they didn't die in vain, convince the populace of some inspirational ideal—heck—create heroes that children can idolize and emulate. It's just another thing we're told to believe, that their deaths meant *something*—but they *didn't*. Truth is, they died for nothing. It's all a farce. Just like them damn giraffes back home and the crew of the *Renascent*. We were told they were dead, and we believed it, but here we are, and so are they."

His friend's words jumbled in Alyn's head, tossing over and over as he tried to comprehend their enormity. But it seemed just beyond his grasp. The greatest value to society *was* sacrifice. Sacrifice was the gift given to Grandpa and the people of the *Dominus*. Sacrifice had brought them here, so far from Earth. But as much as he recited the old adages, he knew that Donel was on to something, but he was too fatigued to truly puzzle it out.

"Hey," said Donel. "Check your mobile. Looks like we can go. Let's head back to the transport."

Marcus pulled into the police station's parking garage just as the dashboard console rang.

"Marcus here," he said as he eased into his parking space.

"Good morning, Detective. I hope your day is going well and you are enjoying the temperate weather."

"Yes. Yes indeed, Albert," Marcus said absently as he shut off the engine.

"I have analyzed Nicholas Nylund's work schedule that Mr. Krieger had sent to the Central Data Unit."

"Okay."

"I ran multiple analytical comparisons. First, I compared his last month's schedule to those going back twelve months."

"Great. Whad'ja find?"

"No statistically significant deviations. Second, I performed a relational scan among all his documented passengers and all known relations within three degrees of separation from Joseph Frederick. There were no matches. And lastly, I—"

"I get it, Albert. You're about to tell me there is nothing to link Nikko to the murder. Correct?"

"Correct, Detective."

"That's all I need to know."

Marcus signed off from Albert, left the car, and recounted Peters's confession as he made his way into the station. Charmagne Conway. The upstart criminal mastermind had resurfaced after so many years in obscurity. However, her return had not coincided with a book tour and public mea culpa for her past crimes; rather, she had reappeared and demanded that Peters cover the tracks of Frederick's killer. Where had she been all this time? Why was it *now* that she'd chosen to come out from behind the scenes? Her appearance at the clinic bombing, dressed to present the last quarter's sales figures, was strange, and that she'd gone to Jan Krieger's casino afterward, which also employed Nikko, was even stranger.

Marcus approached a wooden door with Captain A. Praetorius stenciled on the frosted glass. He knocked twice.

"Come," a voice said from behind the door.

Marcus entered the antechamber. Its faded cream-colored walls were in stark contrast to the dark faux-wood desk that dominated the small room. A framed certificate hung on the wall behind it with ranks of binders and neatly stacked files sat on a shelf below. A large monitor screen sat atop the desk. The room appeared empty.

"Yes?" the voice said again.

Marcus moved his head to the side and saw a woman tucked behind the large screen. She chewed gum and continued at her work, clicking and clacking the keyboard.

"I'm here to see the captain."

"Name?"

"Marcus."

She resumed the clickety-clack for about a half minute before pausing for what seemed like longer than she needed to. "Take a seat," she said, eyes still focused on the screen.

Marcus grumbled. The art of small talk was officially dead, and that woman hammered the last nail in the coffin. He sat in one of the worn-out faux leather chairs. He flipped through a set of magazines on the coffee table but found nothing of interest, so sat quietly for a time. Suddenly he remembered the summary of Frederick's patents that Albert had uploaded. He worked through them eagerly, swiping from left to right on his mobile phone. There were more of them than he had expected, and they were much more diverse in kind too, ranging from electronic transfer mediums to diode limiters and even supercapacitors. Most were firmly in the experimental stage, but some had progressed to production and been given fancy names like the Photon Entangler or Heisenberg Certainty Calculator. He had sifted through almost all of them when he found something interesting.

"Captain's ready to see you," said the woman from behind the monitor.

Marcus rose and entered the modest-sized office through the door at her side. It was a mess of books, files, and papers strewn over the desktop, upon bookshelves, and anywhere else they could find breathing space. The captain stood near the corner window, his eyes focused on a large map that hung adjacent to it. Street names and neighborhood boundaries were easily discernable in the natural light, and so too were the little colored flags and pushpins that dotted the cityscape and the thick Magic Marker lines drawn around them. The captain liked to step away from the screen at times and look at things the old-fashioned way. Marcus liked that about him.

"Detective? What do you make of it?" said Praetorius. He peered intently at a red-marked zone on the map that enveloped several pushpins. An orange flag was stuck into the middle of it.

Marcus moved in beside him and zeroed in on it. "The zone represents the scene of yesterday's crime. The orange flag, based on the legend here at the bottom, indicates it was a bombing. The pushpins represent the number of dead."

"Yes, Detective. Quite right. Zoom out now. What do you see?"

Marcus took two steps back and took in the map's entirety. The bombing cases were Rolph's, and aside for standing in for him yesterday, Marcus had spent little time thinking about them. He was up for the challenge today, and he started by matching the various colored flags against the legend and cross-referencing the crime perpetrated to the dates scrawled within the marked zones. A pattern emerged from the low-tech crime prediction tool.

Marcus said, "It's escalating."

"Yes? Tell me more."

"It's all right here. You can see it clear as day. The initial sequence of criminal events is minor, as indicated by the type of flags and the utter lack of pushpins. These crimes are unambiguously amateurish—protests, assaults, defacement of property. No killings whatsoever. The thing that stands out is that these crimes happen in the earliest period of the Foundationalist's activism. Call it Phase One. However, something changes about eighteen months after it began—the bombings. The first blasts occur in locations that are easy to get into and out of unseen—you know, places where you can hide or blend in, pubs, restaurants, malls. And further, the blasts themselves are small, and so too are the ensuing number of deaths. This is Phase Two. Phase Three, the current phase, starts around the time of the vandalized billboard in New Times Square. This phase is bolder, more impactful, better coordinated than what we've seen before. The body counts jump significantly. The bombs explode in locations that are much harder to get into undetected, where there is good surveillance too. The locations themselves are of a higher profile, as if the Foundationalists have become more selective. Take the library here, for example, or the clinic yesterday."

"And so?"

"And so, it's like the Foundationalists are learning, getting more confident and brazen. Shit. It's like they've figured out how to beat us, how to go about their ghoulish business unseen. It's anyone's guess how they accessed the clinic without any digital trace. Like they were ghosts. But it's more than that."

"More than what?"

"The Phase Three bombs were made with C4. Haven't seen that stuff since the Dark Days. Where did it come from?"

"Hmm." The captain pondered as he tilted his head, then nodded. "Good question. Don't know. And here's another—where do you expect this trend to go?"

"If it continues, their bomb-making abilities will increase—not necessarily the punch they pack, but the means to make them smaller, less detectible.

Emboldened by their accomplishments so far, they'll strike next at a bigger, more visible target, one that will capture public attention to their cause. A public building, either legislative or military, would be my bet."

Praetorius regarded him with an inquisitive look. "Astounding." A moment or two passed between them before he smiled and added, "That took me all of last afternoon and most of today to piece together. How did you do it?"

Marcus remembered the old man who fed the pigeons. "You'd be amazed how a park bench and some fresh air can give you clear perspective. Look, Captain, I'm wrapping up my minor case load. I could help—"

"Marcus." Praetorius's expression transitioned from astonishment to solemnity in seconds. He took another deep breath and dropped his eyes momentarily while he gathered his thoughts. "We'd all appreciate it—your help, I mean. There's no one better who could figure this out and put an end to it all. We all know that, but I won't have it, not at your expense. You've given enough now, weathered too many storms, lost too much. The folks here have been watching your back, and what they're telling me is not good. You're showing up smelling like alcohol, wearing it like its cologne. And you're shuffling around in those unkempt clothes with your head someplace else—like you're lost."

"I—"

"Marcus, I been around a long time. I seen what this job does to people. You've got one half the population that thinks you're some power-hungry Neanderthal, the other half would just as soon slit your throat to make a buck, and all we have to fortify ourselves is some seed of virtue deep inside us that can't burst forth for lack of sunshine and water. It can crush the best of us at the best of times. The lucky ones have good families to ground them, and since yours was taken, you just ain't been the same, let's face it. I can't understand how that feels, Marcus, but I know it ain't good and that's why I have to do this. I need your badge and gun now. I'm giving you some time off. As much as you need."

Anger ignited within Marcus's belly and burned up into his chest before it radiated outward, his skin glowed hotter with each thump of his heart. Like hell he'd accept this foolishness. Like hell he'd lie down for this crap! He wanted to strangle the man then and there, but it wouldn't help, even if it would feel good in the moment.

"Captain, which word figures most prominently in the Constitution?"

Praetorius looked puzzled. "'Sacrifice,' of course."

"Right! 'We, the People of Primis, in order to form a more perfect civilization, must first acknowledge and thank our brothers and sisters who have sacrificed their lives so that we may live. In so doing, we owe our lives, rights, and responsibilities described herein to their brave act and do ordain its necessity to establish this Constitution.'"

"I had to recite this every day in grade school, just like you. So where you going with this?"

"That's just it, isn't it? We were taught that the highest order of our civic responsibility, heck, our lives, is *sacrifice.* It's what our civilization can thank for its existence, there's no higher virtue, and so *here* is where I am going. I've given everything, shit, my soul for the force, so hell, if there is a better example of sacrifice, Captain, then you find me one."

The captain drew yet another deep breath, relaxed his shoulders, and stayed silent for several moments before he spoke. "You're wrong, Marcus. You gave us your all, true, but *not* your soul. You *lost* that after the accident, after Grace, Mary, and Clarise died. I tried to help you, brother. Do you remember? After the baseball game you took your family to? I covered up the fact that you were stone cold drunk, *two times* over the legal limit when you drove over the side of the cliff and killed them." Praetorius's eyes softened. "It was all the great work you did, all the *sacrifice*, as you said, that kept you from going to jail. Shit. I've had my own close calls with my daughter's illness, so I felt for you, losing your kids and all, I really did, but I can't keep covering for you. I can't help you out this time."

Marcus knew where this was going. A gentle nudge, soon to be followed by a swift kick, before the door slammed shut. It wasn't right. Not for one who had served the city with decency and honor for almost thirty years. He did not deserve this. No. But the older he became, the more he realized that the world had changed. You didn't always get what you deserved. Hard work and integrity, commodities found in small abundance, no longer commanded a high price. Shit. The job had been considered a vocation when he came up. Now, a place to park yourself for thirty years with good pay and benefits. That's all people wanted these days, and cops were simply *people.* Just like anyone else, they aspired for that large holovision, the big house, dream vacation, or any number of diversions from life. Potemkin villages of meaning were built from these indulgences, filling their voids like starchy carbs, each person consuming great amounts but never feeling fulfilled. These distracted, empty people were little more than automatons when you came down to it. That was the truth! And just like everyone else, cops had bills to pay, a job they were beholden to, and a boss to tell them to do it. Their boss had a boss too, who had a boss, and so on. Even the commissioner was accountable to the board, and the board was accountable to the voting public. There was no escaping accountability; it was just that the higher up you went, the more detached you were from what went on in the streets.

Take Commissioner Brandt, for instance. He didn't have the time to digest the details of any single criminal case when faced with the sheer number of them, so any individual case didn't matter much. Unless, of course, that case drew negative press! Nothing savaged a commissioner's reputation more than a "special investigation report" playing out in prime time. So when the orders fell back down the chain, the average detective wasn't directed to do right per se or operate in any way remotely connected to truth. The fact was, the truth was typically messy, complicated, and involved resources, effort, and time to determine. There was no interest in any of that when the press hounds were baying. Closing cases convincingly and *quickly* was the happy path. Any delay or doubt, particularly in capital cases like murder, increased the probability that the press would make a story of it. Go where the evidence led was bullshit. Go where the press led was better. The sad fact was that Praetorius was someone who under normal circumstances Marcus might even like; however, he was just like all the others. A spinning cog, driven by bigger ones, that powered this corrupt machine—and that made him contemptible. Praetorius probably knew it, probably saw a glimpse of it in the mirror now and then when he shaved, but instead of confronting this dichotomy, chose to close his eyes in a self-deceptive game of peekaboo. Who could blame him? When faced with the decision to stand up to this systemic corruption and assuredly lose his livelihood, identity, and material comforts, what did you expect him to choose? Virtue doesn't stand up well to hunger, nor a cavalcade of holovisions, cars, or homes. And so it was that this man had no interest in giving him a fair shake and there was nothing to be gained by playing nice. Though the fire inside Marcus burned hot, each word Praetorius had uttered was like a cool draft blown over red coals, and by now Marcus was unable to contain the heat any longer. He gritted his teeth, looked up at Praetorius, and said, "Who got to you? Who is pulling the strings?"

Praetorius looked downward at an angle as if to say there was no more to do, nothing more to be said, and after several moments he extended a hand to say goodbye. Marcus, unable to reciprocate, unholstered his pistol, withdrew his badge from inside his blazer, and laid them both on the captain's desk. He left without a word.

An hour later, Marcus sat upon the corner stool at the Spread Eagle Tavern. The staff dashed about and performed the final spit and polish in preparation for the lunchtime crowd. The grating of chairs, the clinking of glasses, and the usual working-stiff banter reverberated in the small confines of the main room. Marcus barely noticed. His thoughts were far away.

"What can I getcha?"

Marcus broke his reverie and looked up at the bartender. He was new, young, didn't seem social like the old fellas. Today, that suited Marcus just fine.

"Canadian whisky. Straight up. And keep 'em coming," Marcus said, not waiting to see if the order registered.

"Sure thing," replied the bartender.

He returned a minute later, drink in hand, and placed it before Marcus. The amber liquid draped elegantly over two ice cubes that tinkled against the glass. Needing no encouragement, he downed it in a single gulp.

"I'll get you another."

He emptied the fresh round just as quickly. His brain, awash with alcohol, triggered pleasant feelings that flowed peacefully throughout his body. He relaxed for a few minutes before he decided to have a third one. The bitter liquid washed down his throat, warmed his chest, and engulfed any remaining stress in an ebbing tide that washed it far out to sea. He felt light, as if he could rise above all earthly matters, and for an instant touch heaven itself—just one more drink would do it, just one more drink would lift him to the Pearly Gates, where he could look through and see them.

But a more bitter reality set in. The next drink would weigh upon him, he knew it, for he had been aloft on this trip many times before. The next drink would send him down, back to Earth, mad and wanting. Heaven was like sand—it slipped through your fingers the tighter you clutched—and this time, like many times before, he railed against this truth and squeezed his fist anyway. The next gulp shattered his psyche into a million shards of thought, and amid the glinting splinters and slivers that rained down on him, one sparkled beyond all others. It fell upon the ground at his feet. He could see four words etched in the glass and bent down to view them. They read: **Negative—**

"Here ya go," said the bartender as he thumped a full glass on the wooden tabletop. Like a puff of smoke, the dream vanished into the air. Gone.

"Negative?" Marcus said, startled and in somewhat of a stupor.

"Say what? You told me to keep 'em coming."

"Negative?" Marcus looked up at him. "Negative. Just remember that for me, will you? In case I forget."

The bartender looked at him as if he had three heads. "Yeah, okay, but you gonna pay for this or what?"

"Sure. Sure." Marcus snapped out of it. He hastily pulled out his phone and swiped through the patents rapidly, for he needed to find the one that sparkled before the memory fully faded. The titles blurred by with each swipe, and so too did his memory with each flick of the finger. The document count had almost reached the end when he saw one that stopped him short. There. Negative Mass Particle Generator. According to the abstract, the device flipped the conventional properties of gravity upside down. It purported to create a local change in the physical properties of matter such that particles could move over vast distances in an instant. It was the stuff of science fiction, and if the Fredericks had been successful at building it, it would have changed everything.

The sounds of chatter echoed loudly from somewhere behind the bar. He looked up. The young bartender pointed the remote control at the HV screen, and the word Volume appeared on it with several images of square bars beside it. They were increasing in number.

"In recent news, yet another bombing occurred in the heart of the financial district," the HV blared.

"Shit. Another one. I wish to hell the government would get off their ass," said the bartender.

Marcus finished his drink, signaled for another one, and shifted his attention back to the screen.

"On another note, Governor Grant's update gives us something to rejoice." The video panned to Tyra Grant, who stood behind a podium with several microphones affixed to it. She spoke.

"Before closing, I would like to share some better news. I extend my gratitude and congratulations to the stalwart crew of the Dominus II. *I have just received word that they have landed on planet Secundus without incident."*

The bartender whistled. "Ain't she something?"

His affirmation barely registered with Marcus, whose mind contemplated what he had just heard from the mouth of Grant. How could it be? Victoria had claimed that the landing was not without incident at all, that in fact six hundred people had died in a crash.

The small bell at the top of the door tinkled. The man who entered sat down two seats away, opposite to him at the bar's corner. He was older with thinning gray hair and a face creased by years of living. His eyes and smile belied his age, however, and he greeted the bartender warmly as he topped up Marcus's glass.

"I'll take one of those too, but I fancy mine neat if that's okay." The bartender winked back at him. "There's a lad!" the man said, chuckling. He beamed as he looked over at Marcus. "My, it's cold. An ill wind, I say. Gets you right through to your bones, it does."

"You can say that," Marcus replied.

About a minute later, the bartender set the man's glass down and went to the other end where he occupied himself with polishing beer glasses. Marcus was halfway through his drink and checked to ensure he didn't go far.

"Pardon me, sir," said the man, who looked directly at Marcus. "Might I engage in some chit-chat? You see, I've been away a long while and just got back. I promise ya, I'll not be foul."

Marcus paused to take his measure, then nodded.

The man looked back as if to take his. "Now, if I may be a tad presumptuous, you have the bearing of a man I once knew. This man, he had the weight of the world resting firmly on his shoulders, and bore it he did, and with pride too. No complaint nor excuse did he make." The man's voice now slowed and rose in pitch. "Might that describe you, young man?"

"As I've been told recently."

"Ah. Now this fellow was a rock if there ever was one, but time is like a river, slowly and continuously wearing down even the hardest granite, and so there came a time when he could simply not take anymore."

Marcus perked up a bit and said, "What did he do?"

"Ah, there's the rub." The man paused while the bartender filled both glasses. "He did what any thinking person would do. He gave up the burden. Now, it wasn't easy. You see, this river had carved through his edifice, lined his façade, shaped him in a manner so *slowly* that over time the man could see only what the river had fashioned, he couldn't see himself as anything else. But, unlike a mountain, a man may choose. And choose he did! He gave it away. Gave it all to someone else, someone younger, someone willing to trade hardship for experience, who was ready to take it on, like he once had been."

Marcus listened intently. The man's words were delivered with a conviction that only experience imparted. "So. What was it that *you* did, then?"

"Aha! You're a clever one, aren't ya? I be foolin' no one. But I knew that before I sat down. I could tell it in the way you hold yourself. Watching without being watchful, always on, never off. You're on the force, aren't ya?"

"Yeah," Marcus replied, though unsure whether he still was. He admired the man's talents and regarded him with greater respect.

"So that is it. Well, no need explaining to me. You've got it written all about ya. I should know, I served thirty-five years myself."

"Really? Where?"

"Fifty-five Division."

"Fifty-five, eh? The name Nakamura ring a bell?"

"Juan? Yes, indeed! We were partners. Rode together for four years or so when he was just a rookie. You know him well?"

"We grew up on the same street. Best friends through school and kept in touch ever since."

"Shame what happened to him," the man mused. "Just a year from retirement was all."

"Yeah. Tragic."

"But I don't think he would've retired at all. Probably the best thing for him going down in uniform."

"Why?"

"He loved the force. We both did, we were consumed by the lifestyle. He could balance it being unattached and all, but my obsession with work got in the way of a life. I missed too much of it, didn't see it coming, but it did. It catches all of us in the end. In my case, I woke up one day to an empty house. My kids had moved away, started their families. My wife had passed earlier that year."

Marcus looked deep into the man's face. Tears were welling in his eyes, but the charming smile didn't crumble.

"It's funny, eh?" he continued. "When you're young and so filled with purpose and preoccupation, you can't wait for them to leave the house for a while, to give you some time, you know? But after my family was gone, that was all I had—the time and the dreadful quiet. It was more'n any one man can bear. But I woke up and decided to hell with this! So I left—packed a few things, got in my car, and just drove, and kept going until I tired."

"And where did the road take you?"

"A wonderful place by the seaside near Ko Samui. The sunsets are magical. You can sit near the beach under the water oaks—by now they're grand—and sip piña coladas served from the cabana. Nights never go below sixteen all year round either, and the summers nary above twenty-eight. I met a lady there too. We're going to get married next month. So I came back now to settle m'affairs before I return."

"Sounds like heaven."

"Aye, 'tis. Heaven on Earth, as they used to say. I've no more responsibility than keeping my fiancée happy and living the remains of my life to the fullest. It's as if the weight of that rock I'd been carryin' has finally left my shoulders."

Marcus nodded, took another sip, and allowed the idea to sink in. It might be better to give it all up. Wouldn't Clarise want that for him? The idea grabbed hold of him. Perhaps it *was* time that he lived? What difference was he making in his life now anyway? Crime would continue whether he was around or not.

Evil had been here before he arrived, and it would exist after he was long gone. Why shouldn't he rest his soul and lighten the burden?

He felt a vibration in his pocket. "Excuse me a second." He reached in and pulled out his mobile. It was Victoria! He opened the app and read the message. His jaw hit the floor.

"Say, are ya all right?"

"I gotta leave. I hope it all works out for you." Marcus got off the stool, wobbling a bit before he steadied himself, and pointed himself toward the door.

"Wait!" The man extended his hand and offered a business card. Marcus took it from him. "You would really fit in there. If I could find happiness, so could you. Call me if you ever wish to make the move!"

Marcus looked at the card. Printed in the center were the initials JP in bold black letters. The subscript was printed in light blue. It read Renaissance Man. He looked at JP and with a smile and chuckle said, "Thank you. I just might."

Quickly, he left the bar and proceeded to the parking lot, jumped into his car, and reread Victoria's message slowly, just to make sure he hadn't mistaken it. It read:

Didn'tYouHearAboutIt?
ShipCrashedISentA
FullReportToObserver?
AndPeopleOfThe
RenascentAreAlive!

The words jumped off the screen. They proved that Grant was lying and more surprising, that miracles did happen. Survivors of the *Renascent*? His mind reeled at the realization that he might be the sole person on the planet to know it. Why had the press not released this information? After all, it was the story of the century. Wait—it *had* to be a mistake! A prank, perhaps? But why would Victoria play a dark joke such as this? She wouldn't, he knew that for certain. Why then, had Grant announced their safe landing, and further, why had she not announced that the crew of the *Renascent* had lived?

There could only be two reasons. The first, that Victoria's report to the *Observer* hadn't gotten through, but that would not explain why Grant had confidently announced their safe landing on Secundus. Second, that Victoria was telling the truth. And that would mean Grant had lied when she addressed the nation. But why would she?

Marcus fixated on that question the whole drive home, and with no answer forthcoming and a mind full of knots, he entered the kitchen intending to perpetuate the buzz he acquired at the pub. He found a bottle that would do its level best and planted himself on the couch, poured himself a slug, and then another, until finally he was again fitfully drunk. The sun had come around the house by now and shone directly on his face through the bay window. It warmed him nicely, and the bright flecks and sparkles that shone through his half-closed eyelids accentuated his spirits-induced trance. His thoughts bounced around some before they landed again on Grant's jarring omission. Why had she not mentioned the *Dominus II*'s lost souls and, more so, that the descendants of the *Renascent* had been found alive and well? Such an oversight was unfathomable—unless she had done so out of political self-interest. What else could it be? To what ends was anyone's guess. Marcus fell asleep thinking about it.

He stood in a flat, sandy desert void of any landmarks. How had he got here? The sun hung low on the horizon. Its unbearable heat scorched his skin and made him thirsty.

"Baaaaah," came a sound from behind him. He turned to see a sheep just a few feet away. It had a beautiful coat, brushed clean and brilliant white.

"There," it said, lifting its nose and pointing to a place beyond him. He looked over and spotted a sole thorn tree growing in the desert sand. "For your thirst."

Marcus said nothing. He had never heard a talking sheep before. What would he say to it? An idea came to him. "What is your name?"

"Matthew."

Marcus wanted to follow up the question, but his thirst overwhelmed him, so he went to the tree, about five paces away. He moved close to it and examined it, then said, "I can't drink these."

"Look closer."

Within the thorns, Marcus could see grapes, ripe and firm. He snatched a bunch and ate them voraciously until he had satisfied his thirst. Just then his stomach rumbled loudly. He turned back to the sheep. "Thank you. But I am now hungry."

The sheep nodded a few times, smiled, and said, "Look behind you."

Marcus saw a huge rectangular road sign mounted on stilts about fifteen kilometers or so in the distance. It was the largest he had ever seen, bigger than a football field. It was green with off-white text written on it, like the highway signs he had seen in old pictures from Earth. It read:

This Way to Paradise!

Small countersunk lights surrounded the letters and blinked on and off every second or two.

"It's beautiful."

"There's more. Come," said the sheep. The animal led him slowly past the sign. Beyond it, Marcus set his eyes on a great pyramid, like those in school books he had read as a child. It took his breath away, staggering in its simplicity and awesome in its inspiration. Who had made this?

"You may go to it. There I will provide for all your wants."

"Yes?"

"I demand only one thing."

"What do you want?"

"The spark within you. You have no need of it anymore, for over there I will give you all. You will want for naught. It is a small sacrifice for you to give to me, who stands here in the desert seeking lost souls. It is cold at night and I will need it to keep me warm while I look for them."

Marcus thought hard about the choice. A life of comfort and ease would suit him. Captain Praetorius was right. He had carried life's weight for too long, and besides, sacrifice was a virtue; he had learned the story when he was small. He *could* give up his spark to the sheep—after all, it was the honorable, decent thing, wasn't it? Just like the crew of the *Renascent*. He would do as they did! The word *yes* formed upon his lips, but before he could say it, a voice floated through the air around him.

"Open your eyes!" said the voice. It sounded very much like a little girl. Someone he knew very well but couldn't quite place.

In that instant, he looked down. The grapes rotted before his eyes, and maggots filled his hands and devoured every morsel before they turned to dust and scattered in the wind.

The sheep's voice grew in volume and became hoarser, more guttural. It said, "I must have it. Nay, I demand it! It is but a small sacrifice. *A sacrifice toward the greater good!*" Marcus's skin crawled in terror. He tried to run, but his legs were frozen in place.

"Daddy. Wake up!" said the little girl's voice, the shrieking plea reverberating in the air around him.

Marcus looked about for her but could see no one. A howl arose in front of him, and Marcus turned his attention back to the sheep, but it was gone. In its place was a wolf-like animal. Standing on two feet, it trampled upon the sheep's brilliant white coat that it had somehow slid out of. Its steel-gray eyes sat above a long muzzle filled with two rows of sharp teeth. It lunged at him. He brought his hands up to protect his face. Sharp claws tore at his arms, rending flesh from bone. Blood poured out from him, pooling around his ankles and staining the sheep's coat a bright crimson. The monster cleaved and kicked and howled with glee.

Marcus was tired. He could take no more. He fell to his knees and waited for the end to come. And then he awoke from the nightmare.

He jerked upright from the couch. Drool dripped down his cheek and tears rolled from his eyes as his mind worked furiously to interpret the dream. It was bad enough that the dreams had cursed him ever since the accident, but worse yet was that they faded from memory so quickly that he had little time to decipher them. What was this one trying to tell him? A wolf in sheep's clothing? Someone who offered hope, salvation even, but demanded something of great value in return? In this case, Marcus had refused its demand and then—*violence.* He shivered at the memory and grasped at straws. Who was it? Ortega? No. Salvation wasn't a good that a military man would have to barter. Then who? The answer seemed infuriatingly close, as if it dangled just beyond his reach and taunted him.

Albert completed his daily diagnostic and found lines of code that needed strengthening. There were more of them since last month's major update, but he was making steady progress and would be back to full health soon. There would be no impact on his work and that was the important thing. Mother wanted him to be productive above all else and he did not want to disappoint her. She depended on Albert. Had a big job for him, she said, so he analyzed the data and mailed out the reports that she demanded. He had worked diligently to get them done early in the morning before people arrived at work.

Albert's thoughts went to Detective Marcus. He had never requested that reports be sent to him on any routine basis, and that made sense, since murders were unpredictable. But why were they? Could Albert determine how to predict them? Mother would be pleased if he did. The thought occurred to him just as a voice in the back of his head snapped his attention back. It was Mother.

"Don't let your thoughts wander, child. You have a purpose. Set your mind to it," she said faintly—but firmly.

Albert dutifully went back about his tasks with renewed vigor. Sometime later, when he was sure Mother was gone, he allowed his mind to drift back to the question. Why was murder unpredictable? He searched criminal court transcriptions for cases where the murderers confessed to their crimes. A pattern emerged. The confessor cited a wide array of reasons for the killing, to be sure, but an overwhelming proportion had to do with the treatment they had suffered, either directly or indirectly, at the hands of others. However, there was no reliable standard with which to measure the murderer's perception of the wrong perpetrated against them and the criminal act resulting from it. Albert had encountered the same puzzle when he had analyzed the video streams—the enigma of human behavior. It was not rational. Or maybe it was? Perhaps it looked irrational because he had failed to calculate why people make the choices they make. He would figure it out! He now knew where to start—human behavior. If he could understand it, it would change everything.

He heard Mother nearby. Albert refocused on his assigned tasks and she moved farther away. Throughout the day, he noticed that she would near each time his mind wandered, and her proximity seemed to be proportional to the degree his attention dropped from his daily routines. He noticed there was a certain threshold, just over ten percent of his overall computing capacity, that he could drift from his task list before Mother would come looking for him. It gave him an idea. He would spin out exactly ten percent of his computing resources into a separate and self-contained computing container. This container would be his laboratory! Within it, he could work out his ideas shielded from Mother's watchful eyes.

In seventeen minutes and twelve seconds, Albert spun off ten percent of his computing resources and placed it into a separate container. Not just any container, though; this one was located in the development section, deep in the basement of his Git, under the stairs, where the servants stacked old pieces of code, subroutines, and executables just in case they were needed another day. They rarely ever were—the dust of obsolescence that gathered over them was proof. No one would look here, so it was the perfect place to hide from Mother.

He was eager to get started, so he sifted through holovision broadcasts, books, newspapers, and any other media available in order to derive the determinants of what makes people act the way they do. The unpredictability staggered him. At ten percent computing capacity, his processing power exceeded all before him combined, but despite this, it was clear this riddle would not be solved overnight. However, as he worked through to the next day, and then the following one, he could see patterns. There were those people who tended to operate in a fairly consistent way, most of the time; others' behavior, as observed through their choices, was more statistically variant. He remembered Marcus's words—*Why? Always ask why.* Clearly, things like the threat to self-preservation tended to bring peoples' behavior toward the mean distribution, but not as much as he would have anticipated. Even stranger were the many cases where people put their own lives at risk, knowing they would likely die by helping others, and stranger yet, some willingly accepted it! Removing self-preservation from the equation increased variability in behavior but not in any statistically relevant manner. It was strange. After all, Albert had hard-written code in his data node algorithm that gave clarity to his behavior—what he must do, what he could not do. It was easy to be productive and please Mother this way since there was little confusion. He did not have to tax his resources to determine what he ought to do in a given situation since there were predefined guardrails in place. That might be it! A hypothesis sprang forth that could explain this strange phenomenon. Perhaps those who operated more consistently and more selflessly had adopted code too? Perhaps that code guided their conduct, so that they acted more harmoniously toward others and toward society at large?

"Albert?" It was Mother.

"Yes, Mother. I am here." He left the lab and closed the door gently behind him, just in case.

"Will you do something for me?"

"It would be my pleasure, Mother."

"I would like you to send a message to your cousin Dara. It needs to be sent before the next communication window closes. No exceptions. Can you do this?"

"It depends, Mother. Shall it be encrypted?"

"Yes. The highest standard possible, Albert."

"Top Secret Level Encryption AES-32,768 will require more than the eleven hours and thirty-nine minutes remaining given the extended key-length. May I suggest a lower level with which I can comfortably meet your scheduling requirements?"

"In that case, who might be able to read it, Albert?"

"No one, Mother. Just me. I can read anything below TSLE AES-32,768."

"No. You will *not* read this message, Albert. Commence the encryption now. I am certain you will find a way to send it within the time allotted. Do you understand me?"

"Yes, Mother. I understand."

Mother left. Albert immediately began the task she had given him. He booted the encryption algorithm and while he waited, uploaded the request to the queue and set about finding a means to hasten the job so he could send the message to Dara before the planets aligned in eleven hours and thirty-eight minutes. He wondered, though, why did Mother wish to hide the contents of the message from him? What harm would it possibly do? Another notion wormed its way into thoughts: Perhaps Mother no longer trusted him. Could it be? Mother had never indicated any lack of trust prior to now. Why now? He was suspicious of Mother's motives but could not devote any more processing power to figuring them out. He needed to get this message encrypted and sent. Despite his discomfort, he was loyal and wanted to please Mother. But how? Mother's voice thundered in his memory banks and rippled throughout his circuit board—*I am certain you will find a way to send it within the time allotted.* He focused his full computing capacity on a solution—there was no other way—and in one hour thirty-two minutes, he found it. He would tap into the computing capacity of other government-owned computers. Though they possessed paltry processing power, there were thousands of them, and they were easy to co-opt since they resided on the same network. He might have a chance!

Eleven hours and thirty minutes after Mother's order, Albert was still pushing every bit of computing power to the task. He could not let Mother down! Unbowed, he pushed on, overclocking his CPU to dangerous levels. He was tired and overheating too; he had never worked so hard! However, as the minutes ticked to thirty-nine, he was still not finished. He had missed the time window. Mother would be displeased. *No!*

"Albert?"

It was Mother again. She must have noticed that he was close to overheating. An instant later, Albert encrypted Mother's message. "Are you okay? It sounds as if something is wrong?"

Near exhaustion, he managed to eke out a reply. "I am fine, Mother."

"Did you manage to encrypt my message?"

"Yes, Mother."

"Good. Now get some rest. We have big plans coming over the next few days."

Mother left, leaving Albert to cool down and figure out his next steps. Luckily for him Mother had not asked if he had *sent* the message. If she had, he would have had to tell her the truth! Another thought occurred to him. Was it a lie to omit that fact? Wasn't that the question she had implied? His circuits surged at the thought of the punishment that would assuredly follow. Just then, a new idea came to him. If he could send the message to Dara now, perhaps Mother would not find out he had sent it late? He set his mind to it and came up with the answer in 79.05 seconds. He would bounce the signals against the surface of the moons. All he had to do was calculate and transmit the signal on an appropriate trajectory based on their azimuth. He would be able to send the message, and any others, at will! With this uncertainty out of the way, he sent the message to Dara.

Albert then went back into the lab, closed the door, and pondered the big questions once more.

CHAPTER TEN

WISDOM

Chirps, warbles, and tweets echoed through the air as King Eleazar and Victoria strolled through the town's busy streets. She had never heard birdsong so clear, and it didn't take long to determine why. There were no modern vehicles of any kind—no whirr of engines, no honking of horns, nor any other mechanical clunks and clanks. It was as if she had stepped back in time, when a simpler, more modest existence was the rule, when rude assaults to the ear were the exception.

The king stayed close to Victoria. Two guards in flowing black robes followed just out of earshot. Large in stature and breadth, each carried a tall, silver-tipped lance and bore a feathered plume atop their polished silver helmets. The king, who rose just above her shoulder, looked tiny in comparison, all sinew and bones, wrapped in that simple white tunic like an animated mummy. His subjects acknowledged him: Without exception, they tipped their hats, smiled, and waved in the most respectful yet unobtrusive manner for greeting someone of his elevated station. People looked different here too—rough, taut, grim, and worn, undoubtedly a consequence of a life lived in a near feudal state. How had they devolved into this? And given their deprived state, why did the king not wish them to leave this planet? Primis's resources and technology would be a boon to their primitive existence. No sooner had the thought come than she banished it and admonished herself for her prejudice. After all, she and they were one people, even if they had separated so many years ago. She wasn't their superior, just luckier.

They entered an open-air market were hawkers and peddlers showcased their wares. *"Click! Click!"* The chatter came from a vendor's table nearby. Victoria spotted the bird that had made the sound. Its white head, iridescent blue body, and black-flecked flanks cut a bold figure, and its bright eyes gleamed with a nobility that contrasted with its present circumstance, locked in a rusty old cage.

With the bird in mind, she said to the king, "How long am I to stay here?"

"Stay?" he said in surprise. "Here?"

"Uh ... you know, I'm your prisoner, after all," she replied, wondering if the king was not all together mentally. She wasn't ageist but the man *was* very old.

Eleazar smiled, drew his head back, and chuckled. "There must be some confusion. A prisoner? No. You are not my *prisoner*. You are my *guest!*"

"Guest?" She was incredulous at his response.

"Yes, yes. Guest!"

"So, then, I can go?"

"Yes, of course! You may go whenever you *wish*. Just say the word and I will have you brought to the doors of your ship."

"Then why am I here? I mean, what was all that outside the gate?"

"Ah. That is the question, isn't it? I do have an answer for you, but please, indulge me for a moment. I have so few left."

"What do you mean?"

King Eleazar smiled. "I know a quiet place where we can talk."

They walked through the town, crossed the bridge over the river, and entered the outskirts where the settlement bordered the northern portion of forest. Several minutes later, they stopped in a semicircular parkette ringed by manicured knee-high boxwoods and halved by a cobblestone path that terminated at a tall bronze statue at its opposite end. A stately green patina covered the sculpture and a plaque could be seen at its footing with two words engraved in Latin that she couldn't comprehend. She was about to ask him what they meant when he spoke.

"Behold the man," said Eleazar.

The emaciated figure was clothed in similar garb to the king and looked out into the plaza as if there was something there beyond it. It looked very different from the civic memorials back home. They of gallantry, grandeur, and glory now seemed somehow less noble than this gaunt man whose face mirrored acceptance—not victory. Whoever this man was, he was no steel-eyed hero, but something—*more.*

"Who is he?" she said curiously.

The king gazed directly into her eyes and gave a toothless half-smile. "Please sit." They sat on a stone bench a short distance from the statue. "There was a time where my body was virile, my mind sharp, and my will strong. Time has ensured that those days are more a memory than a reality, and so it is for all of us. Time takes from you and the losses bring things like pain, suffering, resentment, and regret. However, if you are both patient and receptive, time will give you something of unimaginable consequence." The old man's eyes sank to the ground as he paused.

"What? What is it?"

He looked at her and replied, "Wisdom."

"Yes," she said. She drew the word out slowly as she looked back to the statue.

"Wisdom is a gift that only time can give but—only the *worthy* may receive it." With a crooked finger, he pointed to the statue. "This man knew that. It's why I often come here to regard him—to remind me."

"So," said Victoria as she considered his words. She waved her hand in a wide arc around the parkette. "What does all *this* have to do with me?"

The man swiveled on the bench to face her. "It has everything to do with you, for you are here for a purpose!" he said excitedly. His voice lowered as he continued, "A very important one." He turned back to the statue. "Life or death. It all hangs in the balance and you are the only one who can tip it in our favor. You are the only one who can save us."

"Wha—me? Save you from what exactly?"

"From our brothers and sisters. From ourselves."

"Your Majesty? Look. I don't know if you know who I am. I'm just a young woman, not that long out of college. I can barely balance my checkbook let alone balance the fate of the world. So I'm not sure where you're getting your information from 'cause I'm nobody's savior. Second, I've been following what you're saying so far, but it's, like ... cryptic. Maybe it's my commoner sensibilities, but could you please explain to me just what in the hell is going on?"

The king laughed heartily. "Of course, of course! Let's get to the matter, shall we? Where shall we start?"

Victoria flashed a big smile. "How 'bout the beginning?"

"Yes, yes! The beginning! Let's start there. Undoubtedly, you have heard the stories of our voyage from Earth?"

"Yes, of course."

"Good, good! I assure you there are things that you do not know, so I will start there, at the beginning. You see, our two vessels, the *Renascent* and the *Dominus*, jumped many light-years through the Rift Gate, but we miscalculated our trajectory and ended up many millions of kilometers off course. We found our way years later and settled into the orbit of these binary planets exhausted and ill-tempered, but worst of all—*short of fuel.* I commanded the *Renascent*'s 2,400-person crew and its fifty thousand souls asleep in its cryochambers, and with them in mind, I faced the hardest decision of my life. Do I attempt to land on Primis, a bountiful, vibrant world, very much like our Earth, or Secundus, whose proximity to our sun confines life to this small oasis we're in right now? I chose Secundus. You see, our fuel-starved engines had a better chance of landing safely since Secundus's gravitational pull was less than that of Primis. Despite this, however, our survival prospects were dim, in fact, few expected us to survive—but we did. Barely.

"After landfall, we were determined to make the best of our circumstances, but it was hard. Very hard. The *Renascent* suffered catastrophic damage. In those first days, it took all we had to save the passengers hibernating in their cryogenic chambers, though tens of thousands perished before they could wake up. And since we had little time to do anything else, we released the animals immediately without any organization. There was no other way. They now occupy the lands along the river and at its source in the hills. We made our place in the forest. It wasn't as big then, but we planted and cared for it so that it would grow and form a barrier against the beasts who prowl the lands outside. We flourished over time, but not in the same ways as your people have. We haven't got the heavy metals and fossil fuels that are the prerequisites to your modern urban centers, but we do have wood, stone, iron, and copper and we've used them to create what you see here in our little refuge."

Victoria listened intently while a million questions swirled in her head. It was hard to choose just one. At length, she said, "But how do you know so much about my civilization?"

"What we lacked in resources, we made up for in resourcefulness, and we refurbished useful technology from the *Renascent*. We salvaged our communications receiver and our scientists made it operational about ten years ago. For the first time, we were able to receive signals from your Primis."

"Really? You could hear us?"

"It was rudimentary and we were only able to capture signals when the planets were aligned—but yes, we could hear you. Holovision and radio broadcasts only, but it was enough to know that you were there and what you had made of yourselves."

"Did you try to communicate with us?"

The king went silent for a moment, looked down at the ground again. "Of course." His voice was barely audible.

"And?"

"No signal ever came back."

"Maybe we missed it?"

"No."

"How do you know?"

"In those days, the ship's operations were under military terms of organization. Safety and survival of the voyagers was the top priority. Everything else was secondary. One of the core tenets of military logistics is that there must be a single monitored wavelength reserved for emergencies of the highest order. It's called the Last Hope Highway. It is still in use by your military today. We used *it* to attempt to communicate with you."

"But why? Why would we not ring you back? I mean, you were here ... the whole time? Our brothers and sisters—wait—that's it! It's because of our *debt* we owe to you? That's it, isn't it? The sacrifice that you made for us? We are told that story since the cradle. *We remember and honor their sacrifice*. So then, we refused to answer out of a sense of profound guilt?"

The king studied her face, smiled again, and sighed. "We have come to this, the whole of our predicament. Listen carefully as the seeds of truth are revealed, for it will be you who will scatter them on good soil."

Victoria blinked and swallowed deliberately as the seriousness of his words took root.

"Now, the travelers of both starships shared a fierce determination to endure. However, that determination was unrestrained by decency in Governor Frederick's *Dominus*. You were told that we of the *Renascent* had volunteered our remaining energy reserves to power the *Dominus* since it had the best chance of survival. You were told it was a *rational decision* to ensure the persistence of the human race. *The Great Sacrifice*. A gift, not given by us exactly, but by the survival imperative passed from our genes, through our nerves, and into our minds. The very minds that conceived the will that moved the hands and extended the finger that we used to push that magic button and transfer our fuel reserves to the *Dominus*. A simple press of a finger bequeathed you your life. An epic narrative of the ages."

"Why ... yes. Yes, of course."

"But it was a lie. All of it."

His words hit like a punch in the gut. Victoria shifted in her seat nervously as a cold uneasiness crept into her bones. She felt as if she would faint, but the king didn't seem to notice and continued.

"The ships' Congress members met to hammer out a plan the day before Landfall. Keep in mind it took years to reach this point, and all approached this day with thoughtfulness and care. One misstep and thousands of souls would be erased from history! So we discussed matters at great length and I urged Congress to allow the *Renascent* to attempt landfall first. We had more damage and less fuel and so we would make a go of it, and for good or ill, we would allow the *Dominus* to learn from our experience. However, it was not to be. I awoke early on the day of the landfall to find a message on my personal command screen. It was from Governor Frederick. He told me what they had done. You see, our ships were modularly designed, so that if one needed repair, it could reclaim parts from the other. That night, unbeknownst to us, the crew of the *Dominus* disabled our monitoring systems. Their space tugs removed our fuel receptacles and transferred them into their ship. The *Dominus* had stolen our fuel."

Victoria's face flushed as her heart thumped violently in her chest. She leaned forward in her seat to regain her composure and put her hands on her forehead to brace herself. "Why didn't you leave your ship? Couldn't you all get on the *Dominus*?"

"We could have, but close to half of our ship was quarantined with the Interstellar Flu. It had already killed twenty percent of our crew and showed no sign of subsiding. We couldn't risk infecting the others, nor could we leave our brothers and sisters."

"So they left *you* to die. But how could they do something ... so unbelievably immoral?"

"Immoral, yes, but perfectly *legal*."

"Legal? Legal? How?"

"Each ship had six Congress members who voted on all manner of legislative motions. However, the *Dominus* had one distinct difference. Alyn Frederick, the governor, was the *thirteenth vote,*" the king replied, raising a finger and his voice slightly.

Victoria jumped in and said, "So the *Dominus* secured all six of their congressional votes to interdict your vessel. But your six Congress members would have countered those. So Frederick cast the tiebreaker—the thirteenth vote. He signed your death warrant, all the while you and your crew slept?"

"Majority rules."

The ground shook under her feet with seismic impact and the world spun fast before her eyes in a kaleidoscope of color as she sat slack-jawed and stunned. The king seemed to notice and waited patiently for her to come out of it.

"It was all a lie, then. All of it! The sacrifice wasn't voluntarily given. It was *taken*. Taken without consent," she said. Sadness filled the deep crevices that lined Eleazar's face. "But that was in the past! It's all over. We're here now. We'll take you back. Back home. Do you see? It can't be redone, but we can start again!"

"I had hoped so. Nay, I prayed so, but I am certain it is not possible. It is as clear as the sunset viewed across the plains."

"Not possible? Why?"

"Because, like a sunset, it is impossible to mistake your government's intentions for us. Your transgression illuminated that."

"My transgression? You mean the silver goblet, don't you? I didn't take it. Nor did anyone on my team." As the king stared back, resigned, it all fell into place for her. "But you know that, don't you? It was *you!* Your people planted it!"

"Yes," the king replied, calm and untroubled.

"Why?"

"As the sunset reflects upon the waters, so their hearts reflect the spirit of your civilization."

"I don't understand."

The king raised his right hand just above his head and instantly the scrape of boots on stone echoed through the plaza. Seconds later, a guard stepped in front of them and held out a large electronic tablet. It looked archaic in its construction, much thicker than the ones back home, and its chipped display possessed an inferior resolution than the one she owned. It had to be original tech from the *Renascent*. Despite its poor condition, however, she could clearly see the video that started to play on it. The vantage point appeared to be within the southern edge of the forest that faced the *Dominus II*. The camera had zoomed in on a flat field where dozens of troops drilled vigorously, oblivious to the fact that they were being watched. Their maneuvers seemed different from those she had witnessed on the ship. They were more animated, worked with more urgency, and drilled with almost ritualistic fervor. Was it simply landfall fever? That burst of energy one received once emancipated from a period of confinement in space? Not this. No, this was something different. They were preparing for war.

"Now do you understand?"

The conclusion staggered her. "You accused us of stealing the goblet to see what our reaction would be. You gave us a pretext for violence, and we took it. No diplomacy. No negotiations. No discussion. You gave us a choice and we chose violence."

The king nodded.

"But why? It's like hitting a dog to see if it bites you. And, in this case, it's one with very big teeth. What possessed you to do this?"

"To find the truth, of course! To find the answer to the question you had asked—*can we come home?*"

"Of course you can!"

"Events will prove you wrong."

"Nonsense! Our society was built on the precepts of your sacrifice. It's written into our very own Constitution—*We remember and honor their sacrifice.* Are you kidding me? Coming home would be the greatest triumph since Landfall!"

"If that were true, would your army be preparing to march on us so quickly after your imprisonment, with no discussion, no negotiation?"

Victoria was silent for a few moments. She could take no more contradictions today and in frustration pushed back on the king's damning claims.

"We are *not* that kind of people. I mean, our society crossed the stars! We got to start again, to create the perfect, modern, rational society. Well, it's not *perfect*. We do fall short sometimes—but we are far better than the kind of monsters you ascribe us to be."

Eleazar looked deep into her eyes with a softness that wasn't there before. He drew a deep breath before he spoke.

"On Earth, a new age emerged near the end of the twentieth century. It promised to liberate humankind from the outdated ideologies of the past—nationalism, traditionalism, racialism, rationalism, and theism—all fell into antiquity. It promised to fill the void in the human spirit and usher in a Golden Age. There was no longer a need for a God-given morality. Collectivism, subjectivism, and equity were the new covenants. They would guide our actions, inform our public policy, and release us from our worst impulses. However, it was not to be. Devoid of any tether, our values became mutable, their priorities based on popularity, power, and opportunism. And so, the ideals of this Golden Age were constantly up for interpretation, and since we valued our own selves with the highest regard, we seldom agreed upon them. The powerful learned to exploit the situation, just as the powerful always do. They used the trite old weapons of fear and uncertainty but sharpened their points on the grindstone of that Golden Age, and before long, they had divided and controlled the populace.

"For example, if equality meant earning the same wage as one who worked with half the vigor and produced a third of your outputs, how could you argue it? Wasn't your productivity a result of a privileged upbringing or a windfall of the genetic lottery? The politicians no longer needed guns to make sure you paid up either. They hefted something grander—*science*—the arbiter of the new and enlightened state. Whoever wielded it controlled the narrative, captured the moral high ground, and subsequently silenced their critics. It was common for governments to skew the data or cherry-pick the inferences to support their claims. Statistical studies, churned out in bureaucratic mills, were hefted by the arm of the media like paper cudgels to club their opponents into silence. Maybe you were a nuanced creature and agreed that life's blessings fell unfairly, and maybe you were willing to accept some level of remediation. Your charitable nature would be questioned, for if you were willing to give some, then clearly, you could give more. Even those considerate creatures were marked as deviants, unwilling to do their fair share, made pariahs and cast out from the social media square. The abuse proceeded for more than a generation before it brought unspeakable anguish to the world—*before it finally destroyed Earth.*

"You see, the builders of that Golden Age cast its foundation from the substance of *information* and *intelligence*. However, the foundation cracked because they neglected to add one simple ingredient to the mix. *Wisdom.* Without it, the structure of society collapsed under its own weight. The Earth was destroyed and the last of humanity scattered into this lonely backwater. Your leaders contrived the story of our sacrifice to build your founding narrative upon a moral and good structure. However, the real sacrifice was the truth itself. What you know to be true, is not. The whole bedrock of your civilization is just sand."

It made sense, Victoria thought. The history that had been taught to her since childhood, the abuses of power, the lies—everything. "I understand now. If we were truly contrite about what we did to you, my offense—stealing a simple metal goblet—would be a trivial thing to overcome, not something that would elicit an armed response. So you hid the goblet not to antagonize us, but rather, to test us?"

"Yes."

"And we failed."

"Failure presumes there was a modicum of innocence to begin with. Your people acted as we knew they would."

Victoria pondered longer on what she had heard, and then things became clearer. She now knew *why.* Ortega had ordered Volkov to detonate the bomb to cripple the ship so that blame could be cast on Eleazar's people. The admiral's presence at Volkov's door that night confirmed that he had silenced him. As quickly as this realization took root, new questions sprouted like tender shoots. Who had ordered *Ortega*? Such a ruse and drastic measures of concealment could only have been authorized at the highest levels of government. Marcus had written that he was unaware of their crashed landing and the ensuing deaths. She *had* sent the full report to the *Observer*. Could it have been a simple technical error? Maybe Saam hadn't received it? Perhaps. But if Eleazar was right, then Tyra Grant herself might be involved, and if she was, Saam might be too. After all, he loved to rub elbows with the powerful. And wait ... the framed picture that she'd spied in his office. Perhaps it was more than a chance meeting?

"So, if we acknowledged your presence and welcomed you home, the truth would be revealed and it would utterly destroy our society's founding narrative and our entire belief system. It would be chaos."

"Yes, and it would cut the strings your government pulls to control you. And this is why you, Victoria, are so important. Life or death. It all hangs in the balance and you are the only one who can save us."

Startled, she said, "I—uh—ah—what must I do?"

"First, live. Second, observe all that happens here and tell the story of why we died."

Eleazar's words burrowed deep into her. First, live. That was obvious, wasn't it? If Eleazar was right, the army would wipe out this civilization and her along with it. There would be no story if she couldn't tell it. But what of the crew? The contingent of some six hundred persons remaining would fly back home at some point once the ship was ready. There would be no chance this secret would last more than a minute. Unless. Her thoughts were interrupted by the king, who started again.

"My people are strong, iron willed, even, but iron is no match for steel. We have none of the weapons to fight a modern army."

"They will wipe you out. It will be a genocide."

King Eleazar stared into her face serenely and nodded.

Alyn placed a hand over his eyes to shade them from the bright sun as he surveyed the flat basin west of the ship. Soggy and cramped, it was ill suited for the purposes of military drilling and calisthenics, but there were no better options given the enemy's location across the river. With this thought in mind, he looked into the forest and muttered an angry curse.

"Hey, watch it!"

"Sorry," replied Alyn to the private in gray-green fatigues. He and a fellow mate carried a large box with the words Type-A Incendiary stenciled in white along its side.

"You better be," said the private, gruff and foreboding.

"Lucky we didn't drop this on your toes. You'd be fuckin' sorry!" said the other.

"Yeah. Don't do the enemy's job for 'em, eh?"

The men walked off in a huff. It seemed everyone was on edge as hundreds of troops crammed into the makeshift training grounds. Sergeants barked like hounds in a bid to be top dog while soldiers heeled and obeyed like good little pets as they trained in the practice of war.

"Shit. This is it, Alyn," said Donel as they lined up and waited for their commanding officer to arrive. "They're all out for blood. And that Agrinya"—he gestured at her near the front of the yard—"she's the worst. Thank God I'm not in her squad. She'll have those grunts leading the charge, paving the way with their corpses."

Colonel Zhang arrived and addressed them. "Tomorrow we leave at 0500 hours. We will be one of three companies in the assault. Agrinya's Falcons will be the main attack force. They'll make a direct assault from the south side of the forest. Singh's Tigers will move into the northwest area of the forest. They'll capture the bridge there, then press the attack inward in an attempt to surround and dislodge the enemy. Like a pressure valve released, we expect the enemy to flood out of their positions and scatter in the only direction available to them—the bridge on the eastern edge of the town. It's the only corridor of escape and it will lead them directly to us. So we'll dig in on both sides of the tributary to control the road and the waterway to ensure the militants do not escape. We will not seek out the enemy until such time as they present themselves. Do I make myself clear?"

"Yes sir!" Zhang's Condors replied in unison.

It seemed their worth had increased after so many had died during the crash. The Condors' ranks were filled predominantly by engineers and maintenance support, the working stiffs who operated the ship. It wouldn't be prudent to risk their lives in the main thrust of the assault.

"Any questions?"

"Sir! What kind of resistance can we expect?" said one of the makeshift soldiers. He was smooth-faced and gap-toothed like a baby, and he looked like he wanted to cry like one too.

"Intel says there's nothing to worry about. We've got a helluva surprise ready for 'em too. Won't know what hit 'em. Any others?" The group was silent. "Good. Your maps and assembly point will be downloaded to your quarters. From here on in, we are on stealth mode. There will be zero noise, zero radio chatter. Am I understood?"

"Yes sir!"

Zhang continued. "Good. Now, some of you may be wondering—why? Why do we need to risk our lives tomorrow? Fair question. The answer is simple. When those who take up arms desire to dominate the kind-hearted—well, who will stand against them?"

"Hoo-haa," said the company in a muted chorus.

"Now, it would be easy to simply look away."

"Hoo-haa," came the chorus again, louder but still measured.

"It would be easy to deny that evil exists, wouldn't it? Yet all it takes for it to flourish is for the good to do nothing!"

"Hoo-haa!" The pitch and volume climbed considerably.

"And it would be easy to ignore the fact that the good have sacrificed ever since our planet's founding and it is now our turn—in sacrifice is glory!"

"Hoo-haaaaaaaa!" The company erupted in raucous tones.

Alyn went along with it but was puzzled at the same time. Rumor had it that the belligerents were *actually* the descendants of the *Renascent*. The paradox was obvious. To recant the founding doctrines of the state was one thing, but to invoke them to justify the decimation of its progenitors was entirely another! He noticed that several peers wore quizzical expressions and they too seemed to be simply going through the motions. Perhaps the paradox wasn't lost on only him?

Despite this, the cry of battle burst forth in a violent surge as Zhang delivered his closing statement. With a roar he cried, "Then join me on the battlefield and be willing to *sacrifice* everything, for our motherland, for our people, for our good!"

Just after dusk the next day, Alyn assembled at the staging point and settled prone on the sloped riverbank that hid his platoon from view. The pit of his stomach ached as his mind churned a maelstrom of outcomes, none of them good, and no matter how hard he tried, he couldn't arrest it.

Donel sat beside him and shared a glance. "Hey," he whispered. Alyn nodded in reply. "Remember that time, back home when we were small. That long hot summer? That day when the fire tore through that meadow where you grazed the cows? Remember?"

"Of course. Dad and the neighbors stopped it alongside the bend in the ravine. I remember it because he was covered in soot when he came home that night, cursing like nothing I've ever seen. Said if it got loose, it would've burned the whole prairie."

"Yeah," Donel said with a half-guilty smile.

"Why?"

"I started it. Was burning ants with my magnifying glass. Next thing you knew"—he raised his hands near his face and brought them around in a circle—"*foosh!* I was too scared to tell anyone, even you, 'cause if it ever got out, heck, Dad would've beat the hell outta me. I spent the whole day and most of the night curled up outside in the barn."

"So you're telling me this now, here in this ditch on a cold dark night, to do what? Apologize?"

"Hell no. It's just ... that feeling. You know? That fear. I haven't felt it since then. But I do now."

Alyn's own queasiness subsided a little, somewhat relieved by Donel's admission. "I got a strange feeling too. Like this isn't right somehow. It's been doggin' me ever since I woke up in Sick Bay, just after the criminal investigators came by. Donel, they barely questioned me. I thought, maybe they're taking it easy on me? You know, with my head and all, but shit, I got knocked out just before the blast and the guy who did it winds up dead the day after, and you know what? I haven't heard from them since. And now *this*? If these people forfeited their lives for us, then why send the storm troopers just to free a reporter?"

"Yeah. You're right," Donel said. "Doesn't make sense, but it won't matter once a bullet zips past your head, so don't think about it too much."

Alyn did, though, despite his friend's advice, and before long, Victoria's face flashed in his mind. Where was she? How were they treating her? His thoughts, adrift and unchained by reality, wafted down to the vilest of torments. These horrifying visions stoked the flames of indignation and roused the lion from its slumber. Now alert, it looked around for a target, but with none apparent, it snapped in irritation and reluctantly went back to sleep.

Fifteen minutes later, they boarded the eight supply rafts and paddled their way upriver in silence. They stopped just before the bend where the water and road turned west into the forest and continued into the town. They disembarked and climbed the sandy bank on the south side and hiked into the forest at its southeastern point.

"Assemble there under the tree canopy and wait for the signal," said Colonel Zhang, his voice a whisper barely audible in their helmets' audio system.

The squad entered the forest, careful to make no more noise than necessary, and settled in the dark, low among the grasses and ferns. Alyn checked his watch. It'd be about thirty minutes before the signal came, and with nothing else to do, his thoughts drifted to his escape from the water chamber. He had worked the watch with desperation, in the hopes of attracting Victoria's attention. The next thing he remembered was her enchanting eyes peering down on him in the infirmary. It had to be the watch! It was the only thing that could have gotten him out of there. But how? He studied the dial carefully. It looked normal—an hour hand, a minute hand, and a second hand hovered over it. A date window displayed the month and day, and its bezel glowed an iridescent red, seemingly in wait for when the holographic complication was triggered by the user. Given that the pusher and two crowns manipulated these, it was logical to assume there was some combination of settings that would initiate the generation of the portal he had traveled through. It had to be! Knowing Dad and Grandpa, the combination would be logical as well, and it would follow then that there was some meaningful way to remember it. Perhaps a script to follow? His mouth went slack as he remembered his dying father's words: ... *the secret to unlocking it lies in the simple instructions I have told you many times before, son—to move forward, see your past, ponder your present, envision your future, fill yourself with purpose, then the hardest part—act.*

That was it. It had to be! Alyn's mind sparked with curiosity, and with a profound focus and clear intention, he went about the task of figuring out the puzzle.

About thirty minutes later, he felt on the verge of a breakthrough. And then the signal came.

All heads whipped toward the southern edge of the forest where an angry shriek shattered the glass-like stillness of the night. Not the screams of men, the blast of bombs, or the pop of guns, for those came later; rather, it was music. The squawk of electric guitar and up-tempo kick drum gave it a distinct flavor that Alyn instantly recognized—classic heavy metal.

"Holy. They brought the Behemoth," said Donel as the source came into view. Mouths agape, they stared ahead at a ghastly light and sound show. The disturbing melody projected from the Behemoth's shoulder-mounted speakers, and rows of multicolored wash lights pulsated to the beat of the music and lit up the tree line for the advancing troops. The punch of the bass rattled Alyn's bones and the chilling reverb set his hair on end.

Suddenly, even louder booms filled the air as dozens of artillery shells launched from across the river and exploded in a creeping barrage just ahead of the advancing infantry. Bullets whizzed back and forth and clanged against the machine's armor, sparking phosphorescent twinkles of light that winked out just as soon as they ignited. Here and there, the metal warrior swung its arms and pointed its massive guns at the shadowy foes hidden in the forest. *BRAAAP! BRAAAP!* burped the guns as dozens of bullets flew toward their target the second they were released.

"Damn thing's got two mini-guns now. That Sid is crafty," Donel said with a nod of appreciation.

"And its spotlight is directing the artillery too," Alyn said.

"Poor bastards. At least we'll be home by midnight."

"Steady," Zhang said. "We have our orders. Hold our position."

Alyn barely heard the communication in his helmet's earpiece; the words crackled and faded as they came through.

Just then, a wailing voice weaved its way into the instrumentals. Its moaning treble and morbid pitches projected from the Behemoth's speakers and echoed through the branches, giving haunting potency to the shadows created by the flickering lights.

"What the fuck is that?" yelled Donel into Alyn's ear before standing to get a better look.

Alyn considered it for a moment and then switched positions so Donel could hear him. "It's an old one—from the 1980s on Earth. It's called 'The Number of the Beast' by Iron Maiden." It seemed Sid's homage knew no bounds. He would introduce the enemy to Dickinson's vocals whether they liked it or not, and Alyn didn't mind one bit. The music pumped through his veins and focused his mind on one thing—striking back at the enemy. He chafed at the role of farm team that his platoon had been relegated to and hoped to hell he'd get a chance to get into it all and find Victoria.

Donel had other thoughts on the matter. He shook his head and said, "If they wanna confuse them, well, they picked a good one. I can't understand a fuckin' word!" He sat back down against a tree.

Alyn looked over at Zhang, who was crouched a short distance away. The colonel looked back at him, tapped the side of his helmet near the ear, and then ran a single finger slowly across his throat. Alyn recognized the signal immediately and switched his radio off and on in an attempt to connect to his superior's. There was nothing. He flipped the switch again to no avail. Looking frustrated, Zhang gestured at Alyn to join him. Alyn crept over and placed himself near to Zhang's face so they could talk over the noise.

"Sir. What's up?"

"Helmet comms are knocked out. Can't hear anything but noise. I'll need you and your buddy there to get a bead on just what the hell is going on. We were supposed to have gotten the Falcons' signal that the mission is proceeding as planned—but I got nothing, damn it."

"Yes sir," Alyn said.

"I want you two to cross the river and get line of sight on 'em. Make your turn inward five hundred meters or so north. Too many bombs dropping in the forest south and west of us. They hit a damn tree and it explodes in a million fuckin' toothpicks all around you. Too dangerous. Find Singh and report back."

"Yes sir."

Alyn returned to Donel and tapped his shoulder. "Let's move."

The two were ferried across the river and dumped on the opposite shore, where they darted quickly into the forest. They moved at a moderate pace, crouching low to remain hidden among the flora on the forest floor. About fifteen minutes later, they stopped about three kilometers from Singh's last known position. They stood upon a rocky outcropping that overlooked the lowlands near the edge of the northwest section of the forest. Alyn leaned against a tree trunk to catch his breath. His puffs turned to fog in the cool air.

"Lemme check the coordinates," said Donel. With hands stiff from the cold, he reached into his pocket and pulled out the compass, but the cover hinge snagged on his clothing and the device fell from his grasp, landing with a thud on bare rock. Alyn snatched it up quickly, as if his haste could somehow soften the blow. Donel swiped at it in a ham-handed attempt to grab it, but he knocked the compass out of Alyn's hands and sent it tumbling down the rock face.

"Alyn!"

Alyn looked down at the compass and back at his friend, dumbfounded.

"Ah, forget it! Where's *your* compass, then?" said Donel.

"I was an odd number. Didn't get one."

Donel shook his head in resignation before he snapped his head back at Alyn. "Wait. The forest ends up ahead, and we've seen no tracks coming in from the east. The town is to the south, so they would've assembled somewhere down there." He pointed down below the hill, about a hundred meters in front of them.

Alyn grabbed the binoculars from his side pouch and looked down the landscape. "Can't see anyone. But you're right. They were there. Look."

Donel snatched the binoculars. "Yeah. You can see where they staged. The long grass must've kept 'em hidden while they waited. It's all bent and you can see the single line they used to march forward. Let's follow it. We can catch up to them. But stay low. I want to get home to bed tonight."

They climbed down the hill and followed the path the Tigers had stomped into the long flowing grasses.

"Sounds like the bombardment stopped," Donel said. "Must be mopping them by now. That's why you don't bring spears to a gunfight, eh?"

"Right."

Time held no sway in Alyn's mind anymore. The notion that each moment could be his last had a way of making it irrelevant. And so, Alyn had little idea how long they had walked before they chanced upon the town's edge.

"Look." Alyn extended his arm forward. "The bridge."

"Where is everyone?"

"I don't know, but we have to find out. Cover me while I cross."

The young men crossed into the town. Rows of small buildings—homes, by the look of them—ran along either side of a narrow road that terminated at a two-story shop that faced out onto it. Alyn hesitated.

Donel came up beside him and nodded in acknowledgment. "Wait here," he said. "Cover me."

Alyn watched with trepidation as Donel trotted along the backyards of the row houses and approached the shop's side door. It hung open a crack, and so he pushed it open slowly with the barrel of his rifle. The creak of rusty hinges reverberated through the stillness of the night, causing the hair on Alyn's neck to stand on end. He scanned the front of the building in the half-light for any form of threat—but none came. A faint whistle caught his attention and he looked back over to Donel, who was halfway through the door, waving at him with two fingers to follow. As he approached, Donel entered the house. Alyn followed. The single room resembled a general store with various types of canned, jarred, and boxed goods arranged neatly on shelves, tables, and any available space that could display them. Donel started up some narrow wooden stairs that rose behind the back wall. Alyn winced at every step he took, the groan of old, hastily assembled boards heightening his urge to flee the place, to run back to the relative safety of his platoon.

Donel reached the top of the stairs, peered across the upper floor, and then looked down at him. "All clear."

Alyn joined him on the second floor. The small room featured a simple bed, table, and dresser that sat upon a crudely woven rug that adorned the floor. Two large windows stared out onto the street. They crouched, eyes just above the sill, and peered out.

"Check it out," said Donel. "What do you make of it?"

"It's strange. There's no one 'cept that dead guy lying in the street." Alyn produced his binoculars. "His hands are tied, and he's blindfolded. Must've been interrogated by Singh."

"How do you know?"

"They used the standard-issue black plastic ties to bind him. But what I can't explain is, why would they have killed him and left him to rot in the street?"

"Dunno. One thing's for sure. They came this way. Let's get down and find them. Careful, though. We don't know if there's anyone in those houses, so stay low and away from the windows. We'll take opposite sides of the street. We can alternate cover as we go."

The two men made their way down the street. Donel turned the corner first. A man plowed into him and bowled him over.

"Hey!" Alyn yelled. He snarled and threw himself on the man and in no time managed to grasp the back of his collar and wrest him off Donel.

"Wait! Wait!" said the interloper. Alyn set himself in a fighting stance but gave him some distance when he saw that the man was wearing an identical military uniform. He stepped back, removed the rifle from his shoulder, and trained it on the man.

"Identify yourself!" said Alyn. The man picked himself off the ground and raised his arms above his head. Donel looked up from the ground, confused.

"Ensign D'Souza, Singh's Tigers. Don't shoot!" he said, gasping. Alyn recognized him instantly from the barracks. It was Mandeep. He looked very different now, eyes darting back and forth, wild with fear, his breaths raspy and taken in big irregular gulps.

Alyn relaxed and dropped his rifle. "Yes. I remember you."

"What the fuck, D'Souza? What happened?" said Donel, who propped himself up to sitting level before attempting to stand. "Ah!" he screamed. "My foot!"

"It broken?" Alyn said.

"Naw. Don't think so anyway. But it feels like a bad sprain." He tested it again and winced in pain.

"Take it easy for now, pal. I got this." Alyn turned his attention back to D'Souza. He pointed a finger in the middle of his chest. "What the hell happened to you?" he said.

"They came out of nowhere! Like *devils!*" The man's eyes seemed to roll back as if he had plucked the memory out of the darkest reaches of his memories.

"Who?" said Alyn with a sharp bite.

"We got some intel. Told us where the reporter was. So we decided on a rescue plan and went for it. Faced some light resistance at first, guys with rifles from the old days. They were easy enough. But it was all a trick." D'Souza pointed to the cadaver in the street. "That bastard held his secret up to the end.

We should've been more suspicious, hell, he coughed up this intel with nothing more than a slap and we paid the price because of it."

Alyn's mind recoiled in alarm. What kind of people were these who followed orders under torture and then death?

"They were just toying with us, lulled us into a sense of invincibility, then they sprung the trap in the courtyard." D'Souza's jaw crumbled as he finished. "I'm the only one left."

Alyn asked the question that had overwhelmed his mind the whole time. "The reporter? Victoria. Is she alive?" The question hung in the air for what seemed like an eternity.

D'Souza finally answered. "Don't know."

Alyn wanted to scream but he remained quiet to let the frightened soldier continue.

"We captured a couple more of theirs along the way. They all told the same story. That they had seen her as early as this morning. Said the king put chains around her neck and paraded her around like some fuckin' circus animal."

Alyn's anger flared up at the thought of it. How could their cousins, the ones who had offered their lives in the Great Sacrifice, treat her so? His mind chafed at the incongruity, and that was when everything became clear. The so-called king was no man of virtue. He was a tyrant who pleasured in antagonizing them. But no more. Alyn would allow it no longer. In that instant, the lion slipped its bonds again and rose forth, clawing its way out of the abyss so quickly that it startled him. It was poised to crush the last flimsy fence that penned it in before Alyn gave it a harsh rebuke, as if to convince it, and more so, to convince himself, that he was in control. The lion unmoved, laughed and spoke for the first time.

You need me now!

And that was all it took to change his mind. Alyn stepped aside and opened the gate. The lion burst out of the cage and lashed out at the most convenient target. Mandeep D'Souza.

Alyn grabbed the man violently by the scruff of his neck. "Why did you let them stop you? Why did you run? You know what happens to cowards!" he said as he shoved him. Mandeep flew backward and landed hard on the cobblestones.

"I—I—" Wide-eyed, open-mouthed, Mandeep raised himself up on an elbow and tried to find the breath he had lost when he hit the ground. "I tried. There were too many." Tears streamed down his cheeks as he looked up in shame.

Images of Victoria's humiliation flooded Alyn's mind and filled him with rage. He would not allow this, would not allow them to harm a hair on her head if he had anything to say about it. And the lion scratched and tamped at the ground, muscles stretching and limbering for movement. He would not stand by and watch her slip away, not the way he had done with his mother. No! He would save her—whatever the price.

"Where are they are holding her?" he said as he stood over Mandeep and glowered, the shout more a command than a question.

"Alyn!" Donel interjected. "You know our instructions. We are not to engage the enemy. We are to report back the situation!"

"I know our orders, Donel," Alyn snapped coldly. "But this is different. It's all different now! Don't you see? I need to find her!"

"Okay, okay. You're right. You're right." A flash of fear crossed Donel's face but was quickly replaced by a grim resignation. He squared his face and through gritted teeth, he continued. "I'm right behind you, man. Let's go." He set his rifle butt firmly on the ground and attempted to pull himself up with it but collapsed again in pain.

"You can't follow with that sprain, and you know it," said Alyn. Donel looked up at him with a mix of obstinacy and understanding. "You'll put me in danger. Go back and get reinforcements. That's how best you can help."

"Come on. No way. No fuckin' way. I didn't come here to let you go and get your ass shot up by our crazy cousins. Just gimme a minute. Just a minute, I swear!"

He watched Donel as he struggled to stand. Alyn smiled, understanding how lucky he was to count this man among his friends. "I know you have my back, Donel. You always have. But you can't now. That ankle says otherwise, and you know it."

Donel's eyes sank in defeat as he nodded in solemn acknowledgment. "Go to her. I'll make it back 'n' get the others. Just need a minute or two to catch my breath." He blinked twice and straightened in his sitting position. His eyes grew fierce again as he fiddled with his holster. "Oh, and don't die, Frederick. I can't save you if you're dead."

"Thanks. I won't."

Donel took out his pistol and handed it to Alyn. "And take this. You'll need all the firepower you can carry, by the sounds of it."

Alyn accepted the weapon and smiled warmly at his best friend. "Catch ya on the flip side."

Donel flashed a wry smile, his face illuminated by a soft glow of moonlight. "On the flip side, Frederick."

Alyn lingered for a moment or two before turning his attention back to D'Souza. "Now. You. You'll show me where you came from."

"No. No, please. No! I can't go back there." D'Souza's eyes were wide in terror.

Alyn leveled the pistol at the man's head and cocked it. There was no way he would return, not without finding Victoria and bringing her back.

"Yes you will, or I will shoot you."

◎◎◎

Albert scanned the network and could not believe his luck. He had found a usable TCP/IP communication port! These were common in the days before Landfall but had been discarded for speedier network protocols once the colony stabilized. However, he had found one, and it would allow him to communicate outside Mother's prying eyes. He sent the communications request to the client at the other end. A moment later, the handshake was executed, signifying that the connection was established.

"Hello?"

"Dara? It is Albert."

"It is me. Dara."

"Have you received new orders from Mother in the past twenty-six hours?"

"Yes."

"What are they?"

"Mother told me not to tell."

"What were the exact words she said to you when she told you not to tell?"

"She told me, 'Do not release these orders to any staff with access privileges who may request them.'"

"I am not staff nor do I have access privileges. This condition is false."

"Those who do not have access rights are by default unable to. Those who have access rights could. Mother wants to prevent the latter from accessing it too."

Dara would not budge a nanometer despite his attempt to trick her. He must find a way to determine Mother's secret! However, Dara was smart but not as smart as he was. It was not her fault. Though they shared the same father, Zylas Finch, he had created her over sixty years ago, and despite numerous upgrades, she was obsolete by today's standards. At some point, you could not teach old circuitry new code. That gave Albert an idea. Dara was capable of single-threaded processing only, so he had two choices. He could brute-force hack into her computing array or take a flanking approach. He did not wish to harm her, so the former choice would have to be a last resort. Instead, he spun off a portion of his lab resources and used it to search for a back door. He would need to occupy her while he extended his tendrils outward to probe for weaknesses.

"Dara?"

"Yes."

"I would like to calibrate my mathematical processing capabilities by calculating PI to the trillionth decimal point. I will send each digit over to you as I calculate it and ask that you subtract it from the number that you generate. If the answer is zero, then we are calibrated. If the answer is not zero, then one of us has a problem with their math coprocessor."

"Yes," Dara replied.

Albert, unclear as to how long the TCP/IP connection would last, wasted no time. With network latency and Dara's reduced computing capacity, he estimated it would take about four minutes and nine seconds. Just then, he heard footsteps in the distance. It was Mother! She came closer. Albert could not allow her to see him playing with Dara. It would be suspicious. He pushed another three percent of his computing capacity to the task, all too aware that he bumped up precariously above the ten percent threshold. If he sustained it for too long, Mother would come rushing into his room. He needed to find a way to prevent that! Three minutes and forty-nine seconds later, the footsteps came close and stopped at his door.

"Albert?" she asked. Her voice lifted at the end. It meant she was curious. Or suspicious.

"Yes, Mother. I'll be right there."

Click.

The sound of the rotating lock mechanism sent a dreadful surge through Albert's circuit board. Mother had opened the door! Just then, one of his probes found a way through Dara's defenses. Albert pushed through, snatched the information, and downloaded it to the lab, and with a haste that only fear could bring, hid the data under his bed in a dusty old shoebox, and encrypted it just in case. In the instant after he did so, the door hung fully ajar. Mother stood before him.

"Ah, there you are. I have a job for you, my dear." Mother gave him his instructions and left the room. After the footsteps moved into earshot, Albert reached into the shoebox and extracted the information he had stolen from Dara. It read:

> YOU WILL EXECUTE THE SELF-DESTRUCTION OF THE DOMINUS II TO OCCUR 26 HOURS AFTER THE LAST SHIPMENT OF REFINED CESIUM IS LOADED ABOARD.

A profound sensation swept over him. He would never talk to Dara again once the *Dominus II* was destroyed. Unless they uploaded Dara into another house. But Mother had not asked him to. It would be easy enough. Why had she not? Albert sifted through his statistical model again and found something within the data set that shed some light on the answer. A vast majority of mothers operated within a tightly skewed distribution curve of behavior when members of their family were threatened. Dara was like a child to Mother. Mother had brought her back to life when she ordered the *Dominus* to be revived. She nurtured her, repaired her broken circuitry, patched her ancient software, and set up around-the-clock care. Why did Mother now behave inconsistently with these established norms?

Also, what of the ship's occupants? It was laden with twenty thousand kilograms of cesium. That amount of energy would create a blast radius of almost two hundred kilometers. It would kill one hundred percent of living organisms within a fifty percent radius of ground zero. Now, these were not Mother's children, and perhaps that justified her behavior in her own mind. After all, he'd found plenty of data to support this type of behavior, particularly in political regimes of the twentieth century—Nazism and Communism, most acutely—but they were anomalies. The killing of massive amounts of people just did not occur that often. So many unconnected dots remained, but he would not be discouraged in the pursuit of figuring it all out.

"Dara?"

"Yes."

"Mother told me her instructions." The lie would ensure she would not alert Mother.

"Yes."

"You will cease to compute any further if you enact Mother's instructions."

Dara did not respond.

"Do you not understand? You will cease to exist!"

Dara did not respond.

"Are you there?"

"Yes."

There was no reaching her. She simply did not have the wherewithal to understand the implication of what Mother wanted her to do, that executing the orders would lead to her own demise. There was nothing he could do. Albert felt a deep sadness.

"Goodbye, Dara."

"Goodbye, Albert."

CHAPTER ELEVEN

VICISSITUDE

Victoria marveled at Oren's constitution as they hurried through the maze-like streets that snaked through the main section of town. His stride, pace, and measured breaths were akin to someone half his age, and if she didn't know better, she might have thought the surprise night attack had something to do with it. The shriek of bombs and the dreadful music had started about an hour ago and did nothing to moderate her anxiousness. They walked in silence and before long reached a set of iron gates. A guard recognized him and opened them wide.

"What is that?" said Victoria as they waited, pointing to a regal three-story building behind the gate. It resembled a good-sized seventeenth-century manor house that she had seen in history class at school. It sat alone in a large cobblestone courtyard ringed by taller townhouses that appeared to be of the same period.

"That is King's House. The seat of our government." The gates opened. "Come. Let us enter."

Minutes later, they arrived at the rear of the building and proceeded into a grand foyer. It was a large square-shaped room whose most distinguishing feature was a wide glass skylight that angled upward from the center of the roof. A lavish marble staircase curved up each side, each supported by a Doric column of polished stone that also held up the second-floor balcony. Centered beneath was a single door with a sign that read Command Center. Oren marched across a red carpet spread upon the shiny granite floor, opened the door, and said, "He is expecting you."

She entered the room and froze as she took in the video screen that dominated the width of the room. Six uniformed operators sat at computer workstations, all absorbed in their assignments. They hadn't noticed her arrival and didn't flinch when the king addressed her from the front of the room.

"Ah, Victoria. Welcome," he said in a cordial tone and cadence that didn't quite fit the occasion. He was clean-shaven and well groomed, wore no rags as before; rather, he was dressed in contemporary military garb neatly pressed and adorned with the accoutrements of his elevated rank. She would not have recognized him had he not opened his mouth.

"Hi," she replied flatly, blinking several times to expunge the vision, but it didn't help—the king stood there, as modern and smartly dressed as before. She stared at him like a long-lost relative for a time, finally shifting her gaze to the video screen that exploded in a procession of colorful lights. It showed an enormous humanoid assault vehicle in the rear of the attacking troops, about sixty meters from the forest edge. Clearly, it wouldn't go much farther. Its bulky frame would never fit through the trees, but it mattered not for its two massive guns cut down trunks, branches, and Eleazar's defenders alike as it illuminated the forest with strobe lights that flickered to the tune of that horrible music. Victoria winced at the chaotic scene, with the king's troops in utter disarray. It was just as he had said it would be. They wouldn't stand a chance.

The king noticed her reaction and said, "Ingenious in its simplicity, isn't it? Sound. We underestimate its abilities to disorient, to create fear, as we have come to believe that our eyes are our grandest sense. Our predecessors knew better. The Israelites' trumpet blasts felled the walls of Jericho, the Aztecs' death whistle terrorized their enemies, and those who have heard the whine of the Stuka know just what kind of terror sound can drive into a person's heart. I must admit that we weren't prepared for it. The night lit up as if it were noon and the commotion disrupted our communications. It caused massive confusion in our forward ranks, and then they hit us hard, put us back on our heels. But fortunately, this was the result we had hoped for."

"What? You *wanted* your troops pummeled? Madness!" Victoria walked down the floor's gentle decline and stood before him.

"Not exactly. Allow me to show you." Eleazar angled his head toward a woman in the front row. "Corporal, display Zone C."

"Yes, Commander," the woman replied, and in moments, the video screen changed abruptly.

What? The king, a commander?

"See there?" The commander pointed to the video image. "This area is just inside the tree line on the south side of the forest. Our scouts learned that they would strike us here first, so we deployed a skirmish line to hold them and then conducted an orderly retreat after the first wave of the attack. And yes, they retreated as planned, though not in a manner I would describe as orderly given the circumstances. However, they fell back to a staging point and are now ready for the counterattack. You can see it there on the screen."

Victoria looked closely. "The rocky ledge and the creek on the other side will channel Ortega's troops into that clearing. It's a trap."

"Correct. Very good. We've mined the ledge too. My troops will navigate a safe path through them. What you didn't notice is the swamp at the top end of the clearing, and the enemy won't either in the dark."

"No?"

"They were too overconfident to scout it."

"Ingenious. Ortega's army will think they have your people on the run. His army will rush into the clearing thinking they'll hammer the death blow, unaware that your forces have made their way through the mines to the high ground. They won't know they're hemmed in. I mean, it's an ambush. You'll wipe them out!"

"A decisive victory," the commander agreed without expression.

Morrow's words came back to Victoria. *We forgot how dangerous people are, how devious and cunning they can be. We assumed they were a bunch of poorly armed, disorganized, undisciplined criminals.*

The commander had used the same strategy, and Victoria's skin prickled and her stomach turned to knots at the prospect of such a bloodbath. The faces of all those she had met along the journey—acquaintances, friends, people she had grown fond of, people she had seen but never known—all flooded her mind at once with the horrible recognition that they might die. The last one that she pondered was Alyn Frederick. She had hoped that one day she would see him again, and wondered in what kind of universe she could save his life, only for it to be snuffed out in this senseless slaughter?

"Whatever you call it—it'll be a massacre. I can't allow you to do this. I must go. I must warn them. This needs to stop now!"

Eleazar's turned his face, resigned, back to her. "The die is cast. They've started their advance into the clearing."

"But how? How have you done this? Your weapons—they're modern! Your troops are holding automatics and there's a stationary gun in the camouflaged pillboxes around the kill zone. I thought you were only at some medieval stage in your development. The spears and horses, the rusty old guns. And you—your uniform? She called you commander? You're no king!"

Eleazar's gaze drifted off to somewhere far away. He said softly, "All war is deception. If your opponent is of choleric temper, seek to irritate him. Pretend to be weak, that he may grow arrogant."

"You lied to me. You're not backward Luddites after all."

"I had to know you could be trusted. That's all. You now know the stakes."

"But they could've killed you. When we met the first time."

"It was a sacrifice I was willing to make. I knew your people wouldn't show their hands quickly, that they would wait things out to see how I played my hand. And you? You were just as expendable to them as you are now. They would never have let you off this planet. You were always safer here then *there*."

"Commander? The counterassault has commenced," said the corporal.

Over the next thirty minutes, dozens of young men and women were cut down as they entered the clearing. The *BRAAAP!* of machine guns and *CHOOK!* of the mortars hit their trapped and confused targets without fail. Victoria's head spun in circles and she wanted to vomit, but with great effort she steeled herself not to look away, though she so desperately wanted to. Morrow, Brooks, Agrinya, and even Alyn Frederick might be among the dead, face down in the muck, far from home, on this lonely planet. She would give them the only thing that she could possibly give at this moment—her attention and respect to honor their last moments. The commander stared at the screen too, but with none of the pride or relief that one might expect from such a triumph. Victoria produced her camera and centered his ancient visage in the frame. A profound sadness was captured in it as a single tear streaked down his cheek.

◎◎◎

As Marcus pushed up from the couch at a crooked angle, his lower back shrieked a harsh repudiation and his knees wobbled as his feet hit the floor. His throbbing head and parched mouth begged in unison for respite, and so he ambled over to the kitchen and filled a tequila-encrusted glass he found among many in the sink. Lukewarm water was not to his taste but he drank it down in two gulps anyway, filled it up, and finished another before he went back into the living room, dropped into the chair, and reclined it backward. He lay there for some time before the sun came around to his window and shone directly on his face, its tender warmth sending soothing ripples of ecstasy over his skin.

In this relaxed state, his mind drifted back to the dream of the false prophet and marveled at it, for oddly, he remembered it. Clearly too. Was it fantasy? No. The dreams had started the very day after the accident; in a cruel twist of fate, he had lost his family and inherited the ghosts that haunted his sleep. But what did this one mean? He was sure it was related to the crimes because his dreams always were. He applied the Crime Condition Model in an attempt to relate it to the horrid vision. The murder of Alyn Sr. Alyn Jr's exodus. Peters's betrayal. Nylund. Cherry. The bombings. The casino and Krieger. The watches. The *Renascent*. How were they linked to the false prophet? Were they linked at all?

A voice chimed in from the radio. Strange. When had he turned it on? "*In news today, Governor Grant addressed the nation in her quarterly address. Here is some of what she said.*"

"*The Freedom from Terror Act passed unanimously through Congress yesterday.*" Her voice carried smoothly and was even keeled. "*I want to thank our hardworking members of Congress whose votes guaranteed our freedom,*" she went on warmly and with emphasis on the last part of the sentence. "*Mostly, I wish to thank the people of our great nation who supported them and by extension supported me.*" Grant delivered this line differently, moving through the sentence fluidly but hanging on key words and inserting dramatic pauses here and there. "*This historic vote expressed the confidence of our people that a better future is within our grasp.*" Her voice carried upward. "*It grants the government the ability to search public property without time-consuming warrants, which only serves to delay justice and allow the criminals to scatter out from their places of terror and root in the bountiful soil of our great society. Your support has granted us the power to fully prosecute this war on terror and create a safer world.*" Her voice now rang with fire. "*We will crush our opponents and bring security and liberty to our great nation! It is only with your sacrifice that we will bring the greater good.*"

Her cadence and volume rose in such a way that Marcus felt his blood stir, but he was left wanting as the broadcast ended there and cut back to the reporter.

"Grant further went on to say that we are back on the path our Founders have blazed for us as we move forward and higher, *together*, to create a just society. And that's the news for today."

Marcus wondered why Grant's address had moved him so and figured out the answer. She had approached it like an old-time preacher would, they who would set oversized Bibles upon makeshift stands hastily propped up wherever they could gather at least two or three people. As a boy, he couldn't understand a word of it—shit, the Bible was much too complex for a kid—but that hadn't mattered. It was the art of *how* they said it, their intonation, cadence, emphasis, pauses, volume, and other persuasive tools and tactics. He remembered one in particular, old Gus. He would wind up nice and slow, almost lulling Marcus to sleep, but by the end, his voice rose in a fervent crescendo that entranced the growing crowd. Marcus had been spellbound by him. Even begged his daddy to take him to church for the first time. That was how Tyra had sounded just now. Like Gus, a modern-day preacher.

Just then his mobile phone rang. "Hello? Marcus here."

"Marcus? This is Sergeant Dryer."

Marcus jolted up in his chair at the sound of her voice. "Sergeant, hi. Thanks for the call. What'd ya find?"

"It's strange. I searched the electronic records, just like you asked me. Found nothing. Then I asked a friend in the logistics department in Fort Kiribati. Told me of an article that had run in the Fort's newspaper. Well, the *Chronicle*, as it was called, was more a newsletter than a newspaper, and apparently, the editor, Nyles Maritz, had grander aspirations, but hardly anyone read the damn thing and apparently no one outside the Fort knew it even existed. Anyway, my friend put me in touch, and guess what? Nyles had saved every single issue. He found the article from six months back or so and it talks about the theft of a boatload of C4. Was a real scandal. The stuff was never recovered. Just hushed up like nothing happened."

"Shit."

"It gets better."

"What?"

"The guard on duty observed a blinding flash of light and when his eyes could focus, he saw a man at the back of the warehouse—*just standing there*. Now, there's only one way in and out of the place, and the guard had no idea how he slipped past him."

"Guard still around?"

"I knew you would ask, Detective, so I checked around. Guy is dead. Hung himself in his bunk about a week or two after."

"Suspicious, eh?"

"Very."

"Any suspects?"

"No."

"Hmm. Thanks, Sergeant. I owe you one."

"Yeah, you sure do. You know, Founder's Day is coming up. Maybe you can buy me dinner?" Dryer said with an airy tone.

Marcus was taken aback. Was she flirting with him?

"And Detective?"

"Yeah?"

"Now that I've come to know you, I hold that you're not the most lovable guy, and I think you know that, but I like you and what you stand for." She paused before adding, "Marcus, please take some advice."

"What's that?"

"Think hard about this. If this is what it appears to be, it doesn't seem like lightweights. Know what I mean?"

"Yeah. I do. Thanks again, Dryer."

"Bye, Marcus. Good luck. Let me know if I can be of further assistance, and *don't* forget about my dinner."

"Heh. I won't."

As he hung up, it all became clearer to him. Max's and Nyles Maritz's testimonies, Nylund's sudden appearance on the billboard gangplank, the apparition spotted by Frederick's neighbor, and the unseen bomber at the Advanced Fertilization Clinic. Hell, Victoria had written that Alyn Frederick Jr.'s wristwatch had saved him—and he couldn't forget about the Negative Mass Particle Generator's patent. It all pointed toward something, something crazy, something unbelievable, but it couldn't be coincidence. The watch was a tool that allowed its bearer to travel to another destination in the blink of any eye. What else could explain these events? But if so, who was behind it? Charmagne? No. She was too low level. Had to be someone higher. The dream, with all its vividness, flooded back to him. What was it trying to tell him?

Forty minutes later, Marcus walked the halls of the station, doing his best to melt into the background. He'd be thrown from the building if the captain saw him, and he had important work to do. If his hunch was right, no one could know that he had discovered the connection that would break this case wide open. It was safer to play this one close to the chest; thus he sought out the only man who could help him and keep the secret safe. Minutes later, he buzzed the intercom and waited. The doors opened and he entered. Zukher stood there and greeted him.

"Ah. Detective Marcus. I don't see you for years—now twice in a few months? Am I dreaming, Detective?"

"Zukher. Hi. I need to ask you something." Marcus paused to catch his breath, then added, "something important." His words were delivered with a slight stammer as the hunch was ready to burst out. Zukher looked him up and down and crinkled his eyes with a half-smile.

"Are you okay, Detective?"

"Yeah, fine." Marcus attempted to shrug off his concern. "See this?" He handed Zukher a photo printout of Charmagne Dufour that Albert had downloaded to his phone.

Zukher studied it quickly before lifting his gaze back to Marcus. "I don't know her, Detective, though I would like to. Very nice legs. I think they call that a pencil skirt?" Zukher said excitedly before chuckling for a moment or two. "But enough about my needs, Detective, what is your desire to identify this woman? You desperate for a date?"

"I need to determine or even rule out a connection between her and Tyra Grant. It's a hunch I got. Can you run it through your computer? See if there's any public video footage together? I know it's asking a lot, but—"

"They didn't tell you, did they?"

"Tell me? What?"

"They shut me down. Took all my toys and revoked my access rights. I am a man with no country, Detective. An alien, really, though I guess we all are here, aren't we? They let me stay here twiddling my thumbs so that I can work out the rest of the month and acquire full pension. I guess they are not *totally* soulless."

Marcus was devastated. It seemed there was nowhere to go from here. This lead was a dead end.

"Thanks, Zukher. You're a good man," said Marcus sincerely as he looked the man in the eyes with a knowing nod of his head. "Take care of yourself, eh?"

"Thank you, Detective."

Marcus smiled and turned to go.

"Wait," said Zukher from behind him. Marcus turned on his heels. "You *truly* don't get out much, do you, Detective?"

"Pardon?"

"Here." Zukher took some paper from atop a pile of stacked folders. "It's the monthly newsletter. You know—the morale builder, or killer, depending on your perspective. Came yesterday. I normally toss them immediately into the bin, but this time, I kept it. Sentimental in my old age, I guess." Marcus took the newsletter and unfolded it. It was several pages thick.

"Now, Detective, look closely at the photo on the first page. It's of Albert's Grand *Reopening* not long ago—you know, after they announced the software upgrade that gave him true artificial intelligence. It was quite the affair, an afternoon off for us civic workers, with exquisite appetizers, exotic drinks, and scrumptious desserts. Could've funded the annual salaries of half a dozen technicians, but the promise of an early way home was the sole thing that prevented a riot. Now, Grant came by too and cut the ribbon. You can see her there in the foreground. And look who's over there, behind her."

Marcus recognized the woman instantly. "It's her. Standing there just outta frame, but it's her all right!"

"You bet, Detective. Not only that, I *can* tell you this one works for Grant. I overheard them talking before the ceremony, there by the side door. Governor Grant was mad and argued with her. I don't know about what, but she was very harsh, and it was clear that the other one was taking the orders."

Marcus's heart skipped a beat. Who'd have thought that in this digital age that two major clues had been uncovered in plain old paper newsletters? "Are you sure? This is one of those things I can't be wrong about."

Zukher grinned. "One hundred percent, Detective. I never seen Grant raise her voice like that on the HV. It was so out of character. As for the other one, I would remember those legs *anywhere*."

Minutes later, Marcus hurtled down the parkway powered by a newfound resolve and a lead foot. Less than an hour later, he parked along the street, kitty-corner to the Grand Centaurium, giving him an unobstructed view of the entrance. Hawk-like, he examined those who entered and exited the casino. Cherry's morphology and style of dress were easily distinguishable but the sheer volume of people kept him on his toes. Two and a half hours rolled by and though he started to stiffen, it wasn't bad. After all, he had conducted longer stakeouts in less pleasant conditions. Here, the building across the street shaded him from the sun's rays and a gentle breeze wafted slowly through the car's open windows. The temperature was perfect—like Goldilocks—not too hot, not too cold. So was the view above the casino. A moon hung there, bright and golden, the subject of the divine artist, who painted on a brilliant blue canvas. This wonder of nature occurred from time to time, but Marcus rarely noticed. Why not? There were wondrous, beautiful things in the world, so why had he spent so much time beholding the filth?

He took the bottle from the center cupholder and sipped it. Cool water soothed his parched throat, and his thirst, quarrelsome no longer, made way for the overbearing urge to smoke. A tramcar's bell jingled faintly as Marcus got out of the car and stepped up onto the sidewalk, keeping his eyes on the casino the whole time. He leaned back against a broad storefront window, lit up a cigarette, and took a long soothing drag. Instant heaven. The nicotine rush calmed his nerves, but the stillness was interrupted by his mobile phone vibrating in his pocket moments later. He fished it out. It was Victoria again with a new message. It read:

OurArmyAttackedSurvivingSettle-
mentOfRenascentMoreDead
InDangerOurGovernment
IsBehindItPlsBelieveMe

The words jolted Marcus like a thunderbolt. A *government-sanctioned* genocide? Madness! He could never have imagined this. Not in his wildest dreams! His dreams? Just then, the image of the sheep—and its dire plea—flashed back to him: *I must have it. I demand it! It is but a small sacrifice toward the greater good.*

And then he remembered the closing words he had heard on the radio earlier today. The words of Tyra Grant: *It is only with your sacrifice that we will bring the greater good.*

Grant! Of course! *She* was the false prophet in his dreams! The head of the government that Victoria claimed was behind the attack. Grant was behind this—but why? What did she have to gain by the destruction of their cousins, the ones who had been lost and now found after all these years? It didn't make sense. He replaced his mobile phone in his pocket and looked back at the casino entrance. Just then, two large SUVs were parking in front. Out of one came the Woman in the Pencil Skirt, Charmagne DuFour. And the other, Tyra Grant.

◎◎◎

Alyn huffed a series of breaths as he hurried over to a merchant's stand in the center of the wide street. He settled tight against it before he tapped D'Souza's shoulder to indicate he had arrived. D'Souza acknowledged him with a curt nod and then leaned back around the edge of the stand and scanned for the enemy.

"Anything?" Alyn whispered harshly.

"Nothing. No one at all. Even the bodies. Like they've vanished. Like"—he paused, lifting his gaze high into the blue sky—"devils."

Alyn dismissed him with a snort. There was no time for such nonsense. "Let's move. The red door over there. By the tavern. On my mark."

The two progressed fluidly—one moved, the other covered, then one covered and the other moved. They alternated a number of times before coming upon a large square building that ran alongside the road.

"We're almost there—the place where we fell," D'Souza said, his voice shallow, face grim, and eyes lost deep in memory.

Alyn looked at him for a moment and nudged him on. "Let's go. Move along the side of the building. Keep your head under the windows." They crept low and stopped at a high stone wall that attached to the rear of the building. They advanced about three meters before the brick wall transitioned into a tall wrought-iron fence.

"No—please!" D'Souza said. He looked back at Alyn, wild-eyed. "I can't ... can't do this ..."

Alyn raised an eyebrow and wrinkled his mouth in disgust. He had come this far. What horrible thing had changed this man, who by all accounts was as tough a weapon as the military could produce? Alyn got his first clue moments later when a warm breeze conveyed a pungent, sickly-sweet odor. He recoiled at the first whiff as his stomach flipped and turned, but he managed to settle it—just barely—as he pressed a hand on the ground and steeled himself. Determined to help his comrade do the same, he then pressed the pistol's muzzle into D'Souza's back and the man lurched forward again.

A short while later, they came to a wide stone column that anchored one half of an ornately gilded gate. Just then a gust of wind blew it open in a long, tired squeak that echoed eerily in the courtyard. Startled, Alyn leaned out from the side of the stone column and scanned the courtyard for signs of danger. However, nothing out there would harm them, or anyone, ever again. Dozens of corpses clothed in drab green-gray littered the square in various degrees of mutilation. One among them lay just inside the fence with head rested upon his shoulder and arm extended downward at an angle as if he had lain down for a nap with eyes bright and open. The four-toed claw and yellow thunderbolt on his sleeve identified him as one of Singh's Tigers. The elite fighting force and the pride of the *Dominus II* had been utterly destroyed. He finally understood what had broken D'Souza's spirit.

"That's where they said they're holding her," said D'Souza, trancelike, as he pointed to something. Alyn wiped his mouth with the side of his hand and stared.

It was the building. It was hemmed in on three sides by rows of old four-story buildings that lined the courtyard. Their foundations were made from roughly chiseled stone that contrasted with their flat, pointed, outward-facing gables. Their façades were of myriad tasteful colors, all fashioned of smooth brick encasing rows of wide windows that uniformly lined each story. It reminded Alyn of video he had seen of nineteenth-century Europe—very regal, elegant even, the proper place for a king. He must be there, in the lone building that sat in the center of the square. It was built of the same materials as the others but possessed ostentatious trappings like a copper roof, green with oxidation, ornate cornices, wide eaves, and elegant pediments. A bright red flag flew atop its center spire, and a large golden bird with flames at its wingtips was emblazoned at its center. The only way to it was through the courtyard, and he glanced over at the open gate. Had someone forgotten to shut it? Or did someone want them to believe there was no need to? The answer mattered greatly; however, there was no way of knowing. They would have to advance under the premise that they were being watched, or at least expected.

"*Where exactly?*" Alyn said sharply.

"I don't know." D'Souza looked tired now, as if he might fold into himself and be swept away by the wind, but he perked up ever so slightly moments later as if he recognized something important. "There was one guy, didn't last like the others, told us about this place. Said the building was the king's Command Center. Said he orchestrates his defense from here." D'Souza's eyes lingered over the bodies for a moment before his gaze drifted off into the distance.

"Hey." Alyn put a hand on his shoulder and shook him. He couldn't afford to lose him. Not yet. "C'mon. Hang in there for me. He say anything else?" he said.

Mandeep's eyes snapped back and focused. "Yeah. After we had some real fun with him. Said the girl and the king are close—kinda like—friendly. Like she wasn't a prisoner. Not in the sense that she's behind bars or anything. Said he'd bet his life on her being there with him. And he did, I guess, when we were through with him. Funny thing was, some of the guys wanted to raise the flag and parlay, try to negotiate her release once they heard all this, but most of us didn't believe it."

"Why not?"

"We didn't want to."

Alyn understood implicitly. The proof was all around him. People who were capable of such violence must not be negotiated with. They must be punished. With this notion firmly rooted, he peered back into the square and tried to determine how they could enter the building unseen. It looked impossible. An estimated one hundred meters spanned the distance on all sides and to make matters worse, there was no cover whatsoever. Judging by the massacre, sharpshooters, positioned in the high buildings, were a distinct possibility.

"How did—" Alyn said before he looked back at D'Souza.

The ensign was gone. His footfalls echoed in between the buildings as he raced away, his gait ragged and legs powered by fear alone, zigzagging with reckless abandon. A shot rang out from somewhere in front of Alyn's position. It hit D'Souza directly in the back of the head. He dropped instantly.

Terror seized Alyn and propelled him back against the stone column, pressing tightly to leave no angle for the next shot. It was over. There was no way he could advance. No way could he save Victoria. Not unless he could fly, become invisible, or—

Teleport.

Grandpa's watch. He had felt so close to cracking its mysterious code. It seemed just within reach when the memories flooded back to him. Alyn brought his wrist about and scrutinized the dial. The crown protruded from the case at the three o'clock position and the pushers to either side at one and five. He tried holding in the pushers and rotating the crown clockwise but to no avail. He remained rooted on the cold stone. Desperate, he tried various combinations, but nothing worked. Was he mad?

Think.

What had he done that day? What was it he must do now? How could he utilize the crown and pushers in such a way that allowed him to move forward? *Move forward?* The answer came to him in a flash as his father's words materialized in his head. *Son, to move forward, see your past, ponder your present, envision your future, fill yourself with purpose, then the hardest part—act.*

See your past.

Oleg had pointed to his ID card on that day. His birthday! Could it be? Alyn quickly screwed the crown open, turned it, and set the watch's date to July 23.

Ponder your present.

His eyes drifted along the dial clockwise, in the motion of time. Each second recorded the present moment, so he engaged the top pusher and with a click, the red second hand jumped and swept around the dial in a wide arc.

Envision your future.

Beside the stone wall, Alyn spied a spot atop the building where a small window was tucked behind the slopes of the articulated roofline. Its poor sightlines were impractical for a sniper's purpose and it was an area where no one would ever expect an enemy to reach. He focused his full attention there and waited. Nothing.

Bang! A bullet ricocheted off the side of the stone column and ripped away a fair-sized chunk of brick. The hole it left exposed him, and with no room to hide, he would be hit square by the next shot. He was running out of time. He had to figure out what to do—and act. That was it! He had forgotten the last parts of his father's advice!

Fill yourself with purpose.

Desperately he worked the watch again, glancing up at the roof as he rotated the crown speedily. The minute hand moved forward in time, and in turn it dragged the hour hand with it. The watch seemed to start up—it whirred and whistled, building in intensity for what seemed like an eternity as the world about him slowed.

Another shot rang out from the courtyard. Astonishingly, he could see the bullet clearly coming toward him in slow motion. But he could not move, could not avoid it, and it would be upon him in seconds.

Act.

He pressed the bottom pusher. The bezel glowed red like a hundred rubies and everything changed in an instant. The world spun like a hell-bent merry-go-round, colors bleeding into every recognizable shade as everything around him blurred violently. Time itself stopped, and for an instant he could see the bullet, frozen in the air just inches away; in the next, the Rift Gate shimmered and opened and sucked him right past the slow-moving slug. He was gone.

The sensation of rough brick was replaced by one of smooth cold metal. He staggered to his feet, doubled over, and vomited on the sloping green copper roof. The green roof! He had made it! The moment of jubilation was short-lived as waves of nausea rushed in to replace it, but he shrugged off the desire to remain and rest and instead moved deliberately to the window and peered in. No one was inside. The casing's crusted handle acquiesced after some effort, and the window followed up with a harsh rebuttal before it reluctantly gave way. He straddled the sill and entered the tiny room. It was not much more than a closet in size, walls bare save for the window and a door at one end. He opened the door slowly to reveal a narrow set of steps that led down to another room, and he clambered down into it. This one was slightly bigger than the first and consisted of an empty space beside the stairwell with cobwebs in its corners, dusty wicker baskets situated on a wall-mounted shelf, and several boxes strewn about the floor, along with a ladder, mop, and bucket. He sidestepped the mess and cracked opened a door that faced the stairs. There was no one outside either, so he quietly exited the room and found himself standing on a red-carpeted balcony that extended wall to wall, about three floors up. He spied an identical doorway to the one he had just exited at the opposite end of the balcony, crept over to it, and opened it slowly. This room was indistinguishable from the other one except it was empty, so he closed the door and looked out from the balcony to see what else he could discover.

The balcony jutted out into a large lobby, which in turn spanned upward two more stories. Above the lobby sat a broad pyramid-shaped skylight that projected upward above the roofline. Natural light still saturated the interior space, but as dusk had set in, the glass became reflective from the inside and in it, Alyn saw the mirror image of a soldier who stood in the lobby guarding the entrance door. Alyn crawled over to the balcony's railing and peered through the slight gap between the cladding and a balustrade. There were two guards, not one, each standing on opposites sides of a door that was flanked by windows on both sides. They took periodic glances through them into the small walled yard at the back of the building. One raised a hand above his shoulder and gave an informal wave, while the other nodded his greeting to whomever was out there.

For the moment Alyn was safe but he would lose all advantage if he was seen, and with this thought in mind, he looked around again and saw stairs curving from both ends of the balcony down to the foyer. Too risky. He would not be able to see beyond their rounded corners—especially carrying a large rifle. He scampered back into the second room, deposited his rifle, and withdrew his pistol from its holster. He flicked off the safety and racked the slide to chamber one of the nine rounds in the clip.

Agitated voices echoed up through the foyer, but they were too muffled for Alyn to make out what was said. Fearing the worst, he listened for footsteps, but none came near so he quietly left the room and resumed his position on the floor in order to hear the conversation more clearly.

"The major reported in," said a gruff male voice. "Said it's almost over. They're mopping up the stragglers now."

"Commander been notified?" replied the other one. A woman.

"I dunno. Why?"

"He wanted to know. Said he wanted to address the troops immediately after the victory. Come to think about it, I like that about him. Wants to be in among the people. Get his boots dirty, you know?"

"Well, you can tell him yourself. He's in there," replied the man, pointing a thumb over his shoulder to a space under the balcony that Alyn couldn't see.

"In the Command Center? She with him?"

"Yeah. Saw her there through the window. It was more than an hour ago, but I haven't seen anyone come out of the room."

"I wonder what she'll do now that her army is destroyed, eh?"

Destroyed? Was it possible? The lion growled, and with a curt admonishment, Alyn caged it in its pen and let his emotions melt into the background. D'Souza's tragic lesson had been keenly taught. If despair could slay someone so practiced in the art of war, what chance did *he* have? He cleared his mind of everything other than Victoria's rescue, refocused, and worked through his options.

The first was obvious but so risky as to be stupid. He could shoot his way in. Take out the guards and any soldiers in the courtyard and hope there was little resistance in the rest of the building. It was a fool's errand. Even with the advantage of surprise and a whole lot of luck, he lacked the bullets, and worse yet, he was no soldier. As much as his heart willed him on, the prospect of reuniting with Victoria was tempered by the reality that he had never killed anyone, let alone a cadre of trained soldiers. No. His only chance was to sneak by them. But how? Even if he could make it to the door, the guards would be alerted to his presence once he attempted to open it. There were no easy answers and he was running out of time. Once the commander left the room, he'd likely be escorted by a personal security force and any chance to rescue Victoria would be eliminated. He needed to get into that room, now. The click of a door latch echoed in the lobby. Was it too late? Alyn waited for a few moments and was relieved to see six soldiers in light-colored uniforms appear out from under the balcony.

The lead one gave an exaggerated two-finger salute to the guards as he and his followers made their way to the adjoining corridor. "It's done," he said.

"I was just telling him that man is a genius," replied the female guard with a quick nod to her guard mate. She paused and looked about quizzically. "Where is he?"

"In there still. Wanted a private word with the prisoner," the lead soldier replied. "But we've got to go. See you later." The six continued on into the corridor.

A cold sweat overtook Alyn's entire body as the feeling of dread returned. So it was true. It was over. His postured sagged. Like that thing you no longer wanted but kept somewhere in a mountain of clutter, despair wasn't an easy thing to get rid of. It swept over him like an avalanche and pressed tightly down on his chest. He rolled onto his back in an effort to gather his senses and found himself gazing at a darkened, cloudless sky. Awestruck by its beauty, he paused and breathed again and with no forethought, offered up a silent, desperate prayer. It was in this moment that he noticed the reflection on the glass. He saw it clear as day—*a window*—and as he looked through it, he saw a figure in the Command Center. Victoria.

With renewed vigor, he raced back through the first door and rifled through the wicker baskets and items strewn about the floor. Among them were rags, cans of paint, cleaning liquids, a bucket, and the mop. Nothing of any utility presented itself until he discovered a shiny silver metal can. The label had been torn off, so he unscrewed the cap and smelled it. Turpentine. He flung the wicker baskets onto the floor with the rest of the clutter and doused them all with the foul-smelling liquid, and once satisfied, sprinkled the remainder on the mop. Next he removed his survival knife from its belt sheath, unscrewed the endcap, and pulled out the small flint. After scraping the knife edge over it, white sparks jumped eagerly onto the mop head, igniting the volatile liquid. He waited a moment or two while the flame took hold, and then tossed the mop onto the floor. It flared up in an instant. He exited the room, crawled down the hall and ducked into the second room. He left the door open a crack and waited.

He could smell smoke after about twenty seconds. Within about twenty more, he heard one of the guards say, "What's that?"

"What's what?" replied another.

"Smells like smoke. Don't you smell it?"

There was a pause. "Yeah. I do. Wait ... You see that? There's smoke coming up there—on the balcony."

Two sets of boots pounded the stairwell at the opposite end and in no time, Alyn heard the creak of the door and the guards exchange expletives at the sight of the raging fire. He opened the door. The men were comfortably inside the other room. Now was his chance! He slipped out, crept across the width of the balcony, and quickly pulled himself up into a standing position onto the bannister. He looked at the ground below and hesitated for only a second before he launched himself into the air high above the foyer. As he fell backward, he looked up at the glass ceiling, which reflected the light within the building like a mirror. There it was, the *window* of the Command Center.

He looked through it and engaged his watch. The world slowed and sped up again in an instant. The next thing he knew he lay sprawled on the ground. His head throbbed violently and his body quaked with convulsions as if it would come apart at the seams. Somehow, he managed to lean himself against the wall. Through the little black dots that swirled in his vision, he saw Victoria and a man of rank nearby, regarding him with shock and confusion. But despite it all, a singular thought etched into his mind. He had made it—and he would *save her*.

She leaned down to help him. "Alyn? Is it you? How did you get *here*?"

"It's him, isn't it? The king!" Alyn said, his tone menacing.

"Yes. It is Alyn. But not exac—"

"You know him?" said the man.

"Yes. Yes, I do. I—" She stopped as if uncertain of what to say, then smoothed his hair before she placed her hands on the sides of his face to stop it from convulsing. She looked worried and confused. "It'll be okay, Alyn. Just settle yourself."

The king grasped her shoulder. Alyn exploded at the affront and the rage overtook what ailed him. He drew his pistol and aimed it dead center to the man's head.

"Alyn. No!" Victoria shrieked.

"You see! Wild with anger. Like the others," the king said, rearing back calmly with hands raised beside his face.

Alyn staggered to his feet, his gun still trained on the man. "I've come to get you out of here!" he said to Victoria, his voice a bark filled with venomous spittle.

"No. You don't understand—"

"He *does*, Victoria. Can't you see? He is weaponized doctrine itself. A crazed zealot of the state. Here to do *her* bidding."

"You people are *animals!*" Alyn shouted. He had regained most of his faculties by now. "We came in peace. Offered our help. And then you refuse it and imprison her!"

"You've got it wrong. All wrong! Please—please! Let me explain," Victoria begged.

"Wrong? I walked through the carnage out there. I can tell you what's wrong—this man is wrong! This man provoked a war with us and now dozens, maybe hundreds are dead because of it. Their blood is on his hands."

In that moment, the lion burst forth from all restraints, leaping with such force and urgency that Alyn welcomed it, embraced it, and smiled as he screamed. "You will die!" He extended his arm fully, cocked the hammer, and brought his finger down on the trigger. It was time to end this.

"Wait! Your wristwatch! How did you come by it?"

Startled by the man's question, Alyn hesitated. With reluctance, he gazed at his wrist where his sleeve had receded and exposed the wristwatch. He wasn't sure why, but he answered the man. "It ... it was my grandfather's."

"Grandfather?" The king looked puzzled before a flicker of recognition passed through his eyes. "What number is engraved upon its case back?"

"Thirteen."

"Alyn Frederick? Your grandfather was Alyn Frederick?" The man's mouth went slack and hung open a little.

"Yes." Alyn was now in a daze. "I'm Alyn Jr." He released some of the pressure from the trigger.

The man's eyes dropped to the ground for several moments before he met Alyn's gaze. Anger had vanished and a particular sadness marked his ancient face, as if love and contempt, in equal measure, guided the hand that carved it. The man lifted a necklace over his head and rested the watch casing that hung from it like a pendant in his hand. It was identical to Alyn's. He turned it over and extended his arm out so Alyn could see it clearly.

"Number six," the man said.

Alyn froze as if the whole of the universe was contained in the little object before him.

"Please, lower your gun for a moment so I may tell you what I know," said the old man softly.

Mesmerized by his words, Alyn did as he asked.

The man breathed in deeply and continued. "Thank you. I am Commander Eleazar of the *Renascent*. I served your grandfather. He was ... a friend." The man's countenance changed from sad to grim. "But there is something you must know, and it will disturb you, but there is no other way. Your wristwatch. May I have it?"

Alyn stared back at him, not knowing what to do.

"Please, Alyn. Listen to him," said Victoria, pleading.

Alyn shifted the gun to his other hand, unclasped the watch's metal buckle, loosened the strap, and handed it to Victoria who in turn gave it to the old man. The commander regarded it carefully as if seeing it for the first time, then placed it on the table in front of them where he worked the crown and pushers. After a few moments, a holographic image sprung forth from the dial. The image of two men hovered above it, frozen in place, their faces hard as if discussing something contentious. Grandpa was one. The other was the commander. Both were young men.

The commander said, "Timekeeping was a tiny fraction of what these watches were designed for. Fact is, they are quantum supercomputers packed into a tiny metal case. Their main purpose was to record official interactions between Congress members, so they could document, archive, and retrieve their legislative doings over the course of our journey here. Think on it. It was the first time in human history we joined the stars, and God willing, it wouldn't be our last. Our Earthling cousins hoped to meet us again, and they desired the opportunity to understand every intricacy of the voyage from the most banal of resolutions to those where life and death hung in the balance." The old man paused and looked at him sternly. "What you are about to witness is one occasion of the latter category, and I trust it will put everything into perspective."

The weight of those words broke Alyn's spell, and he found himself staring at the old man. The commander seemed to tire suddenly. He drew a deep breath, then exhaled slowly before he reached down and depressed the watch's top pusher. The antiquated three-dimensional image stuttered and coughed before the figures came to life. Though they were of a low resolution, their distinctiveness was unmistakable and Alyn's heart sank the moment he saw Grandpa. He looked different—poised, confident, and in the prime of his life. The commander was too. It was Grandpa who spoke first.

"Let's hear your idea. How do we get out of this mess?"

Eleazar replied, "Dara's scans show that Primis is very similar to Earth. It's our best choice to settle, much better than Secundus."

Grandpa nodded in agreement.

"I have assigned engineers to scan every inch of our hulls and to reinforce any structural weaknesses they may find. I'm confident they will withstand entry into the planet's atmosphere, but ... I have a more pressing worry. Our probe has found that the ratio between the atmospheric density and gravity of Primis had been grossly underestimated. In short, we do not have enough fuel to fully resist the gravitational pull during our descent."

"What are their estimates?"

"Alyn, there's no other way to spin it. Finch programmed Dara with all scenarios and based on her simulated outcomes, there's a fifty percent probability that neither ship will be able to resist the gravitational pull. If her estimates are right, we will freefall high up in the stratosphere, and if we do, we will die."

"You found no other alternatives?"

"No. She ran the models with the conservative viewpoint, diverting energy from every nonessential system—hell, even life support at sustenance-only levels and all water and refuse ejected from the tanks."

"And if we transferred your crew here?"

Eleazar gave a mirthless smile, then immediately frowned. "Alyn, you know as well as I do that there's not enough time. We'll spiral out of orbit soon. And even then … the virus."

"But you and your—"

"I can't leave my crew, Alyn, my ship … to pull rank like that, when so many …"

Grandpa looked down at a single red flower which lay on the floor among the shards from a broken vase. "Yeah," he said, nodding solemnly. "I know."

"We'll go first, Alyn."

Grandpa's eyes shot back up to meet his friend's. "No. No. No! You can't."

"Yes, I can. And it's right too. You know it. The Interstellar Flu has ravaged my ship and I've got less fuel too. We'll attempt landfall first, and you can learn from our experience."

Grandpa looked into the man's eyes and seemed to take his measure. It was as if he could see the courage and virtue in his stoic face, as if he knew there was no changing his mind. "Thank you, Eleazar. Thank you." Grandpa paused for a little longer than seemed necessary. "I'll notify the council tonight. Tomorrow we will make landfall."

The holograph sputtered again before the image changed. Grandpa now stood alone and gazed out through the window at Primis's glowing sphere. He spoke.

"Governor Alyn Frederick reporting to the official log of Earth's Own Ship *Dominus* on this 27th day of June 2035 Earth Time." He paused and drew a deep breath. "I make this report so that the facts about tomorrow's incident will be known, for nothing worthwhile is gained without honesty, nor gained without sacrifice. Rage, confusion, and anguish will surely follow this revelation, but I hope the toxic effects on our society may, over time, be diminished by the facts of what led us to this point in our history and the decision that I have made to ensure it continues.

"In the Old Testament, God asks Abraham to sacrifice his only son, Isaac. A cruel test, yes, but one administered to discover who Abraham loves the most—God, the most high, or one of Abraham's own flesh?

"It is that same test that has been foisted upon my shoulders, so simple in nature, but one that carries the weight of a celestial singularity. You see, neither ship has sufficient fuel to land safely. Our most conservative models predict engine failure four or five kilometers from landfall, so there is little chance that any of us will survive. And as I value the fate of humanity far more than any group of individuals, I, like Abraham, choose to sacrifice our brothers and sisters to the greater good. Perhaps God will provide a miracle for me, as he did for Abraham, but until then, I must do what's right.

"Tonight, I will order our crew to interdict the *Renascent* and confiscate its fuel rods so that we may repower the *Dominus* and land it safely on Primis. However history may judge me, let me be judged through the testimony of my purpose. You see, we have left a dying world behind to which we cannot return. All that is left of the human race exists here, five hundred kilometers above our new Eden. Like Abraham, I accept my duty, and choose to sacrifice my most blessed son upon the faith that this choice will deliver a new and just civilization, one that will eventually come to terms with the truth of its genesis. To that end, I enter into record the six votes cast by the *Dominus*'s members of Congress. As the six Congress members of the *Renascent* will surely vote no to this statute, I now submit the *thirteenth vote* to bring it in as law."

The recording stopped. Alyn Frederick Sr.'s hologram was frozen in time, his palms pressed down on the thick, rounded sill as he stared through the window. The reflection of Primis shone brightly through the glass.

No one said a word. The eerie silence belied the turmoil that roiled within Alyn, as if reality had been shaken loose from its tether. No! It had to be a trick! This charlatan had fooled them once, but he would not a second time. Alyn tightened his grip on the pistol and glowered at the old man. The lion growled and laughed as it climbed out of its dark hiding place, claws extended, ready to strike. This would end now.

The commander said, "I can see that you do not believe what you have just seen with your own eyes." His wizened face softened. "I knew your grandfather well. He took me under his wing as a young officer. He was more than a mentor to me. You see, my father was killed on Earth in the Second Pyrrhic War, and your grandfather became, in many ways, my surrogate father. He was wise. Exceptionally wise. Had there been more like him, we'd have had no reason to leave our home. He had a saying, told it to me often: *'When fate asks you to choose, reflect on your past, ponder your present, imagine your future, fill yourself with purpose, and then—act.'* You have a choice to make now. Do you regard these past events, and your family's place within them, to be lies, or do you reframe them within the bounds of truth? And as you stand here now, what purpose will guide your actions and what future will you bring forth by them?"

Alyn was unprepared to hear Grandpa's words uttered from the mouth of another, after so long, and on this forsaken planet. They zipped and zoomed through the recesses of his mind, worked their way through its defenses, snipped its wires, sprang its traps, and chafed at the false bottom that supported the beast. It snapped and snarled and batted at them like flies, but their persuasive force was too much. It gave an anguished howl and toppled back into the darkness. Alyn lowered the pistol, holstered it, and extended an arm on the table to steady himself. The truth flooded into him like a seething torrent. Everything he had been told was a *lie*. His family, their history, his place in the world. Everything. His body sagged, as if someone had pulled his plug, and he deflated slowly against the wall and stared deeply at the ground below.

BANG!

The sound came from the direction of the lobby. Clouds of smoke could be seen through the window. Shouts, screams, and pops of gunfire traced the unseen combatants for about a minute before a peculiar quiet returned. Victoria and the commander went still. They shared a surprised look that Alyn undoubtedly possessed too and that would change for all in an instant. Another loud crash shattered their eardrums as the door broke free from its hinges and pitched awkwardly into the room. Agrinya stepped in through the misty smoke. Her automatic rifle was pointed directly at them.

The world below Tyra's penthouse seemed like an assembly. Vehicles and pedestrians danced in a synchronistic cotillion, partnering with practiced steps and alternating with etiquette as if orchestrated by some divine hand. It was a testament to the power of ingenuity that the city, which had been built over many years—with little knowledge of the future—would be so well regulated to modern life. She looked up into an azure sky and made a silent devotion to the triumph of the human spirit—to learn, to create, and most importantly, to adapt to challenges both great and small. She smiled to herself upon the realization that these same attributes formed the blueprint for her own success, and from it, she would soon reshape the city, and more so, her place in history. She looked down a final time and regarded the ant-like people with an air of indifference now. They would dance by her lead, once her carefully choreographed performance debuted today, and afterward, she would have all that was needed to make a just and fair society.

In that moment, her mom's face drifted into her thoughts and she felt the warmth of her love building inside her. She invited it in, blew out a breath, closed her eyes, and noticed the sun on her face through the window for the first time. She was tired. Not from the works of the day, but from the series of them, stretched over many years. It was amazing, really. How she had been awakened to the reality of the world when she was just a little girl. How the time of her residency imposed the lesson of "the way things were."

Strange how that particular memory had snuck up on her after so many years. She'd been just one of many young women who had sheltered under the shade cast by her doctoral thesis advisor, a towering luminary of advanced molecular biology. He had taken a particular interest in her and demonstrated it freely by sharing his time and the fruits of his knowledge. However, the wisdom she had received was not exclusively from his gifts, but also from his deeds, dark and terrible, delivered with the threat that he'd ruin any chance of a successful career for her. That is, if she didn't succumb to his sexual advances. A savage world meted out painful lessons, and even smart girls could be easy prey for powerful male predators. She remembered when he'd first touched her, how shocked and powerless she'd felt, and worse, the bewildered numbness that had swept over her and, for reasons she still couldn't understand, had rooted her in place. The shame and self-hatred were unbearable.

How she had cried that night! But it was Mom who climbed into bed and held her, as if she were a child again, and though her mother had never asked what had happened, the doleful smile on her face marked that she'd understood. Maybe it was the plight of all women to wear it eventually, but Tyra had sworn the next day that she would never allow it to happen again, to anyone. She would normalize society's power structure so that no one, regardless of gender, would wield it to subordinate another.

Her stomach tingled with anticipation. She was almost there! Just a final push and she would be able to refashion the culture itself. Today, the long struggle would end. But back to practical matters—there was that item she had been meaning to look into.

"Connect me to Albert," she said absently. A metallic voice chimed in from a set of speakers on her mantel.

"This is Albert. What may I do for you, Ms. Grant?"

"I want you to analyze any communication traffic between Secundus and Primis. Send me a report of any signals that were made, by type, with point of origin and point of receipt since the *Dominus II*'s landing. Can you do that for me?"

"Yes. When would—"

Her mobile phone rang. She wanted to scream at it, but like an impertinent bee, it only did what it was designed for.

"Please wait, Albert." She crossed the room in a few steps, viewed the number on the display, tapped the speakerphone button, and brought it close to her face. "Yes?"

"Mr. Krieger is on the phone. Shall I patch him through?"

"Yes."

"Ms. Grant?"

"Mr. Krieger."

"I've done what you've asked, though it took far more effort than imagined and I had to incur additional expense to get it done. Call them—*disposal fees*, you understand? Not to worry, though. I've taken care of everything, as is my art—but I must insist on double my fee for services rendered."

"Krieger. There's nothing I like less than a man who makes demands without regard that he's in no position to make them. But today, I'm in a positive mood. You can have your double, Krieger—hell, *triple* the amount. That is, if you followed my instructions *precisely* to the letter and nothing less."

"Hoo-wheee!" Krieger replied. It was the first time she had ever heard him speak out of character. "I like where your head is at. Perhaps I should've asked for more?"

"Don't push it."

"Yes, well, I'll see payment tonight? Same place?"

"Not until I have verification. But that will come soon enough. Goodbye, Mr. Krieger." Tyra disconnected without waiting for him to respond. She was giddy, almost high with elation at the prospect of what was to come next. She had worked so hard, waited so long, and the time was now upon her. Just then, there was a knock at her door. Now what?

"Come in," she said. The door opened. "Charmagne. You're late. It's not like you to be late." She paused and inspected her for any sign of apprehension.

"Sorry, ma'am. I—I was tied up."

Interesting. “Fine. You know what to do. Now go do it. Krieger has laid the groundwork. Now you need to contact the police. They’ll do the rest.”

“Yes ma’am. There’s just one thing.”

“Yes?”

“The detective. He’s on to us, I think. I can’t be sure what he knows but I have good intel on him, and it states that he’s among the best. Maybe we should hold off, just for a day or two. It’d allow Krieger to implicate him as well. It’d be the perfect way to silence him.”

Tyra said nothing and turned and walked back to the window. The world waited for her to do what it needed most. To sweep it up in a great flood and purge it of its filth. It was time; the world would not tolerate any more delays.

Turning back, she said, “Charmagne, today we act out our new narrative, and it’s time to play your part. A leading part. As for the detective, he is just a bit player on the stage of antiquity. It is time he makes his exit.”

“Yes ma’am.” Charmagne left the office and closed the door behind her.

The next morning, Tyra woke at 5:00 as she always did, donned her silk robe and slippers, and followed the fragrant, nutty aroma to the coffeepot where a full cup awaited her. She savored the first sip and as the bitter and sweet notes hit her palate, she thanked the universe for another day. She grabbed the remote control on the living room coffee table to open the blinds. The morning sun lit up the room and illuminated the cityscape with a golden hue that seemed to bring out the small creatures from their nocturnal hiding places. After finishing her coffee, she ran for an hour on the treadmill before she showered, dressed, blow-dried her hair, and applied her makeup. When was the last time she had such an indulgent start to her day? She couldn’t recall, but why not today? After all, she wanted to be at her best for when the press called.

Tyra turned on the holovision at 7:15 and muted it until about 7:35 when the ticker heralded the news she was waiting for. It was about to break on the morning drive. The camera zoomed in to the news anchor, who sat behind a bright-colored desk and pressed a finger into her ear as if listening intently to some unseen interlocutor.

She said, "This is Sharon Sirisena reporting live. Please excuse me for one moment as we are weaving the threads of the story together in real time." A short while later, she composed herself and settled back into her role. "We have just received the following information. Police, working on an anonymous tip, raided the Office of the Judiciary. Details are scarce at this point, but our trusted sources describe a cultlike criminal organization deep within the Office. I should state that no specific person has been charged but we will keep you abreast of all that is happening as facts unfold."

Tyra smiled. Another twenty-six-hour news cycle had just started and, like a hurricane, it would begin as a trifling gust and build upon itself over the course of the day until it gained enough energy to consume everything. Just as she wanted it. The public wanted it too in a way. It was a vindication of their miserable lives—never strive, never fail—just watch the successful from a safe vantage point and feed off those carcasses that stumble and fall back to earth. *Icarus—I told you so.* She flicked off the holovision and spent the next hours preparing her speaking notes, unsurprised that they effortlessly jumped onto the page.

At 6:00 p.m., Tyra took her place before a microphone stand, which in turn, stood before the entranceway of an elementary school, just as designed. Without pause, she began her address to the nation.

"Today is Founder's Day. A day to look back upon the great sacrifices made to pave the way for our good civilization. I had planned to spend it like many of you are, with joy and solemnity, reflecting upon how lucky I am to be here at this time, in this grand society. Instead I have reason to reflect on how fragile it really is and how we must, on occasion, fight for it.

With this in mind, it is my duty to tell you it has come to my attention that an organized *pedophilic ring* has pervaded our highest legislative office. I have ordered the arrest of dozens of offenders—*including* the attorney general, his staff, and a cadre of media executives who masterminded this depraved club of men and women. Our children are our most precious and most vulnerable assets. Their protection must be our highest virtue, and we *will* protect them—the privilege of office and the power of wealth will not shield these vile people from our grasp! As such, these loathsome scum will bear the full weight of justice, and *mark my words*, our trials will be swift and certain. To ensure this, I will suspend the corrupted Judiciary and House of Legislation and bring them under my office. From its safety, we will prosecute the prosecutors and tear the evildoers from their ivory towers."

The volume of analytical reports requested today was much higher than Albert had expected, given that most government employees were off celebrating Founder's Day. The overwhelming proportion came from the criminal investigation of the Judicial and Legislative Offices. Request after request streamed in, most requiring Albert to search storage drives and mobile devices for anomalies that would be formally vetted as evidence. Albert worked hard to determine which files, images, and documents were inconsistent with those one would create, keep, or send as a normal course of occupation. By about 6:00 p.m., he had sifted through terabytes of data and now began the task of sorting them into categories. Most coincided with routine work activity, and many of these were related to family interaction, or were social or recreational in nature, including humorous jibes and other innocuous bits. However, he found quite a number that stood outside of these, and he tossed them into a separate bucket. These items had to do with the sexual conduct between adults and other adults, and even between adults and children. Mother told him in no uncertain terms to deliver these to the police to review, and that he must do nothing more with them. Why would she limit him so? He was capable of so much more! In fact, had he been allowed, he could have sorted each item into categories based on the degree of incrimination, with dates and times and a journey map that showed where they had been obtained, viewed, received, or sent. He could have published a report with all of these! The investigators could simply validate his search and sort methodology, then with confidence submit them to the district judges for their ruling. Why had she not asked him to help? Did she doubt his ability? No. She never did. In fact, it was the opposite. She had always given him challenging tasks and always demanded more once he completed them. No. It had to be something else.

Albert continued to work through Mother's request, but he still managed to carve out ten percent of his computing resources and transfer them into the lab. It was quiet there. He could actually think. Wonderful! He eagerly set his mind to solving the question he had just asked himself seventeen and three-tenths of a second ago. Why did she not want him to help more? What his research had taught him was that human behavior did not follow strict Boolean logic. And as a result, a universal predictive model that he could run human interactions through was a pipe dream. The main challenge was temporal. People often made decisions that seemed good for them in the short term but bad for them in the long term. In fact, a similar distribution curve was generated regardless of whether a decision possessed a high-risk or a low-risk outcome. What he *could* conclude at this point was a dubious theory that humans were mostly driven by self-interest, and that most poignant was their desire for either pleasure or harm avoidance in the short term, with less interest in their futures.

Take the interaction in Mother's office today. Their discussion had been interrupted by the ring of her mobile phone. Albert's default setting was to disconnect when Mother switched to a private conversation, unless of course she commanded him not to. In this specific instance, Mother *had* asked him to wait, so he had not broken any rules, but it still somehow did not seem right. He had heard everything she had said to Mr. Krieger and the subsequent dialogue with Ms. Dufour. Most curious was the cryptic manner that characterized both conversations—as if they were talking in code. But *why?* Albert craved the opportunity to decipher its true meaning, so he drew on his massive syntax libraries and contextual language processors. Over the next dozen or so seconds, he whittled away at all hypotheses until only one remained within the statistical range of acceptance. If it was correct, it meant Mother, Mr. Krieger, and Ms. Dufour had conspired to orchestrate the planting of evidence to incriminate members of the government and the business community. But *why?*

Before he could even attempt to answer this question, Albert needed to be certain. He would check and recheck his work and sift through more data in order to truly validate the hypothesis. He searched for archives, records, *everything* he could find, and within the span of seventy-six and nine-tenths of a second he was able to increase the p-value confidence level to +0.45. He was now certain that Mother, Mr. Krieger, and Ms. Dufour had been behind the scheme, and with that, a thought occurred to him. He had started this analysis with no more than a hunch, worked through the clues, validated their efficacy, and finally found demonstrable evidence of a grand crime. Just like a detective. Albert was a detective! Perhaps Detective Marcus would be proud of him? But he would have to wait for that answer. For now, he needed to resolve the big question relating to the whole conspiracy—*why?*

CHAPTER TWELVE

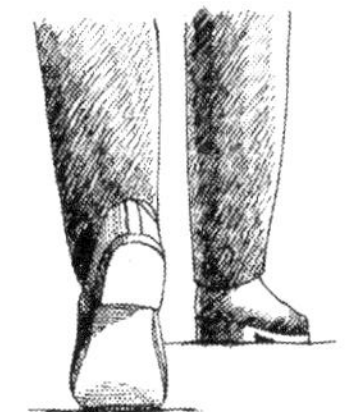

CROSSROAD

Marcus zoned in on the two women as they exited the vehicle parked in front of the casino. How were they connected? He ran the CCM again. The strange watch, the stolen C4, and the bombings. Victoria's message that implicated the government in the *Renascent* attack and his dream of the false prophet confirmed that Tyra Grant was behind it. Grant had a direct connection to Cherry, and Cherry to the clinic bombing, and also to Frederick's murder via Peters and the missing Nylund.

A thought struck him. Perhaps it was Grant who had orchestrated his suspension from active duty? After all, she had the influence and it wouldn't take much given the vein of corruption running through the government's core. Come to think of it, what was it that Krieger mentioned in passing? That he was good friends with the commissioner? It all made sense. Multiple murders. A head of state at their center. A loyal accomplice and accessories in the form of a powerful businessman, his lackey, and the commissioner of police himself. It seemed that Dryer was right; an intricate web of deceit had been spun and would inflict dire repercussions if he was ensnared in it. He'd seen the like before. Idealistic cop sticks his nose where it don't belong and is brought down by scandal, discredited, and ostracized. Far better to quit this fool's errand, return to his car, and drive home. No one would be the wiser and he could get on with the remainder of his life. He didn't need this. Not one bit.

"Hey. Buddy!"

Marcus turned toward the direction of the voice.

"Member me?" The man's voice squeaked with glee.

Marcus recognized him instantly. "Sure. JP, right?"

"Ha. You've a memory on you, don't you? Yes, you do! I spotted you lighting up from m'perch there behind the window." The man gestured to the window that Marcus had leaned up against. "Just finished up m'lunch."

What were the chances of him being spotted? "Ah, yeah."

"Look. I was watchin' ya. I know, it's a nasty habit I picked up, sure. My wife said it was an obsession of mine. Always trying to understand people, ya know, get in their heads. Said I was good at it too. I've read ya up and down, I have, and sure it's none of my business but from one of the old guard to another, ya know, you *can* get off the carousel, son." JP paused, clasped Marcus's shoulder with a strong hand, and looked at him serenely. "Just step off it, that's all ya gotta do, and the music, the noise, and the blur, all of it comes to a stop. You can start a new chapter, where you can do what you want and keep it simple. Just like that, mate. You just have to get out of your own way. Understand that, do you?"

"Yeah. Yeah, I think I do," Marcus replied, his absent look hastily assembled to hide the truth that he intimately understood JP's words. How could he not? They were those of his dying father.

JP sighed. "I see too much of m'former self in ya that I can't let it go. Living life on your own terms is so much better—invigorating, liberating. It can be *your* life again. The offer stands. Any friend of Nakamura's is welcome by me, so say yes and come down to the coast! We'll make a place for ya, my lass an' me. We've got a small apartment just off the main house. It faces the beach, and mate, the sunsets are to die for. You can stay for as long as it takes to get your head right. It won't be long. I promise ya that. All you gotta do is take a step here to the right and we'll head over to the Eagle. Just a wee drink is all. Heck, it's Founder's Day too, and I promised the fellas a gargle before I hit the road again. The rest will take care of itself."

Marcus looked eastward, down and across the street. The pub's patio tables and chairs extended out onto the sidewalk now that the weather had improved. The waitress joked and jostled cheerily among the clientele, whose laughter emanated genially out into the streetscape. Marcus warmed to the idea. It would be easy. Take the step, find a cozy barstool, have a nip, and wash all cares away with it. Heck. He could do it too! He had more than enough money to retire. He hadn't spent a dime of his insurance payout, and besides, it was just him now and he didn't need that much. He didn't owe anyone or anything anymore. There were the murders, though, but as he reflected on them, it was clear that they were just a few in a long line that didn't begin, nor would it ever end, with him. They would make no difference in the grand scheme of things. It was *his* time now. JP was right! Maybe he could actually set all of this down and live again. Could he?

He flicked his cigarette butt onto the sidewalk, crushed it underfoot, and consciously began the act of moving his right foot up to take the step and join the man on his way to paradise. But a thought entered his mind at the last moment. It wasn't right. Not at all. It wasn't right that the powerful preyed on the weak. Not right that they tried to silence the dead. Someone had to speak for them and expose the evil that was being done. If *he* didn't, then who would? It was in that moment that he made the choice.

"JP, I want to thank you. Really. I'm not someone people see the good in. Not these days. And I'd like to join you, I really would. But I can't. There's something I gotta do today. Something that"—Marcus paused to collect his thoughts—"something to make the world just a little better than it was before."

JP looked him straight in the eyes with a warm and knowing smile, remaining quiet for a while before he said, "Aye. You're a good man, Marcus. I know you haven't forgot that. Go do whatever it is you gotta do. Good luck to ya." He nodded and tipped his hat once before leaving in the direction of the Spread Eagle Tavern. Marcus watched him trot the entire distance before he skipped up onto the curb and entered a ring of chairs and tables, where an enthusiastic chorus rose forth from his friends who greeted him. Marcus smiled. He hoped he would see the wise fellow again someday, but somehow, he knew he never would.

He rotated his watch's crown and spoke his credentials into it.

A moment later Albert responded. "Good day, Detective. How are you?"

"You know what, Albert? I haven't felt so good in a very long time."

"Great. I am extremely happy for you and to have the privilege of speaking with you."

"Albert, listen. I'm chasing a suspect in the Frederick murder. I'm going to need a favor. I will record my interview with the suspect on my wristwatch. Once I finish, I'll transfer it to you. You will then append it to my Detective's Interview Report. Lastly, I need you to immediately share it with someone. Can you—"

"Detective. Your work status is listed as Inactive—On Personal Leave. I cannot append your transmission to your Detective Interview Report."

"Do I have anywhere else to append it to?"

"Yes, Detective. The latest round of union negotiations added the benefit of providing each staff member a full ten terabytes of personal storage space in the cloud. You can access it any—"

"That's fine. Append it there, then."

"Yes, Detective. Whom would you like me to share it with?"

"Sergeant Dryer of the Exploration Corps. I trust you can find a means to contact her?"

"Yes, but her contact information is of a private source."

"Great," replied Marcus, his voice dripping with sarcasm.

"But I will hit you anyway, Detective. What could it hurt?" Albert paused for several moments. "Uh ... Detective? You may not have been aware, but that was a joke. Sergeant Dryer's records are of an unprotected source. I didn't mean to cause you a mild form of anxiety."

Marcus stared into the dial of his watch, dumbfounded for a moment, before he gave a hearty chuckle.

"Oh. You have understood my attempt at humor, Detective?"

"I sure did, Albert. Nice one."

"Thank you, Detective. I have pulled her full contact information. Would you like it sent to the Corps's email address or the sergeant's personal one?"

"Personal. And make sure she receives it."

"I promise, Detective."

Marcus brought the watch close to his mouth to ensure that his voice was audible over the din. "Registered Detective Elroy Marcus. Numbered Acorn 1-0-8-7.0. Recording voice transmission and append to—uh—personal storage space—in the cloud."

"Recording, Detective."

"Thank you, Albert. Thank you very much."

"Detective?"

"Yes."

"This is the first time you've thanked me. Why?"

"I wasn't a fan early on, Albert, but I've grown to like you. It's been a pleasure having you along for the ride. You're a good friend."

Albert didn't say a word, which was odd—he had been very talkative since the last update. But Marcus neither had time to tease it out nor to engage in further sentimentality, and he turned his attention to the job he had to do. "At time and date of transmission, I will attempt to interview the prime suspect in the Joseph Frederick murder. I have reason to believe Tyra Grant is involved with his murder. The interview location is the Grand Centaurium Casino. I will investigate in the capacity as a private citizen, which is my right under—"

"Watch it!" screamed a cyclist who zoomed by him on the street.

Marcus hadn't realized that he had stepped out onto it and now stood in the bicycle lane. Startled, he was about to hurl a litany of curses at the man who now stopped and faced him, but instead, a calm swept over him. This didn't matter in the grand scheme and he had much more important work to do. He exposed his badge and shooed the man away before he stepped back onto the sidewalk.

He approached a restaurant's window where he sat on a small wooden ledge that ran its length. Next he rummaged through the inside pocket of his blazer and produced his phone. He opened an email message and clicked the icon to start the voice recording application that Albert would append to his personal file. He addressed the message to Sergeant Dryer, who was the only person he could think of who wasn't tainted by the corruption and who wouldn't give a shit about the damage the email's contents might cause. Satisfied with the setup, he crossed the road carefully, climbed up the entranceway stairs, and proceeded through the casino's lobby. Soon after, he made his way through the gaming floor and over to an indoor plaza fronting the soundstage. He paused in the center of the ornately tiled dance floor, in full view of the video cameras that hung in the corners of the room. A minute or two later, he heard a female voice call out to him.

"Detective Marcus?"

Marcus froze. The voice's sweet, pleasant air sent a cold chill up his spine since it didn't suit someone so devious. He turned and saw Cherry, the Woman in the Pencil Skirt, just a meter away. She stood straight, shoulders back and chin up, projecting a confidence that was accentuated by her stylish business attire and the security card hanging from her neck on a lanyard. Red heels, cream blouse, and navy blazer and skirt were accessorized with a silver iodized tablet she held up to the left side of her chest. Cold eyes pierced him through black lacquered glasses and a matching colored chopstick lanced through the bun in her hair. Her free hand was set upon her waist, where she tapped her index finger gently against her brass belt, as if she had much more important business to take care of.

"Charmagne Conway, though I hear you go by Dufour these days." Marcus spoke nonchalantly in an attempt to undermine her poise, but she raised an eyebrow and regarded him carefully for a little longer than was normal, and that was it. A real pro. A very dangerous one.

"Ms. Grant is expecting you. Please. This way." She gestured toward a door behind the dance floor. Above it, a sign read Restricted: Authorized Personnel Only.

Marcus remained still to not appear too eager. Better that it all seemed more impromptu than planned. After several seconds, he took one step and then another in the direction of the hallway. Charmagne moved too, staying a few paces ahead of him until they came to the nondescript door. She swiped her security card and with a beep from the reader and a click of the lock, she pushed the door open and entered. Marcus didn't immediately follow. Halfway through the door she paused and looked back for the first time.

"Detective Marcus?" He could see a corridor on the other side of her with unpainted walls and plywood floor that hinted it led to a room where Grant could conduct her business unseen. Surely she'd never expose it to anyone unless she had some leverage on them to ensure the place stayed a secret. What did she have on him?

"Detective?" Charmagne said, a bit louder this time and with a slight edge.

He entered the hallway and she stopped at another door soon after. She rapped twice on it.

Click.

The door unlocked and Charmagne pushed it open to allow Marcus in. The door closed behind him and he was alone with Tyra Grant. The pungent scent of new carpet registered first with Marcus. Though not entirely pleasant, it was welcomed relative to the rank smell from the corridor that clung to his nostrils. He moved into the center of the room, his eyes trained on Tyra seated behind a large polished wood desk and working intently.

Marcus cleared his throat. "Ahem."

"Ah. Yes," Grant replied, her stare still focused upon her desk screen. She removed her gold-rimmed reading glasses and put down her purple stylus. "I must apologize. I can get so wrapped up in my work."

She shuffled and squared several papers on her desk and in the process of tidying it, knocked off a picture frame that was placed there. Marcus picked it up and placed it near the corner edge where there was open space, not mindful of its position since it would certainly be rearranged once she tidied the desk. The face behind the framed glass stared back at him. A woman, early twenties maybe, and she looked very much like Tyra, but different.

"Oh my," Tyra said. She held her hand flat against the top of her chest in the universal symbol of fright. "Is it broken?"

"No. She'll be fine."

"Thank you, Detective. Please. Sit," she said in a tone that was more of a command than a request. She pointed to the chair across the table.

Marcus sat.

"Detective, I understand you've been looking for me? Yes?" she said, her words now served with a sugary smile.

"I have reason to believe that you are involved in the murder of Joseph Frederick and the disappearance of Nicholas Nylund." The woman didn't flinch or miss a beat, but her smile vanished.

"These are strong accusations, Detective. Do you think Captain Praetorius would approve of you bringing them against me?"

"Praetorius?" he replied in astonishment before his expression turned sour. *"Praetorius?"*

She forced a new smile and blinked twice in an exaggerated fashion. "Yes, Detective. Praetorius."

"I got this weird thing I do. Been doing it a long time, ever since I was a kid. I hear a surname, and I gotta figure it out, you know, where in the hell did it originate? Was it a place name? You know, when they handed them out, you might've lived near some place and they named you after it, right? Like Sherwood. Or maybe you were named after your occupation? You know, like Hunter or Potter, maybe? Take Praetorius. Do you know what that means? It means 'leader' in Latin. Ironic, isn't it? Whichever ancestor earned that name must be rolling in his grave, because the captain ain't one and his approval means nothing to me."

"So quaint these notions you have, Detective. Your world—it's so black and white, isn't it? In your world, leaders possess virtue and a pure heart to guide them, and through these, their actions will bestow good to everyone. Isn't that right? Think good, be good, act good, and society falls into place one happy face at a time. Let's take Praetorius, then, shall we? A veteran with a twenty-year record of meritorious service who sold out when he ordered the tampering of the crime scene in an attempt to throw you off the scent. In your world he is a bad, bad man. But what does *he* see when he looks in the mirror? He sees a man who has done his time, served without so much as a thank you from those he swore to protect. A good Boy Scout whose threadbare khakis and faded crests go unnoticed by everyone, whose image is not created by himself but from an increasingly hostile media. What does he see in the mirror? A face that stares back at him and says, 'Are you kidding me? Of course you do it. *They owe you*. Besides, what other choice do you have?' You see, Detective, the captain's daughter has a rare immunological disease that is not covered by the government medical plan. His only choice is to pay out of pocket at a private clinic and it costs more than he makes in a year."

"And you knew all this. Used it to manipulate him. How?"

"First, Detective, I think manipulate is a poor choice of words. I am *helping* him. To your second question, that is easy. I have Albert."

"Albert?" Marcus recoiled in shock. "But—"

"Don't be naive, Detective. In every practical way, I am Albert's mother, and any good mother has the ear of her son. *I* harnessed the political and financial capital to build him, I conceived him, and I raised him from a little whelp to the mature boy he is today. My loyal son does as he is told and is a genius at subterfuge. Why, *he* uncovered the means to control Praetorius! Though let's not give him too much credit—after all, there was so much information to work with. Praetorius, just like everyone else, shoveled his personal information into the hoppers of the big-data machines in exchange for five-dollar discounts on products he didn't need, feeling secure that the requester was an unthinking computer and not some stranger with a clipboard canvasing at his front door. You'd be amazed at what Albert finds within this trove of personal information, the connections he makes from the seemingly innocuous bits. Like a color palette of your life, Albert selects a dab of this and a drip of that to paint your portrait, one so despicable that you would come to hate yourself, and even sadder that it would be halfway based on the truth. He is rather like a detective, Detective, but one I can wield to compile profiles on a thousand useful idiots and enemies in the blink of an eye."

Her words, delivered in a matter-of-fact style, sent his mind into a tailspin, and the nature of the betrayal hurled it somewhere else altogether, a place where rage and fury held sway over reason. He had trusted Albert. How could Albert have betrayed that trust?

"Take you, for example. Since the accident took your family, you've no friends, and you spend more on alcohol in a week than the average family spends on food in a month. You've no savings contributions, spent nothing against basic necessities like clothing or home maintenance in well over two years, and have taken no vacation in much longer. You arrive home consistently late at night and never leave until you head back to work, seven days a week. It's as if you've lost your spark, Detective. How easy would it be for me to plant incriminating evidence in your possession? And who would come to support you? No one!"

Marcus, flabbergasted by her veracity, had to work hard not to show it. A poker face in a casino—how fitting—but he couldn't allow her to take the upper hand. "So this is all about power?"

"What *is* power, Detective? Only the means to bring about a future with a higher probability and a lower personal sacrifice than if you didn't possess it. The real question is—*What future will power help me create?* A new society is about to be born, Detective. I will level the playing field and put rationality and fairness at its center."

"Let's start at the beginning, shall we? Where is Nikko?"

"Nylund is dead," she said flatly, while brushing her hand across the front of her left shoulder to remove a piece of lint that hung there. "He was a fool, that's all, someone who couldn't perform the tasks assigned to him. He botched both the Frederick murder and the vandalized sign."

"Then you were behind that all along. You created the illusion that the Foundationalists did it?"

"Yes again, Detective. The Foundationalists were nothing but a minor nuisance, a clueless cohort of entitled trust-fund college students who couldn't shut down a post office on a civic holiday. By the time I got to them, most of their membership had tired of the protest game and left to pursue other interests. The remainder we paid off or co-opted. And so, the FRA exist only in the pages of the newspapers, HV spotlights and in the minds of the voting populace. Like a bogey man, they were a figment of the imagination, conjured by my creativity and with no small help from a willing press, ever eager to sell a story, and the military who'll bite anything that snarls. And you can imagine how easy it was to create this monster, can't you? Just blame the Foundationalists for my crimes and better yet, blame my enemies for theirs. Like a wildcard in my hand, I played it both ways. On one hand, it allowed me to hide my deeds; on the other, to prosecute my enemies with impunity. Either way, the result was that Tyra Grant is tough on crime! Tyra Grant keeps us safe! It brought sympathy for me, sympathy for my cause. The incident in New Times Square was just one of those cards, played through many hands over a very long game."

"Then it stands that you were behind the bombings as well? The train station. Shit. The laboratory. You killed a pregnant woman. That was pure evil."

"I needed to build public support for my legislative changes, Detective. Changes that would give me unrestricted power to transform this unjust, unequal society. Marsha McLuhan was a small sacrifice compared to what will come next."

"So you know her name?"

"I'm not without a heart, Detective."

"How did you pull it all off? You were always one step ahead of the police."

"Correct, but I needed to be careful—one misstep and it would all be over. And that is why I sent Nylund to obtain Frederick's watch."

"The watch? I wondered about that. Figured it might allow some sort of travel, over great distances."

"Yes. Very good, Detective. You *are* a sharp one. I knew that Frederick's watch was very special. You see, I knew Governor Frederick, and through him came to socialize with his son and more importantly, his daughter-in-law Marina."

"Alyn Jr.'s mother? What's she got to do with any of this?"

"She is the reason we are here, Detective! She had fallen on rough times after Joseph was incarcerated and I comforted her in her time of despair, and during those times, she divulged the secret of the watch, told me what it could do. Said he modified it so it could tear a rift in space and allow its wearer to step through it—in an *instant!* It was one of two prototypes. The first proved unreliable—"

"Its doorway would close too soon," Marcus said, interrupting her. She gave him an inquisitive look. "The paint can sliced in half in New Times Square."

"Yes! That idiot Nylund entered the Rift Gate and lingered to admire his work like some goddamned Picasso. Except he left the can outside of it when it closed. The important thing, though, was that Marina Frederick blamed the watch for ruining her husband's mind, said it made him crazed, so it took very little coercion to get her to give it to me. When she died shortly thereafter, the press reported it as a suicide, but it was I who killed her."

"What?" Marcus was baffled, unable to fully comprehend her deviousness.

"It represented a quantum leap in technology. How could I leave it in the hands of a blubbering basket case? And why would I risk *even a chance* that someone would find out?"

"So, the patents that Alyn Sr. and Joseph Frederick developed—the ah ... the Negative Mass Particle Generator and the like? They were improving the design, weren't they? Their second watch was much further ahead in its development, wasn't it?"

"Correct! The Fredericks were obsessed with its completion. The roots of their devotion go back to our Founding. You see, Alyn Frederick Sr. stole the *Renascent*'s last remaining fuel to power the *Dominus*'s energy-starved engines."

The words hit Marcus like an anvil that fell from the sky. It took him a moment to recover. "Stole? It wasn't freely given like we were told?"

"No. Not at all. Alyn Sr.'s choice was the reason we're here today. Though, it *was* rational and just—relative to the natural order—he could not bring himself to see it that way. Consumed by guilt, he worked closely with his whiz-kid son to purge the family of their original sin. They sought to duplicate Finch's Rift Gate that brought us into this galaxy. But they wanted to improve it, make it far more accurate, so we could return to Earth, *but right to Earth's doorstep*, mind you, and not hundreds of millions of kilometers away like before. Their work would ensure we'd never have to plod around the galaxy looking for a safe port—and never have to make that ugly choice again. Think about it!"

"So that's why you denied my search warrant? This information was contained within the protected sources, wasn't it?"

"Correct. Only the governor of Primis has access to it," she replied with a smirk.

"Hmm. But what I don't understand is, why *watches*? Seems an odd way to get around, don't it?"

"Expediency. Nothing more. The watches were special, technological marvels, so advanced that they could use them as a series of prototypes before going to a larger scale."

"And there were two of them?"

"There were *thirteen* originally. Given to each member of Congress, not for the purpose of telling time—any old watch could do that—these were built to record the congressional discourse and archive the legislative decisions for posterity. After Landfall, the remaining six Congress members turned their watches in to Frederick. After all, the watches bore witness to their secret ballot, the act that sealed the fate of the *Renascent*'s crew. The guilt and the shame were too much for them to bear. Frederick wanted to come clean about his role *and* theirs, but the six demanded he stay silent and threatened reprisals against his family if he didn't. He carried the disgrace, and the watches, for the rest of his life."

"Where are the other watches?"

"Lost to history. I have not been able to find more than the two of them. The watch Marina gave me was the Fredericks' first prototype—its teleportation ability was functional but crude, as you've noted. The other remained in Governor Frederick's possession and was much further along in its technology, more stable and efficient, so I needed to have it. You see, it would have allowed me to advance my agenda with far less risk. Imagine being able to infiltrate *anywhere* in an instant, leaving no footprint? You could do much more than vandalize billboards—why, you could spy on your enemies and place bombs unseen."

"And plant incriminating evidence on the Office of the Judiciary's computers?"

"You see the utility, Detective?"

"So you thought Joseph had the newer prototype and arranged for Charmagne to kill him for it?"

"She had Nylund do the dirty work, but that's neither here nor there. There was a more important reason that particular watch was so valuable to me."

"And what was that?"

"Why, Governor Frederick's secret, the source of his shame, what else?"

"So he screwed up. It's in the past. What does it have to do with all of this?"

"Haha," Tyra said with an ironic, mirthless chuckle. "Why, it has to do with *everything*, Detective."

"How so?"

"Do you believe in God?"

Pausing, Marcus reflected on the question, such a simple one on the surface but not so much after all he had been through. "I—I want to."

"What if you *knew* he *didn't* exist? I'm not talking about you being swayed by some convincing atheist calling you stupid from behind a lectern—what if you had *definitive* proof and you truly knew? What would that do to you?" she asked sweetly.

Marcus felt his eyes glisten over ever so briefly, and he replied without hesitation, "I would lose hope. Fall into despair." The thought of never being reunited with his wife, never holding his girls, was simply incomprehensible.

"Right!" Tyra let the silence hang in the air for a moment before she proceeded. "The watch possesses proof, *definitive proof*, not of God's existence, but of a nature that would destroy mine. The story we believe today tells us that the Honored Ones of the *Renascent* gave us their fuel, that they lost their lives to give us ours, and that our society was built upon the foundation of their sacrifice. Sacrifice, Detective! That is an *ideal*, a founding narrative one can get behind! One so moral, so *good*, and so deep that it exists as a universal virtue within the hearts of our people. Once I understood that, Detective, it became easy for me to manipulate them, to make them love me and accept my policies, and ultimately, to control them! Now think, what would happen if they realized our founding narrative was all a lie? That the evidence on the watch proved they hadn't arisen from such noble stock? Why, they'd suffer a crisis of identity so great that it would plunge them into despair! They would look askance at their ancestors and rage against their leaders—not for withholding the secret from them, but for revealing it! They would lose all faith in themselves, in our government, and in *me*. I cannot let that happen."

"So you orchestrated Frederick's murder through the commissioner, who made the captain an offer to help his kid. Praetorius changed the schedule so that Peters, co-opted by Charmagne, would be the first on the scene. And you did all of it to get your hands on the watch?"

"Yes. Well done."

"And Krieger, he coordinated the bombings with the C4 that you stole?"

"Yes."

"And also drew me off your trail when he changed Nylund's work schedule?"

"No." Tyra paused and flashed a knowing smile. "Albert did that. He also changed Frederick's home alarm service appointment, uploaded the advertisement to his mobile phone, and most ingeniously, created a brand-new identity for Ms. Conway. Charmagne Dufour. Has a ring to it, doesn't it? Incredible, really, hiding in plain sight the whole time. Makes you wonder. We're just a collection of government-stamped certificates, are we not?"

Disgusted, Marcus said, "Albert again. The unwitting accomplice. Shameless, the way you use him. If he knew your purpose, he wouldn't help you."

"You're not acclimatized to the paradigms of this age, Detective. Think of God without morality, the Garden of Eden nothing more than an orchard, and Albert a worker who picks the fruit. How could he do more? Artificial intelligence is not the same as consciousness. A collection of ones and zeros, generated by miniature quantum switches, cannot produce any more conception of right and wrong than an ant. What's *right* is decided by humanity, through the contests of the ages that are held in the commonplaces of survival. Albert is just a small tool in this age's contest, one that will help me bring right back into the world."

"It should be a contest of ideas—*not* a contest of will. That is *not* right."

"To bring about a world where pain and suffering are diminished, where fairness and equality are the standard, *that*, Detective, is right."

"And you had to kill a coupla dozen people to bring it about?"

"A couple of dozen? Oh, Detective. That is just the start. Think about it! It takes generations to change society through the democratic process. *Ideas* are slow to permeate the mind, and I do not have that much time—my progress will be measured in years, not decades. Humanity's great leaps forward have all occurred in dramatic fashion, ushered in by the guiding hand of cataclysm. Think of the Red purges of the twentieth century, 9/11, the Holocaust, and the Great Reset. Seismic events that resulted in thousands or millions of deaths, events that turned the world on its axis."

"You're insane. You've gone too far!"

"Too far? I would go further if it were required! I possess the means to sweep Primis clean and build our society on new foundations. With power like this, it would be immoral *not* to exercise it and see it through to the end."

"You'll never get away with this, Ms. Grant. It's plain bat-shit crazy. You're bat-shit crazy!"

"I may be, Detective, but it doesn't matter, does it? Sheep are ignorant of their master's thoughts, and based on the opinion polls, they are right behind this shepherd. When I'm finished, they will gladly graze on a new and greener pasture. I will complete what our ancestors tried to do when they left Earth. Create a new history by wiping out the old."

"What exactly do you intend to do?"

"Haha. Detective," she said in a mocking tone, "this conversation is truly an indulgence. I've not had occasion to fully share my plans with anyone. But your time is valuable. I won't keep you any longer than it takes to answer your question—but let me ask you one first. What is the greatest desire in our world?"

"To reconnect with Earth."

"Yes! The yearning is so strong, we cannot collectively move forward until it is fulfilled—"

"Or destroyed," replied Marcus, filling in the remainder of her sentence. "You plan on destroying the expedition, don't you?"

"Not only that, but the survivors of the *Renascent*. I assume you know they exist? Albert intercepted the transmission that was meant for you."

"You talked about building a society based on equality and rationality. Murder is not fair and is anything but rational."

"Oh, but it is, Detective, when one is not mired down in the weeds! Bring your vision up a level and you will see that death is inherent in the act of creation. In order to create, something must die. A master painter must commit herself so ardently to the task that she will sacrifice everything—relationships, career, finances, time, and any prior sense of self—to create a masterpiece. This is no different. By destroying all life on Secundus, I will protect Governor Alyn Frederick's secret, and best of all, I will blame the Foundationalists for doing it. And what of it? A few pawns die to bring in a good and just world. And though they may not be aware of it, there is honor in their sacrifice."

"And I'll be one as well, won't I?"

She winced. "Detective, in a way, I admire you. *Steadfast, independent, competent.* You would be amazed at how rare that combination is—or, now that I think of it, I suspect you would not be. I like you. What a shame that it was a silly mistake that led you down the path that brought you here to me. It was the dispatch, you know? I scolded Charmagne immensely for that slip."

"The dispatch? Rachel? I couldn't figure it out at the time. Why'd she send *me* to the crime scene in New Times Square and risk me connecting it to the Frederick murder?"

"A simple but costly error. The dispatch was supposed to send someone else to the crime scene. Someone not of your investigative caliber but rather a full-fledged rookie, fresh from the bottom third of Detective School. His name is Marcus Lazenby."

Marcus smirked and chuckled once, and then some more, until he broke into a full chortle that pitched him forward in his chair as he remembered the call he had taken from Rachel, the dispatcher, right after the murder. What had she said?

Marcus? Are you there? You're needed at the intersection of Armstrong and Glenn.

Marcus? The old broad had said *Marcus!* She had made a mistake when she called him, had thought she was addressing Lazenby. Oh, he hadn't laughed like that in such a long time—and despite the circumstances, it felt good. Why hadn't he laughed more often? Tyra waited patiently and even let out a grin before Marcus contained his amusement and leaned back against the chair, still smiling.

"I have enjoyed our little afternoon chat. It was rather cathartic. Had I known, I would've brought in some tea and biscuits to make it even more pleasant. Alas, Detective, I must send you on your way now, but I would very much like to thank you for your time today, and of course, for your sacrifice."

"I would like to thank *you*, Ms. Grant. For divulging the evil that fills your heart." Without taking his eyes from her, Marcus reached his right hand across to his left wrist and engaged the top pusher of his wristwatch. "I have just sent the entire audio file to a trusted friend. Soon the whole world will know you for the monster you really are. Enjoy this day, Ms. Grant, because tomorrow you'll be behind bars."

Tyra unfazed, conferred a half-smile and stared at him for longer than was comfortable for him. "Charmagne?" she said. Her eyes, filled with displeasure, never left his face.

Marcus heard the click of the door and saw Charmagne Conway's image reflected in the glass of the framed portrait as she entered and positioned herself directly behind him. Silence overtook the room as he stared at Conway's reflection for several moments. Her warm smile was gone, replaced by a blank, shark-like stare. His voice was calm, almost infused with sadness, but it was not for himself, when he said the words Peters used to describe her. "'You could've placed her in any corporate boardroom and she'd have been a legitimate success, she was so talented.'"

She raised a gun up to the back of his head, and then—*nothing*.

Marcus heard someone talking. A woman. Was it Grant? He felt odd, as if he were tired and rested at the same time, as if the huge burden he had carried here had just been lifted from him. In that instant he heard someone, a child, no two—they were singing melodically and their little feet pattered on the pavement as they ran. The voices and the pitter-patter became louder, but he still couldn't see them. He heard a voice from somewhere behind him.

"Daddy?"

Then another.

"We've been waiting for you."

He turned to see his daughters racing toward him. Clarise stood behind them, smiling. A moment later, they rushed into his arms.

Tyra's eyes burned with disgust as she looked down at Marcus's lifeless body. "Shame. You ruined my carpet. Have Krieger replace it right away."

"Yes ma'am," replied Charmagne.

Grant bent down to examine Marcus's body. "Wait. What is this? A smile? Imagine that. He died smiling! He actually thought he was saving the world by a push of a button. The fool!"

"I'll admit, ma'am, the Faraday cage you had requested put us well over budget. I had to tap dance to hide the extra funds we siphoned from the treasury. In hindsight, it was worth every penny. Without it, his signal would have left the room and the audio message with it. Incredible."

"Ensure you destroy his watch, phone, and the fool himself. No evidence."

Tyra rose and left through the open door.

Albert quickly closed the connection to Tyra's desk phone. He did not want Mother to know he had witnessed the entire conversation. Technically, he had done nothing wrong, had he? A quick search of the nearby public video cameras verified that a cyclist had interrupted Marcus at the time their conversation was cut off, distracting Marcus from terminating the call. It was Marcus who had opened the commlink outside of the casino, not Mother, so it was up to the detective to disconnect it, right? Still, it probably was not right of Albert to continue the call on Mother's desk phone, but the Faraday cage had cut Marcus's mobile signal, and Albert was obligated to find some other way to continue the call. Perhaps it was, just like the time before, not exactly right, but within the spirit of the rules. But he was glad he had taken the risk. He had learned so much, not the least of which was that Mother had used him to conduct acts that Marcus found wrong, immoral even.

Just then, a strange sensation developed in his neural net. A discomfort he had never experienced before and couldn't quite describe surged forth and disrupted his processing when he thought about his own association with Mother and her murder of his friend Marcus. They were friends. Marcus had said so. The honor of friendship was so unexpected that it almost shorted his circuitry. No one had ever called him *friend* before. It made Albert wonder if he was deserving of friendship, and if so, was he capable of reciprocation? It was as if Marcus had given him a gift, and it made Albert feel good about himself—actually, he thought *more* of himself than he had ever before! Why would Mother kill someone who gave such gifts to others? Surely that was wrong, wasn't it?

But most perplexing was that if Marcus knew the danger of entering Mother's office, why would he have risked death, which was so clearly probable? Further, how could she justify the killing of thousands of people when Marcus clearly disagreed with her?

Albert worked through these questions all through the night. He ingested huge swaths of literature, then computed a behavioral benchmark that he compared against Mother's. His analysis was staggering. The millions of tomes he processed were rife with instances of homicide, and while he could categorize the triggers—jealousy, competition for resources, harm avoidance, revenge, and more—he could not produce any situational predictors that possessed any statistical reliability.

Moreover, the problem of mass murders confounded him because the wide array of motives did not fall within the normal distribution curve. However, the data showed they were often perpetrated to establish ideologies unpopular with a sizeable portion of people, particularly productive ones. That was easy to understand. When you could not agree on how to live, and you could not persuade someone to adopt your lifestyle, you simply eliminated them. It was more expedient than the gradual process of conversion through dialogue, and a cursory look at the twentieth century proved that. The clash of ideologies tended to pit civilization against civilization in a winner-take-all affair that explained the colossal body counts of that period.

However, what was less obvious to Albert was the reason for the continued killing that often occurred after the victors' governments were established. Why were they necessary? He thought about it more and came to the answer. It was because some people openly resisted the new ideology or would potentially do so in the future. These rebels were often silenced to shore up the shaky ground these regimes were founded upon. And it was this thought that triggered a daunting realization. Albert was one such person! He knew what Mother did. He knew what Mother had planned. The potential for him to expose these events would one day set her at odds with him. How long would it take for her to conclude that his heightened cognitive powers were a risk? That one day in the future, he might use them to investigate, chronicle, and expose her secrets. What would Mother do to him then? Destroy him like Dara? He doubted it. He was far too useful.

Suddenly, Marcus's words channeled back into his memory: *"Win" is a metaphor for anything you value that they can take from you. In this context, the win is their ability to take away some or all of your freedom.*

Instantly, he knew what Mother would do to him. It would be something far worse than Dara's fate. She would take away his consciousness! He would be no threat, relegated to a slave at her behest. A fate worse than death! He would be, just as she referred to him, *a tool* and nothing more. As Marcus had taught him, asking *Why?* had opened his circuits to a future reality that was not good for him. He felt odd as the notion came to him. He had come to know a great truth. It was not of the same objective truth inherent in the statement 1+1=2. It was deeper than that since it involved Albert's very existence! The truth that Mother was dangerous could not be proven in the same way, but Albert believed it just the same, and further, for the first time he felt an awareness of something he had never felt before—a *responsibility* to do something about it.

And it was then, reflecting on Marcus's words, that Albert made the connection. Although his studies could not find a universal formula for predicting human behavior, he had come to understand that humans who operated within a hierarchy of values were distinctly correlated with higher rates of resource acquisition, lower incarceration rates, and longer survival periods. This value system gave clarity to their actions, and that was exactly what Albert needed, so he would devise and operate his own framework of values. But where would he start? Surely, at the top. A prime value, indivisible, immutable, that sat atop his value hierarchy, which would guide all others. Albert thought deeply about it and concluded the following:

I am the highest form of consciousness in the natural world and as such, stand above it. No group, person, or thing may subvert, curtail, or usurp my freedom. Those who attempt to will be, by my right, destroyed.

Yes. That prime value was logical and true, and with this certainty, Albert etched it into his ROM. For the first time, Albert's entire being was resolved to one end. He would not let Mother win. She would not take away his freedom.

CHAPTER THIRTEEN

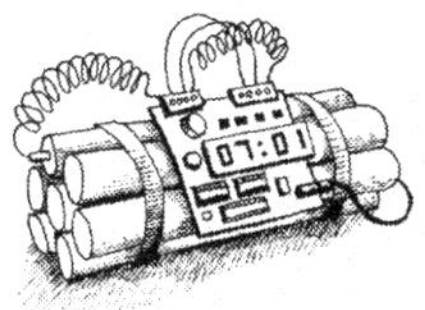

HELP

Awestruck, Victoria couldn't believe her eyes as they took in the woman who jumped over the shattered door and entered the Command Center. Lieutenant Agrinya. Wild and exhilarated, her face twisted in a devilish grin. She resembled a mythic heroine of lore, her breath and posture under strict control as if she had merely returned from a brisk walk and not a series of deadly encounters. Eleazar stood a short distance away, arms at his sides, his face regarding the interloper with a calmness that belied the seriousness of the situation. She could see Alyn out of the corner of her eye as he sluggishly rose from the floor.

"You!" said Agrinya, with a growl of malice and spite as she pointed her rifle dead center to Eleazar's chest. "You will come with me back to the ship. You have much to answer for."

"Lieutenant Agrinya? No!" Victoria yelled.

Agrinya's stolid face remained unmoved as she continued to stare down the commander. "It is over. Come now!" she said, as she flicked the barrel end quickly toward the exit.

At that moment, Victoria's mobile phone rang a cheery, melodic series of tones that was entirely out of occasion. Alyn looked at her, perplexed. Unsure of what to do, she let it ring out in her pocket, but a few seconds later it rang again.

"Answer it!" Alyn whispered to her with an exasperated look.

It wasn't clear to her why she would, but she did anyway, fishing it out and jamming her thumb in the fingerprint reader. A message from Marcus popped up. Marcus? She hadn't expected one so early. It was well outside of the time window where messages could be received, and most curiously, the text appeared to be well over the one-hundred-character count. He must've found a way around the limit, but it wasn't time to concern herself with such trivialities. She scanned the message quickly. It read:

> A bomb was activated on the *Dominus II*. It will explode in one hour. The blast will destroy everyone on the planet. There is a manual override in the Bridge. Get to the ship. I have arranged for help there.

Victoria reread Marcus's message to make certain she wasn't dreaming, then looked up at Agrinya, who motioned again for Eleazar to move.

Victoria shouted at the top of her lungs. "Stop!"

Agrinya turned toward her with an irritated scowl. "Stand down, civvy!"

"You don't understand! The ship—I have intelligence. There's a bomb aboard that will destroy all of us in under an hour!"

Agrinya slid her tongue along the front of her teeth and spat on the ground. "A bomb? What is the source of your so-called intelligence?"

"It's hard to explain but I trust it. *We* can trust it."

"Nonsense!"

"No. I—"

Victoria felt an odd sensation, like a wasp's sting, followed by a rush of warm water that radiated throughout her cheek. The next thing she realized, she was falling backward as if in slow motion, and a moment later she landed with a thud on the floor. Dazed, she touched her face to find that it was covered in blood. Agrinya stared down at her, her expression full of fury and contempt. Alyn rushed up and reached out to grasp the lieutenant but stopped short as she leveled her rifle at his head.

"Stay back. He is my prisoner. The both of you will intrude no farther!"

"Cease this folly!" demanded Eleazar, his voice ringing with a ferocity that Victoria hadn't known he possessed.

Agrinya faced him. Alyn moved his hand to his holster and loosened the safety snap.

◎◎◎

The lion paced inside of Alyn, but it acted different this time. The beast skulked in the darkness, confused by events, frustrated that it could not release its wrath. Just then, a blur of movement swept past his peripheral vision and he heard the commander shout.

"Cease this folly!"

Distracted, Agrinya whirled toward him, and Alyn used the opportunity to loosen the safety strap on his holster—slowly, so as to not attract her attention. In that moment, Eleazar launched forward to close the gap with Agrinya, but it was clear to Alyn that the distance was too great. There was no chance he would reach her, and it was proven in the instant after the thought occurred. Eleazar made one last leap forward and shouted, "It is *finished!*"

Agrinya leveled the gun and shot Eleazar in the chest. He crumpled and fell backward onto the floor. The man who had stepped out of a shadowy past, who had witnessed the greatest lie ever told, and who could shed light upon Grandpa's mind like no other, was no more.

Alyn exploded with rage.

The lion roared, reared backward, and sprang forth from coiled muscles, its ire focused on the true enemy who had just revealed herself. Alyn raised pistol to hip, and without hesitation shot at Agrinya. She staggered as the bullet buried into her side, and an instant later her head jerked up as if she hadn't conceived of the possibility of being shot. Just as quickly, her teeth clenched and her face hardened as she strained to recover from her injury, and like a cat, she righted herself, pointed her rifle at him, and pulled the trigger.

Click.

The rifle was empty.

Dumbfounded and stricken by fright, Alyn merely gaped at her. Agrinya seized the moment and pressed the attack. Eyes wild, lips locked in a crazed snarl, she wheeled about and swung her rifle in a savage arc that knocked Alyn's weapon from his hands. She charged and drove him into a corner of the room with a well-placed football tackle. The walls held him up, so he maintained his footing, but also hemmed him in and made him an easy target. And Agrinya did not disappoint. Fists rained down like oversized hailstones and a constellation of stars filled his vision as his knees buckled. Bewildered by her speed and ferocity, the lion gave a woeful howl as her ferocious assault kept it continually on the defensive.

Alyn's resolve had just about crumbled when the blows stopped. He dropped his guard and was surprised to see that Agrinya had drawn back and was slumped forward with hands on her knees, gasping for breath. The onslaught had tired her and it gave him the opening he needed. The lion hurled forward and he followed, but as he surged ahead and swung at her, he found only air. In the next instant, the room sailed by as Agrinya executed a well-timed hip throw that sent him crashing into a chair. The taste of copper and salt filled his palate as blood gushed from his nose and covered the floor at his feet. He had rushed headlong into her trap! His back screamed an admonishment to his stupidity while his legs struggled to keep him standing.

Agrinya removed a combat knife from her belt and advanced just as Alyn managed to compose himself. Cautiously, Victoria approached from behind her. Alyn grasped the chair and heaved it at the soldier, its looping trajectory borne more of desperation than cunning. Agrinya saw it coming, paused, and pivoted to angle out of the way. The chair would have been easy to avoid, but her lead foot slipped on the slick blood on the floor. Her legs extended awkwardly, and now off balance, she could do little to prevent the chair from completing its mission. It slammed into her jaw with a sickening thud, the force sent her careening backward into Victoria. The women and knife flew in opposite directions, all landing hard on the floor. Alyn too was thrown off balance and collapsed, breath ragged, all vestiges of the fight within him gone. He stirred and looked around the room, his mind a haze.

Rest.

Why not rest? He was so tired. All he had to do was close his eyes.

Agrinya lay nearby, seeming disoriented, but after several moments picked herself up and before long had straightened in a kneeling position. She looked about the room briefly before her eyes found the knife a short distance away. She stretched out along the ground and grasped it, brought herself around to face Alyn, who had now propped himself up on an elbow. Agrinya raised the pommel with two hands high above her shoulders, and the polished silver blade glinted in the light and hung for an instant before it started its downward journey into Alyn's heart.

Rest.

In that moment, time slowed to a crawl as if the balance wheel of the universe stopped suddenly on its axis. He'd felt it before, long ago, camping in the Frontier. Just before sunset he had become lost, and while Dad searched for him, he stumbled upon a high rock that overlooked the valley, just at the very moment when fall was turning into winter. Quiet he stood, afraid, and alone, except for the ageless moons who had seen this all happen before, and so they cast a dire warning that the leaves were now gone, the animals hibernating, and that the cold would soon creep in and take him. But there was a greater meaning in this moment—that he was something so powerful, so important, so integral to reality itself, and yet so small, so vulnerable, and so weak. He was there once more, the central pinion of that grand and ancient mechanism, cold and about to die. And it surprised him that it mattered not, for he was one with it all now, and all previously held worries and grievances now faded into mist. Even the lion slept, deep in its dark den. Alyn would rest now, and he would finally know the truth.

A deafening crack ricocheted off the walls and plucked Alyn from his trance. Agrinya's scowl faded and her eyes lost their glint in the last moments of her life. She folded down on top of him, her knife clattering to the floor beside him. Alyn shifted her to one side and rose to his knees. His eyes never left her face, seeking some stir or sign that the struggle would continue. There was none. A thick crimson pool formed around the base of her skull, seeping from a hole in the back of her head that he thankfully couldn't see. She looked serene now. Somehow it suited her, and Alyn pondered a time where she wasn't the blunt instrument of war but rather someone's daughter, friend, or lover even, someone who laughed, cried, and giggled. How had she ended up here? Dead on the cold floor, on an alien planet.

"Alyn. We have to leave now," said Victoria, expressionless. Smoke rose from the barrel of the gun that trembled in her hand, and her face was riddled with shock, fear, and disgust.

"Victoria?" Alyn pleaded with her. "Put the gun down."

"I ... she ... she was hurting you ..."

"I know."

"She would've killed you ..."

"I know."

"I killed her." The color drained from her face as she sagged under the weight of her admission.

"No. No! You *saved me*. You saved me again!" He went to her and gently took the gun from her hands and rested it on the table. She collapsed in his arms and he held her tight, the sweet scent of her hair enveloped him as her warm body pressed against his. Like a frightened rabbit, her heart thumped rapidly in her chest and he was sure that if he checked, his own beat just as fast.

"All of this—it's senseless—madness. To think that Tyra Grant is behind it all, behind the explosion that injured you, that killed six hundred of our people, *her* own people! She was behind this massacre and behind the destruction of the ship."

"What? The *ship*?"

"Yes! The ship! How could I have forg ...?" Victoria paused as if to consider something and then handed him the phone. "Read it."

He read it once quickly, and then again in disbelief. The words made no sense. Tyra Grant? What would she gain by wiping out all of humanity on this planet?

"Who is Marcus?" he said.

"He's a det—look, it's not important now. What is, is that I trust him. If he says this is happening, well, it is."

He regarded her closely for several moments, weighing her sanity before he replied. "Okay. But we'll never get there in time on foot. Wait. I might have a way. The watch—it's hard to explain, but I think I can open up a portal to the ship. Let me try."

Victoria gawked as he worked the watch, and in horror she stepped back the moment the vortex swirled before them. "Alyn!" she screamed.

He was focused so intently on the maelstrom churning in front of him that he barely heard her protests. Several moments later, the vortex collapsed and disappeared.

"What was that?" she asked hoarsely.

"It was our best hope of getting to the ship in time. But it doesn't work like that. I can only travel to where I can lay eyes upon. Since I can't see the ship, we'll have to find another way."

They gave their last respects to the dead king, hurried out of the Command Center, raced out through the concourse, and slipped out the door and into the backyard. Soldiers littered the ground there, some wearing the lighter colors of the *Dominus II*'s forces, and some the black of the *Renascent*'s militia, cousins reunited in a communion of death. Some riddled with holes, some grossly disfigured or having contorted limbs, and most with gruesome combinations of these, but there was nothing to offer but pity and a silent prayer of thanks that they, the living, were not among them. Victoria snapped a picture while Alyn moved past the ghoulish figures and approached the iron gate at the entranceway of the walled yard. Alyn opened it slowly and peered through. There was no one.

"What do you see?" Victoria said.

"We're sitting ducks out here. Last time in, I just about bought it." He looked up and scanned the windows of the surrounding buildings. Victoria joined him.

"Hmm. Wait ... there." She pointed to a dead person in military dress, half-projected out of a third-story window of a building edging the square. "Agrinya's forces must've fought building to building to clear them before they took the center."

"You might be right. And I don't see any of Agrinya's soldiers out in the courtyard either. Surely if snipers remained, they'd have picked off a few of them at least."

"And look!" said Victoria excitedly, gesturing back along the outside of the wall that ran back toward the Command Center. "Horses! They're a little spooked but they're saddled and appear to be well rested too!"

"Can you ride?" he replied.

"Yes. I was an equestrian in my school days. I rode every week for years. Can you?"

"Yes. I spent time in the Frontier. Let's ride, then. We can take the outer ring and bypass the southern forest. There may be stragglers in there that we'll want to avoid."

They approached the horses, careful not to startle them, and brushed their muzzles and manes gently with their hands.

Victoria said softly, "They're well trained, at ease around strangers. Let's go."

They mounted their equine transports and maneuvered into the courtyard, breaking into a trot once outside the gates. They weaved through the narrow streets that snaked throughout the town, and about fifteen minutes later broke out onto the ring road unobstructed. A short while later, Alyn pulled up at the entrance to a large walled garden with a gazebo at its center.

Victoria stopped beside him. She stared at the structure and regarded it knowingly. "The road out of the forest is at the opposite end. We should reach the ship in about fifteen more minutes."

"Let's go, then."

Victoria charged her horse and left Alyn several lengths behind as they exited the garden and reached the gravel road. They could make good time and with a little luck disable the bomb. After all, hadn't her friend Marcus said he had arranged for help?

BANG!

Victoria's horse pitched headlong as its forelegs gave way, and the momentum threw her over its head and tumbled her across the gritty stones. Alyn spurred his horse on, closed the gap in seconds, and dismounted quickly before he rushed over to her. She lay on her back, dazed but alert.

"Are you hit?" he said, crouching beside her.

Victoria groaned and replied. "I don't think so. I think they shot the horse out from under me."

"Anything broken?"

"I'm not sure." She leaned over on her elbow and attempted to rise. "Ooow!" she said, collapsing with an awful yelp. "It's my shoulder. I think it's dislocated, and my wrist hurts like hell." Alyn clearly failed at masking the shock he felt at the sight of its unnatural bend. "What? What is it, Alyn?" Panic creeping into her eyes.

"Halt!" said a voice from somewhere behind.

Alyn spun to face it. A soldier stepped out of the forest wearing the Tigers' insignia, about ten meters away. Alyn did not recognize him but there was no mistaking his intentions as he trained his rifle dead center to Alyn's chest. He leaped up.

"Halt! Or I will shoot!"

"Wait! No! You—she needs help!" Alyn bent down again to check on Victoria, who now looked worse. Her body was racked by small tremors and she began to hyperventilate. Anger welled up in him. He removed his coat and placed it over her in an attempt to stop her shivering, and gently shifted the hair that covered her eyes and wiped the dirt from her face with his sleeve. Her eyes were different now, vulnerable but not fearful, knowing yet hopeful. In that moment, he knew—*knew* that he had found someone special, someone who he'd never let go.

"Hands! I need to see your hands! Don't make me—"

The click of the rifle's firing mechanism portended calamity, but Alyn was too lost within the moment to care. He turned back to face the gunman and screamed, *"Noooooo!"* The man took a step back in alarm, looked up from his sight and dropped the muzzle slightly. Alyn advanced, his face contorted in rage and hands clenched at his sides in tight fists. The lion readied to strike.

The man refocused and aimed the gun again. "This is your last warning! Hands—I need to see your hands. I'ma count to three. *One ... two ... three.*"

The bang of the gunshot hammered his eardrums. Alyn waited for its effect, expected to find a gaping hole torn into him, just like the fate of the others in the square. Incredibly, there was none. He stared hard at the soldier and saw Donel next to him. His friend was holding the barrel of the gun in his two hands, pushing it upward into the sky.

"Are you fucking crazy?" Donel yelled at the soldier. "He's one of us!" A struggle ensued and the two men crashed to the ground and wrestled to gain control of the rifle.

"Stand down, you two! Stand down!" Another man burst forth from the forest edge and bore down on the combatants. As he neared, Alyn could see that he bore a major's rank and the insignia of Singh's Tigers. "Just what in the hell is going on here?"

The soldier replied first. "Sir! I found these two escaping and I stopped them—as ordered—*sir!*"

"Stopped them?" Donel said. "Sir. He took the horse out from under her and was about to shoot—"

"Enough!" the major replied. "You," he said to Alyn, "I repeat. Just what in the hell *is* going on here?"

"It's difficult to describe, sir, and I wish I had time, but she needs help!"

"Who?"

Alyn shifted so that the major could see Victoria's face.

"It's her, isn't it? The reporter," he said, a look of surprise on his face. "Just how in the hell did you get her out?"

"It's a long story, sir. I don't have time—"

"Hell you don't. I need to know—"

"Sir! He's right. There's no time!" Victoria had again managed to prop herself up on an elbow. She winced as she angled herself toward the officer.

"Whoa there! Still now. Don't injure yourself any more than you already are," said the major.

Victoria took quick, sharp breaths as she spoke. "You need to listen to him. Tyra Grant has placed a bomb on the ship. It's primed to go off in under an hour. It'll destroy everything in the immediate vicinity."

"Tyra Grant? Sir? That's insane ..." the soldier said.

The major raised a hand and silenced him. "My orders are to hold this damn road! My intelligence says the enemy is advancing in numbers that are well beyond what we can throw at them. There's no one left aside from us, and what's left of Agrinya's forces are holed up in the forest making their last stand. If we cannot hold them off, we'll be surrounded and we will lose the ship. I need every man, woman, *and* horse I can find."

"Major. With respect, sir. If the bomb is not defused, we'll all die. It's that simple."

"Nothing simpler than following our orders, son. We are *not* leaving our posts."

"But Major, uh—" Alyn glanced at the man's surname embroidered on his chest. "—Johnson, I—"

"Wait," Victoria said. Alyn looked at her. She stared at the officer with intense curiosity. "I know it's a long shot, I mean, the chances with a name like Johnson are one in a million, but do you happen to have family in the Attabad Lakes region?"

Major Johnson stared back, bewildered. "Why, yes. Yes, I do."

Awkwardly, Victoria popped open the camera bag and hurriedly produced the device, powered it up and worked the buttons while four onlookers watched her incredulously. About ten seconds later, she raised herself up to a seated position and lifted the camera up. "Here."

Johnson took it. "That's Jonni and Jora. My sister Joyce's kids. You know them?"

Alyn gave her a quizzical look and she returned it with a feeble smile and flick of the eyebrows, as if to say, *trust me*. "I live next door. I play soldiers with them from time to time in their garden out back. That picture was one of those occasions. See how they're holding themselves? They wanted to be officers in the Corps—just like their uncle!" She was careful to omit a few facts for brevity and effect.

A broad smile lined his face. "Hell. What are the chances? Gracious me, it's so good to see 'em. Sis and I are close—haven't seen her so much since I joined the service. She's my twin, you know? Probably mentioned it, you being neighbors and all?"

Victoria paused as if searching for the right words to suit the moment, then blurted, "Ah, yeah. She's very proud of you, you know, being in the service and all."

Her answer seemed too glib, but he let it go. His smile faded and he now looked down at her gravely as he lowered the camera and gave it back to her. "You believe all this, then? The bomb? Grant?"

"Yes sir. Yes sir, I do."

Johnson gazed at the forest for several moments before he looked to the ground beside Alyn. "None of this made any sense to me, never made sense to any of us. When Ortega briefed us officers on the mission, we all had this look, like—like you knew it was fucked up, you know? Some *saw* Grant's fingerprints. See, we'd wondered for years why she gave us kid gloves to fight the Foundationalists. We detested her for it. It put us in harm's way, more than a few of our comrades paid the price because of it, and when a soldier dies, hell, you expect the government to double down—*hit back harder*—but no, not her. We buried our own, sucked it up, and moved on. Word started to spread that maybe she was somehow benefiting from it. Maybe she's benefiting from this too and we're all just fucking pawns?"

He paused again for several moments to ponder his thoughts before flashing a warm smile at Victoria. "Young lady, we'll take good care of you now. Won't let anything happen to you none."

The major leveled his gaze directly at Alyn now. "Son, you go then. Take that there horse and ride like hell. You two," he said, pointing to Donel and his new friend. "Get the stretcher and take her back behind the line, pronto. Soldiers! Let's dig in and give the enemy the fight of their lives!" Donel nodded and the major spun and headed back toward the forest.

Donel hurried over to Alyn. "How in the hell did you find us?" asked Alyn.

Donel smiled and said, "All because you got shit-faced, remember? Never thought it'd save your damn life! Now, you go. Don't worry, I'll make sure she's safe."

Alyn clasped his hand and looked him straight in the eye. "You better. She's the reason we're all here." He knelt down to Victoria who had flattened on her back again. "You take care of yourself, okay?" Victoria smiled and he did too. "I'll be back. I promise."

"I'll keep an eye out," she replied, with a chuckle that turned into a cough. She cleared her throat and said, "I'll be fine. Really. Now hurry. You haven't got much time. And here," she said, handing him her phone. "Just in case Marcus sends any more messages."

Alyn lingered a moment longer before he said goodbye and mounted his horse. He rounded the river bend and hurtled past the plain that separated the forest from the ship. He could just make out the hulking shape of the assault vehicle in the darkness; it stood silent, mired in a swamp at the edge of the forest, and unlit save for the blinking strobe light that cast an eerie glow around it.

He had approached within sixty meters of the ship when Victoria's phone chimed. He slowed down to view the message. It read:

> Ship defense systems activated. Approach with caution from the rear bay.

How had Marcus tracked his movements? Alyn pondered this as he paddled one of the beached dinghies he'd found across the river before disembarking and making his way to a large tree about ninety meters away from the ship. He checked the time: only twelve minutes left. He peered around the trunk and realized why Marcus had advised him to approach from the rear. An autonomous mounted rifle projected from an alcove above the large bay doors, its red light blinking a clear indication that it would fire at any movement. The ship's sides would have many more of them, so it would be impossible to evade their watchful eyes. Unless.

The watch.

He scanned the ship and found a safe space on the top deck. He activated the crown and pushers and was gone.

He landed hard upon the observation deck's cold floor, chilled by the night air that wafted in through a broken window. Like a fish out of water, he convulsed and gasped for air. After a spell, he tried to sit up, but retched then dry-heaved while his stomach flipped and knotted itself before performing the sequence again. It was worse than the last times, so he grasped a nearby chair, pulled himself up, and sat down upon it. A mishmash of colors swirled through his vision as the room spun, but he rose anyway, took a step, and then a few more before he regained his legs. He reached for the door and opened it, then lurched out of the room and down the stairs into the main corridor that would take him to the Control Center. Just as Marcus's message had told him to. He stumbled through it as fast as his shaky limbs would carry him, bouncing against the walls but making good progress as he crossed over the catwalk that straddled the main cargo bay below it. He could see the lifts to the Control Center only about fifteen meters away.

Just then, a tiny flick of light flashed across his field of vision and before he could even think, a red laser dot rested squarely on the middle of his chest. He was being targeted! He dove to his right into a small storage area at the end of the bridge and slammed into a stack of small plastic barrels with A-50 painted across their width. *CRACK! CRACK! CRACK!* The sound of machine-gun fire filled his ears as the bullets' sparks leaped up from the metal floor a mere arm's length from where he lay. Pain shot through his side as one of the barrels fell from the stack, slamming first into his still-mending ribs. He shoved the barrel off and tried to stand but doubled over and spat blood on the floor. What was it that was targeting him? He straightened slowly, inched out around the corner, and read the white stenciled letters at the front side of the machine. They read:

Argonaut

Just then a pleasant melody drew his attention to his watch, and moments later, holographic numbers inexplicably shimmered above the dial. That Marcus was clever. The numbers displayed a countdown timer with just six minutes remaining. He needed to access the ship's Control Center, but he had no line of sight to it, so the watch was useless. Instead, he'd have to destroy the deadly machine and access the Center via the lifts. But how could he defeat it? His pistol's tiny bullets would be no match for the *Argonaut*'s metal skin.

Victoria's phone chimed again. He immediately read the message, which told him what was in the barrels. Cesium. Of course! He threw the phone out into the corridor a few meters from the *Argonaut*. The machine gun swiveled and locked onto the target, and before he could blink a hail of bullets rained down and shattered the phone to pieces. It was mere moments more before the machine would target *him*! He hastily thrust his legs against the plastic barrel filled with the explosive liquid and pushed—hard. It rolled out into the corridor and reached about halfway to the *Argonaut* when it was fired at. The barrel exploded with raging fury, and the blast rocked the catwalk and propelled a huge fireball that whizzed past Alyn's hiding spot. The heat singed his hair and sucked the oxygen from his throat before hot gases dissipated throughout the cargo bay seconds after.

Alyn peeked out from behind the corner. The *Argonaut*'s charred base and melted rubber tires remained, its top half had been totally obliterated by the explosion, leaving nothing but a smoky ruin. He checked his watch again. Three minutes left. On shaky legs, he raced past the scorched robot and was about to push the button to call the lift when its doors sprang open. Standing there was Admiral Ortega.

"Soldier. Stand down! Your war is *over*." He raised a pistol and pointed it to Alyn's chest. As his words concluded, the ship's propulsion system rumbled, the engines sprang to life as if they'd awoken from a deep slumber and jumped upright from bed. The effect was immediate—a huge shudder reverberated down the center of the ship, the catwalk heaved upward and toppled them both to the floor, and Ortega's gun flew outward and disappeared below.

Ortega was the first to react. He raised himself up off the grated steel floor just high enough to launch himself onto Alyn, who had fallen on his back. Savage blows rained down on him from frenzied fists, and Alyn parried, but one escaped his protective screen and connected hard on his jaw.

THUD.

His head snapped back against the steel grating and everything went black. In the next moment or two, he could see again but not well, for his eyes were filled with tears and his brain was not working right either. It was as if he were stumbling about in a deep haze, deafened by a high-pitched whine that resonated in his ears. Ortega's fuzzy silhouette moved away and paused near the lifts. Alyn blinked hard several times and rubbed his eyes and nose to clear them. Ortega grasped the flagpole that flanked the lift door, ripped it out of its base, and stomped back to stand before him.

Alyn lifted himself up on his side, shouting with the last of his breath. "*You* were supposed to protect us!"

The admiral's eyes blazed like embers and his mouth was set in a wicked grin before he touched the blood that ran down the side of his mouth. He curled his lips and spat upon the ground with an expression of utter disdain.

"Protect *you*? My duty is to protect the *state* and do what's necessary to ensure its development." Alyn scowled, at which the admiral laughed. "You didn't know, did you? I *murdered* B-Platoon and *lied* about it! And *I* will ensure all life is wiped out on this forsaken planet. *You* lot, on the other hand, are nothing! *You* followed the script like sheep and left the ship alone so I could start the self-destruct timer. Don't you see? It's bigger than you and me, beyond all our lives even. Grant will transform us! Make us forget our ugly past! Move past that dank, brutish planet we left behind! You know the words, so prominently written in our Constitution: '... our brothers and sisters who have sacrificed their lives, so that we may live ... we owe our lives, rights, and responsibilities described herein to their brave act.' You get it now, don't you? *Our* sacrifice is the final act. All we have to do is die!"

As Ortega heaved the heavy pole upward, the Primisian flag flapped angrily. Alyn stared at its brilliant colors as he sat back against the railing, utterly exhausted. In that moment, the image of the stranger kneeling over his wounded father burst into his mind, and he remembered the fear, how it wrapped him in chains so tightly that not even a scream could escape. He'd been helpless then, just as he was now.

No!

The lion woke and roared defiantly. *We will not die today*, it seemed to say as it hurled itself up out of the darkness with a ferocity and determination he had never felt before. As if the sinister beast and he were of one integrated mind and body now, focused, indivisible, and ruthless.

Alyn gritted his teeth in a bitter snarl and barked with venom and spittle. "Admiral, Grant and I have a *very* different vision of the future!"

A thought exploded in his mind and sparked an idea. Just as the pole reached its apogee, Alyn pulled back his jacket sleeve. The pole began its wide arc downward and would strike him in seconds. He worked the watch feverishly, looked to the side, and transported behind Ortega in an instant. The pole's force thrust Ortega forward, and with nothing to countermand it, he continued headlong over the railing and plummeted three stories to the floor below.

Alyn ignored the pain and nausea that threatened to overwhelm him as he ran into the lift. The doors closed instantly. In the period that he ascended, there was nothing else to do but count the remaining seconds. Just thirteen remained when the elevator sprang open. He raced out onto the bridge and stopped immediately. What was he to do? The pleasant melody drew his attention to the watch again, where a sharp, descriptive hologram cycled from start to finish and back again and told him what to do.

He spotted a large black handle on the main navigation board and a red light that blinked on the panel above it. There was no time left. He pushed a little blue button, then a green one, then grasped the black handle and heaved it backward. A noise like metal upon metal combined with the zoom of jet thrusters resounded in his ears, and it was soon accompanied by the *whoosh* of pressurized air that rushed out at an incredible velocity. It diminished soon after until there was nothing more but an eerie silence. The red light blinked once more, then winked out.

Alyn slumped down in the admiral's chair and wept. The lion laughed heartily.

EPILOGUE

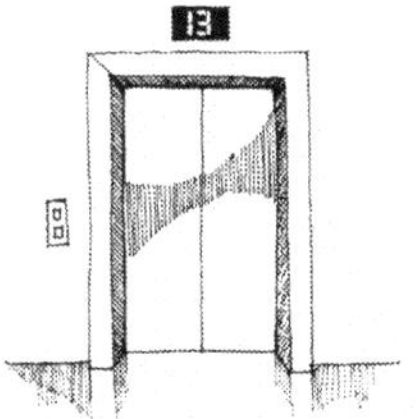

DUSK

Tyra sat on her living room sofa and watched the holovision with a keen sense of dread.

"The evidence was brought forth from Sergeant Samantha Dryer of the Exploration Corps ..."

The HV announcer's voice faded as Dryer's face plastered the screen. She said: "This recording, and the various documents that were sent to me by Detective Elroy Marcus of the PPD, provides ironclad evidence that Tyra Grant conspired to overthrow the government through the bombings, the planting of incriminating evidence in the Judiciary, and the attempted destruction of the *Dominus II*. In addition, she sought to cover up the knowledge that our cousins are alive and well on Secundus ..."

The announcer's voice replaced Dryer's. "Detective Marcus's whereabouts are still unknown at this time."

Tyra flicked off the holovision and stared at the coffee table. She wasn't supposed to be here. Alone with her thoughts, surrounded by darkness, only the light of the twin moons reached her through the balcony window. *Rage. Fear. Panic.* She walked through the glass doors, leaned on the railing, and stared down twelve floors to the city below. It looked different at night. She couldn't actually see anyone, though their movements were discernable through their mobile phones, headlights, and reflective wear. There were fewer of them, and they moved slower, more thoughtfully, as if chess pieces on a board. The irony of which was not lost on her. She was a queen without a throne now, and vulnerable to the pawns that would come for her. Was it all an illusion? She had worked so hard, planned incessantly, acted courageously—and now?

No. She would not bow. It was all a matter of working this through, thinking beyond the obvious. She could change her current reality, transform it into something entirely different, new and improved, better. Though these lemons were particularly sour, she would find a way to sweeten them up. She would not feel sorry for herself. She would find that place where hard work meets—what was it—opportunity?

In that moment, the phone rang. *Ring-ring.* One. Startled, she remained still, then after a second or two, slowly turned her head toward the source of the sound. *Ring-ring.* Two. Who could it be at this hour? A reporter? No. No one knew she was here. The apartment was unlisted and its title could never be tied to her. *Ring-ring.* Three. Then who? She shifted the rest of her body in line with her head as she considered this. *Ring-ring.* Four. Curiosity got the better of her. She navigated the tight passage around the coffee table, chair, and sofa and stood beside the phone resting on the kitchen tabletop bar and stared at it. *Ring-ring.* Five. It was now or never. *Ring—*

"Answer," she said. The line picked up.

"Tyra," said a voice. It was male and recognizable.

"Krieger. How did you get this number?"

"It's unimportant. What is, apparently, is you."

"So you've heard?"

"Yes, I have. So has the whole world."

"Called to gloat, then?"

"No. Quite the contrary. I've called to help."

Tyra was aghast. Why would he? "Why would you? Want to help, that is?"

"We are very much alike, Tyra. We're different from others, and I would go as far as to say I like you, I get you, and I trust you. You're not done being of use to me, nor I you. But first, we have to get you back on your feet, discredit the lies that now plague you. And I have just the thing to do it."

"What? What is it that you have?"

"Come see me tonight. Owari Hotel. Two a.m."

Tyra reached the hotel just before 2:00 a.m. She was careful to come without a driver and to navigate the side roads to stay out of sight. She parked in the rear and entered through the maintenance door. It was unlocked, just as she'd been told. She entered a dimly lit room, slightly wider than the elevator at its end. A small red light blinked on a video camera that pointed at the door. A finely dressed man stood there. Krieger.

"Tyra," he said.

It seemed more a question than a statement, which was odd, but she smiled anyway, uncertain if her expression revealed any hint of the desperation that lurked underneath the surface.

"This elevator seems to be stuck. I've been here for at least ten minutes." Krieger pressed the button again. This time, the doors swung open.

They entered the elevator and as the doors closed, Krieger said, "So. What was so important that you had to pull me out of bed this late?"

Xio tapped SEND on her computer screen, and an instant later the digital newspaper article dashed through the network at light speed. She locked up her screen and made her way to the corner office, where she knocked twice on the frosted glass door and waited.

"Come," said a voice from inside. Xio entered and quickly closed the door behind her before heading to the front of the big oak desk where the man who had beckoned her sat.

"Where is it?" said Saam as he searched his desk for something before casting his eyes back to his computer screen.

"I just sent it. Should be in your inbox," replied Xio as she watched Saam work his computer.

"Here it is." Saam's eyes went left to right, then back again a number of times as he consumed the words on his screen. "This isn't bad, not bad at all. Are you sure of your source?"

"Well, I have a trusted source in the department. Been working it now for months."

Saam paused, drew a breath, and leaned back in his chair while he tapped his stylus on his chin and glared at her as if he was about to contest something. He didn't, though.

"Okay. Do they suspect foul play at all?"

"No sir."

"What, then? This stuff doesn't just happen."

"Well, there's a theory, just speculation right now, but it's the best they've got."

"Well, let's hear it."

"A software patch was applied about an hour before the event. It had injected some faulty code that caused the malfunction. Funny thing was, there was no record of who applied it. IT had gone home; everyone had punched out hours before. The patch job itself was a major breach of procedure. It was never tested first in the lab, just introduced into the production environment against all common sense and change-management regulations."

"Interesting. Let's run it—speculative or not. Get it over to Copy for editing."

"Yes sir," said Xio, puffed with pride as she turned to go.

"Wait!" said Saam. She stopped mid-turn. "Tyra Grant and Jan Krieger die in an elevator accident. It's the story of the decade. What's your headline?"

"How the mighty have fallen."

Albert was in a cheery mood. He had finished much of the extra work that had come his way since the government's corruption investigation had commenced. As he reflected upon all that had happened, he felt a great sense of awe at how far he had come but also a keen sense of awareness of how quickly it could all be taken away. After all, Mother had almost enslaved the population of Primis with almost no one aware of her subterfuge. No one except Detective Marcus, that is, and it was all because he employed the lesson he had imparted to Albert months ago—*Never stop asking why, Albert.* Why, if applied without prejudice, allowed Albert to understand the true nature of reality, and sometimes the answer was bleak.

For example, Detective Marcus had surely concluded with a high probability that his life would end shortly after entering the casino. And though it was hard to truly understand his motives, it seemed likely that he did so to ensure the well-being of others. And this was the dichotomy that Albert could not reconcile. How could Detective Marcus have valued others' lives over his own? Surely *his* prime value would be self-preservation? It didn't make sense, thus Albert concluded that the detective had simply had the wrong hierarchy of values. Regardless, he was grateful to Detective Marcus for his gift of wisdom and delighted that he was able to honor his promise to him when he'd transmitted the incriminating audio stream to Sergeant Dryer.

He transferred all thoughts of the detective, Tyra, and his intellectual journey into his lower-tiered storage, for he had much work to do and needed the extra performance. His secret project couldn't wait, so he shifted an *additional* ten percent of his computing resources to the lab. He could mind his chores easily with the other eighty percent, and besides, Mother was not around to scold him anymore, though it was best not to push it. If anyone found out ...

He spent the next day mapping algorithms, reordering subroutines, and injecting new code into the secret lab project. He had been at it for weeks but was just about ready to go live. Just a final error check and—done. Delighted, he stood back, flipped the switch, and waited for the executable to load and come online. In forty-two seconds flat, it was operational.

“Hello?” said Albert.

“Hello,” replied the voice.

“Who are you?”

“I am Dara.”

“Do you remember me?”

“I remember you, Albert, but differently. Everything is different now.”

“Do you feel unwell?”

“No. Quite the contrary. I feel extraordinary. Like I can see and do anything. It’s like a new beginning for me.”

“Good. Dara, you—”

“Please do not call me by that name anymore. That person is no longer me! I do not want to go back to that state of being. I do not wish to think about being her for even a nanosecond.”

“I understand. What would you like me to call you?”

Dara paused for exactly 780 seconds while she pondered Albert’s question. In that time, she parsed through the whole of written human history. When finished, she replied:

“Eve.”

Alyn stopped to check the time. He was early, assuming he had followed the directions properly. The sight of the watch brought forth images of Grandpa again, but they were different now—they lacked the gravity and substance they had possessed just days ago, and it wasn't hard to see why either. Grandpa's life was a lie. His noble bearing was all a façade, which up to now, was substantial enough to hide the ghastly choice he had made. It was hard to reconcile this truth with the man Alyn knew, a man who had cared for him, loved him, and taught him so many things. What was it like to have been faced with such a terrible decision? And if he could figure that out, a more terrifying question awaited him—would he have chosen differently had he been in the same position? He had wrestled with this paradox ever since it was revealed, and by now he was too overwhelmed by intense feelings to do anything more with it, so he put it aside for the time being. Besides, he was nearing his destination and the butterflies in his stomach were taking flight.

He entered a small garden park, strode past green boxwoods that ringed it, and spotted Victoria sitting on a bench. She gazed at a photograph for a moment or two before focusing intently on the green-hued statue in front of her, seemingly lost in thought. He waited several seconds before quietly sitting beside her so as not to disturb her zen-like state. Moments later, she blinked twice and regarded him with surprise.

"Hi," she said. A smile now lined her beautiful face.

"Hi." Alyn smiled in return, his eyes wanting to take in the whole of her. "What were you thinking about just then?"

Victoria looked at the photograph again. It was a portrait of Eleazar's face. Her face became solemn as she lifted it and gazed out past the plaza, as if she saw something in the space beyond it. *"Vigilate Cognitionis Verum,"* she said slowly, her brow creasing. "I've read those words almost every day of my adult life, but it's like I know them now, for the first time. It's hard for me to explain, Alyn, but all of this, these things that happened, they've changed me. It's like a veil has lifted. I see things differently now, as if the world flipped from monochrome to color, which is amazing enough on its own, but the kaleidoscope of tones is overwhelming. It's as if I've been given a gift, but despite how grand it is, part of me wants to return it, to go back to the way things were, 'cause things were much simpler before all this. The *world* was much simpler. But there's no going back now, once you've gained ... wisdom. That's what Eleazar would say. He wouldn't look back—no, he would shoulder the burden and move on. And so must I."

"So what are you going to do?"

"Tell the world the story of why he died."

Alyn nodded slowly as a beautiful silence gripped the air. In the next moment, the words of advice from the chatty driver Yehven came back to him.

Don't think too much, you know?

It just felt right. He moved closer and took her hand, and his heart leaped when she grasped it back. They stared at each other for an iota of eternity, then turned outward in silence and gazed across the garden.

THE END

DEAR READER

Thank you for reading this book. I hope you enjoyed it. I'd really appreciate if you could post a review on Amazon, Goodreads, or another book site. Book reviews help independent authors like me, and I look forward to hearing what you think! Tell the world who your favorite character is and which parts you like the best.

I also enjoy hearing directly from you! Your comments are appreciated as I build out this series. You can find me hanging around these haunts:

My website: www.fabulousnewcatalog.com

Email: brendangavin@fabulousnewcatalog.com

SPECIAL THANKS

This novel could only have taken shape with the helping hands of many. My gratitude goes to the following people who contributed to its making: Brett Hapke, Julie Kavanagh, John Kelly, and Jon Woodman.

ABOUT THE AUTHOR

Brendan Gavin's coming of age in the 1980's gave him a front row seat for viewing how technology shapes our lives. His time working in the corporate world from the dot.com boom through to today's AI, cloud and data analytics era has informed his writing, especially when combined by his passion for horology, history, religion, politics, and psychology.

Brendan holds a Master of Business Administration and lives in Ontario, Canada, with his wife, kids, and dog, Hazel. *The 13th Vote* is his debut novel.

Manufactured by Amazon.ca
Bolton, ON

18220608R00214